# Play Dead

*For Sally —*
*Love the hair! Rolf forever!*

*Michael A. Arnzen*

Michael A. Arnzen

RAW DOG
SCREAMING
PRESS

Published by Raw Dog Screaming Press
Hyattsville, MD

Hardcover Edition

Cover & Book design: Jennifer Barnes

Printed in the United States of America

ISBN 1-933293-04-7

Library of Congress Control Number: 2005901932

www.rawdogscreaming.com

# Also by
# Michael A. Arnzen

# Dedication

To my lucky charm, Renate
&
For Margaret Annie Jessie Moneyeyes

"It is only by risking our persons from one hour
to another that we live at all. And often enough
our faith beforehand in an uncertified result is the
only thing that makes the result come true."

—William James, *The Will to Believe*

# Acknowledgments

I've got debts. Most of all to two people: Lance Olsen—my mentor during the original stab at this novel many moons ago—and Renate, my rock steady partner in the big game. I deeply appreciate the help of The Committee—Lance, Ron McFarland and Dennis Colson—and all the good people in the English Department at the University of Idaho who contributed when I first dealt out this dark deck for my Master's Thesis. Here's to the many friends who contributed during the birth, rebirth, and afterbirth of this novel—especially: Barb & JC Hendee, Greg Rucka & Jen VanMeter, Wayne Edwards, David Hale Smith, The Abject and everyone at UO, Bruce Siskawicz & Becca Baker, Mark McLaughlin, Kurt Newton. Here's to raw dogs John & Jen at RDSP, the street pack, and the folks at Z Malice. I want to thank my Mom for taking me out for a fine steak and the conversation we had that planted the initial seed for this project. Thanks, too, to my Dad, whose influence is everywhere, always. A shout-out to my good old friend and poker partner Mike V., who is a ghost that floats all over this book, too. Hell, here's to all my friends. And here's to you, for reading this.

The city of Vegas in this novel is highly fictionalized, and is not intended to represent the actual city of Las Vegas, Nevada, by any means.

An excerpt from this novel originally appeared in *Palace Corbie*, with rights retained by the author.

Gambler's Anonymous Helpline: (213) 386-8789
http://www.gamblersanonymous.org

# Joker

*The gun barrel confronts him. The inevitable blast roars inside of his ears and light blares between his eyes as if his head was the chamber of the pistol all along. The screen flickers: red to black, red to black...*

# part one
# CLUBS

# A♣

Johnny Frieze knew it was coming long before it was dealt: a dead hand, nothing but Suicide King high. He peered up over his cards, ignoring the dealer and the pot before him, glancing pathetically at the guy across the green felt of the poker table—a jerk who called himself "Jimmy the Gun" of all things—who was holding the majority of Johnny's chips. The Gun was an arrogant player—couldn't keep a poker face—and was melodramatic about every hand, like something straight out of a bad gangster film.

He grinned at Johnny like a head-bobbing vulture. Johnny grinned back, flashing him his gold front tooth, keeping his head in motion, rising, rising, his neck craning up as he purposely stalled, going through the motions of stretching, eyes finally locking on the mirrored security dome above like some alien mothership planted in the starlight sparkle of the casino's ceiling.

His reflection: a fish-eyed mutant, fun house features absurdly mimicking his panic. His ears hummed with that horribly silent and infinite pause of knowing one's fate right before the kill.

Jimmy The Gun coughed. Johnny could feel him staring at his bared and straining neck, his shifty eyes like greasy fingers feeling for a pulse. The dealer sat at the table like Death: silent and patient, hauntingly anonymous, wise.

Johnny wondered if whoever was watching from above—the eye in the sky, spying on every table in the casino—knew that Johnny was about to lose the last of everything he had. *Everything*. Every fucking asset he'd pawned, every damned chip he'd bought and spent. Every. Mother. Fucking. Cent.

*Sky's the limit*, he thought, grimacing at his fun house reflection above.

He heard the clink of plastic chips. "I'll bet the rest of whatever you got there," The Gun impatiently said, motioning with his chin at Johnny's embarrassingly tiny stack of reds. "This game has gone on far too long, and I'm sick to death of teasin' ya."

Johnny sighed and lowered his head. His skull felt as heavy as a bowling

9

ball. "I'll see ya," he said, smartly swiping the last of his chips forward into the pot to make some noise. "Even though you're robbin' me blind." He dropped his cards face-down and rubbed his pockets with both hands, feeling the naked skin beneath.

The Gun stuck his large chin forward over his cards. Johnny stared him back as if seeing him for the first time—even though they'd been playing since the afternoon and it was now four a.m. The Gun's eyes were beads of black and green—wet and shiny—gleaming with the flash of the casino like plastic eyes on a statue. His over-moussed, jet-black hair clung to the lumpy, light bulb shape of his head, as matted as cat's fur after a rainstorm. His ugly chin was a stone stuck in his lower lip, plump with tobacco. And worst of all, he smelled like Pine Sol and polyester.

The Gun blinked—a slow motion recharge of darkness—then whispered: "I ain't took nothin' from you yet, boy. Nothin'. Just your money, your fake plastic." He peered down at the challenged chips and rolled his eyes back up to meet Johnny's. "I still haven't taken the *game* outta you." He prodded his cheek with his tongue, stretching the flesh so much that Johnny could see the blackheads in his pores. "I still haven't beat ya, boy, 'cause you still got the balls to sit here and act like a player, bluffin' with your last chip like you still got a chance in hell."

Johnny felt his nostrils flare. He raised one in a sneer like Elvis, not quite knowing how to respond.

"I don't want your fuckin' money, kid," The Gun continued, leaning back. "Think I'd sit here all damned night and day just to take your damned money? That'd be like takin' a Butterfinger from a diabetic baby." He menaced a smile. "Nope, I don't want your money." He dropped his cards and crossed his arms, waiting. "I just want you to *fold...*"

A sudden knot of energy pulsed inside of Johnny's chest. It was a warm, familiar feeling—the whole reason he played, a feeling he'd been trying to get back ever since Reno. This is why he did it: for The Itch, The Fever...*Action*, baby, Action with a capital A...

"Break," Johnny said to the dealer, who not only looked like a mortician but nodded like one too as he placed a marker on the table beside the pot, solemn as a tombstone. The Gun cursed and slapped down his cards as Johnny pushed his chair back and rapped on the table with his knuckles for luck. "Back in a flash."

As he began to walk away, Johnny noticed that a small mob of on-lookers had gathered around the poker pit like a crowd at a car accident. All of them seemed to look him in the eyes at once. He bummed a cigarette off a skinny Arab who was all too eager to give one up, light included. Johnny didn't thank him. He just nodded and breezed away, sucking the smoke deep into his lungs like it was fresh air even though it tasted like shit. He was careful not to walk too fast or too slow—looks were everything, and he didn't want to look like he was running away, beaten. He maintained his cool, keeping his hands out of his empty pockets, focusing all his attention on the cigarette between his lips and the smoke that curdled in his lungs.

*Fuckin' menthol*, he thought.

He marched until he reached the bathroom, pushing forward on the green-marbled sign that read GENTLEMEN in golden letters. The bathroom was immaculate and empty—as if the janitor had just finished polishing the porcelain sinks and urinals. Everything shined, spoiled only by a subtle tinge of impure white. The doors to the stalls had gold knobs and the tiled floor reflected them like a mirror of melting ice. Not bad for a casino at four in the morning, but...

It smelled an awful lot like the asshole he was playing poker with. Pine-scented and oily.

Johnny spit the menthol butt from between his lips and stamped it out on the floor. It fizzed the rubber sole of his tennis shoe. He grabbed a knob on the nearest sink and triggered the cold water, running his fingers beneath its stream, waiting for his hands to numb.

His reflection was there, looking at him like a stranger from behind the glass of the mirror. He didn't look as good as he thought: blond hair browning from too many runs of the hand over his scalp. His eyes were baggy, bloodshot, someone else's pinned up over his nose. Old sweat stains etched tan topographical maps across his once-white shirt, strange continents around his armpits, sick islands between his nipples. A shadow of hair stippled his

# Play Dead

jawline, running too high up his cheeks—anyone could see that no one had ever taught him how to shave properly. And that ugly gold tooth, glimmering inside the dark cave of his mouth, a shiny gem that only deepened the yellow of his other teeth and gave his breath the stench of old cat food cans.

He smiled a pirate's grin. The gold tooth shined beside the rest, his mouth the exact color of the bathroom decor.

But he liked it.

Because it helped him keep his confidence. No matter how far down he was on his luck, he'd always have his tooth, always have something golden inside him where no one could touch it. Plus it scared people. People who couldn't read his face. People who squirmed when they realized they were sitting at a table with a guy who knew what money tasted like. A guy who chewed on that hunger deep inside which every amateur tries to prod and tease. Johnny wasn't hungry for money—he ate players for breakfast *with* money, usually their own stacks.

At least...he *used* to.

And he used to wear a fancy suit and tie. And a ring with diamonds and crusty golden nuggets. And a money clip. And all the other things it took to get that look right, that young-kid-on-the-make look that frightens wannabes and ruffles old pros into making the wrong moves, calling the wrong bluffs, and forgetting how to read the cards because they're too busy trying to read *him* instead.

"Right," Johnny said to himself—half-question, half-sarcastic jab at his reflection.

Johnny left the water running while he ditched his reflection, pissing in the urinal, holding himself with cold, wet fingers. He couldn't feel a thing but the pulsing heat of the thick steady stream as it hissed between his legs for what seemed like forever. He hadn't been to the bathroom since he sat down at the table. An old—but strategic—habit: make the other man get up from the table first. Remind him that he's human. And therefore, bound to lose.

Finished, Johnny returned to the running water, the reflection.

Nothing left. No scratch. Nothing.

He knelt before the sink. The tiles felt cold, like cubes of ice grinding against his bony kneecaps. He stared forward, watching the stream flow into the polished basin like a waterfall of diamonds just above the rim of the sink. He felt majestic, bowing like this, as if before some god.

He placed his hands behind his neck, sit-up style. Like being arrested.

Smiled a pained smile.

And then slammed his open mouth forward against the edge of the porcelain sink as hard as he could.

Again.

Again.

Until the last thing he had on earth to bet with cracked out of its bony socket and dangled somewhere above the bloody puddle of drool and enamel on his tongue.

The cold water of the sink washed the pain away, numbing his cheeks and gums, buzzing across his entire face. And as he walked back into the game — the small crowd of on-lookers scowling around the poker pit as they noticed the blood trickling between his lips — he suddenly knew that this numbness inside would never go away. Never.

Even when he lost his gold tooth to the arrogant asshole who couldn't keep a poker face.

Even when he told The Gun he was gonna need it.

Even when he punched him squarely in his enormous chin and stormed out of the casino, wondering what the hell he was going to do next to survive.

*Sky's the limit*, he thought, the numbness in his head spreading around his jawline and racing down his neck. *Sky's the limit...*

# Play Dead

"Vegas," The Preacher was saying, "is in the middle of a desert. Where the heat is worse than hellfire, because it lets you think you're living, leads you to believe that you can beat the devil by escaping into some air-conditioned casino where comforts and coolness abound! Vegas is heaven smack dab in the center of hell. But don't think you can beat that devil. No one can. He's a tricky sonuvabitch, and I tell you now that this place is one giant trap of sin, where the heaven *is* the hell, where that tricky bastard teases and tempts us all as part of his sneaky little game! Dice, cards, cigarette girls, hookers, slots...they're all part of his game! And so are we—we weak men who turn to vice and sin. Simply pawns in his twisted game...a game that can't be won by the likes of a man without God!"

The Preacher, having marched up and down the rows of beds to wake everyone up with his sermon, paused and leaned down over Johnny Frieze's face. "So don't you play it, boy! I'm warnin' ya. You pick yourself up by the belt and haul your own ass outta here!"

Johnny closed his eyes, droplets from The Preacher's cheap liquor breath burning into them like grains of pepper. "Fuck," he said groggily, "you."

The Preacher pivoted, heels squeaking on the floor of the homeless shelter like ice skates on concrete. "It's a mirage, I tell ya. A mirage! All of this! A hallucination, brought on by the devil himself, to confound our senses and seduce us like he did to Jesus in the wilderness. Pretty lights, beautiful women: ain't it all a dream come true? Hell, no. It's a trap, I say again, to play his sick game. A mirage in this god-forsaken desert, a ruse you can't escape, once you step inside. Just a little diversion for that tricky bastard. 'Cuz he's bored stiff out there with the rest of the world. The whole world is full of sinners, chock full of 'em, and so the devil's so bored he's gotta pick on us, the weak ones. For entertainment!" The Preacher twisted his neck, staring all the sleeping bodies down. "Well I say 'No more!' I'm gonna be strong! I'm gonna allow God's strength to pass through me and beat that devil. 'Cuz God's the only one who can beat him. God's the one who created

14

this world. *He* set this stage, and because he's a loving God, the devil can play all he wants to on it, but God knows damned well he's just a bad actor. And what's more..."

A tennis shoe hit The Preacher in the face, a flat slap of rubber against flesh.

The Preacher double-blinked, brought a finger to his nose. Saw blood.

He twisted accusingly to face the rows of beds in the dimly lit room. "Who did that? Who fucking *dares* to commit this sacrilege?"

Snores in reply.

The Preacher swiped a hand across his face like a boxer, then held up his palm to display it to the entire room of sleeping, bearded faces. "This is God's blood you've spilled today, heathens! God's blood!"

Then he stormed out of the shelter, his heels click-clocking the concrete floor military-style, the aluminum door slamming back into its hitch with a loud CRACK.

Johnny flipped over on his stomach, the springs of the bed drowning out his chuckle. It felt good to shut that fucker up. Every day since he came here it had been the same morning ritual: a wake up sermon on the sins of Vegas. As if they all had to be told how badly they'd screwed themselves.

Johnny knew from day one that he wasn't the only one at the shelter as a result of a bet gone bad. In fact, they all were gamblers, as far as he could tell. And that included The Preacher himself. The story with him, according to Shorty, was that he'd bet his congregation's entire tithes and offerings at The Circus Casino. Believing, no doubt, that God's hand would roll the dice in his favor. Since it was God's money he was playing with, the good Lord above would naturally want to turn a profit, wouldn't he? But The Preacher had lost everything—everything but his faith and towering voice—and ever since then he'd been here at the shelter, acting as if every poor slob here was a part of his new church, his new congregation.

Johnny, on the other hand, held no such beliefs. No beliefs at all. He went into the game that final day riding solely on luck. Everything, he believed, was luck: fame, fortune...and the flip-side of those coins, too: poverty and death. Luck was the difference between God and Devil, heaven and hell. And luck was what brought him here—bad fucking luck.

# Play Dead

Someone was clapping, applauding him for shutting The Preacher's trap. Johnny opened his eyes—he was awake now anyway—and looked over across the rows of army-blanketed bodies.

"It's about time someone did that," a warm voice said. Johnny spotted a familiar man two beds away: bleached red bandanna around the neck, long sandy brown hair...and a stony face with features chiseled in, crisp wrinkles surrounding soft baby blue eyes like gems in a statue. The eyes were eerie—so clear they looked like plastic water bottles. Johnny didn't know the man, but he'd seen him around the shelter, especially at feeding time. The guy scared him a little—partly because of that face of his, but mostly because he was always *clean*. Always shaven, his face had a shine that none of the others had. His skin was always light, not tanned from dirt and grime like everyone else. In general, the man did not look like he belonged in the homeless shelter—and Johnny knew that the key to surviving in a place like this was to not stand out from the crowd, so he stayed clear of Mr. Clean. But now—since everyone else was sleeping—he really had no choice but to talk. And he *was* curious.

"I dunno what his damned problem is," Johnny said with forced anger, copping an attitude. "He's more fucked up than everyone else here, but he thinks he's so high and mighty."

"Well," Mr. Clean said—his voice was soft, too, Johnny noticed—"I think he does that sermon of his to get a bed. He's out all night, preachin' probably, and doesn't get back here till all the beds are taken. So if he wakes someone up, he thinks he might get a cot."

"Ah," Johnny said, understanding. His first night here he had run into a similar problem, nearly getting into a fistfight with a bum who thought he owned every bed in the joint. "I knew he was just an asshole hypocrite." He prodded the space between his teeth, missing the taste of gold. "But I just thought he was used to lecturing folks who were snorin', him bein' a preacher and all."

Johnny looked up at the ceiling, waiting for a reply or a snicker, but none came. The silence was uncomfortable, nervous. Shorty's pet rats made clicking sounds from somewhere across the room. "So what's your name?" he finally asked, giving in to his curiosity.

"The name's Winston," he said, pulling a cigarette from somewhere underneath his pillow and stroking it straight.

"I'm Johnny. I've only been here a week or so, but it's just like home already. Don't know if that's good or bad. Seen ya around here, but..."

"I've seen you, too," Winston said, his deep voice calm in comparison to Johnny's nervous introduction.

Johnny rubbed his face as if adjusting a mask. In for an ounce, in for a pound. He swung his legs out over the side of the bed and sat up. "Got another smoke?" he asked, and instantly regretted it—cigarettes were like poker chips here. Valuable.

"Sure do," Winston said, immediately tossing one over to his lap as if he knew Johnny would ask. Johnny examined it as he dug a book of matches from a back pocket: WINSTON, the filter read in bold golden letters. Johnny doubted it was Mr. Clean's real name.

The nicotine shot straight to his temples, thrumming consciousness behind his eye sockets. It had been days since he'd had a real cigarette—ever since the night he sucked that menthol down his throat like a last request, he'd had nothing other than a half-finished generic butt from the sidewalk to chill his nerves. But instead of enjoying the flavor of the Winston, he sucked it down quickly, bringing the filter to his lips as frequently as a spoon from a bowl of soup. The smoke shotgunned to his lungs, aided by the locomotive gap of his missing front tooth. His face still felt numb—there was no flavor to the smoke. The fix was all that counted—just like at the tables: keep it comin', keep the dice rollin', keep stokin' those flames.

Winston sidled off his bed and went through an extended morning ritual of sliding on his boots. Shiny cowboy boots, all snakeskin and silver buckles. Johnny gave him his privacy, staring blandly at the walls and snoring cots around him.

The shelter looked much like a prison: drab gray walls of painted cinderblock, a brick removed here and there to give the illusion of windows. These small openings in the walls were air vents more than panes, not quite efficient enough to keep the stench of Thunderbird and Mad Dog and piss and sweat from clouding the shelter like an exterminator's lingering vapor. Johnny was glad he could only barely smell it—his face was still blessed with that numbness from chunking out his gold tooth. But he swore that in the early morning he could see the stench raising from the cots like steam.

The beds were bolted down and lined up military style, dress-right-dress, with stained white sheets and olive green Army blankets handed down from the Vietnam War. *US* they read in black, fuzzy letters, faded from industrial bleach to get out the urine and jizz and vomit. About thirty beds total, all filled with victims of the economy. Gamblers, no doubt, every one of them; losers sprawled like dominoes already spilled, one tumbling after another in some absurd race to a finish line that didn't exist.

Johnny heard the light fizzle of eggs frying on the grill, the strong stench of grease cutting its way through the shelter's more human smells. The kitchen was in an annex to the room that housed the beds, accessible from a hallway that also led to the toilet stalls and community showers. Everything was styled after an Army barracks. But there was no mess hall—they ate at their cots. Amid the stink.

"Smells good. Wanna grub?" Winston stamped his boots on the floor and slapped his knees.

Johnny salivated at the thought: a good breakfast, perhaps some conversation, and—if he was lucky—an after-meal nicotine fix from his new-found buddy. He stood and followed. On instinct, the bodies in the other cots began to stir, the others awakening around them as they crept quickly toward the kitchen to be first in line. "Early bird gets the worm," Johnny said, and Winston just nodded, grinning as if he'd already caught it.

Gin stepped out of the walk-in freezer behind the counter, hauling a large chrome pot. Johnny saw sweat on her forehead, clear beads matting the blond sticky strands around her temples and ears. She wore a filthy apron that only emphasized the pert curves of her breasts, and through its fabric Johnny could see the emblem of a college stretched out on her T-shirt. But she looked almost too old to be in college—a little older than Johnny—late twenty-something. And as usual, Johnny thought she was working harder than she should for free. He tongued the space between his front teeth, staring at her.

Winston nudged Johnny in the ribs with an elbow and his tongue poked forward through his lips. "Looks like that little chile pepper there's got the hots for ya."

"Knock it off!" Johnny blushed, immediately seeing what Winston was leering over: Gin's nipples were hard, pointed purple nubs that jutted from the front of her damp T-shirt like sideways strawberries. The chill from the walk-in freezer was responsible, naturally, but Johnny couldn't help but feel a slight twinge in his stomach. He'd been fantasizing about Gin since the first day she spooned him some mashed potatoes, flashing him a reassuring smile that said something like *Anyone with pockets knows how it feels to be empty—don't be embarrassed*. It was the first and only friendly smile he'd received since arriving. She was the first kind face he'd met since he'd lost everything to the Suicide King, a faint glimmer of hope that he latched onto in his dreams.

But he knew she was unreachable, a fantasy. What woman in her right mind would be attracted to a worthless bum without the ability to smile back at her?

Gin looked over at him now, acknowledging his presence with a nod before handing the cook—who everyone called Cookie—the pot, and helping him butter slices of burnt toast.

"Did you see that look, Johnny? I told ya, man. Chef Boy-*hard*-ee is boilin' for ya. You better get you some of what's cookin' back there before it cools off."

Johnny was still blushing as he shook his head. "Hey, just 'cause she's a volunteer doesn't mean she gives *everything* away."

Winston snorted, elbowing him in the ribs. "But that don't mean ya can't take it anyways. Women ain't like draw poker—you don't get no second chances. You gotta cut her cards before she even knows she's dealin' em, if you know what I mean."

Gin turned from the cook and headed towards them, a steaming paper plate in each hand. Johnny could feel the blood in his cheeks intensify; Winston was grinning again, looking back and forth between Gin and Johnny, rolling his eyes, making Johnny feel awkward as an adolescent.

Gin ignored his motions. "Here's your breakfast, boys."

Winston leered at her, winking.

Gin smirked, tossed Winston's plate down on the counter in front of him, and handed Johnny his. "No seconds today, fellows, so eat up while its still hot." She went back into the freezer, all business.

"See what I'm sayin', Johnny?"

They turned, headed back down the hallway toward their cots. A line had formed at the counter, bearded men rubbing the slime from their faces and the crud from their eyes. The Preacher had returned for his daily bread, flecks of black blood lingering around his nostrils from Johnny's shoe slap. He was praying to himself, eyes clenched tightly as he clutched his Bible. The others were doing their level best to ignore him. Johnny nodded hello at the few he considered acquaintances, but they were basically sleep walking—a zombie line-up—and didn't notice him at all.

"Hey, Johnny!" one of them called from behind.

Frieze turned to search for the voice, and found Shorty sticking his big head out sideways from the line, not willing to lose his place for conversation.

Winston kept walking toward the cots as Johnny stepped over to Shorty. "What's up, man?"

Shorty—whose nickname related not to his size, but to his attention span—lifted a hand in secrecy. His voice was sluggish, and Johnny always thought he sounded a little bit like a retarded John Wayne. "Don't forget to save any leftovers for my little buddies, okay?"

Johnny smiled and nodded. "You betcha." Shorty had a few rats for pets; his only friends, besides Johnny, who pitied him more than enjoyed his company. He was a bit slower than the rest of the cutthroat players at the shelter. Shorty was nothing but a kid whose body had grown up faster than his mind, a pocky black beard covering the zits on his chubby face like a bad disguise.

Shorty returned a full-faced grin. "Thanks, Johnny. You're the best."

Frieze sighed. "Cards later?"

"Sure, big guy." He looked at another man in line, who completely ignored him. "He's the best."

Back at his cot, Johnny shoveled the hot food deep into his mouth so he could chew it with his back teeth. The eggs were freeze dried, and the bacon was all shriveled fat, and the hashed browns were rehashed *blacks* made from three-day old leftovers, but it tasted so damned good that he almost drooled while he ate. He had forgotten how empty he was—how hollow inside. Winston sat a bunk away: not eating, but cleaning his fork and spoon with an immaculate handkerchief, as if the food mattered less than his image.

Johnny thought about Gin—short for Virginia, no doubt—wondering what she was doing here at the shelter of all places. She was too young to be a state employee—or a trustee out of the state pen like Cookie, the head cook. Considering her T-shirt and age, he figured she might be a college student out at UNLV, probably getting some sort of credit out of volunteering her time for the soup kitchen. She seemed smart enough. And whatever it was, she was getting something out of the job other than the satisfaction of having a bunch of bums slobber over her. No one, he knew, would do what she did—or put so much effort into it—for free. He wondered what she was studying, whether she had a boyfriend, whether she'd consider going out with him once he got out of this place.

Yeah, of course she would. Right after he won the lottery, got elected president, and won the Nobel Prize for being the world's biggest screw-up.

He prodded a fleck of eggs from the gap between his incisors with his

# Play Dead

tongue. If he had enough money to at least get a new gold tooth, maybe she'd consider at least talking with him over a cup of coffee. Money. Scratch. It always came back to having some greenbacks. Money controlled everything—from survival to sex. More important than air. If he just had some, just a little bit, just *five fucking bucks*, he could get both Gin and a new set of gold teeth. A whole mouthful. All it would take was one smart bet and a little tease from Lady Luck...

Johnny set his fork down and rubbed his eyes. He hated thinking like this—it didn't feel natural. It always happened when he ate. He'd start thinking about the future, filling himself up with crazy ideas about having some sort of life to live. Maybe it was the food that did it, thumping in his stomach as if he had more things to think about than just *surviving*, making it alive from day to day.

Winston looked down at his plate, his face stretched in perplexion. Then he smiled up at Johnny who was slurping the remainder of his eggs. "You like bacon?" he asked.

"Nope," Johnny swallowed. "I like *food*. Any kind."

"Then how about a little wager?"

Johnny swallowed. "Say what?"

Winston set his plate down on the cot between them, as if displaying a trophy. "I'll bet you this entire plate of food that you don't have the balls to go ask that little peach in the kitchen for a good time."

*No one around here offers to give up their food.* "What is it with you, huh? How can you possibly not wanna eat?"

"But I do expect to eat, Johnny. Because I think I'll win the bet."

Johnny finished his plate. He stopped himself from lunging at Winston's food and quaffing it down as it sat steaming in front of him. "And what do you get out of this?"

Winston looked up at the ceiling impatiently. "The satisfaction of knowing I'm right."

Johnny looked down at the offered plate. It was getting cold. "Oh, come on. What are we? A couple of dumb teenagers? Get out of here!" Johnny waved the idea away with a hand. "Eat up before it gets cold."

Winston sighed. "But we all *are* like kids, aren't we Johnny? Everyone here, a child inside a man's body. Like your pal, Shorty. We're irresponsible. We're desperate. We think the world owes us something. And we like to play games." Winston pulled a cigarette from a pack, lit it, and tossed the pack beside the plate of food, upping the stakes. "That's why you're here, isn't it? Because you like to play games?"

He felt the muscles in his face loosen and sag. A plate of food and a pack of cigarettes, free for just asking Gin something he'd been wanting to ask her for a long time anyway. It was too easy. And too juvenile. But then—maybe luck had come his way? If so, then maybe he was on a roll. And maybe Gin would say yes.

Someone screamed.

It was Shorty, standing over his cot in the corner of the room, his fat nipples shaking as his plate spilled runny eggs and potatoes on the blankets.

Johnny ran over to him. Winston shrugged and casually watched him run, smoking.

Johnny grabbed Shorty by his plump shoulders, forcing him to look up. "What the hell's the matter, man? You okay?"

Shorty's furtive eyes audibly squished in their sockets, flittering side to side as if bees were swarming his face. He'd broken out into a sweat, his face pale and sallow. The DTs, Johnny thought, till he saw what was on his cot.

Four dead rats.

Butchered: guts dangling from caved-in yellow and pink cross sections.

Patterned: arranged geometrically, four wet furry bodies chopped in thirds and systematically laid out in each corner of the cot, each ornamented niche a small puddle of wet blood turned black by the green fibers of the Army blanket.

Johnny just stared, disgusted. He scraped the sides of his tongue between his teeth, trying to rid himself of the taste of rat guts on his tongue.

From behind, he heard the fizzle of Winston's cigarette being pressed into his prize eggs. It didn't matter. He wasn't hungry anymore.

# Play Dead

Johnny pulled the corners of the blanket down over the dissected rats, giving them the same respect he would a human. He knew how important Shorty's rats were to him—they were his only friends here in the shelter. His pets and more: his family. They all looked the same, but each had different names. Patience, Blackjack, Klondike, and Trix. Shorty would feed them nibbles from his own food, he slept with them...he even took *showers* with them.

It was an easy identification to make, Johnny figured. Rats and bums: both scavengers, both filthy and hungry, both just trying to survive in a world that didn't give a flying fuck whether they lived or died.

The room filled with the sound of smacking lips, scraping forks, and growling bellies. Everyone was eating, keeping to themselves, hoarding their food into their stomachs as if they might never be fed again.

Johnny put an arm around Shorty's shoulder, giving him a quick hug of confidence. "It's okay, Shorty. We'll find you some new pets, okay?"

Shorty's eyelids clenched painfully shut, holding back tears.

"Awwww," a deep voice bellowed. "Isn't that cute?"

Johnny looked over at the heckler. He was dressed in flannels and jeans, long johns beneath it all despite Nevada's desert heat. He looked like a lumberjack or a coal miner, with a thick black beard that ran too far down his neck and up his face. Two heavy forearms bulged out from his plaid sleeves like hairy baseball bats. "You got a problem, Paul Bunyan?"

The man grinned, his beard crinkling up the sides of his face. Johnny saw old bits of food and beads of spittle trapped in the beard and green stuff between the cracks of the man's yellow, rotting teeth. "Whatta you? Faggot like Shorty? Like to stick rats up your ass and have 'em nibble the crud off your nuts?" He stood up—his head could have hit the ceiling. "Huh, pretty boy?"

Johnny swallowed a mouthful of hot, angry spit.

Shorty's eyes shot open, his neck snapping towards the man. His voice was ludicrous John Wayne: "You gone and did it, didn't you, Axe? You killed my rats!"

"What if I did, queer boy? Whatchu gonna do, buttfuck me to death?"

Shorty jumped, bouncing off his cot and into the chest of the man. Both spilled to the concrete floor, the crackle of bone smacking stone echoing in the shelter. The homeless continued to eat, ignoring the fight while the two grunted and punched at one another.

Johnny moved to assist Shorty, but Winston—suddenly rushing to the scene out of nowhere—beat him to it, easily wrenching the two of them apart. "You fuckheads are spoiling the *game*," he grunted, pushing them away from each other and holding them at bay with splayed fingers. His cool blue eyes accused them both, and, frowning, the two men looked down at the floor guiltily, like brothers being chastised by a parent.

Winston placed his hands on their shoulders and pulled them forward into a huddle. Johnny turned an ear to hear Winston whispering: "...if you can't play correctly, then you'll fold. *Involuntarily*. Got it?"

The two men nodded. Shorty was flexing his fists, the veins on his arms standing out deep blue.

Winston whispered something else, and then they both turned and went separate ways, the jerk named Axe kicking his cot on his way to the showers, and Shorty returning to his dead rats.

Winston strolled back to his cot, grabbing his cowboy hat from beneath it. He pulled a cigarette from the hatband, stroked it, and popped it between his lips, looking curiously at Johnny. He stared him down as he lit the cigarette, winked, and then flipped the hat atop his head, walking toward the front door of the shelter. He slammed the door shut behind him as he left.

Johnny wondered if he was really awake. "What the hell was that all about, Shorty?" he asked, looking down at the man who was bundling the stained blanket around his pets into a makeshift sack.

"Nothin'. Let me and my little buddies be, okay?"

"But..."

"But nothing." Shorty faced him—his eyes maniacally searching Johnny's. "You shoulda kept an eye on 'em, Johnny. You shoulda watched out for 'em. Friends watch out for each other, don't they?" He turned away, staring down at his bloodied bed. "I don't think you're my friend anymore, Johnny. The only friend I got around here anymore is my *self*. So just go away." He crouched down before the bed, whispering, "Just leave me alone."

Johnny returned to his cot, stunned. The trophy breakfast plate was there, atop his pillow, a cigarette butt standing up in the direct center of the untouched eggs like a flagpole that said WINSTON.

"Fucker," Johnny said, pulling a strip of bacon out from beneath the eggs and shoving it into his mouth. He watched Shorty crying to himself, petting the wet blanket on his cot. He'd never seen Shorty so violent before. He'd lost his temper plenty of times, especially when he was losing at cards, but this time it was different, disturbing. In a sense, Shorty had just accidentally dropped the cards he was holding, showing something hiding all the time beneath that innocent retarded look on his baby face. And this new side of him was intense and in control...almost *normal*. Shorty might have been a bit slow, but when he lost his temper he regained his self-control. Something about that frightened Johnny.

And what, he wondered, is all this crap about folding from some game? What was Winston up to?

The Preacher stepped over to where Shorty knelt and placed his hand on his shoulder. Shorty looked up into his eyes, pleading. The Preacher opened his Bible and closed his eyes, reading aloud from the book as if fingering Braille. Shorty hung his head and bawled. It looked to Johnny like he was reading the rats their last rites or something.

*This place is a friggin' insane asylum.* Johnny stood and headed for the door, eager for escape. And as he made his way out of the door and into the blinding Vegas sun, his mind couldn't help but remain straitjacketed with questions about Winston's game.

*The Five of Clubs.*

Ferret slipped his arms behind his head and thought deeply about the Five of Clubs. Five measly little Clubs—the ugliest suit—but it was the card he needed to draw next if he wanted to stay in the game. It had to be the Five of Clubs and it had to be good or he'd be dead in the pot without it...

"Whatcha thinkin' about, honey?"

Ferret turned his head to rest in the crook of his left arm, facing away from the woman in bed beside him. The bed was too soft. Much too soft, like a big pillow. He'd gotten used to the hard denim of his cot back at the shelter, which he preferred. He looked at the cushy mattress, then let his eyes rest on the wooden post that held up the headboard with a stupid floral pattern engraved in it. "I'm thinking...about the Devil's Bed Posts."

"What's that?" She whipped a leg over his spread thigh. It was itchy, unshaven. "Somethin' about my bed?"

He faced her. He didn't know her name. Her face was wide, green eyes like stained marshmallows poking out of her sockets. Too much make-up for such bug-eyes. Her Southern accent—which he always thought was sexy—somehow made it worse. "No," Ferret said, still not quite believing he'd slept with such a woman on a whim. "The Devil's Bed Posts. It's a slang name for a card." *My last card*, he thought, reminiscing.

She frowned. "Huh?"

"A card. The Four of Clubs. It's nicknamed the Devil's Bed Posts."

"That's funny." Her eyes bugged out some more as her facial muscles released her frown. "I guess the Four of Clubs does kinda look like four bedposts, don't it?"

Ferret chuckled, thinking of the last card he'd created. It certainly did look like four bedposts—*literally*. "Mmm-hmm."

The bug eyes retracted again. "Why are you thinking about a silly thing like that?"

He wondered if he should tell her. Even if he was dumb enough to show her his hand, he wouldn't know where to begin. Or end. "I dunno," he said. "Just thinking about a poker game."

She kissed him on the shoulder. "That's what I love about you real players...always thinking about a game. You're so intense. Like, there's a game going on in your head all the time. It's just so...in-*tense*." She toyed with a thick strand of his curly brown hair and rolled a finger down the long shaft of his nose, as if cautiously probing his skin to see what an Indian's flesh really felt like, and being surprised that it was the same texture as her own. "I knew you were a high roller, the second I saw you outside the casino. You looked right at home. Casino means home in Italian, did you know that? Anyway, there you were, standin' there by the front door with that intense look on your face. Like you were planning for some big game or somethin'. I knew right then and there I had to have you. Had to feel that intensity of yours. But intense as you are, I took your mind off of silly games, didn't I?"

"You sure did," he lied. Ferret craned his neck forward and sighted another bed post near his foot. "I forgot all about poker, about money, about cards and chips...hell, all I could think of was you, darlin'." He slid down an inch. Toed the bedpost. It was hard wood. Oak, probably.

"And you couldn't get enough, could you?" Her hand trailed down his neck, caressed his shoulder, slid down to his chest. "Why don't you let me take your mind off that silly old Devil's Bed Posts, too, huh?"

She leaned over and kissed his chest, tonguing his nipple. For a moment, Ferret imagined the wet flicking muscle to be a brush of her obese eyeball. He writhed and shimmied down the sheets, hooking his foot around the bedpost, using it to pull his weight further down until he was face to face with the woman.

She looked up from sucking his neck and met his eyes. "Maybe you'd like to tie me to them Devil's Bed Posts, huh?"

"Nah," he said, swinging his leg back. "I need a five this time."

He brought the sole of his foot forward as hard as he could. The bed post cracked, half of it dangling from a long, sharp splinter.

The woman's eyes were humongous marshmallows puffing in surprise. "Wha..."

Ferret was up on his knees and swinging the oak club at her forehead before she could finish. She fell back onto her pillow, a large purple welt spreading quickly across her temple, the circular bruise rippling in three different directions. Like a Club. Her eyes sunk deep into her skull, as if sucked into the space he'd just opened up.

"Much better," Ferret said, wondering what intense games were going on in *her* head before clubbing her in the skull again with the oak post, counting out loud as he swung.

Precisely.

Four.

More.

Times.

# Play Dead

The sun was bright, nearly melting Johnny's eyes, like a gigantic blinding spotlight resting right on the edge of the sand and gravel lot in front of the shelter. Johnny stood before the aluminum front door, rubbing his eyes, hating it. He wasn't used to the light of early mornings yet.

"Beautiful day, ain't it?"

Johnny turned, blinking.

Gin tucked a leg back beneath where she leaned, noisily scraping a tennis shoe against the concrete wall supporting her. As Johnny's eyes focused, he felt his face flush red with blood. Blushing—his weakness with women. As a rule he never gambled with them. He hated being caught off guard. And blushing.

He kept his distance, digging his toe in the gravel. "I wouldn't know. I'm a night person, myself."

"Aren't we all?" Gin pulled a crumpled pack of cigarettes out of the tight back pocket of her jeans and lit one. "But there sure ain't nothin' like the morning sun on a smoke break." She offered the pack to Johnny. "Like one?"

*I'm on a lucky streak, all right. Getting cigarettes left and right.* He walked to where she stood—the gravel crunching under each footstep—and leaned beside her against the wall. The concrete was hot against his back. "Sure." He slipped a Benson and Hedges from the long green and white paisley pack of 100's. Menthol. She lit it for him.

They silently smoked.

"So what's the deal with your friend?" she asked, staring into the sun.

Johnny took a drag, keeping the palm of his hand over his mouth to cover his gaping teeth. "Someone went and knifed his pet rats."

She didn't budge. "Figures. He *looks* like a rat, all slicked back. Acts like one, too." Gin sucked on her smoke. Blew. "Is that why he looked at me that way, 'cause he thought I did it?"

"Huh?" Johnny pivoted on his shoulder and cocked his head painfully against the bricks. He tried his best to keep his eyes off Gin's beautifully pink lips as much as possible while she spoke.

"You know, this morning. Lookin' all lovey-dovey at me and winking like he was gonna get me back for something..."

Johnny paused and thought. Grimaced. "Oh, you mean *Winston*. I thought you meant somebody else." He looked down at the gravel and kicked at one of the many butts ground there. The black and white foam pellets were a habitual give-away: this was Gin's break spot. "No, Winston's just some sort of schemer. He likes to play games with people's minds. Ignore him." He chuckled, thinking about the stupid bet Winston had laid down about asking Gin for a date.

But then...what did he have to lose?

"Gin, how would you...." He stopped, feeling like an idiot. He started laughing.

"What's so funny? Would I what?"

"Nothing," Johnny said, trying to cool down and change the subject. "It's just that you seem different out here, when you're not behind the counter with a plate of food in your hands."

Gin smiled, then crunched her cigarette in the gravel with a heel. "So do you," she said and winked, walking away.

Johnny could feel the blood rushing to his cheeks again as he watched her enter a door that led to the kitchen. He smiled to himself and spit between his teeth, dropping the cigarette and shaking his head. "Menthols," he said, looking at the scattered butts at his feet. "Figures."

He crossed his arms and tried to look at the sun. It was still too bright. But he forced his eyes to get accustomed to the light. He had to, if he wanted to meet her out here for a morning cigarette again. Maybe next time he'd have enough guts to ask her to join him over a cup of coffee without cracking up and making a fool out of himself. And he'd do it for himself, too. Not on some childish bet with Winston. Winston and his silly games.

*Game*, Johnny thought, recalling the early morning fist-fight. *What was all that talk about "spoiling the game" that Winston had said to break up that fight between Shorty and Axe? And what did he mean by saying they'd "fold"? Just what kind of game was Winston running?*

# Play Dead

The aluminum front door of the shelter crashed open. Axe stepped out onto the gravel lot, grunting as he marched toward the sun, large arms swinging at his side and slapping his thighs. Johnny noticed that he was leaving a trail behind him: his black hair was wetted back and his beard was still dripping from the shower he'd taken. He still wore the same filthy long johns and jeans he'd apparently slept in. These, too, were wet and clinging to his skin.

Axe lumbered off the loud gravel and onto the sidewalk, heading south.

A familiar voice of instinct whispered in his mind: *Something's going down.*

Before he knew what he was doing, Johnny followed him. He wasn't quite sure what sort of game Axe was involved in, or if he'd even find out what it was by trailing him, but that didn't mean he couldn't play a silent game of Hide and Seek with Paul Bunyan. He could waste his whole day following him if he wanted to—he had nothing better to do—it didn't matter.

All that mattered now was that—perhaps—he'd finally found some Action.

Axe was easy to follow: he stood out from the crowd, the epitome of home-lessness. Johnny trailed him from a block's length, ducking around the occasional lamp post or billboard whenever Axe took a paranoid glance over his shoulder.

Axe didn't know he was being followed. But he was paranoid that he might be, snatching peeks over the lump of his collarbone like a kidnapper with a baby in his arms. Johnny knew what that meant: something was definitely going down. Something *hot*, or else Axe wouldn't be dropping his poker face like this. Johnny eagerly quickened his pace.

The streets were crowded with cars—morning rush traffic and early tourist buses—but there was no one on foot besides Johnny and Axe. The sun was still burning brightly; everything glowed with absorbed heat, alive, humming with the action of the city.

But this was the no-man's-land between the downtown casinos and the grand hotels on the Strip: the gap between real Action and The Show. "The Show" was Johnny's phrase for the glitz and glamour of the Strip, the attractions and weird architecture, the shining lights and tourist traps. You didn't have to "go see a show" on stage in Vegas—the Strip *was* the stage, the place itself *was* The Show. And The Show had everything the sucker tourist came to see and do...except gamble to win. Johnny couldn't understand the tourist mentality of wasting good money—*playing* money—just to come all the way out here to an oasis in the desert, only to play a game that's rigged right from the start. People fed on its fever, just to be consumed by The Show itself: blinded by its spectacle the second they opened their eyes. Maybe they liked to lose. Maybe it made them feel like they were purging themselves of their American sin, sacrificing themselves to the big god of glamour. Vegas: one big excuse to be a loser for a day, and be damned proud of throwing their money away in a perverse ritual as moronic as religious fasting.

Axe turned and Johnny ducked. The billboard he dove behind buzzed with a rectangular border of electric lights. NEBO'S BUCKET OF BUCKS

# Play Dead

its flashy silver letters promised atop an image of a fruit machine running three thick golden bars. In the corner, Johnny faced the corniest of logos: a four-leaf clover atop a rainbow tipping a pot of gold with fingers of colored light. The Bucket was a new joint on the Strip. And from what he'd heard about the place, the corny advertising was working.

Johnny wiped a thin sheen of sweat from his forehead. The lights of the billboard were brighter than the morning sun, hot and mystically flashing around him. He peeked around the advertisement and sighted Axe doing his best to cross the street, rushing through the spaces between cars like a New York beggar washing windshields. A few Japanese autos honked at him. A dude in a Chevy pick-up flipped him off. But no one bothered to stop.

Johnny continued to shadow his mark from across the road. They were close to the Strip now, The Show's brotherhood of casinos towering in the distance like pyramids in a desert. And that's what they were: THE SANDS, ALADDIN, THE MIRAGE, THE TROPICANA...all desert names, and everything *but* deserted. NEBO'S BUCKET OF BUCKS was out there, too, the newest, and, therefore, tallest of them all, a flat black mirror standing in the sand as ominous as an obelisk. Unlike the others, though, it made no pretensions of desert imagery—the allure of money itself—a pot of gold at the end of a rainbow—was like water to anyone who came this way. Especially Johnny, who really needed a drink.

Axe picked his nose while he walked, shifting his head sideways in fear of watchers as he passed a seedy-looking bar-and-grill with a collapsing sign that read THE SHANTY and a newly-renovated tattoo parlor called KILLER'S INK.

Johnny spit through the gap in his overbite—he could have won a contest. He smiled and tongued the space in his mouth, prodding the gummy wound as he walked, thinking that it might just be good for something. In fact, it was probably all he had anymore.

And then Axe disappeared.

Johnny skidded his steps, double-taking the scene. He spun in a circle, hoping Axe hadn't spotted him, hoping he'd only misjudged his trail by a few steps. But Axe was gone—nowhere to be found amid the hot concrete and lost in the dawning haze of the neon forest. Cars blurred past where he stood as if Axe had been swallowed up by the flash of taillights.

Johnny cursed, spit, and moved to cross the street. Maybe Axe had ducked into that bar he saw earlier to try and bum some bourbon.

The cars and pick-up trucks made it difficult, but Johnny managed to cross over. After one last look at The Show, he turned back toward the bar and tattoo shop. It would be tricky to keep his cover if he got too close, but he had to know what was going down. Maybe nothing at all, but at least he'd *know*.

From the outside, The Shanty looked like a worse dive than the shelter. But even from this distance, Johnny could hear the clinging of bells and the click-clack-click of spinning wheels—ancient slot machines—which made it sound like heaven. Or Hell, depending on whichever way Lady Luck flipped her silver dollar.

There were no windows. Only mirrored glass. Johnny spit and entered.

The smoke hit him like mustard gas. He quickly sorted its smells in his nose: thick clouds of cigar and cigarettes burning in unclean ashtrays; something greasy fizzling on the griddle in the kitchen, loud perfumes and colognes...and beneath it all the scent of sulfur from so many cheap matchbooks, freshly struck. Near the doorway, a woman in her sixties with large blemishes on her cheeks and curly gray hair shoved a quarter into a slot machine faster than it could take it, just to hear the sound of the rejected coin clapping the dull tin of the jackpot bucket. She blinked rapidly, mascara-clotted eyelids batting away the smoke that trailed up and eddied in her sockets from the thin cig dangling between her lips.

Johnny feigned interest, using her strangely angled body as a shield as Three men—none older than Johnny—decked out in slick black and blue business suits raised thick red drinks in toast. Beside them, another elderly woman, probably the sister of the one whom Johnny stood beside, slouched over a beer. There was no music, little talk. A hairy-armed bald man with apron strings tied behind his back faced away from Johnny, addressing someone in the kitchen. Axe was nowhere to be found.

Johnny considered returning to the streets to try and catch up with him, but the second-hand smoke from the old lady's cigarette—coupled with the smell of food—was too much to pass up. He dropped his pursuit and turned to the woman. Staring at the unmoving row of stars across its board, she continued plunking the coin in the machine's slot.

"You ever gonna pull the lever?" Johnny asked.

The woman flashed him a sliver of eyeball and then continued her routine. "You can never win the next pull after a machine hits the jackpot. Don't you know that, boy?"

He chuckled and looked away.

And he spotted Axe through the thin square of space that revealed the kitchen, his back turned as he washed some pots in a steaming sink. "Yes," Johnny said, staring at him. "I know that boy."

The woman twisted on her stool, cigarette dangling dangerously from over-painted lips. "Huh?"

"Never mind." So this was what was going down, eh? Axe had a job slinging grease for a bunch of lounge lizards in a cheap dive. Big deal. Johnny sighed, desperately wanting a cigarette. He sighted the woman's pack beside the slot machine. "Mind if I borrow a smoke from ya?" He was blushing—he could feel it in his ears. He hated to ask.

"Sure, no problem." She winked at him and returned to the machine. "But I'll be damned if you can give it back once you smoked it."

He grimaced. Stupid question. He tried to cover it up with small talk: "So I take it you're a big spender now that you won the last pull."

"Nah, if I'da hit the ol' JP, I'd be buying a round for the house. That suit over there at the bar done plucked this fruit tree. First time I seen it hit stars in years."

Johnny nodded and smiled. He could feel stale air creep between the spaces in his teeth. The woman grinned back, though she didn't look away from her machine. If anyone looked like they lived in The Shanty, it was this old lady. He patted her on the back. "Thanks for the smoke."

"You asked for it," she said, rubbing it in.

Johnny walked over to the counter and pulled a stool up beside the men in suits, perfectly aligning his vision in the corner of the space between the bar and the kitchen so he could keep an eye on Axe.

*The no-good bum. Three hots and a cot at the shelter, and still he moon-lights here. Shouldn't that be illegal? Shouldn't I tell somebody? Shouldn't I go back there and let him know that I know where he gets his booze money?*

*Or better yet: Shouldn't I get him to make me some lunch?*

"We're gonna make a lot of money today, gentlemen," a suit beside him barked, raising a shot glass. "To the deal!"

"The deal!" his buddies chanted, and drank.

Johnny saw an opportunity. He reached inside his pocket and withdrew three bent cards. "Someone say deal?" he asked, tossing the cards onto the bar, face-up, one at a time. Queen. Ace. Queen.

The one nearest him smirked, avoiding eye-contact. "Do ya mind, friend? We're talkin' business."

"So are these three cards." Johnny began to hand toss the cards Three-Card Monte-style, flicking their edges with his fingers so they'd slap wood when they hit the heavy oak of the bar. "And they're talkin' to you." Johnny went through two rotations before letting them lie. "You up for a wager?"

"What's the con?"

"No con. Just pro." Johnny winked. "You're a pro, aintcha? A professional?"

The man nodded. The other two slid forward on their stools, getting interested.

"Well I reckon you must know what it's like to play the market then, right?"

"What market?" The man leered secretively. "We sell porn vids to sleazy distributors."

"The *meat-market*, Charlie," a buddy snickered.

"Yeah, but I think Charlie here's been playin' with his own salami," said the other, downing his Bloody Mary and belching.

Johnny grinned. "Well, let me put this here market in perspective for ya, Charlie. What we got here is two chicks and an Ace who can't make up his mind which one to fondle."

"So?"

# Play Dead

"So whatta ya say you help him make a decision?" Using the face-up edge of the Ace, Johnny flipped the two Queens over, and then juggled them on the table. "You just gotta play matchmaker. The Queen of Spades wants Mr. Ace of Spades here big-time. They were made for each other. Both being spades and all, they'd make a perfect couple, right?

"And?"

"And the fact is, she never has the nerve to tell him how much she wants his body, because the other Queen's a jealous gal—always keepin' her eye on him." Johnny flipped the cards so they were now all face down on the bar. "But now that both their backs are turned, our Queen of Spades has a chance. Ya follow?"

"I think so." He blinked as if fighting his morning drunk and peered at the cards, enthralled.

"Here," Johnny said, dealing Charlie the Ace. "Take Mr. Ace and put him in your pocket so he doesn't run away."

The man named Charlie kept his eye on Johnny's hands while he slid the card into the breast pocket of his coat.

"All you gotta do is pick the right Queen to rendezvous with the dude in your pocket, while the other Queen's got her back turned." He stopped the shuffle. "Just choose one of these two face-down Queens, and put it in your pocket with the other one, so they can make whoopee in private. If it's the right match for your Ace, I'll buy you and your friends the next round."

"And if I pick the wrong Queen?"

"You'll buy me a hamburger."

Charlie jingled the change in his pocket—leftover quarters from the slot machine. "So it's an either-or situation—one card or the other—fifty-fifty chance. That simple?"

"If only life were so simple, my friend."

Charlie grinned as he reached forward. "Bet you think I wasn't watchin' your little rigmarole while you was shufflin', don't ya?" He laughed. "I got your number, buddy," he said, and picked up the card on his right, sliding it into his pocket.

Johnny said: "Now flip over this lonely Queen."

He did so: *the Queen of Diamonds*.

"Ha! I won!" The others cheered. Charlie clapped Johnny on the back. "Barkeep! Another round on my new friend here."

The bartender moved toward their side of the bar.

"Uh, not so fast," Johnny said, bracing himself. "Don't you think we should check on those lovers in your pocket first?"

"Huh?" Every sound seemed sucked clear out of the room in a pulsing silence as the group of suits turned on him.

"I think someone's having an affair in your pocket."

Charlie reached into his pocket and tossed the cards on the bar. They landed face-down. He reached forward and flipped over the Queen of Spades.

One of his buddies snickered. "See? That's the right Queen."

Johnny flipped over the other card: the Ace of Diamonds, which he'd switched when he handed him the card to put in his pocket.

Charlie guffawed. "This is bullshit!"

"Nope, this boy's match is right here." Johnny pointed at the Queen of Diamonds.

Charlie puffed his cheeks out in anger, his eyeballs ready to spill out of their lids. His hands were flexing into fists. "Fuckin' con artist! I oughta..."

A hand landed on Charlie's shoulder and gripped tightly, squeezing Charlie back down in his stool. His friends jumped out of their seats.

"I believe you owe this man some lunch," a familiar voice said.

The bartender nodded. "That's the way I see it, too."

Johnny turned to see Winston holding Charlie down in his stool. Winston paid no attention; he just looked up at the bartender and nodded beneath his cowboy hat while Charlie winced and dug inside his pocket to start counting out his change.

From across the room, a sole quarter plunked down in the jackpot bucket with a metallic *clunk*. The old lady by the slot machine cackled so loud it filled the barroom.

# Play Dead

Winston motioned with his head, glancing toward a booth of crackled burgundy leather in the corner of The Shanty. Johnny stood, and together they sat down at the booth while Charlie counted out quarters at the bar to pay for the hamburger. Johnny and Winston stared at each other silently across the table, waiting for the suits to leave, which they did grudgingly, cursing among each other as they exited the bar. The old woman continued to drop her single quarter in the slot machine, eyes fixed on the unmoving series of bars while Johnny's lunch sizzled on the grill in Axe's kitchen.

"Okay," Johnny said. "I've had enough of this crap. Something's up with you, and I'm not so sure I like it. It's all too convenient. I come in here and find Axe working in the back like some nine-to-five asshole, and just when I get into a tiny bit of trouble, you magically show up outta nowhere." Johnny tongued the gap in his gums, wondering if he should mention what he saw that morning at the shelter, too, but decided to keep that in the hole for now. "You wanna explain how something like that could happen?"

Winston sighed before lighting a cigarette and dropping the fresh pack on the table between them. Johnny grabbed one and shoved it between his lips without asking. Winston chucked him a book of matches. Johnny lit up, recognizing the logo on the matchbook. It was an exact replica of the billboard he'd seen on the street: NEBO'S BUCKET OF BUCKS.

Winston swallowed smoke and squinted at Johnny, considering both the question and the man who'd asked it. After an uncomfortable silence, he said: "Sure, I'll explain anything you want...if you can show me how you pulled off that con you suckered that asshole at the bar with."

"Everything's a game to you, isn't it?" Johnny pulled the bent cards out of his pockets like forgotten lint. "There you go, look. It's all in the cards. There's four of them, not three. The game's fixed. I switched Aces when I handed him his pocket card. It's a simple hustle."

"No game of chance," Winston said, leaning back, "is ever simple...or truly *fixed*, for that matter." He puffed on his cigarette. "The smart player will always bet on the opposite of what he's been led to believe. Every con can be conned because they think they're in control of fortune. But chance can't be controlled, ya know?" Winston leaned forward, snatching Johnny's cards and pocketing them. "You don't need this shit. Period." His eyes brightened so deeply they appeared to change colors. "You asked me a question, but I've got a better question for you, Johnny. If I explained to you how to play another game, a bigger game than this penny-ante bullshit you pull on morons like a bus station punk, would *you* try to con *me*?"

"Huh?"

"Food!" the bartender called, sliding a steamy plate onto the bar. Johnny fetched it, saliva racing into his mouth as the smell hit him. His hunger surprised him. He sat down and immediately took as large a bite as his mouth could possibly handle, tearing the food sideways like a dog might, because of his missing front tooth. *Axe ain't too bad a cook*, he thought, shoving in another bite.

Winston waited, watching him eat as if disgusted. "That stuff'll kill ya someday, Johnny."

Between bites: "I'd rather die. Of clogged arteries. Than starvation."

Winston shrugged.

When he was done with the burger, Johnny mopped up the brown grease and ketchup on his plate with cold and shiny french fries. His stomach felt full—it was a new feeling, a satisfying one. He couldn't remember the last time he felt so complete. It was like a body part missing since birth had been magically reattached.

He felt ready to play again. Ready for Action.

"What were you talkin' about before? Some kinda game you're in on, or somethin'?"

"No, I'm not 'in' on any game. Just an interested party. I'm not a player, like yourself. I don't like to get my hands dirty, and I don't fool myself into believing I have the skill to master Fate." He avoided Johnny's eyes. "No, I just like to watch. And make educated wagers."

Johnny was on his final fry. He made it last, sucking it down to powder in his mouth. "So what's the game? And what's it got to do with me?"

"Well," Winston said, his voice nearly a whisper. "I've been watching you, Johnny. And I'm willin' to wager that you got what it takes to play a game that most folks would kill to be a part of."

Johnny's face clenched in disbelief. He wasn't sure what kind of con Winston was pulling, but he wanted to know more, even if only to get a better idea of how Winston's mind worked. He let him reveal his hand: "Mmm-hmm. And?"

"And I think that when I tell you how you can be a part of the action, you'd kill to be in on it, too."

Johnny stole another cigarette from Winston. Lit up. "Quit the sales pitch and get to the meat. What's goin' down?"

Winston rolled his fingertips on the wooden table. "I know of a vacant seat that's opening up in one of the greatest poker games ever held. I have the power to get you to sit in on that game. I can't go into much detail yet, because it's too risky to talk about until I know for certain that you're ready to play. I'll need you to do me a favor. An act of confidence, if you will, so I'll know I can trust ya."

*Bait-and-switch.* The oldest trick in the book. Johnny sighed. "Let me guess. You want me to rob a bank or some rich tourist or some such shit. Maybe pull a hustle with ya on some high roller. Then you'll offer to split the take with me so I have enough scratch to buy into this mysterious bullshit game you've made up. Next thing ya know, I'm doin' time in the state pen, while you're the richest bastard in Borneo. Sound about right?"

Winston closed his eyes, and swallowed. A dramatic gesture, but Johnny could see his eyeballs flitting side to side beneath the fleshy lids, as if searching for his reply. Winston—eyes closed—licked his lips, and said: "I see that I've crapped out and misjudged my bet. You were not the right choice." His lips tightened to thin angry lines, which he continued to smack as his neck muscles tensed. "I thought you were a real player, Johnny. A gambler. Not some mouthy con artist who bites the hand that feeds him." He opened his eyes. Deep blue mirrors reflected Johnny back at himself, trapped inside the corneas. "Opportunity just knocked, kid. And weak little you had to slam the door in its face." He snatched his cigarette pack and pocketed it. "Fine, Johnny. If that's the way you wanna play it, fine." He topped his head with his hat. "There are better players than you. And I know where to find 'em." He stood up and began to walk away. When he reached the slot machine, he turned to the woman sitting there and whispered something into her ear. She nodded, eyes glued to the stars on the machine. Then Winston left The Shanty—sun rays cutting into the smoke through the door jamb like a vision from God—not looking back.

A gruff voice: "What the hell are *you* doing here?"

Johnny looked up. Axe loomed over him, wiping his hands on his apron. Johnny grinned. "Enjoying your fine cookin', what else?"

Axe gritted his teeth. "Well I think you better get out, before I cook *you* for lunch."

Johnny remembered the morning fight. "Tell me somethin', Axe. What's goin' on here? What's this game you guys are playin'?"

"Fuck you. I don't know nothin' about Winston's games. Get out of here."

Johnny's smile widened. "I didn't say *Winston*, did I? But since you brought it up..."

Axe had his apron off and around Johnny's neck in as much time as it took to move behind him. He yanked backward on the strings. Johnny struggled, clawing his fingers beneath the cotton fabric. Too late. He couldn't breathe.

*"I didn't say nothin', you hear me? Nothin'."* He yanked again, so hard Johnny's tongue popped out of the gap between his teeth and he bit down on it. His stomach convulsed to vomit but the grip on his throat gave no release, violently trapping the puke in his pipes. Regurgitated hamburger trickled back into his lungs as he turned bright purple. Axe punctuated his words with a violent pull on the strings: "Now you just get the *fuck* outta here, boy. And I better not see you back here again. Or at the shelter, neither. 'Cuz next time it'll be a piece of barbed wire around your throat, or maybe my buck knife. Got it?"

Johnny tried to nod against the swarm of tiny dots which seemed to be drowning his vision.

# Play Dead

Axe let go and stepped back toward the kitchen, slapping the knotted apron against his thigh.

Johnny gagged, spilling his lunch into the sawdust on the barroom floor. He curled up in the booth, writhing on the leather which crackled beneath him, trying to breathe and see and stop the pounding in his temples as blood returned to feed the hungry cells there.

When he had the strength to sit up, the strange old woman was sitting across from him, staring into his eyes with the same expression she used on the slot machine, hypnotized by the stars there.

"Let's talk," she said, sliding out of the booth and tugging Johnny up by an armpit. He dizzily followed her lead, abstractly noticing that she had left a shiny quarter on the table, an absurd tip.

On the sidewalk, the sinner tried to dodge The Preacher, and nearly tripped over his green duffel bag. But The Preacher was relentlessly in his face: "The wages of sin are death! And your sin—playin' games with Lucifer—makes those wages easy money, ill-gotten gain...when you gamble you sin to earn more sin! Repent from this lewd behavior! Repent from gambling to procure sins of the flesh! The only sure thing is your death if you don't! Bet on it! Or better yet, bet on the Lord! The Lord takes care of his own!"

The man's face was bright red as he ducked into the building which read SEX*BOOKS*SEX*TOYS*SEX*BOOKS in black lettering on a stained yellow tarpaulin above its black-tinted glass entrance. The Preacher moved to follow him, but pulled his hand away from the silver doorknob, neither wishing to shake hands with the Devil, nor daring to enter the gates of his Hell. "Damnation!" he shouted and pivoted, looking for more sinners to convert.

The area was deserted for the time being—sin *hides*—so The Preacher sat down on the concrete beside a beaten black hat, visually counting the coins inside which rested atop the tattered leather cover of his Bible. It looked like he'd panhandled about two dollars and thirty-six cents. He picked up the Good Book, spilling the coins into the bottom of the hat, and flipped through its gold-edged pages for inspiration.

A playing card—The Five of Hearts—marked his place in the New Testament: Acts.

Underlined: *Silver and gold have I none; but such as I have give I thee.*

He muttered the sentence to himself over and over as he wiped his forehead with the fat end of his peach-colored necktie. Hell was a hot place.

*Silver and gold have I none; but such as I have give I thee.*

He thought about the coins in his hat—the few tokens of guilty penance tossed to him by occasional passers-by. He knew it was tainted money, ill-gotten gambling gain. But he would return it to its rightful place, in the house of the Lord, as he had done each and every Sunday since succumbing to his own sinful desires and ending up on the streets. Two-dollars and thirty-six cents was hardly enough to offer this week, but if he bet it well, it might be.

He withdrew the Five of Hearts from its place in his Bible and used its dull edge to dig the green dirt out from beneath his left thumbnail. *Four down,* he thought, *and nine to go. Thirteen cards altogether—a suit's worth—the Devil's number. Had to play him at his own game, though, to beat him. Play by his rules, sitting at his table. It was the only way to trick the evil bastard.*

A car pulled over to the curb in front of The Preacher. Black-and-white, with an encircled star on its door. A pentagram—satanic symbol—disguised as police car markings. The Preacher knew better. He tucked his card back into his book and cursed, hoping they hadn't seen it.

*He's found me out,* he thought, and began madly snatching the coins out of his hat.

The cop car opened a window. "Sir? Excuse me, sir?"

The Preacher placed the hat on his head, and turned his head to one side, ignoring them.

"Sir? We got a phone call from the owner of this establishment, and I'm sorry to say that if you don't leave these premises immediately, I'm afraid we'll have to take you in for loitering and pandering."

"Who says?"

"Those are the rules, sir."

"I'm playin' by the rules," The Preacher said, standing up and holding his Bible before him like a cross to a vampire. "God's rules!"

Someone inside the car laughed. "I understand that, sir, but you're in my playground, and you have to go play somewhere else. Now get a move on, before we take you in. Got it?"

The Preacher spit on the sidewalk between them. "I'll leave this den of iniquity, sinner. I'll leave. So long as I have the Lord, I am free. You could drag me down into the bowels of your torturous prisons, and I would remain free. You could shoot me with your guns, and I would be free as a bird. You could beat me and rape me and murder me, and free I'd remain..."

Snickering: "Good for you. Now beat it."

The Preacher picked up his duffel bag and walked away, proud of his victory over the demon patrol as he continued preaching to himself. He knew where to go next—to the PAIR-O-DICE MARRIAGE CHAPEL, yet another sacrilege against the house of the Lord. Perhaps there they'd listen to reason. Perhaps there, he'd find open ears and innocence in young lovers.

No matter. There was business on the way—a particular address he had tucked into the Book of Revelations, which he had planned on visiting today. It was nasty business, but it had to be done. He had promised Shorty vengeance. And now Winston had ordered it. Plus it was the Lord's business, on top of it all, though only The Preacher knew that for sure.

At the bus station, he tried his luck with the two dollars and thirty-six cents he'd been blessed with during the afternoon. He fed the coins into the mouth of the one-armed bandit in the lobby as gently as placing the Eucharist on the tongue of a child, whispering a rite and praying as he pulled the lever. The rush was feverish, each turning wheel a holy vision: a trinity of plums. But for the experience, he lost it all to the one-armed bandit in the lobby.

Leaving the bus station, the passage returned to him:
*Silver and gold have I none; but such as I have give I thee.*

"The trouble, Lord," The Preacher said aloud as he headed toward The Shanty, "is that I have nothing left." He frowned as he considered the implications, walking, looking at his playing card for inspiration.

And the message was clear. Acts 3:16. The book of Acts. As in *Axe*.

And the Five of Hearts.

He prayed it wouldn't take him too long to give the Lord what he could scrounge up behind The Shanty.

# Play Dead

Her name was Violet and she suggested that Johnny stay at her place until he figured out how to deal with Axe who'd warned him not to go back to the shelter. Johnny agreed, not knowing any better.

He was shocked by the extravagance of her apartment: a plump brown vinyl sofa took up nearly the entire front room when they entered, like Jabba the Hutt oozing against the wall; odd paintings, prints, and photographs engulfed nearly all the wall space, haphazardly puzzled together to form a bigger picture of Violet's history and quirky delights; the carpet was deep purple shag, gaudy in comparison to the rich furnishings, and Johnny swore he could feel its tendrils writhing between his toes even through his tennis shoes. There was no rule of decor—in one corner, Indian-styled rugs hung beside three Victorian picture-framed black velvet paint-by-number canvasses of weird animals playing cards, slightly crooked atop polka dot-patterned wallpaper.

Johnny felt his gut lurch, while Violet left him in the front room to visit the bathroom. He felt extremely nauseated and he couldn't tell if it was from the disorienting construction of Violet's carnivalesque living room, or from the strangling he survived an hour ago. Maybe it was from the burger Axe had made him—or what was left of it in his stomach. Or, perhaps, it was the feeling of being in a place that was unmistakably a *home* after so long an absence from anything remotely like one.

Violet returned. "Make yourself comfy, Johnny. You can sleep here on the couch." She smiled to herself. "Heck, that'll be a first. Don't think I've even *sat* on the thing since I bought it. And now I got a sexy man sleepin' on it to break it in. Figures." She shared her smile with him, the blotches on her face purpling with blood. "But you gotta wash that stinkin' ass of yours in the shower before you go rubbin' it all over my nice sofa."

"Yes, ma'am," Johnny said, surprised and embarrassed by her mouth.

She turned away, heading toward a makeshift bar which separated the room they were in from the kitchen. Johnny followed, vaguely feeling like a teenager collecting an allowance for mowing her lawn or shoveling her walkway or something stupid like that. She spoke over her shoulder: "I've got plenty of food and drink, and you can partake of it whenever you want to. Just make sure you clean up after yourself." She pivoted, and he nearly fell into her. "I ain't young, ya know, and I catch germs real quick-like if I ain't careful. So you gotta keep this place cle..."

"Slow down, Violet." He touched her shoulder. "I promise you, I'm not moving in for good or nothin'. I'll just be here for a night or two. And I appreciate all you're offering, but I won't take anythin' I ain't earned."

Violet winked. "Like you earned your lunch today? Or that wringin' of your neck?"

"Well..."

She waved a hand to shush him. "No, no, you ain't gonna earn my respect by connin' me, boy. Let's just say we got an understandin'. I know you ain't no money-maker, and I don't expect you to 'earn' a thing for me. But you *are* a player. I know it just as I know the smell of my own armpits. I got the instinct—I can tell. I know you better than you probably know yourself, kid. And though you probably don't know shit about me, you can trust me. You *know* you can. You got the instinct, too." She paused, frowning at her sermon. "Anywho...We're both human bein's, and we're both gonna respect each other. Right?"

Johnny nodded. "'Course."

"So don't you go connin' no old lady like me. Just be yourself and take what I give ya, no questions asked."

Johnny rolled his eyes. "Okay, I suppose. But I'll get you back for this someday when you least expect it."

Violet began pouring shots of Jack Daniels. "You make it sound like I'm doin' somethin' bad here by helpin' out a man down on his luck." She handed him his glass. "I ain't got much time left and I gots to do all I can to improve my resume for the big guy upstairs..." She raised her glass. "*Salud!*"

Johnny downed his shot, surprised at how quickly it settled his stomach. "Ahh. Been awhile since I've had a stiff drink."

Violet was pouring the next round. "There's more where that came from."

# Play Dead

Johnny watched her, wondering how the hell he ended up drinking shooters with an old slot machine queen. Her face was unpleasant, but Johnny thought she was sort of cute, too. Something about her fiery personality and gruff voice attracted him. And from the looks of her apartment — and the free food and booze — she seemed rich, to boot.

"So what's your story?" he asked, eyeing her kitchen and blinking at the gargantuan size of her refrigerator. "You're obviously pretty well off. Why do you hang out at that Shanty dump?"

"I could ask the same of you." She slid a full shot glass in front of him. "Hell, I got a lot of questions for you, boy."

"Like?"

"Like what in the hell did you think you were doing, giving ol' Winston the brush off?"

"How do you know Win..."

"I know him real well. Works for Nebo, owner of my favorite bar — that joint you just had the balls to call a 'dump.'"

Johnny was blushing. "What kinda name is Kneebone? And did you say Winston was *working* for him?"

"It's Nebo, kid, not kneebone. Get your names right. Don't you know nothin'?" She set fire to the end of a long cigarette, staring at him through the smoke. "I swear. You walk around actin' like you're some big hot shot who knows all the dice, but you sure are stupid."

Johnny didn't know what else to do but shrug.

"Here, have a cigarette and listen." She passed him a pack, cigarettes spilling out in offering like a fanned hand of cards. "Nebo's one of the richest men in town. Got his own casinos and what not. Haven't you seen the signs?" She puffed — locomotive chug — not waiting for his reply. "Owns a lot of chintzy dives, too, like The Shanty. I swear. He plays the real estate market like a crap game, and always turns up sevens." She rolled her eyes, which looked weary beneath the weight of her green mascara. "Wish I had his luck."

Johnny let it sink in. Nebo — *Nebo's Bucket of Bucks*. He'd seen the sign, all right. Got so close to the bulbs that they nearly sunburned him. He wondered where Violet was headed with all this. "And?"

50

She blew. "And you'd do best not to get on the wrong side of Winston. He's a strange feller, but he always deals straight with ya. Nebo wouldn't trust anyone who didn't."

"So what do you know about this game he's got going?"

"Game?" Violet hacked, and stamped out her cigarette, half-smoked. "Winston don't play no games, far as I know. Just wagers. He's nice enough to make book for me once in awhile, though, if that's what you mean. But I don't bet on sport games. Just horses. You can trust animals a helluva lot more than humans." She looked into his eyes—Johnny saw something like sex shining in there, innocence long gone. Then she blinked and it washed away. "Hell, when I saw you two arguin', I thought you'd missed a payment or somethin'. I told ya—he's a straight shooter, and don't take no welchers. I figured maybe you got him steamed when I saw the two of you talkin'— you can tell if he's pissed atcha by the way he closes his eyes and whispers when he talks to you." Violet lit another cigarette, throwing Johnny a look of secrecy. "Anyway, he told me to take care of ya when he left you at the bar, so I did." She chuckled. "But I guess the Axeman took care of you first."

Johnny cracked his neck. "Sure did. I'll get the fucker, though." He finally gave in to the menthol cigarette he'd been palming, and lit it. "What can you tell me about Axe?"

"Nothin' to tell. Winston got him the job at the Shanty is all I know."

"That's all?"

Violet smirked. "Well he smells like baby shit, too, for what it's worth."

Johnny stared at her. Then he laughed so hard the gap in his front teeth whistled like a steam train chugging downhill.

Violet laughed then, too, until tears washed mascara down her face in crazy green lines. That made Johnny think of clowns and he laughed some more. Soon their laughter faded until she pointed at his mouth, and guffawed, spitting out her dentures in the process.

Johnny nearly fell to the floor, his gut in so much pain from the laughter that he thought he'd been kicked in the crotch.

He laughed, control beyond him, trying to remember if he'd ever laughed so much before, or ever been quite so drunk.

# Play Dead

## ♣ ♣ J ♣ ♣
## ♣ ♣ ♣ ♣ ♣ ♣

Johnny awoke in what felt like an ocean of rancid tapioca pudding. He tried to sit, but couldn't, sinking only deeper into the cushions of Violet's brown vinyl sofa. His head was too heavy to lift, throbbing with the morning's hangover and the pain of Axe's strangulation, and he gave up trying.

He closed his eyes and struggled amidst the pain in his temples to remember what had happened. Instead, a vision of Gin came to him: Gin, nude, blonde hair tousled over her face. He reached up to brush it aside so he could look into her eyes, shut them, and, perhaps, kiss them. And then he saw large purple blotches and runny green goo undulating like a puddle of worms in orgy as he parted the hair—Violet's face, stitched onto Gin's body—as her tongue pressed forward, thick and yellow, teeth spilling out onto his lap and nibbling...

He shot up into a sitting position again. His mouth was flooding with watery, undeveloped saliva—the familiar warning of upcoming vomit, as if his body was hungry enough to salivate at the chance of digesting the same food once again—only Johnny couldn't remember eating any food, couldn't remember anything at all as he forced himself to swallow and hold it all down. The room was swimming, and the couch felt like a disturbed waterbed quivering violently beneath him.

He held his breath and swallowed twice, riding the waves. It worked.

He decided not move anymore, to just sit still and think, eyes closed.

His clothes felt funny. Scratchy. He looked down and discovered that he was wearing a pink terry cloth bathrobe with brushed velvet lapels. For a moment he thought that he was in another person's body—a woman's—as if someone had screwed up the seating arrangements on the flight back from the land of dreams. Part of Johnny's absurd reasoning was due to the fact that he was nude beneath the robe. Nude...and undeniably *clean*.

And then he recalled what Violet had said about washing his "stinkin' ass" before rubbing it all over her precious sofa. That was fine—it felt good to be clean for once. But he couldn't remember if he had washed up voluntarily, or if she forced him into the shower. And watched.

"Oh, God," he said, rubbing one side of his face with a hand that smelled of lilac. "What the hell did I do?"

But it wasn't so bad. He might have been hungover, but he was happy not to wake up in the prison-like shelter, with all its stenches and stains. With The Preacher's early morning sermon. And the bad food.

And Axe.

Johnny looked up at the wall. Four pedigree dogs played cards on a field of black velvet, surrounded by an ornate frame. He'd seen the picture before—dogs playing poker was a common one—but there was something different about this portrait that he couldn't quite place his finger on. The dogs were cheating, which was usually the case. They were smoking and munching on snacks—typical. But something was strange...

He closed his eyes and rubbed the other side of his face this time, trying to focus on his situation. Here he was, sleeping at some old barfly's house, in the lap—bizarre as it was—of what could pass for luxury. Winston, her bookie, had told her to take care of him. And she obeyed like one of those dogs in the painting. Winston had offered him a seat in some wild bullshit poker game, which he rejected. Axe had attacked him and threatened his life, just for mentioning Winston's game. And Winston had broken up a fight between Shorty and Axe, just by mentioning the word "game."

Winston had power. Johnny wasn't quite sure how he got it, or how he was wielding it, but Winston had more power than Johnny had ever seen up close before. And he always had his nose in everything, showing up at just the right moment to keep everything in control. Whatever it was he was controlling.

*The Game. The Game you passed up, you friggin' moron.*

Johnny's temples were throbbing.

He remembered what Violet said about Winston working for a guy named Kneebone...no, Nebo, the dude who had Buckets of Bucks—buckets Johnny could have had dug his fingers into if he hadn't pressed his luck with Winston. *Buckets.*

Johnny knew exactly what he could do with money like that. Buy himself a new gold tooth, a fresh suit, and maybe even enough guts to ask Gin out for a night on the town or two. Or twenty. Or a lifetime.

*Opportunity knocked and you slammed the door in its face.*

Winston was right. Johnny felt like an idiot for not listening to his gut, for not giving Winston a chance. Even if he *was* trying to bait him into being a fall guy, Johnny still could have turned the tables on him somehow in the long run. He thought about it — wondering how he could have been so stupid. And he didn't like the answers that were presenting themselves to him, like deals turned sour:

*Because you're afraid of him.*

*Because he has power and you have nothing.*

*Because you lost it all once, and don't have the guts it takes to get it back.*

Johnny prodded the space between his teeth. His mouth still felt numb — the absence was perpetual Novocaine. He thought about the night he lost it, trying to figure out what went wrong, playing the game over and over again in his mind like he had ever since he stepped out of that casino and into the empty, lonely streets. But — he now realized — it wasn't the game that went wrong that night. It wasn't in the cards; there were no bad deals. It wasn't bad luck. It was *himself.*

Because he never expected to lose. He expected to *win*, the second he sat down at the table. Like he always had. And he figured that was probably a backwards way of looking at life, once the cards took a nasty turn. And so in the middle of the game he'd convinced himself that he should expect to lose, always, no matter what he was dealt. That way, anything that did manage to come his way would be gravy. That way he'd feel like he was winning something, even if it was peanuts.

Everything was flip-flopping.

And now things were really fishy. He was *winning*, big-time, even though he'd gone out of his way to lose. One day he was at rock bottom, sleeping and starving in a stinking homeless shelter with a bunch of psychopaths, and the next he was in a glitzy apartment, fresh-clean and full, spoiled ripe with a hangover. He'd turned down one chance, and was given another. Things were goin' right when they were supposed to go wrong.

And *he* wasn't in control of it.

He didn't like it. Johnny stood up and fought his dizziness as he looked for his clothes. He finally found them, filthy, in a funny-smelling hamper in the bathroom. He dressed. Then he checked around the apartment for anything else he'd brought, but remembered that he'd had nothing. Ever. He grabbed an old sandwich and a bottle of orange juice from Violet's refrigerator. He sat down at the bar and began to shovel it into his mouth.

The bar was a mess: empty JD bottle towering over puddles and half-full shotglasses with cigarette butts floating inside. Ash was everywhere, spilled from a touristy ceramic tray that read GREAT SMOKY MOUNTAINS in bold black letters atop a picturesque scene. Johnny thought it'd make a better postcard than ashtray.

A piece of salami fell out of his mouth—a bad habit, due to his missing tooth. He bent down to pick it out of the wormy naps of the shag rug, when he saw yet another strange addition to Violet's mystique: Tarot cards, spilled there as if swept off the bar in anger. No words were on the ones which were face-up. A nude angelic woman, holding a globe upraised in her palm; a man hanging upside down by his ankles; a silly-looking drawing of two ornate cups.

Johnny was never into Tarot cards. He thought they were kind of silly. Still—he wondered what fate had laid out on the floor for him. He couldn't recall using them the night before. Did Violet do a reading for him, fore-telling a future that pissed him off so bad he'd swiped the cards off the bar?

He decided to tiptoe into her bedroom to check on her. Violet snored under satin sheets in an amazingly *un*decorated room with bright white walls and a lamp on a bedside table for furnishings. She looked even lonelier than he felt over at the crowded shelter.

He padded over to where she slept. Thought about kissing her on the cheek. Maybe even crawling into bed with her to cheer her up and make up for whatever he might have done the night before. Saw her purple blotches. Reneged.

Then he left, locking the front door behind him, realizing that the sun had yet to rise. That was good. Maybe he'd bump into Gin. Maybe he'd make it back to the shelter before Axe woke up. Maybe he'd be lucky enough to regain some control and get back in the game.

"You're gonna win," he told himself, still not quite ready to believe it as he headed toward the ever-glowing lights of the Strip. He saw Nebo's new mirage towering over it all, glow-in-the-dark green, the color of money. Buckets of it.

"You're gonna win," he repeated, but the words sounded silly coming out of his mouth. It simply looked like there was just way too much out there to beat.

♣ ♣ ♣ ♣ ♣ ♣  Q  ♣ ♣ ♣ ♣ ♣ ♣

Gin stepped outside the shelter's kitchen door with a crash, cold cigarette dangling between her lips, the moment Johnny stepped off the concrete sidewalk and onto the gravel lot. Perfect timing, just as he'd hoped for.

She turned against the rising sun, lighting her cigarette, not noticing his approach. He took advantage of the opportunity to examine her body, absorbing every detail—blue jeans so tight she had to struggle to get the lighter from her pocket, worn white Puma tennis shoes with the purple stripe, blonde hair curled under the ears, loose and baggy red T-shirt covering breasts which bowed the apron in such a way that he could see their soft pale sides through her sleeves as she lifted her arms...

She turned and caught him staring at her.

But this time he didn't blush. He needed to get a good picture of her in his mind, to cleanse his conscience of the morning's nightmare. And just seeing her made it feel good to be back.

She smiled, blinking at the sun behind him.

"You smoke too much," Johnny said, stepping between her and the door that led to the kitchen, smiling back.

Gin leaned forward, studying his face and neck as she offered him a menthol. Cute wrinkles squiggled up her forehead. "You look different."

"Yeah," Johnny said, somehow *feeling* different, too. "I'm clean for once." He lit up.

"A change for the better." Gin leaned back against the wall, smoking. "Does this mean you're outta this hell hole already?"

Johnny swallowed, thinking about Axe's promise to kill him if he saw him. "Yeah, for awhile anyway." He inhaled the menthol cigarette smoke, realizing that he was getting used to it. Kind of liking it, too. It tasted clean. He wondered if Gin's lips tasted this way—cool metallic mint with a hint of tar. "Didja miss me?"

Gin grimaced, cocking her head sideways at him in response.

"Kidding."

"Thought so." She blew. "So where are you comin' from so early this morning? Did you land a job or score at a club or what?"

*Is that jealousy?* Johnny wondered. "Neither. Fell asleep at a friend's place."

"Uh-huh."

They silently smoked.

*You're gonna win*, Johnny reminded himself. "Hey, Gin. Could I ask you for a favor?"

"Depends." She peered down at the gravel, twisting the cigarette in her fingers as if about to drop it and head back inside in disappointment. "What is it, Johnny?"

"I was wondering if you'd tell one of the guys to meet me out here after breakfast. You could just pass the word when you serve him up his grub."

She lifted the cigarette. Took a cautious drag. "What for? Why can't you just go tell him yourself right now?"

He touched her shoulder. "Please? His name is Shorty. You can't miss him: a big guy, acts kinda retarded."

"I know him. He always asks if I have cheese for his rats." She dropped her cigarette and crunched it beneath a heel. "What's in it for me if I do this for ya, Mr. Mysterious?"

Johnny smiled, shutting his mouth when her eyes trailed down to his lips to catch it. "Anything you want," he said, grinning. "Honest."

She cocked her head sideways and shrugged. "We'll see." She stepped around him. "I gotta get back to work." She opened the door and Johnny could see steam pour out into the lot. "Though I do think I should take it personally that you're skipping breakfast. What's the matter, don't you like my cookin'?"

The blush was returning. He tried not to look like he was staring at her, back arched as she glanced over her shoulder, moist hair sexily draped over her eyes as she leaned against the door frame. "No, I like it lots. It's just..."

She was already inside.

Johnny kicked at the gravel, raising dust with his tennis shoe. He felt like an idiot, again, a dumb shy teenager, a bag of hormones. But at least Gin seemed interested in him, even if only curious. And maybe she'd pull through and get Shorty to come outside to answer a few questions without getting Axe suspicious.

Johnny dropped what was left of his cigarette onto the gravel and stepped down.

And then he saw something that bothered him: other butts, with stained yellow and brown filters in contrast to the thin green lines and lipstick on Gin's favorite brand. Johnny didn't have to look closely to recognize that foreign brand scattered here and there around Gin's break spot like the markings of a dog trying to take over his territory: Winston.

"The fucker's everywhere," he whispered. It occurred to him that Winston was probably sleeping behind the very wall which Johnny leaned against. "If he's such a big-time bookie or whatever, why the hell is he sleeping in a homeless shelter?"

The front door slowly creaked open, and Johnny jogged to the corner of the building in case it was Axe, heading for his job at The Shanty.

Shorty peeked his head out. "Johnny?"

"Pssst." Johnny raised a finger to his lips.

Shorty saw him and his eyes widened, goofy. "John...oh." He lowered his neck, ducked back into the shelter, and then came back out. Johnny noticed that he carried his breakfast with him.

"This is from Gin. She said you should eat up while you still can."

Johnny chuckled, taking the paper plate from Shorty's hands. "C'mon, let's go behind the building where no one can see us."

Shorty obeyed, no questions asked. Which made Johnny nervous. Could he trust a guy like Shorty, who followed orders so easily?

They sat down by the trash bins behind the building. Johnny ate Gin's offerings: biscuits and gravy—a puddle of lumpy gray liquid drowning day-old bread. Too much pepper. But it tasted pretty good on top of the sandwich he'd nabbed from Violet's refrigerator.

"It's good." Shorty said, squinting as he read Johnny's face.

Johnny nodded, and decided to get right to the point. "What's goin' on with Axe, Shorty?"

"Whatta ya mean?"

"I know you guys are playing some big-time game for Winston." He swallowed food. "I wanna know more about it."

Shorty avoided Johnny's eyes and began biting his nails.

"Don't be scared—Winston told me about it himself. He just didn't give me very many details..."

"Why don't you ask him yourself? Want me to go get him? He's right inside..."

Johnny gripped his shoulder. "Not so fast. I wanna hear it from you, first."

Shorty nervously rubbed his pant leg—this was how he petted the pet rats which he used to carry around in his pockets. But now there was nothing beneath the fabric but his own skin.

Johnny chewed. "C'mon, Shorty. Aren't we buddies?"

"Not if you're playin' the game, we're not." He stood up, the pant-rubbing getting frantic now, with both hands. "Uh-uhn, Johnny. I can't say nothin'."

Johnny dropped his fork, looking up at Shorty. "Listen. Every time I ask someone about this game, they say they don't know anything. I'm sick of hearin' that." He set the plate down beside his lap, and crossed his arms. "Can you at least tell me *why* you can't talk about it?"

"No!" Shorty began pacing.

Johnny didn't want to make him upset. It might attract too much attention—especially if Axe was somewhere nearby. "Okay, never mind. C'mon and have a seat. Let's play some cards."

Shorty kept pacing until he realized that Johnny had mentioned the word "cards." Then he sat down beside him, the pant-rubbing slowing down, but ever-present. "Poker?"

"Sure," Johnny shrugged. "Gotta get ready for the big game, don'tcha?"

Shorty stopped rubbing. Looked at Johnny. Started rubbing again. "Do ya know Butcher Boy?"

"Who's that?"

"Not who. Butcher Boy. The card game." Shorty moved a hand to the gravel, and began grinding his palm there. It looked painful.

"Never heard of it. Sounds like a sissy game to me. How do you play?"

"Real easy." Shorty sat up and crouched, eager to get into the game. Johnny loved this moment—Shorty's transformation in the thrill of upcoming Action—which he could read in Shorty's features. His eyes widened, pupils dilating with alertness. His hands took on a magician's dexterity as he pulled a beaten Bicycle deck from his breast pocket and began shuffling. Total coordination and concentration reflected in the tightened muscles of Shorty's neck, cheekbones, and forehead. Action resurrected Shorty from his mental slumber—instantaneous, feral. A quick change of personality, like Superman in his phone booth.

"Super," Johnny said. "Show me."

"All you do is deal—face-up—and bet." Shorty started dealing, all grins, and then looked up, startled. "Hey, what's the stake?"

Johnny had been waiting for this. "Info on Winston's game if you lose. A bottle of JD from me if you win."

Shorty frowned. "Where you gonna get JD?"

"Connections." Johnny raised an eyebrow. "Don'tcha trust me? C'mon, deal, man, deal."

"All right already, don't rush me." Shorty tossed the cards between them, face-up. *Queen of Hearts. Two of Clubs. Nine of Diamonds.*

"What is this? Fifty-two card pick-up?" Johnny fingered his Nine of Diamonds, which was bent and crumpled compared to the others.

Shorty ignored him.

Johnny watched his every move, especially focusing on the hands, looking for a trick deal. But Shorty was legit, flipping the cards squarely from the top of the deck. *Ace of Diamonds. Seven of Spades. Three of Hearts. Queen of Spades.*

"You got another Queen. Now I stop dealing." Shorty set down the deck. "Okay, look. You've got a pair showing. A pair of Queens. Normally we'd bet here, but we've already laid down our stakes. If I got the card you needed, in this case a Queen, I'd have to pass it back to you. Every Queen that turns up goes straight to you. And it keeps going like this, stopping to bet when another Queen turns up, or if I get a different pair. Either way, the game doesn't stop till one of us gets a four of a kind."

# Play Dead

Johnny's shoulders slumped. "Is that all? Just deal the deck till someone gets a four of a kind? Where's the skill in that?"

"It's tougher than you think. Luck of the draw is always the hardest game, ain't it?"

Johnny thought about his losing night, the night he crapped out on his own front tooth. "Yeah, I guess it is." Johnny wished he had a cigarette, and cursed under his breath for not stealing a pack from Violet.

Shorty picked up the deck to continue dealing.

Johnny grabbed Shorty's thick wrist, feeling the fat between his fingers: "Hey, not so fast."

"What?"

"Since I got another Queen, you wanna up the bet?"

Shorty nodded involuntarily. "To what?"

"I dunno," Johnny said. "Whatta ya got to lose?"

Shorty sighed, blatantly upset with having his thrill train stopped to pick up passengers. "I don't have anything. Let's just play."

"Hey, I got it!" Johnny slapped his thigh, feigning revelation. "Let's bet favors. If I win the pot, you owe me however many favors we've tossed into the pot, and vice versa. We gotta keep count, though."

"No problem," Shorty blinked. "But you keep count. I got better things to do. I'm dealin'."

First card peeled off the top: Ace of Spades. That gave Shorty a pair. "Looks like you won't have far to count, my friend."

Johnny chuckled. *How could Shorty change so much, so quickly?*

Next card: Queen of Diamonds.

"Unbelievable."

"Believe it," Johnny said. "And I think you're right—I won't be countin' much longer."

Johnny raised three fingers. "That's three favors you're gonna owe me if I turn another Queen."

Shorty shook his head. "Never happen." He continued the deal, hitting himself first: *Four of Clubs. Six of Hearts. King of Diamonds. Ace of Hearts.*

"I believe that would be mine," Shorty said, plucking the card from

Johnny's tableau and laying it beside his other two Aces. "Just like this game'll be mine in a few seconds."

"It ain't over yet. You're gonna owe me four favors, and the first one is gonna be to eat my shit, buddy."

Shorty laughed. Dealt: *Five of Hearts. Queen of Clubs.*
*Queen of Clubs.*

Shorty cursed and slammed the remainder of the deck on the gravel. "I'll be damned if I'm gonna eat any of your shit whatsoever."

Johnny didn't rub it in. He knew he'd win. Because he'd promised himself he would. All he said was "Butcher Boy, eh?" and crossed his arms. "I think I like it."

Shorty was scooping his cards up, angry. "Beginner's luck. You didn't cut the cards, and that was just a lesson anyway, so that game shouldn't count."

"Every game counts, Shorty. You should know that better than anyone."

The muscles in Shorty's forehead loosened. "Yeah," he said. "I guess I do."

Johnny moved quickly, tapping into Shorty's gambling fever while he still had some left in reserve: "So pay up and tell me about the game you're playin' for Winston."

Shorty fell back on his butt, as if in shock, realizing that he'd just lost. "Uhh." He licked his lips. "I don't know where to begin."

Johnny leaned closer. "Start with the important stuff. *What's the stake, and what's the game? Lemme guess: it's Butcher Boy, ain't it?*"

Shorty nodded. "Yeah, Butcher Boy. One hand. Million dollar payoff."

Johnny couldn't believe he was hearing this. "A *mil*? Did you say a *mil*?" He looked around the empty lot, searching for a witness to tell him he heard it wrong. "For a lousy four-of-a-kind, luck-of-the-draw kid's game? Gimme a break!"

"There's plenty of catches, though. Things I'd rather not say."

Johnny tilted his head. "Shorrrr-teeee." He made a gimme sign with his fingers. "C'mon. Tell me everything."

Shorty seemed near tears. His voice raised an octave: "*I can't.*"

Johnny sighed. "I'll wipe three of the favors you owe me off the books if you just give me what you owe me. All you gotta do is 'fess up. How's that? Fair deal?"

"I'm no welcher," Shorty said, glaring at him, getting his energy back. "I'll do your favors. And I'll tell you everything I know, so long as I know you won't go narcing on me."

"Narcing? No way. I wouldn't rat on you." Johnny winced, remembering Shorty's dead pets. "I mean, you can trust me not to talk. You know it. And you got my word."

Shorty raised a hand to shake on it. They did.

His throat clicked as he swallowed to clear it. "Okay, it's like this. You gotta make your own suit of cards before you can ever sit down at the table."

"Huh? What does that mean?"

"Oh, why don't you just ask Winston, huh? He's got the rules and everything you need to know."

Johnny raised an eyebrow.

Shorty spit. Then he went on: "Winston's the ringleader. He runs the show, and organizes the deck. He gave me a Polaroid camera to take shots with. I take pictures for him, and he puts them on cards, see. I don't know how he does it, but he does. My suit is Diamonds. I gotta take thirteen photos to make a full row of Diamonds. Understand?"

"Think so."

Shorty didn't believe him, and so he began pulling diamonds out of the deck on the ground, lining them up side-by-side, face-up to illustrate his point. "It's hard to explain. Anyway, thirteen photos. Each'll end up on a card. Like this." He waved at the thirteen diamonds: Ace through King. "There are three other players, each doin' the same thing, takin' pictures for their suit. Ya know, hearts, spades, and clubs. Four players, thirteen cards each, one suit a-piece. I don't know who all the other players are, but now I know Axe is one of 'em..."

Johnny interrupted, not wanting to be told what he already knew. "Wait a minute. I see all that. But why do you gotta take pictures in the first place? What's the deal? Pictures of what?"

"Dea..."

Winston came around the corner of the shelter. Mid-sentence, Shorty panicked, kicking his legs out beneath him to run. But he only slid out onto the gravel, scraping his back.

"Well," Winston said, tipping his hat and lighting a cigarette. "I wondered where Shorty went with his breakfast. Figured I'd find the two of you out here." He inhaled, and nothing came out when he finally blew. "Guess this can mean only one thing, Johnny. You've come back to play. Am I right?"

Johnny stood, brushed the dust off his ass with three slaps, and walked toward Winston. His feet crunched loudly in the gravel like a silly show-down straight out of a Wild West movie.

Winston drew, whipping out the ever-present pack of cigarettes and offering it to him. Like bait.

*Sky's the limit*, Johnny thought, reaching forward.

Winston pulled back. "You in?"

"That's right," he said, snatching a smoke and popping it in his mouth. "I'm in."

# Play Dead

♣ ♣ ♣ ♣ ♣ ♣
♣ ♣ ♣ K ♣ ♣ ♣

The Five of Clubs was still burning a hole in his back pocket and Ferret couldn't wait to get rid of it. But right when he was about to hand the photograph of the woman over to him, Winston slipped outside. Something was going down. Probably following Shorty to keep an eye on him.

*Shorty. Bet he still thinks Axe did his rats,* Ferret thought, grinning. *Wait'll he sees my Devil's Bed Posts!*

Ferret knew he'd win this game. Piece of cake. His competitors were morons. A retarded geek. A crazy preacher. And an idiot lumberjack. He couldn't have picked better players himself. They were just like the fools he beat in Butte before taking his winnings and buying a bus ticket to the city. Easy game, easy money. This was just more of the same.

Only the pot was much higher this time.

And it was a helluva lot of fun just working up the deck.

He liked Clubs. They suited him. And they were always good to him. Back in Butte he'd even pulled off a royal flush in a last minute lucky draw, all Clubs. And the face cards themselves were beautiful: no one-eyed Jacks here. All straight shooters and know-it-alls. Lucky Clubs, black as night. Night Clubs.

He couldn't wait to see the finished deck, couldn't wait to wear his perfect lucky suit of *Clubs*.

The rules said he had to work his way up, slow and easy. And at first he did. The Ace was nothing more than a single plucked clover. Simple photo, simple plant life. A modest beginning for a relatively new photographer. But Winston said it wasn't good enough—he wanted more creativity, so Ferret went all out on the Two of Clubs: he'd squashed a million flies in his hands, waiting till he got two with guts pressed in perfect club formation in his palms. It was fun, sure, but it still wasn't enough. Who cared about silly bugs? What kind of life did a fly have? What sort of power? So he moved on to animals for the third card, carefully pressing a decapitated cat's paw into its own puddle of blood and making three bloody footprints on the sidewalk. Two forward, one back. Pat, pat, pat. Picture perfect. Creative.

Then came the Four of Clubs, the Devil's Bed Posts. A special card, deserving special treatment. He didn't know he would use Shorty's rats until the geek left them sitting there on his bed all alone while he went to go stand in the breakfast line. They spoke to him, little demons, little devils, chittering at him to get on with it. So he pulled out Trickster—the Bowie knife he copped in a craps game in Butte—and sliced the devils cleanly in thirds. Placed one in each corner of the bed. Four club-shapes. Even more creative than the others, sure, but the card had *asked* to be made. Those rats had spoken to him.

And what they said was right on the money: Shorty would lose his concentration in the game if he lost his little friends.

And the Five of Clubs...*perfection*. He moved to take the photo out of his pocket for one last look, but changed his mind. Someone was opening the front door—might be an outsider.

But Winston entered the shelter, ceremoniously removing his hat. His eyes quickly sighted Ferret, and then scanned the rest of the room as he approached him.

"Seen Axe?" Winston asked, sitting on the cot in front of Ferret's.

"Nope. I think he's out chopping down trees."

"Funny." Winston leaned back. "How about The Preacher?"

"Yeah, he's here somewhere. Why? You taking attendance or something?" Ferret laughed at his own joke.

"Funny," Winston repeated.

Ferret leaned sideways on the cot to pull the photo out from his back pocket. Shielding it, he passed it over Winston's hat, and dropped it inside.

"Busy man," he said, looking down at the Polaroid. "What's this...five?"

"Yep. The best Five you ever seen. I had fun with this one, man..."

Winston checked for on-lookers before examining the photograph closely.

Ferret grinned. "You like?"

Winston was frowning. "You're jumping the gun, asshole. How the hell you gonna outdo this one?" He leaped out of the cot and sat beside Ferret, wrapping an arm around him. Tightly.

# Play Dead

"You know that the numbers gotta go up, right? Ace-two-three-four-five. *Five*." He dug his fingertips into Ferret's bicep.

Ferret winced in pain. Winston's fingernails sliced into the soft tissue of his arm where three circular wounds—cigarette burns in his bicep—were still evident. Leftovers from a game in his early days on the reservation, when he played poker with a few buddies and a bottle of bourbon. When he'd lost, and couldn't pay up, they all used his arm for an ashtray, fizzing their cigarettes out in his flesh. He'd quit smoking and drinking after that day—and hated fire ever since.

Winston grinned into his face. "The lower the number, the lower the *lifeforce*. But here, I see, you've taken a *human* life for a five. Shit, man, what were you thinking? If this is a five, what's a ten gonna be?" Winston gripped so tightly into his arm it bent his fingernails. "Huh? Are you outta control or what?"

Ferret couldn't take the pain anymore. Angrily, he flexed his muscles so that Winston had nothing to sink his fingers into. "You don't worry about that. You coordinate. I know exactly what I'm doin'. You just stay outside the game. I'm the one that's playin, right?" He twisted his shoulder out of Winston's grip and turned on him.

"Yes, but I'm…"

Ferret seethed, leaning forward. "But *nothin'*. You let me play it my way."

Winston closed his eyes and smacked his lips. "I'm only gonna say this once, Ferret. The game can't get out of control. It's my job to make sure it plays out smoothly. You better keep your shit together or you're gonna *fold*." He opened his eyes. "You won't even see it coming. You got that?"

Ferret swallowed, hearing himself gulp. He held back his anger. "I got it. But trust me, I know what I'm doing."

"And so do I, Ferret." Winston lit another cigarette. "Don't you forget it."

Ferret nodded, eyes locking on the lighter's flame in front of his face. "Peace. Okay?"

Winston just stared at him, smoking.

He flicked down the lid of his Zippo, finally breaking the silence. "I just made arrangements for a new player. It was a pain in the ass, and a waste of time. You just ask the Axeman what happens when someone thinks about fucking up the game, next time you see him." He stood up, puffing on his cigarette and brushing his hat brim. "I don't want to have to make similar arrangements again. But that doesn't mean I won't if you force me to do so."

Ferret nodded, wondering what the hell he was talking about.

"Play straight," Winston said, flicking his cigarette onto Ferret's lap. "Or don't play at all."

*Fire.* Ferret blinked, then violently flipped out of the bed and onto the floor, madly slapping his crotch to put out non-existent flames. The cigarette rolled down the blanket and onto the floor, making its way toward his elbow. Ferret cowered away and then slapped a heel down to kill it like a bug.

"Fucker," Ferret shouted at Winston's back as the door swung shut behind him. "You piece of shit!" He continued rubbing the hot spot on his crotch, thinking about what Winston had said—wondering what Axe had done, and who the new player could possibly be. Then he looked down, and saw that Winston's cigarette had burned three crooked holes into the lap of his pants—the tiniest of holes, branched together like Clubs.

# part Two
# HEARTS

# A♥

*Axe has folded.*

Winston's voice still echoed in Johnny's mind as he entered The Shanty, nervously making his way through clouds of smoke to the bar. He sat down, peering through the slit of space into the empty kitchen in the back, half-hoping that he'd see Paul Bunyan back there, frying bacon and forming meat patties between filthy fingers. No such luck.

The bartender slid a cup of coffee in front of him and winked. "On the house."

Johnny cautiously nodded. Things had changed too quickly. Last time he was here—was it just *yesterday*?—he was strangled and violently forced to return his lunch to the floor before getting ushered out by Violet. He thought he'd never step foot in the place again. Now the tables had turned: he was being treated like royalty. And Axe was nowhere to be seen.

Which, unfortunately, was exactly what Winston had promised.

Johnny sipped his coffee, swishing the hot thick liquid through the gap in his front teeth like mouthwash. He could sense some kind of alcohol in the mix. It tasted like motor oil, but he liked it.

Johnny spun on his stool. The place was nearly empty, save for a cigar-smoking fatso by the front door reading a racing form like a businessman browsing a financial journal. Only two morning drunks sat at the opposite end of the counter, nursing boilermakers. The bartender washed glasses, eyeing them for grit, purposely leaving Johnny to himself. He wondered if the man knew what was going down, why he was here, what Winston had asked him to do.

Johnny slurped coffee. Swished. It was getting cold. Like his feet. He wasn't ready to carry out Winston's mission yet. Wasn't sure if he'd ever be.

The slot machine seemed hopelessly lonely without Violet's presence. And The Shanty was hauntingly silent without the rhythmic plunk-plunk-plunk of her rejected quarter through the slot's apparatus.

He wondered how much leeway he had. "Hey, barkeep." The bartender turned, cocking his chin. "No food today?"

"Nah, I had to give our cook the axe for the way he behaved yesterday."

"I see." *Axe got the axe. Funny.*

"But I can fix ya something if…"

Johnny nodded *no* while he swallowed the rest of his coffee. "Got another cup?"

Silently, he retrieved a round metal coffee pot and poured a steaming refill. Then he passed Johnny a shot glass with dark brown liquid in it. "Thanks." Johnny poured the shot into the brew. It curdled like cream.

"Don't thank me. It's on the house."

Johnny made a face of misunderstanding.

"Oh, almost forgot." The bartender reached beneath the wood of the bar, and then slid a fresh pack of Winston cigarettes to Johnny with a black book of matches that had the NEBO'S BUCKET OF BUCKS logo printed in gold embossed lettering on them. He smiled, winked, and returned to the barflies.

Silently, Johnny fast-opened the pack and lit one. A perfect chaser for his drink. His mouth felt like heaven, and he let himself enjoy it while he could— it cleansed the bad taste that still stuck to his mouth from the morning's exchange with Winston, who let him in on Butcher Boy.

Winston hadn't told him anything more than he already knew, though. Johnny had to prove himself ready to play, before Winston would let him in on the details. He had to give Winston his token act of faith, first.

*You gotta make your peace and bury the hatchet,* he'd said. *Today.*

Johnny slammed back the rest of his coffee and dropped what was left of his cigarette in a nearby ashtray without putting it out. He figured he was as ready as he'd ever be.

He exited and turned at The Shanty's corner, jogging behind the building, hoping he hadn't been seen. He stayed close to the bricks as he walked. They were warm with the morning sun, and Johnny instantly began to sweat from their heat. Or perhaps from the creeping feeling that he was *in the game*, all right, in way too deep long before he even knew exactly what he was getting himself into. But that's how the greatest games were played. High risk, high pay-off. Sometimes you had to bluff yourself and put it all on the line if you wanted to win.

The lot behind The Shanty was surprisingly well kept, compared to the front of the building. Two shiny trash dumpsters stood orderly beside a freshly-painted red back door and immaculate bricks. Beside a new green hose stood a rake and a long shovel. The gravel road that led to the back door itself seemed swept, new compared to the brown hills of sand which sheltered the back of the building, creating a natural alley. Johnny wondered if The Shanty's seedy look up front was just a show, a ruse to attract die-hard drinkers looking for escape from the real Show, the casinos down the Strip. If Nebo did own the bar, like Violet had said, then he was a pretty shrewd businessman, knowing how to trap folks like that.

Johnny held his breath and stood before a trash dumpster. He closed his eyes and swallowed, then lit one of the cigarettes from the pack he'd been given. When he felt ready he lifted the corrugated lid, taking care not to let it crash on the other side.

The smell hit him, but it wasn't too bad—a benefit of the missing tooth and numbed senses that came with it. Large desert flies buzzed inside. Johnny blew a cloud of smoke at them before peering over the edge.

Axe had folded, all right. Doubled-over like a white fetus in a womb of garbage. Caked with dried blood, his yellowing long johns were now spread with a stain the color of chocolate pudding. His fingers were clenched together as if in prayer; his neck craned up in supplication. Flies walked on his open eyes.

Johnny blinked and backed away. He felt dizzy, nauseous, as if the buzz from his drink was intensifying. Death didn't look as bad as he'd imagined it would. It was almost comforting. If it wasn't for the trash and the flies, Johnny might have inspected him more closely.

But there was work to do. He had to prove himself to Winston—had to come through on his sign of faith.

*Had to bury the hatchet.* Literally.

Johnny walked over to where the long spade rested against the bricks of The Shanty.

If he had to bury a body, he couldn't think of a better choice than Axe.

75

# Play Dead

The dust and black flecks of Axe's dried blood felt like ants burrowing nests into his forearms. He needed to shower, right away, and jogged towards Violet's place, taking side roads and alleyways. The shelter would have been a shorter trip, but Johnny didn't want to risk it—if the cops knew that Axe had been murdered, they'd no doubt start poking their noses around the shelter first. And while Johnny hadn't killed anyone, he was now an accomplice to murder.

But as he turned it over in his mind—each slap of his tennis shoe against the sidewalk pushing new ideas through his brain—he figured he'd get away with it. Axe was a nobody. A worthless bum, just like himself. Who paid attention to the homeless? Who would notice if one of them was missing? And who could possibly care?

After all, no one had found Axe's body in the trash dumpster. And now he was buried; swept under the carpet as if he'd never existed. All that was left of Paul Bunyan was the remnants of life that now peppered Johnny's arms and clothing.

He quickened his pace towards Violet's. After a shower, Axe would be gone for good.

Maybe.

He doubted he'd ever get that image of him out of his mind: curled up in prayer, lord of flies and french fry grease. Five stab wounds gouged horribly into his chest. Bathed in blood.

But even worse than that vision was what Johnny had seen when he dropped him into the hole he'd dug: the cavity in the center of his chest. A blackened hole of torn meat and chipped white bone. A man without a heart.

Johnny tried to wash it from his eyes with a blink.

It didn't work.

Johnny turned into a new alley and sighted a long denim jacket on a clothesline in someone's backyard. Not skipping a step, he yanked it and continued running, sliding his arms into its snug sleeves to cover his crime.

He was sweating like hell, but beneath the coat he felt less exposed.

Nearly there. As he slowed his pace to catch his breath, he thought about Winston. He wondered whether he'd done Axe himself, or had someone else kill him. Maybe that smug bartender, who gave Axe "the axe?" But more importantly, he wondered *why* Axe had been so brutally murdered, just to "fold" from the game. It didn't make much sense. Maybe there was more going on in this game than Johnny realized. Winston said they'd meet this evening to talk about the game. Johnny figured that after what he'd just done for Winston, he'd better get some answers.

As it stood, he was only sure of one thing: that he'd be taking over Axe's role in the game. And that meant that he could just as easily "fold" from it, too, just like Axe. He could get *killed* if he didn't play his cards right.

But if he did...

A mil.

A true risk.

Johnny felt a surge of energy thumping in his chest. His lips curled on their own accord into a smile. His skin was hot and tight beneath the damp denim jacket. Disgusted as he was, he hadn't felt this good in a long time, as if he had finally caught up with his old self again. Like back in Reno, where he'd found all those back room games—the late night tables where the real players congregated—like a secret brotherhood, with its own unwritten rules and high-payoff stakes, untaxable, untraceable...and the true payoff was sitting in on some of the best damned poker games he'd ever played in his life. It had taken a lot of work to earn the respect he needed to get into those back rooms in order to cop a seat in the Action: he had to make a rep for himself at the legit tables—had to make friends with those in the know and circulate himself like a dollar bill—and in the end, he was so well-known for being a player that they kicked him out. He would simply *win* too much.

Johnny figured that burying Axe wasn't much different than what he'd done back then: he'd tore the game out of a few player's chests, as if ripping their hearts out; he'd buried many of them in financial ruin. Axe was no different—just a victim of chance, wielded by the hands of a better player.

*And now I'm back in circulation. Back in the Action. And I'm gonna win.*

# Play Dead

*Because I've already got an Ace in the hole.*

He laughed as he turned a corner and sighted Violet's apartment building. He couldn't wait to shower. He couldn't wait to play. He tried his damnedest not to sprint up her doorstep.

He knocked.

Violet opened the door. "Well, I'll be," she said, eyeing his gap-toothed grin. "Whatta you got to be so happy about?"

Johnny shrugged. "You," he said for lack of an answer and leaned forward to kiss her cheek.

Violet's face spiderwebbed purple in a blush. Johnny let himself in while Violet took her time about shutting the door. And he was in the bathroom and stripping before she asked any questions. The shower washed away the past, scrubbed away the blood. This time he'd play it clean.

Violet handed Johnny a towel. "So where'd you go this mornin'? Thought you'd split for good."

Johnny tightened her velvet robe around his waist and covered his head with the towel. He could smell the perfume on it. Lilacs. He didn't mind. Smelled a lot better than Axe; fitting for a funeral. "Had work to do. Got a job."

"Right," she said, lighting a cigarette. "And I'm fucking Phyllis Diller."

Johnny peeked out from the towel and blinked. "That explains your hair-do."

She blew smoke in his face, and he beat it away. Violet nodded at the pile of Johnny's clothes in the corner. "Where'd you get that filthy jacket? Steal it off a dead guy or something?"

Johnny reddened, covered his face. He smiled under the towel. "Funny you should say that."

"Eh?"

"Nothin'." Johnny swiped steam from the bathroom mirror and dropped the towel over a bar. He looked at himself. His hair was disordered like a nest of black barbed wire. "Got a brush or a comb?"

"Should be somethin' behind the mirror." She blew more smoke, as if she'd been holding it. "Wait here, I'll get you some decent clothes." Violet left Johnny to his privacy.

"Like I'm goin' anywhere," he said to himself.

He opened the mirror and saw various brown plastic pill bottles, a pink disposable razor, a large bottle of Advil, and a giant purple brush with gray hairs trapped in it. Just the basics. He grabbed the brush and closed it, and stared at himself in the mirror: a familiar look—himself, the gambling man, before that day he lost his gold tooth to some wannabe poker player. He brushed his hair back to show a lot of forehead. Then he looked for some mousse. Found some beside row upon row of perfume bottles lined up behind the bathroom sink. He cemented his hair back slick.

Violet reached inside the door without looking to hand him some clothes.

# Play Dead

He took them from her. A pair of black polyester slacks which felt oily between his fingers and a Hawaiian-style floral shirt with cork buttons. He put them on and made it a point not to see how goofy he looked in the mirror. It didn't matter: for some reason, it felt safer to dress this way, as if putting on a disguise.

He tossed his own clothes—bloodstained—into the tiny trash can beside the toilet. He'd rather have burned them, but the garbage can would have to do.

Violet was sitting at the bar, pouring rum into a blender. She flashed him a look and nodded in approval. "Not bad, Johnny. Not bad at all."

He pulled up a black leather stool. "Where'd you get these?" he asked, fingering the material of his shirt as if trying to pull the petals of the print free from their stems.

"They're from Dutch, my ex." She swallowed what looked like a frown as she pressed the BLEND button on the machine. The room filled with the roar of thrashing liquids, and Johnny figured that meant that he shouldn't be so nosy about her past.

Johnny lit one of the cigarettes from the pack of Winstons he'd been given at The Shanty.

Violet poured a tall glass of what she was mixing. "Got paid already, eh?"

Johnny blinked smoke from an eye. "Whatta you mean?"

"The cigarettes." She nodded at the pack.

"Oh."

"Winston's brand. You workin' for him now?" She poured another glass, and slid it to him. Her eyes were clear and gentle, but glued to his own. Like she knew more than Johnny gave her credit for.

"In a manner of speaking." He lifted the glass and drank. It tasted like a cross between Piña Colada and banana nut bread. Sour and rancid, too fruity. Johnny forced a grin. "Good drink," he lied.

"It's homemade truth serum," Violet said, winking.

Johnny smiled. "No lie?"

"No lie. So fess up. What's goin' down with Winston? He got you enforcing now, or what?" She rolled plastic fingernails against the countertop like bullets.

"Enforcing?"

"You know, gettin' welchers to pay up, snapping thumbs backward, pokin' people in the eyeballs with cigarettes, stuff like that. That what you doin'?" She drank from her glass. Johnny imagined he could see the thick pulp moving down her thin-skinned throat.

He smirked. "C'mon, Violet. You know better. I am not a violent man."

"Well you sure looked like you been in some kinda scrape when you walked in here all dirtied up and shit."

"I fell."

"Fell in with the wrong crowd is more like it."

Johnny stood up, angry. "Hey, don't mother me, all right? You didn't adopt my ass."

She laughed. "Ain't that a pretty picture. An adopted ass. Imagine tryin' to breast feed *that*."

Johnny didn't get it, but he laughed anyway, blowing puffs of smoke through his nostrils. "You've got one hell of a dirty mouth for a woman your age, you know that?"

"Fuck you," she said. "How old do you think I am, you whipper-snapper?" She chuckled. "Sit down, shut up, and drink. It's early yet."

Johnny shook his head and pulled smoke through the gaps in his teeth. "Early? Early for what?"

She smiled up at him, all dentures: "Hitting the casinos."

Johnny lit another cigarette off the first one, still standing. "You know I don't have the money for that, much as I'd like to."

"But you're a *workin' man* now, Johnny," she said sardonically. "Don't worry—I'll front ya."

"I told you the other day: I don't want your charity."

"Well then give me your charity and go gamblin' with me. I ain't had a partner in years. That's why I've been playin' the horses."

"I don't know, Viol…"

She smirked and looked Johnny up and down. "Well you sure ain't dressed for anything else."

Johnny sat. Violet had a way of beating him, hands down. "Okay, but I've got an appointment tonight."

Violet was lighting a cigarette. "Winston?"

"How'd you guess."

She blew smoke from her nostrils. "I can read you like a book. You musta had too much of this here truth serum." She finished her glass, and poured another.

Johnny rolled his eyes.

"But let me tell you somethin', since it seems you ain't figured it out yet." She leaned forward.

Johnny leaned back—she felt uncomfortably close. He could even smell the rank fruit on her breath. "What?"

"You don't meet Winston for no appointments." She dragged. Blew. "He always finds *you*."

Johnny sighed. "Well, then I gotta be findable tonight."

Violet cocked her head. "Don't you worry none. He'll be there."

He stood up, feeling awkward. He couldn't tell if Violet had already made arrangements for them to meet Winston at a casino or if she was just pulling his leg. Either way, Johnny knew that she was probably right—Winston had a way of simply showing up, expected or not.

He grabbed his glass and walked into the living room to look at Violet's art. He found the painting that had bothered him that morning: Dogs playing poker. He scanned it, looking at the details, trying to decipher its puzzle.

"You like that, don't ya?" Violet said from the bar.

"Yeah. It's different somehow." Johnny sipped. "You're quite the artist."

Violet laughed. "What makes you think I painted it?"

Johnny blushed—he'd assumed she had, since it was an obvious paint-by-numbers job. And then he noticed her signature in the lower right corner: Violet Tresharts. Interesting name. Had a ring to it; sounded like *treasure*. "Oh, I'm only guessing, Violet," Johnny replied. "Since it's such a good painting, I just assumed it was your own handiwork."

"Well I do have a thing for dogs," she said.

And then Johnny saw what it was that bothered him. The dogs weren't dealing with regular playing cards. The cards all had strange shapes on them.

Human figures. Like the Tarot cards he'd found on Violet's carpet that morning.

"Did you read the Tarot to me last night?" Johnny asked.

"The what?"

"I found Tarot cards on the floor this morning. What did we do with them last night?"

Violet cocked her head sideways. She smiled so wide Johnny could hear her cheeks crinkle. "You don't remember?"

"No," Johnny said, finally facing her. "Why? What happened?"

"You asked me about some girl. Whether you'd have a future with her or not."

*Gin*, Johnny thought, his face warming with blood. "*And?*"

Violet's smile widened.

"And? C'mon, tell me, Violet."

She shrugged. "And I can't tell ya."

"Why not?"

"'Cause the cards are always changin' and it's all up to them to do the talking."

Johnny slapped his thigh. "What kind of bullshit answer is that?" He thought about how he'd found the cards spilled on the floor that morning, scattered as if angrily swept aside. Maybe he really didn't want to know what they had promised. "Oh, never mind. I don't believe in that hokey baloney anyway."

"Believe what you want. That don't mean you're right." Violet grabbed a coat from a hook in the hallway. Black leather. "C'mon, let's hit it. I'm feelin' lucky."

"Okay, all right." Johnny grabbed his cigarettes. On their way out, Johnny looked back at the portrait of dogs, wondering how they cheated at Tarot.

# Play Dead

Johnny tried his best not to look excited. But as they headed toward the front entrance of the Bucket—a gap without doors, an ever-open hole in the side of the building like a mouth, grinding Action, taking its fill before spitting out the stripped bones of its victims—Johnny wanted to run and get inside as quickly as possible. He could feel the pulse of the Action from within pressing against his face like a desert breeze. The place was rocking: he could hear winners screaming *JACKPOT!* and clanging bells and spinning wheels and...

"Johnny," Violet said, grasping his elbow. "Hold on a second."

He stopped, finding it difficult to pull his eyes away from The Show. Atop a long row of humongous slot machines a bright sign flashed PROGRESSIVE JACKPOT above an ever-turning digital counter. *34,024...34,296...34,538....*

The casino was hungry. A fast eater.

"Here," she slipped something into his hand. He could tell it was a wad of cash by its feel—fleshy paper between his fingers.

He faced her. "What gives?"

"I told ya I'd spot you." She smiled, recognizing the gleam in Johnny's eyes. "I know you'll pay me back." She nodded down at his hand, holding her money. "Hell, you'll probably triple all that right away. You're a good investment."

"Sure, but I thought we'd play as partners..."

"I know, I know. But I'm probably gonna go a little crazy the second we step foot in there, so if we get separated I want you to be able to hold your own. When I'm playin' I don't like to get interrupted, so make it last, all right? All that should be enough."

Johnny pocketed it without counting and nodded. "You bet. Where do we meet afterwards?"

"I'm sure we'll find each other somehow." She lit a cigarette, turning toward the casino's lights like an actress on the side of a stage. "Let's go." They charged.

Violet sat down at the first slot machine in her path and fumbled quickly in her purse for quarters.

Johnny shook his head and went deeper into the throat of the Casino. The slots and games by the door were for suckers. Johnny knew you couldn't beat a machine, because machines can be rigged. Especially in new joints like the Bucket, trying to make enough to pay off the cost of construction. True, they did throw out the occasional pay-off to try to get a rep for themselves as having loose slots, but Johnny wasn't gonna wait around for the lucky toss. He had to play face-to-face. Poker. Where skill and balls could beat anyone.

He felt naked without his old get-up, though. Decked out like a tourist in Violet's old man's clothes, he considered shopping instead of gambling with Violet's cash for the right look, the look of a high-roller. But then, maybe he could sucker someone into thinking he was just like every other small-time jerk in the place.

He paused and turned to pretend he was watching the spin of a roulette wheel while he wondered how much lettuce he had to cultivate. *Black*, he bet to himself, watching the ball roll and tumble. Sticking his arm deep into his pocket, he fingered the wad that Violet had spotted him. It was thick, but he didn't know if they were singles or twenties. The ball on the roulette wheel bounced twice and slammed into its socket: 22 Black.

Sighs from the sitters. Johnny laughed. He made his way to the table and peeled off a bill from the top of the wad in his pocket and then dropped it on black. This way he could see what denomination Violet had given him without pulling the whole money roll out in public.

It was a hundred dollar bill. Green on black and green. Johnny whipped his hands out to take it back.

"No more bets." The spinner waved an arm over the board like a magician, frowning sadly at the banknote on black as though Johnny's money was already lost.

"Fuckin' A," Johnny said out loud. The ball spun, but Johnny couldn't watch. He was too busy trying to figure out exactly how much cash was in his pocket—if they were all Franklins, then Violet had given him at least two thou.

# Play Dead

"Four Black," the spinner announced, placing a marker on the number.

Johnny prodded the gap in his mouth. *Make that two thousand and one*.

The dealer slapped a multi-colored hundred dollar chip on top of Johnny's bill. "Place your bets."

Johnny stopped himself from reaching for it. "Let it ride."

A few players shot him odd looks. The table's mood seemed to shift— some betting with him, others against—all trying to read Johnny's mind or tap into his wave of luck. He wondered if roulette wasn't a lot more like poker than he'd thought.

The table cheered. He'd won again. Some of the players bitched when Johnny pocketed his winnings—but he knew when to stop. Twenty-four hundred bucks seemed like just enough for a game of cards. And he was *ready*.

*Damn, I feel good*.

He lit a Winston as he made his way to the poker pit in a corner of the casino, back by the racing forum where things were quiet and serious players could concentrate. On a wide screen TV a boxing match played out. There was no sound—the announcer was unnecessary. All that mattered was the winner. Only a handful of hardcore gamblers were watching—it was a bantamweight bout. Sports didn't interest Johnny much: why bet on the fate of others when you can only trust yourself?

The poker pit was surrounded by the usual brass bars, a fence to keep out watchers and cheaters. Only players were allowed inside. Johnny preferred it that way. He stood behind the brass, scoping the games. Twelve players, two tables. Small time. Both were playing Texas Hold 'Em, Johnny's least favorite because he would rather not have half his hand showing. It took all the fun out of it.

But he still knew he could beat every player there.

He stepped inside the pit. No one looked up—he'd have to work his way into a game.

"Sir?"

Johnny turned, and a man dressed like an absurdly tall leprechaun approached him. His uniform had the logo of the casino on it: a pot spilling gold as if tipped over by the fingers of a rainbow and a four leaf clover. Johnny immediately played the part of naive tourist. "Me?"

"Yes, sir. I'm sorry but there's a waiting list to play." The man pulled a clipboard from behind his back. "Can I have your name please?"

"What for?"

He clicked his pen. "To put you on the list."

Johnny tried to think up a title to match his disguise. "Pauly," he said, looking down at his polyester pants and floral shirt. "Pauly Flores."

The man wrote it down. "Very good, sir. You may wait at the bar if you wish." He motioned at the watering hole between the pit and the sports forum. "I'll get you when your time has come."

Johnny nodded, not liking the way that sounded.

The bar was fairly empty: most folks knew they could get free drinks delivered to their table if they were gambling. Johnny, eager to play, thought about checking out another casino rather than waiting, but reminded himself that Violet would need to find him.

He sat on a stool at one end and saw a video poker machine beneath the glass top of the bar. Another machine, like Violet's slots. Probably rigged. But perhaps it would get him in the spirit for the upcoming game...

The bartender brought him a glass of clear liquid and set it down in front of him.

"What's this?"

"Gin," the bartender said, nodding at someone behind Johnny. "Compliments of that gentleman sitting in the booth over there."

Johnny turned around.

Winston tipped his hat at him and smiled.

"Figures," Johnny muttered, picking up his drink.

# Play Dead

"You really shouldn't advertise," Winston said as Johnny slid into their booth.

"I don't follow ya. Advertise?" He pulled out his pack of Winstons and placed one in his mouth. It felt good to not have to bum one off the bookie for once. "Advertise what?" Johnny picked up his matches.

"Yourself," he replied, lighting Johnny's cigarette for him with a silver lighter. "As a player. Especially around here."

"I see," Johnny said, not seeing anything at all. "So what are you doin' here?"

"I should say the same to you," Winston replied. "You sure are livin' it up for a man who just buried his first body."

Johnny winced, amazed that he'd actually blocked it out of his mind all day. *The meaty pit in Axe's chest. The stab wounds. The blood on his hands…*

He downed his gin to erase the image from his mind. "He deserved it," Johnny said, forcing himself to sound tough. "Fuckin' asshole nearly killed me the other day." Johnny snubbed out his cigarette. "But we've buried the hatchet, and now I've got your faith, right?"

"Right, Johnny. You're in." Winston stared at him somberly. And then he smiled and waved. "But let's not talk about the details at this moment. It's too public here. Right now I'm concerned with giving you something in exchange for what you did for me today."

"And what might that be?"

"Everything you need." He slid a key across the table: letters and numbers imprinted in gold read RM 505.

"A room?"

"Just for tonight. Consider it a reward."

Johnny pushed it away, thinking of Violet. "Don't need it. I've got places to stay." *And I'd rather you didn't know where I am, either.*

Winston closed his eyes and swallowed. "Take the key, Johnny. You'll need it."

Johnny crossed his arms.

Winston pressed his lips together into a tight purple line. "You gotta trust me now, Johnny. I'm all you got." He stood up. "Go up to that room now. Right now. Don't go gambling or drinking, just go upstairs. You'll see why in a little while. I'll meet you there shortly."

Winston walked away, leaving his cigarettes and silver Zippo on the table, along with a five dollar tip. Johnny snagged it all, including the key. "Fuck it," he said, sliding the key into his front pocket and finishing off what was left of his gin.

He stood and made his way toward the elevators. His legs went wobbly—the gin went straight to his head, mixing with the remainder of Violet's "truth serum" in his gut. He wondered where Violet was, and whether he should tell her what was up. After all, she was right: Winston found him, just like she'd said he would.

And she had bankrolled him, too, saying they'd be separated. Johnny figured that was a hint—if he had to stay or go elsewhere, she wouldn't mind. He wondered if there was more to it than that, though. Maybe Winston and Violet were closer than she let on.

Still, Johnny glanced around the casino, hoping to catch sight of her.

She should have been easy to pick out: the slots and tables were surrounded by crowds of nicely-dressed young people for the most part. Tourists, mostly. People who came for The Show and not Action. People satisfied with breaking even or losing it all just to say they'd been there, at Nebo's, during its grand opening week. Bullshit.

Johnny did a double-take when his eyes passed a blackjack table.

Gin.

Decked out in a cheesy leprechaun outfit. Standing alone before a smooth felt field of green, shuffling cards. Johnny couldn't believe it. He nearly ran to where she stood. "Gin, is that you?"

She smiled as he approached, her hands still busy shuffling. "Johnny?"

"What the hell are you doing here?"

"I work here. You?"

Johnny ignored the question. "Don't you have homework to do, or something?"

# Play Dead

"Homework?" She frowned. "No. Why, what makes you say that?"

Johnny sat down on a stool. "Aren't you a student at UNLV?"

Gin looked down at Johnny, frowning. "You *playing*?"

"No, I'm serious! I thought you were a student volunteer…"

"No, I mean are you playing." She nodded toward the engraved gold placard on the blackjack table that read $500 MINIMUM. "You can't sit here if you're not playing."

Johnny blushed. It had been so long, that he'd almost forgotten the ground rules. Seats were for players only. He slipped a foot off the footrest to stand, but remembered the money in his pocket. And that he *was* a player now. He was in the Action again.

Gin stared at him coldly, waiting for an answer. He could tell she was getting uncomfortable. Dealers had to be in total control, had to appear unbreakable. Especially since they were always being watched by the eye-in-the-sky up above and the pit boss down below. Eyes were everywhere, staring. Staring at Johnny, too.

*You shouldn't advertise,* Winston had said. *Don't gamble…go upstairs. Right now.*

"Maybe just one hand," Johnny said.

Gin scowled. She didn't believe he had the kind of money it took.

He reached into his pocket and peeled five bills off Violet's money roll. He slapped them down on the table like a pay-off. "There ya go. I'm in."

Gin's eyes shot open—betraying the polished look she had by showing the red veins in their corners. Working too hard again, Johnny thought.

"Great," she said, though he didn't think she meant it as she shot a yellow plastic cut card at him. He picked it up and sliced the long shoot of cards—like cutting a plastic cake—probably fifteen decks shuffled together in the holder…maybe more, since there were so many card counters out there these days, and the joints weren't willing to pay out at $500 stakes. Johnny cut the deck right in the middle while Gin exchanged his banknotes for chips and put them in their chalkline ring on the table. She shook her head from side-to-side, still smiling in disbelief at Johnny's cash.

He lit a cigarette. Tried to make small talk. "So how long you been dealin'?"

Michael A. Arnzen

"A few years. I worked at the Turf Club before coming here. I like it better at The Bucket—it's new. Doesn't smell like old cigars and cheap booze."

"Uh-huh." Johnny preferred the opposite, himself. Old smells meant old money, and plenty of it.

"I like your outfit," Gin said, sizing him up. "You've obviously come into some good money. That job of yours must be *really* paying off." Johnny thought she rolled her eyes in sarcasm.

"Yup."

She dealt. One hole card to each of them and one face up: King to Johnny, Six to Gin.

Johnny lifted the corner of his hole card. A Four. He was holding a lousy fourteen—one of the worst hands you could possibly get. He'd need a Seven or less to win. He saw that Gin had a Six, which meant that the highest she could have was a seventeen—and if that was the case, she'd have to stand on it, house rules. If he didn't bust first.

"Hit me," he said, bracing himself while he made a gimme sign with his fingers.

Another Four, face up.

Smoke shot out of his nose as he waved his hands. "I'm stickin'."

Gin flipped over her hole card. It was a Five, which gave her eleven total. She flipped herself a Queen from the shooter. "Twenty-One," she said, as if it were predestined.

Johnny stood up. "You win some, you lose some." He winked at her.

Gin scraped his chips toward her with his cards. "Sorry, Johnny. Luck of the draw."

"No biggie." It wasn't—he still had plenty of cash in his pocket. And a room key. "Listen, I'm staying here at the hotel tonight. If you want to get together later, I'm in room 505."

Gin grimaced and shook her head. Johnny got the hint—she wasn't saying no, but she was trying to tell him that she couldn't say *anything* with the eye-in-the-sky watching her. Dealers weren't supposed to make dates with their customers. It lent itself to cheating.

Johnny winked. "Thanks for the game, Gin. I'll be seeing ya."

# Play Dead

He walked away while Gin returned to shuffling the cards, all alone.

The elevators were empty when he got there, which Johnny thought was strange for a new glitzy hotel. He stepped inside. When the elevator doors closed, his stomach lurched, and he nearly vomited in the golden ashtray beneath the buttons. Violet's truth serum was getting to him again. That and the hydraulics of a brand new elevator. He watched the digital floor counter tick off stories like the progressive slot machine sign out front. *Everything rises when the sky's the limit*, Johnny thought, knowing how corny it sounded, but how true it was. The truth usually *was* corny, after all.

The elevator stopped. A bell dinged and the door slid open. "Maybe not," he said aloud, and stepped out onto the fifth floor. The hall was richly carpeted with dark green shag which had hardly been stepped on and brass rods lined the walls at hip level, a helping hand for drunks. The whole place smelled new, like money fresh from the mint. Johnny liked it.

Room 505 was easy to find. He slipped the key into the doorknob and entered, praying there was a wetbar inside.

"What took you so long?" asked a voice from inside the room. "I've been waiting."

It wasn't who Johnny expected.

The man sitting at the table in the corner of room 505 had dark skin, tight on his cheekbones, as if pulled back by plastic surgeons. His eyes were beady brown bullets, glossy as gems. His short jet black hair had gray streaks in the sideburns and to Johnny they looked unnatural, dyed. He wore a well-pressed Italian suit with mirror-polished shoes like something straight out of a Mafia movie. But he smiled like a banker—his face betrayed him. He wasn't physically threatening, but he seemed to have his shit together. Exactly what Johnny could have been, had his streak not crapped out on him: rich, with it, and ahead of the game.

"Who the fuck do you think you are?" Johnny asked, approaching him with flexed fists. "And what are you doin' in my room?"

"Please," the man said with a voice as warm as coffee. "My name is Nebo Tarrochi. Have a seat." He motioned toward the chair opposite his.

Johnny bit down on his tongue, using the gap between his front teeth to hold it in check as he obeyed and sat down in the offered chair. But he couldn't stop his mind from racing—if the sky was the limit, he'd just hit it. He was sitting at the same table with Mr. Bucket of Bucks himself. The sky just didn't get any higher than that.

"Are you finding your evening enjoyable, Johnny?" His question was extremely casual. Nebo crossed his hands.

*My God. He knows my name.*

Johnny released the vice on his tongue. It hurt. "'Course I am. This is the best joint in the city. And it's still new." Johnny smiled, keeping his ugly teeth concealed behind his upper lip. "What's there not to like?"

Nebo leaned back, smiling. He'd kept eye contact ever since Johnny had walked in the room. "Yes. It's new. Well..." He shrugged, the city landscape of Vegas ominously bending in through the window behind him like a curled picture frame. "The building might be new, but it's always the same old game, isn't it? Poker. Slots. Craps. The same as everywhere else." He sighed.

"Rarity is what makes gambling a thrill, Johnny. If it's everywhere, it's no fun anymore. If it's forbidden fruit, it's thrilling to pluck. But there really isn't much new under the sun. Or moon." He frowned, as if Johnny had let him down somehow.

Johnny wondered when Nebo would blink. His eyes were still tracked on his, as if Nebo was just waiting for him to turn away. He figured Nebo was the sort of guy who could sleep with his eyes open. "Guess so."

"Yes. You *guess*. That's what I like about you, Johnny. You *guess*."

Johnny couldn't take it anymore. As if he needed to, he watched his own hand reaching for the cigarette pack in his breast pocket. Lighting up, he kept his eyes on the flames. "I don't follow you," Johnny said, his voice sounding forced. He could still feel Nebo's eyes on him.

"You're a player. But you don't fool yourself into thinking skill is all it takes, or that you know it all already. You *guess*. You take *risks*. I like that." Nebo waited until Johnny looked at him. "Because knowing when to take chances is the hardest skill there is to master." He paused, and blinked. "And guessing means you, my friend, believe that there is still something new under the sun, so to speak. Because you still have faith in chance."

Nebo's blink said it all. Johnny stared him down. Time to be up-front. "Tell me about Butcher Boy."

It was Nebo's turn to look away. He peered down at his lap, smiling. "Such a risk taker." He looked up. "You know who I am, yes?"

"I know. You own several joints. Lotsa real estate…and lotsa money. You're staking a poker game, through Winston, who works for you by finding players and running the game and what not. He's invited me to play, and that's why I'm here." Johnny leaned back, feeling relieved somehow. "That's really all I know."

"So you do know a few things about me," Nebo said, obviously impressed. He leaned forward, his eyes targeting Johnny's. "But I'll bet I know more about you, Johnny Frieze, than you could ever possibly hope to know of me." He grinned. "Would you care to bet on that?"

"Nope," Johnny said, trying his best to sound bold. "Because the fact is I don't give a flyin' fuck about you, or your life story." He stamped out his cigarette in the glass ashtray between them. "I just care about the game."

Nebo laughed. It sounded phony.

He stood up, softly pushing in his chair. "But it's all a game, isn't it Johnny? Some say life's a stage, but that's only half right. Life's a *game*, and we're all players. And you know this more than anyone. So I think you care a great deal." He paced the length of the room, and then turned back. "Let me tell you a little of what I know about you. Because I think you'll find it of interest. For example, I know you're missing a front tooth because you lost it in a poker game." Nebo craned his neck, to see Johnny's response. "Right?"

"So? That's obvious, ain't it?"

"Is it? You tell me."

Johnny thought a moment, keeping his lips shut. "How'd you know I lost it in a game?"

Nebo grinned. "Because I watched you play it."

"What?"

"You had a dead hand. Highest card you were holding was the King of Hearts—the Suicide King. You tried to bluff, but the guy you were playing had you. So you made a mistake. You got up from the table and went to the bathroom. You lost your streak."

Johnny turned his head to study Nebo's face. "I don't remember you…"

"That's because you didn't see me."

It hit him. "The eye in the sky…"

Nebo smiled at Johnny's quickness. "Yes, exactly. I was watching from the security cameras. That casino is just one of the six I own, and I just happened to be there at the right time. Quite lucky, actually. I watched your whole game. It was extremely interesting. The suspense was thrilling. You're quite a gambler—you know how to play your cards right, but lady luck just happened to screw you that night. You shouldn't blame yourself—you're a very good player."

Johnny felt himself blushing, feeling naked. *He knows my game…*

"But that's not all. You borrowed a cigarette from somebody. You didn't like how it tasted. When you were in the men's room, you put it out on the floor. You ran the water while you urinated. And then you bashed your own jaw against the sink to break the gold tooth out of your mouth. Just to have some scratch to play."

Johnny twisted violently in his seat. "HOW…"

"I was watching. There's a camera behind the bathroom mirror. You don't think our surveillance stops where the casino ends, do you? Every owner knows that the rest room is where cons and cheats spend most of their time."

Now he really felt naked. Deeply so—as if even the flesh had been scraped free of his bones. The man who sat across from him had seen him at his worst, had watched every excruciating second of the most humiliating moment of his life. "I don't believe this…"

"Believe it." Nebo returned to his chair and held onto its back, leaning over the table. "But that's nothing. I know *everything* about you: your parents back in California, Mickey and Barb; your favorite color, gray; the grades you got in high school, the crimes you committed afterward, and the names of every woman you ever had in your life…everything. You've got a history, Johnny. And it was as easy to trace as reading a book."

Johnny just stared at him. He believed it.

"And I know you buried a body yesterday, too."

The room thrummed with silence. Johnny swallowed. The back of his mouth felt scratchy. "How does a guy go about getting a drink around here?"

Nebo squinted, and Johnny could see the veins pulsing in his olive-brown temples. Then he relaxed the muscles there. "Certainly." Nebo walked over to a dresser and grabbed a bottle of scotch. "This is for you." He handed him the bottle.

Johnny snapped the cap off and chugged directly from the bottle, spilling some down his chin. Nebo watched—not disgusted, but understanding. And satisfied that he'd made his point.

Johnny smacked his lips. The booze felt solid in his stomach. "Okay, so you know what I did. I figured that. It was your idea, right?"

"Nothing of the kind. The cards fall where they fall; some people deal 'em, others play 'em. I don't get involved with that part of the game."

Johnny rolled a disbelieving eye at him before taking another swig. He slammed the bottle down hard on the table. The ashtray rattled. "So what gives? Why are you telling me all this? You gonna blackmail me, or what?"

Nebo sat down. Crossed his hands again, completely calm. "I wanted to meet you in person and to tell you this because I want you to know who you're dealing with. And that I've got your number. You are a lucky man, Johnny, for being invited to play my little game. I'm putting a great deal of faith in you, and a whole lot of trust. I wanted to meet you face-to-face today, to let you know that. And if you don't play by the rules, I can fix you faster than a back alley boxing match. You understand?"

Johnny nodded. His left eye twitched. "I think so."

Nebo nodded, as if cinching a business deal. "Good. I only do this as a formality, you see. Because I know you'll play correctly. When I saw you play poker that night you lost your tooth, I was intrigued. I knew you were the right player for this game of mine. Like I said, you've already got the skill down, and you're not afraid to guess. And you always play by the rules. Winston assures me that you are a cautious player, that you can keep a face, and I trust him with my life. So part of my...um...*research* of your history was simply to see if you were right for the game. I'm really not out to black-mail anyone."

Johnny nodded. He knew Nebo was right—he was lucky. And Nebo was so rich, that blackmail couldn't possibly be a factor. Not like Johnny had anything to be blackmailed for, anyway. "Tell me more about these rules. I'm eager to play."

Nebo raised an eyebrow. "I bet you are."

The door to the hallway opened and Winston walked in. Johnny wasn't surprised. The whole situation seemed staged.

"I'll leave the nitty-gritty details to Winston here." Nebo held a hand out to Johnny. They shook. "It was very nice to meet you," Nebo said, keeping a tight grip on Johnny's fingers, squeezing them painfully together. "Remember, Johnny. I'm the eye in the sky. I'm the man behind the mirror. And I'm always watching." He leaned closer. "So don't you fuck me. You just play the damned game the best you can, and I'm sure you'll do fine."

He let go. Johnny rubbed his fingers. "Nice to meet you, too," he lied.

# Play Dead

Nebo winked at Winston, who had removed his hat and was fingering the brim. Then he made his way toward the hallway door. "Why don't you just enjoy yourself tonight. We'll meet again. You can come up tomorrow morning for breakfast."

"Sounds good to me," Johnny said.

Winston flashed Johnny a look that said he should stay quiet.

Nebo softly shut the door behind him.

"Enough bullshit. Let's get down to business," Winston said, rubbing his hands together and grinning like he was about to rake in a pot of just-won chips.

Johnny lit a cigarette before taking another slug of liquor. His eye was still twitching.

Standing outside the Seven-Eleven, Shorty reached into his wrinkled paper grocery bag, double-checking that his stuff—his life's belongings—were still there. This was a daily routine. After losing his pets, he didn't trust anyone at the shelter.

He tooled around in the bag, reminiscing. The '79 Nolan Ryan baseball card reminded him of his Junior High pal, Eric, with whom he'd traded a Reggie Jackson to get it. The photograph of his mother in an evening gown with her fine diamond necklace always brought the smell of macaroni and cheese to his nose—his favorite food. He smiled and tried to swallow the odor while digging deeper into the bag and finding his trusty hole punch. The metal was cold in his hands. He remembered all the winter days of his paper route, going from house to house to collect, punching everybody's year-long cards with the cold metal hole punch as a form of receipt. That was his favorite part of the job. He liked the sound it made—*ka-chunk*—always followed by the pocketing of a wad of cash. The rest of the bag seemed to be there: an old Polaroid camera, a green light bulb, a lotto ticket from three years ago that had his birth date on it, chips and silver dollars from various casinos, and other little trinkets which meant something special to him. Especially his Mother's heirloom.

He rolled the bag closed and carried it by his side like a huge lunch sack.

The hookers were everywhere tonight. Three of them were standing by the phone on the Seven-Eleven's brick wall. And Shorty could see them lining the sidewalks ahead of him as he made his way down the street, lifting the bag and hugging it against his chest so no one would try to steal it.

As always, they tried to get him right away. He knew the best ones could be found further down the street—near the center of the Strip—rather than here on the outskirts. But it never really mattered. It was safer to play with these early birds.

A girl in a torn black leather skirt turned and cocked her hip, staring him down as he approached. He avoided her stare. Her deep brown eyes were too round. Too young.

"Hey honey, what's in your bag?" she asked, walking towards him. Her shoes click-clocked the sidewalk.

"Nothin'," Shorty said, acting shy.

She reached him, and blocked his path. "You show me yours, I'll show you mine," she said, parting the front of her denim coat. Shorty caught the sight of a plump white breast angling up towards him. He looked down at the ground. This was happening too fast.

The girl moved closer. "Aw, don't be shy. I know you like what you see." She opened her jacket like wings and leaned into him, engulfing his sack with her breasts, which pushed and wiggled their way around his tight, clenching fists. She leaned her head up and kissed his chin. "You do like Candy, don't you?"

Shorty could feel his head quaking. "You have Snickers?"

She laughed, She laughed, brushing between his legs before pulling away and snapping her coat closed over her chest. "No, silly. Candy's my name."

Shorty found himself laughing, but it sounded funny—choppy bursts of nervousness.

Candy winked at him. "But if you got the money, you can eat me or chew me or suck me or anything you want." She buried her hands in the slit-pockets in the side of her jacket as she leaned forward, smiling. "Snickers *really* satisfies, lover."

"I don't have any money," Shorty said.

Candy stiffened. She dropped her jaw and then said, "So why the fuck am I wasting my time with you?" She stared at him, waiting for an answer.

"Well," Shorty said, nervously rolling his bag open and reaching inside, "I do have this." He withdrew his mother's diamond necklace. The one the pawn shop wouldn't buy because they said it was cubic chrome or something like that and not made from real coal which was crushed to form diamonds. He had hoped to get the cash from it to play poker, and didn't quite understand why the pawn shop wouldn't buy it from him—it might be fake, but why couldn't he cash it in like a plastic poker chip for real money? But now it had its uses in another game, which was fine with Shorty. "You like it?"

Candy's eyes popped open. "Put that away." She reached forward and grabbed him by the arm as he shoved it back into his bag. "Let's go."

She led him into the building they stood beside, taking him down dimly-lit stairs into a room that looked like a basement. It was dark and Shorty couldn't see her anymore.

A yellow light came on, dangling in the center of the room where Candy was screwing it into a socket. Her jacket was unbuttoned and Shorty watched as the sides of her breasts slapped together. Her stomach was smooth and tight—and she had a little knob of a belly button. An outie.

Shorty took the necklace out of his bag again. "Can I put this on you?"

She approached him. "For those rocks, sweetie, you can do anything you want to little ol' Candy."

"Turn around."

She obeyed.

Shorty wrapped each end of the necklace around a fist, making sure the diamonds faced him, and pulled the chain taut.

"Is it true what they say?" Shorty asked, waiting for the energy to come.

"What's that honey?" He heard her spit out her gum.

"That diamonds are a girl's best friend?"

"You bet your life," she replied.

"I sure do."

He brought the necklace down in front of her face and pulled back as hard as he could, forcing her backwards against his chest. Candy struggled, first gripping Shorty's fists, and then trying to pry her fingers underneath the chain. But it was too late.

Shorty's muscles were burning. He tightened the choker. Her legs were still kicking. It was taking much longer than he'd planned.

Soon, her body stiffened and relaxed as she fell asleep into his arms.

Shorty began to move the necklace from side to side. He didn't want to strangle her to death. It wouldn't make a good card. Instead, he relied on the diamond's cutting power. At first it was too hard—like using a string to saw on a tree trunk, but soon the lubrication of blood helped the necklace slide.

Candy's voice box sang.

# Play Dead

The smell of macaroni and cheese was strong in the room. Shorty closed his eyes and sang along.

Winston and Nebo had left, but Johnny felt like they were still in the room, their spirits lingering in the humming absence of their wake like a winner in a poker game who hauls away a big pot and leaves a dose of good luck behind him for the remaining players to wrestle over.

Things were moving so swiftly that Johnny had to chain smoke to settle his nerves. The scotch bottle was half-empty. He was in the game now, and Nebo's version of Butcher Boy was a helluva lot more complex than the game he had played with Shorty behind the shelter. It had the strangest rules and the most risky set-up he'd ever heard of in his life—and he'd played his share of outrageous games in his day. But this Butcher Boy thing was the strangest. It was a game where a player gambled with life. And not just his own.

The rules were simple enough for even Shorty to understand, but they were stunning in their intricacy:

There were four players.

Each one was responsible for a suit of cards: Clubs, Hearts, Diamonds, and Spades.

Each one had to *make* their suit of cards by taking pictures with a Polaroid camera (and Winston had left one behind for Johnny). Thirteen cards per player.

Johnny was assigned the Spades.

Whenever a photo was taken, it was to be given to Winston, who would somehow transform the photograph into a playing card, ready to be dealt.

Each photo had to—how did Winston put it?—"capture life."

And the more creative a photograph was—the more it succeeded at "capturing life"—the more chips a player would get to play with when it came time to play the game (and because he was entering the game late, he had only one month to get ready). A player earned his bankroll by his wits, like an artist. The amount of this reward for creativity would be up to Nebo.

After the deck was complete, the four players would sit down at a table to play Butcher Boy with the deck of cards they had created. The individual suits would be shuffled together, no longer important. When the time came to sit down, winning Butcher Boy was all that mattered.

Winston would deal, but not play. Nebo would simply watch.

The winner would walk away from the table with a million dollars.

And all losers would be killed.

It was that simple. That black-and-white. Just like life: *winners lived, losers died*. Survival of the fittest.

The thing that nagged at Johnny, though, was *why*. What did Nebo have to gain by staking such a game? Why did they have to go through the trouble of creating the deck of cards themselves? And why did the cards have to "capture life"? What exactly did that mean, anyway?

What it came down to in the long run was that Johnny had absolutely nothing to lose. The prospect of being killed if he lost didn't appeal to Johnny at all, but he wasn't really *living* anymore anyway. Yet Winston had given Johnny one last chance to back out of the game after explaining all the rules to him and giving him the equipment he needed. And Johnny didn't quit. He agreed, surprised at how eager his voice had sounded when he said "I'm definitely *in*." The money was just too much to pass up. And he figured they wouldn't *really* just let him go out on the streets, knowing what was going on, if he wasn't going to play. That's what Nebo had warned him about—knowing more about Johnny than vice-versa. Johnny would have been screwed in more ways than one if he backed out of the game now. And probably not just killed, either. Mutilated. Like Axe.

So he was in. And he knew he could win.

No, not *could*. He *had to* win. His life depended on it.

He lit another cigarette, and took a quick inventory of the equipment Winston had given him, spread out on the bed. A Polaroid camera. A Bicycle deck of cards with blue backs—just like the deck Shorty had played with behind the shelter—for "inspiration." A carton of Winstons. And a red and yellow capsule. Johnny didn't know what was in it, but he was sure it was deadly. "That's in case you get caught and I can't help you out," Winston had said when he handed it to him with a wink.

Johnny sighed, and took another swig from the bottle. He still felt sober. Way too sober.

He picked up the pill, and rolled it in the palm of his hand.

A suicide pill. Nazis used to keep cyanide tablets in their gear for the same reason.

He considered popping it. He was in the game, win or lose, no way out. He'd never been in that sort of situation before. It felt like losing itself— trapped, unable to do anything about your circumstances. Like being homeless, caught up in a game where you were bound to lose. No escape. You couldn't get a job because no one would hire a non-skilled bum. And you couldn't get out of town because you didn't have the money to buy a ticket.

And now Johnny had a pocketful of money and a roof over his head at Violet's if he wanted it. He was back in the Action. And he was more ensnared in a trap than he was when he started.

Yet there was always the chance he might win. Just the existence of that one possibility was enough to cancel out any worry.

Someone knocked on the door.

Johnny felt blood warm through the curl of his ears. He yanked open a dresser drawer and tossed the stuff Winston had given him into it. Then he covered it all up with a towel from the bathroom and shut the drawer.

He opened the door to the hallway. Gin stood there, leaning against the frame, cocking an elbow to rest a palm on her uniformed hip. A long unlit cigarette dangled from a pouting pink lip. "Hurry up and let me in, before I get caught." She brushed past him. Johnny could smell perfume. "Shut the door. I'm not supposed to be doing this, and I don't want anybody to see me."

Johnny obeyed.

And then he pulled the blankets off the bed.

"Geez, you're fast," Gin said. "What makes you think…"

"It's not what you think," Johnny said, draping the blankets over the room's mirrors. "I just don't want anybody to see me, either."

Gin lit her cigarette and picked up Johnny's bottle of scotch to read the label. "You're a strange man, Johnny." She set the bottle back down and stared at him. "Very strange."

# Play Dead

Gin looked beautiful. Even in her green Bucket of Bucks uniform, with the embossed gold-at-the-end-of-the-rainbow patch above her left breast. He could tell that she'd been working her ass off—as usual. The heavy make-up and jewelry couldn't cover for the sweat stains in the armpits and the rings under the eyes. If there was one thing Johnny didn't miss about work—and it seemed like years since he'd done so—it was the visible damage the daily grind did to the body that you had to face every morning in the mirror. But Gin looked beautiful, and Johnny guessed that her commitment to work was part of what attracted him to her in the first place. Work: something he didn't understand, something he didn't have, mysterious in that all the other suckers in the world fell for it—but he could tell that Gin knew better. Like it was all just a game to her, and she was somehow winning.

Johnny had filled the ice bucket while Gin cleaned up. He poured scotch into the tumblers he'd grabbed from the bathroom, figuring she wasn't the sort to drink straight from the bottle. Heck, he didn't even know if she drank at all. But he hoped so.

He waited for her on the bed, arms crossed over his chest. But when the sound of running water stopped, he hopped out and sat at the table, guessing she wouldn't like that very much.

She entered the room, snapping her purse, and blinked at him. "How do I look?"

"Just fine," Johnny said, motioning at the empty seat in front him. "As mysterious as ever."

She pulled the chair back and sat down. "Just what is that supposed to mean?" She reached for the drink Johnny had prepared for her and sipped.

"You know," Johnny said, lighting a cigarette. "I keep finding new things out about you every day. Digging up little mysteries."

"Like?"

"Like working here at The Bucket, on top of slaving in the soup kitchen every morning." Johnny leaned forward. "And I think I just discovered your eyes."

"Lucky you." She sipped again, ignoring his sweet talk, but allowing him to gaze at her as she surveyed the room. "What's with the blankets over the mirrors, anyway?"

"You should know," Johnny said, puffing smoke. "You work here."

"Come again?"

Johnny waved around the room. "There's security cameras behind every mirror in this joint."

She smirked. "You're paranoid."

"Maybe. But paranoia is a safe bet."

"You gamblers. Everything's a bet to you. It gets old after awhile." She unsnapped her purse and withdrew a long Benson-and-Hedges. "I don't suppose you want one of these?"

Johnny shook his head. "Nah."

She lit up. "So are you bettin' you'll bang me tonight, too?"

Johnny nearly spit his drink. "Excuse me?"

"Never mind." She rolled her eyes. "So tell me how a guy like you lives in the streets one day and stays in a fancy hotel room like this the next. What's the story?"

"Didn't I already tell you I got me a job?"

"What sorta job pays this good on the first night? Don't con me. I don't like it."

Johnny smoked. "A gamblin' job."

"Figures." She poured herself another drink, splashing the scotch violently against the ice. Then she took a sip while Johnny watched the muscles of her lips and throat as she swallowed.

She met his eyes and set the glass down. Hard. "You know, I really don't appreciate having to work my tail off for guys like you. I mean, shit, I donate my friggin' free time for a good cause, and I get screwed. Who the hell do you think you are, sleeping in the shelter and playin' Mr. High Roller at night? Acting down-and-out just so you don't have to waste your next bet on a hotel for the night. Like it's an open house or somethin'. That makes me sick." She cooled down as she lifted her glass and took another sip. "But I bet you'll be back. Guys like you always come back. And pretty soon it'll be for good."

Johnny couldn't believe he was hearing this. She was voicing the guilt he had felt for ditching Violet, not the shelter. "Hey, what's the problem? I'm one less mouth for society to feed…"

"Not society. *Me*. I do the work. And you were never worth my time."

Silence. They stared at each other, pretending to ignore the sound of a television through the wall.

"Listen," Johnny finally said. "Aren't we friends?"

Gin smirked.

"Really. Aren't we? You know me pretty good by now. And you've treated me like a friend. You came up here to be with me tonight. You gave Shorty my plate the other day. You've given me smokes when I needed them. You're like my best friend—about the only friend I got—and I'm willin' to bet you feel the same way about me. Am I right?"

She flipped her palms face up on the table in response. "I don't know why I did those things. I musta been out of my mind."

Johnny leaned forward and dared to hold her hand. It was limp. Cold. He bluffed: "Because you like me. And I like you. We both know that."

She didn't move. "I guess you're right. Hell if I know why, but you're right. I do."

Johnny gripped down on her hand before pulling away. He poured himself another drink. Things were going well. "It's a helluva lot better in here than in the shelter, Gin. Anyone in their right mind can see that. But you gotta understand: I didn't use the shelter as some sort of rock to crawl under till I found my legs. I was *seriously* down on my luck. To tell ya the truth, it really hasn't even sunk in that I'm here at all right now, or that I was ever really there at the shelter at all." Johnny looked around the room to confirm its reality.

"Me neither," she said, her eyes like full clouds. Suddenly, she leaned over the table to kiss him.

Her lips felt like warm bread. Holding her head against his, refusing to let her face go, he stood and made his way around the table to her side. He opened his eyes. Gin kept hers closed as she pulled herself against him and held the small of his back, massaging the bones there. Johnny parted his lips and Gin shoved her tongue deep into his mouth, nearly choking him. She tasted like a warm worm of menthol scotch.

She gently caressed the gap in his teeth with edge of her tongue, before madly fucking the space there with it.

It tickled the roof of his mouth. Hurt a little.

Johnny let her do it.

# Play Dead

The phone rang.

Johnny slapped the headset off its cradle and tried to bring it to his ear, but its buzzing end seemed continually just out of reach. It had been awhile since he'd answered a phone. When he finally maneuvered it next to his ear, the metallic voice on the other end was already speaking: *This is your wake-up call. Good Morning! Thank you for choosing Nebo's Bucket of Bucks. This is your wake-up call. Rise and shine! We have the loosest slots. This is your wake-up call. Up and at 'em! Featuring Vegas' largest sports forum. This is your wake....*

He hung up.

He didn't remember requesting an alarm. "That's weird," he said, turning on his side, but Gin was already gone, already out of the picture. And that seemed even stranger.

Johnny slid out of the sheets and sat on the bedside for awhile, running his fingers through the greased clumps of his hair. His temples throbbed with last night's scotch, but it seemed to be a feeling he was getting used to. The bottle was beside the phone, with just enough left to get him going. He downed it.

Headache gone.

He stood and checked the dresser to make sure that the goods Winston had given him were undisturbed. Satisfied, he grabbed his clothes from a pile by the table and went into the bathroom. He showered until the pipes ran out of hot water and toweled off, looking at his naked self in the body-length mirror. He was looking better and better. Private showers—a luxury just a few days ago—were working wonders for him. He thought it was a shame to have to dress in the same clothes he'd worn the night before—the get-up Violet had given him. But it was all he had.

Johnny brushed his teeth with a cheap plastic travel brush the hotel had provided. The toothpaste tasted stale. When he spit, a green-red splatter hit the sink. His gums were bleeding terribly, and the gap where his tooth should have was stinging as if needles had been slipped into his mouth. He let it scab while he shaved with the complimentary razor and packet of gel, and he could feel the dirt being scraped out from his pores with each stroke. It burned to use the Brut the hotel provided, but the burn was good. It made him feel alive. That was a feeling he was beginning to appreciate.

A light tap on the bathroom door. "Are you gonna take fucking forever, or what?"

Johnny recognized Winston's voice. He wasn't surprised. And he figured Winston had ordered the wake-up call, too. Still, he acted pissed: "Who let you in here?"

"I did," he said through the door. "So hurry up. I ain't had my coffee yet." Winston coughed. "And I have a little gambling debt to pay this morning."

Johnny opened the door, and he could see that his cleanliness caught Winston off guard. He smiled and winked as he made his way past him. "Debt?" Johnny said over his shoulder as he looked for his shoes. "I thought you didn't gamble."

"I usually don't." Winston rolled his cigarette between his fingers, watching its end burn. "But it appears I lost that little bet I made with you awhile back, about askin' that soup kitchen girlie out on a date."

*How does he know Gin was here?* Johnny grabbed his cigarette pack, double-checking the blanket-covered mirrors with a glance. No reflections.

"So, come on. I owe you breakfast." Winston took a drag. "Only it's gonna have to be on Nebo, since he's invited us both upstairs."

"Uh-huh." Johnny slipped a foot into a tennis shoe. "It's all on Nebo, ain't it?"

Winston shook his head. "You're lucky, kid. Nebo likes you. You shouldn't be so ungrateful."

"Ungrateful?" Johnny motioned at the room. "So far, I gotta say I like Nebo, too."

Together they walked to the elevators.

"So how was she?"

"None of your freakin' business."

Winston smiled as he pressed an illuminated arrow pointing up. An elevator door opened at their right. Johnny moved, but Winston held him back by the shoulder. "No. Wrong elevator."

"What's the difference?"

"You'll see."

They waited until an elevator on their far left opened. Johnny followed Winston inside. It didn't look any different than the others. Winston opened a metal door which housed the telephone and emergency call buttons. Beneath those was a slot, into which Winston shoved a plastic card. An electronic key.

The elevator rose swiftly and Johnny's stomach sunk as though he'd swallowed a thousand marbles. The digital read-out didn't bother flashing floor numbers. And it didn't matter. He knew where they were headed. To the penthouse. To Nebo's place.

Winston stared at the floor as the elevator rose, silent. He looked tired, bags around his eyes like a badger's. Weak, shoulder blades thin and drooping. Johnny wondered if this was how Winston always looked when he was alone, and didn't have to put up a front.

"Hey," Johnny said, trying to get his attention. "You never told me the deal with Axe. What was up with that?"

Winston smirked, not bothering to look at him. "I told you. Act of faith. Bury the hatchet. All that crap."

"Yeah, but who killed him? Was it you?"

Winston faced him, an eyebrow menacingly raised. He just grinned.

The elevator lurched to a stop. Johnny's stomach kept rising. The door quickly opened.

And they were inside.

The living room was immaculate. Johnny could feel his feet sinking into the floor through his tennis shoes. A bright white sofa—with room enough for ten people—stood on his right. A fireplace—something completely unnecessary considering the climate—burned across the floorway from the couch. The walls were papered with a simple black-and-white pattern of stripes—almost like prison bars, but not quite as thick. Gold-framed paintings covered most of that space, though. Windows through a cage.

"Wait here," Winston said. "I'll see if he's ready."

Johnny stepped over to the couch, feeling as though he were creeping on tip-toe. The thickness of the carpet was spooking him for some reason. He curled his toes. The place smelled like money, and Johnny felt like a thief.

Before he sat down on the couch, he noticed the frames on the wall. They didn't hold expensive art at all, as he had first thought. They held *cards*.

In the frame nearest Johnny, a plate of gleaming glass pressed an entire open-faced deck against green felt. They were old cards, crackled, yellowing, and bent. And quite simple: no numbers or letters, just drawings—pen and ink on parchment—depicting ornate scenes in intricate detail.

Johnny moved closer, so near he could see his reflection in the glass.

Ten leaves stemming from a branch that ran the middle of the card, like a tree. The leaves were grotesquely larger than the trunk, though, veined and plump with thick stems that webbed together to form the background like strange Gothic ironworks. It reminded Johnny of church for some reason—stained glass and capital letters from ancient bibles.

"I see you like the Ten of Spades," Nebo said from behind him.

Johnny stopped himself from jumping. "Spades? Oh, I get it." The leaves were the same shape as Spades from a regular card deck. The other suits were just as strange: acorns and balloons. "Yeah, these are pretty neat. How old?"

"Germany, Renaissance era."

Johnny preened his shaved chin, as if he knew what Nebo was talking about. "What did they gamble with 'em for? Food?"

Nebo softly chuckled. "Come, let's eat. You must be hungry."

Johnny obeyed, stealing glimpses of the other framed decks along the wall as Nebo led him into the dining room. Most of them looked hand-painted, homemade. And Johnny figured he was right the first time: those frames held art, all right. Decks of it.

Steaming plates were waiting for them on a square table shining with sunlight that stabbed into the room through glass walls. Johnny ignored the skyline view and stared down at the food. Omelets with cheese and chunks of ham draped over the top. Hash browns and coffee. As Johnny sat on the opposite side of Winston—who was chugging a cup of coffee from a tall mug—he was more interested in the plates that held the food: they, too, looked hand-painted and ancient. Johnny felt like he was sitting down to grub in an Egyptian tomb.

Nebo opened a cloth napkin and placed it over his lap. Johnny followed suit, trying to keep his manners. The smell of the omelets was creeping into his nose, and Johnny swallowed its scent, eager to get started. But he waited for Nebo to take the first bite.

They ate in silence. Johnny shoveled the food into his mouth, swallowing chunks of ham whole without chewing. He'd never eaten a meal that tasted so good.

Soon, Nebo lifted his napkin and patted his lips with it. "I take it Winston has told you everything you need to know about my little game?" He eyed Winston, and then turned his head towards Johnny.

Johnny nodded, finishing a bite. "Everything except why."

"Yes," Nebo replied, replacing his napkin and reaching for the pot of coffee. "*Why*. The eternal question." He filled his cup, and gently set the pot back down. "I'm curious. What guesses might you make, to answer that question?"

Johnny grabbed the pot and poured his own coffee. "Well," he said taking a sip, "you obviously want to add another deck to your collection."

Nebo nodded, smiling at Winston. "Very perceptive."

"But I don't see why the game is important." Johnny played with the napkin on his lap as he spoke. He felt totally out of his element, chatting over breakfast with a rich bastard in a penthouse suite. "You could get anyone to capture life or whatever. Creative people. Real artists, not bums like me. And I bet you'd save a lot of money that way, too. But a million dollars for one poker game..." Johnny stopped folding his napkin, and looked at Nebo. "I just don't get it."

"I think you do get it, but you just don't know you do." Nebo stared Johnny down with his almond eyes. He spoke with his hands, like playing with dolls: "You're a gambler. I am, too. You play cards. I play people. It's how we both make a living."

Johnny nodded. Winston was lighting a cigarette, so Johnny figured it was okay if he did the same, listening closely.

"But without a certain risk, there is no gambling. Without the possibility of loss, there is no game. Winning or losing, either way it's a joke if there isn't something riding on the line. You understand?"

"Of course I do," Johnny said, dragging on his smoke. "But I don't see what this has to do with making cards."

"You will, as the game progresses. After all, it's only just beginning for you. But there are lives riding on the outcome of this game. And life is the ultimate gamble."

"But what's that got to do with you? You're just gonna watch, right?"

Nebo pulled his chair closer to the table and leaned towards Johnny, as if to whisper. But he didn't. "You and I are quite alike, Johnny Frieze. We both have ridden that bull named luck. It threw you off its back, but it has taken me for quite an unexpected journey. That's the only difference between us. How we've ridden luck. I'm just helping you back up."

"Only if I win."

"Right. You can't help a man who doesn't help himself. But I think you'll do just fine, Johnny. You've got what it takes. The game should be quite interesting. And as to why I want to watch it play out…" He slid back into his chair. "Well. Let's just say I've got a vested interest in its outcome."

"Like what?"

Nebo pulled on his cuff, and Johnny knew he was making him nervous. "I can't possibly explain it all to you. But suffice it for now to say that I'm simply bored with games. I've played every game under the sun—from business to bingo to back alley craps—even games you've never even heard of. And they all bore me now. Like I've said before, if a game isn't new—isn't rare or fresh—then there's really nothing to it. And the risk is minimal. I've seldom got anything to lose. And who can play at my level anymore? There are probably only ten people in the country who could play at a stake high enough to interest me."

*What a snob*, Johnny thought, but he knew everything he was saying was truth.

# Play Dead

"There's an old saying in the gambling world, Johnny. I'm sure you've heard it: 'the more a man's got, the more he has to lose.' But it simply isn't true. It's a myth. The fact is, the more a man's got, the more he's *gonna* get. And the less he's got, the less he's *gonna* get. That's the system. The way progress and power works—one direction or the other. Call it destiny if you wish."

Johnny shrugged as he put out his cigarette in a silver ashtray.

"Anyway, you asked why I'm staking Butcher Boy. The reason is simple: *it's my game.* Since no other game excites me, I've decided to play my own game, with my own rules, and my own vested interest. I've got my reasons. And I'm keeping them to myself. But I'm sure you can appreciate the simple rarity of this game."

Johnny nodded. "Understood."

Nebo played with his tie as if trying to get himself back together. He'd revealed more than he wanted to. "I enjoyed our conversation. Now if you'll excuse me, we've both got work to do."

Johnny slid back his chair and stood. Winston did likewise. "Thanks for breakfast," Johnny said.

Nebo nodded. "Thank you for visiting me. I'll see you at the game."

Johnny made his way out, with Winston at his heels. As he passed by the framed decks of cards, he noticed that each set had one card flipped over, to show off the decor on the back of each deck. The back—the cover—the tease—the only part of a hand which everyone got to see in the game to wonder what was on the other side. The part that faced you when you wondered what a player had in the hole.

Like people, every card held its secrets.

Nebo liked flipping them over.

Johnny wondered if he could do the same.

"C'mon," Winston said, slipping his key card into the slot from inside the elevator. "We've gotta get your stuff, so you can get started. You've got a lot of catching up to do."

The Seven of Clubs was the luckiest card in Ferret's suit...and the most frustrating.

He'd spent hours staring at the card from his practice deck, trying to find a pattern or purpose to the lay of the design. Roughly formed in the shape of the letter M, the pips were lined up in two parallel lines of Clubs, with one club between them—five on their stems, two upside-down. From a distance, the card sort of looked like a makeshift map of a forest of seven trees. Or seven keyholes to some madman's idea of a door. And....

That was all he could come up with.

A very uncreative card.

He decided to hang out at a nearby park to try and find seven trees arranged in the same pattern as the Clubs on the card. No such luck. The park was barren of anything but palm trees, which looked absolutely nothing like Clubs. More like drooping, flattened Spades. Some had bunches of coconuts. But that was pushing it.

He made his way back to the shelter, hoping Lady Luck would give him inspiration.

And she did. In the form of a large sign above a dark disco doorway: THE LUCKY SEVEN CLUB.

Ferret had to laugh. He went inside.

The place was relatively crowded and noisy for late afternoon, and Ferret guessed that it was happy hour. People crowded around the bar like pigs at a water trough, squirming around one another to get the barkeep's attention. Behind this crowd was a space no bigger than the shelter's cot area—a dance floor—where so many people were dancing that they didn't look like people at all to Ferret—just an undulating mass of arms and body parts, a large alien organ, pulsing to the beat of some thumping bass and synthesizer shriek that called itself music.

Ferret felt dizzy. The place was confusing him, but he knew he had been sent here for a purpose. He moved away from the slot machines that lined the entranceway and found himself standing on the edge of the dance floor, trying to keep his balance.

Spinning colored spotlights taped together like glowing grapes in groups of three beamed into his eyes. When he blinked, he found that the dancers seemed to writhe in parties of three—clothed public threesomes—grinding groins, heads over shoulders and hands on hips—sweating above a dance floor covered with the symbols from playing cards like step-patterned footprints. But there was no order to the dance. The moves were as random as a deck of cards in the act of shuffling.

*Pick a card*, Ferret thought, trying to conjure Fate's magical assistance as his eyes roamed the dancers. *Any card.*

He focused on faces, counting them in freeze-frame blinks in the shutter of his eyes:

*One*—a Latino man with a pock marked face and razor stubbled chin, bumping his erection against some girl's ass.

*Two*—a redhead with long curls and a dress revealing too much flatness on her chest, wobbling on each step on her purple high heels, ready to topple at any moment.

*Three*—a drunk white businessman with silver hair, a large spot on his blazer from spilling his Martini while he swaggered, trying to get a young boy's attention.

*Four*—a kid in a Nike T-shirt, obviously underage, dancing alone, grabbing his crotch with one hand and chugging a can of Budweiser with the other. He was smiling widely.

*Five*—an alcoholic woman with large freckles and dark rings around her eyes, trying to focus on the man who was hanging on to her ass to hold himself up while they danced.

*Six*—a big fat guy, leaning against the wall between the DJ's booth and the rest rooms, flexing the biceps of his crossed arms—proud to be a bouncer—looking for some action.

*And lucky...*

*Seven*—a man wearing a gray sport jacket and T-shirt, rising on the balls of his tennis-shoed feet to dig into the front pocket of his much-too-tight-

and-revealing blue jeans. He was flashing the edge of a folded stack of hundred dollar bills that stuck out from his pocket to the blond standing next to him, before tucking the money back inside. He cautiously cased the room, making sure no one had seen. The blond nodded and grabbed him by the elbow, leading him into the crowd.

Ferret moved. He could follow. Be patient. Wait.

The couple cut across the dance floor, not to dance, but to get somewhere. The blond seemed to be in quite a rush, tossing her hair behind her and elbowing folks out of the way, but the man was taking his time, forcing her to drag him behind her by the hand.

*That blond looks familiar*, Ferret thought, watching as they moved closer and closer to where he stood. She was wearing a black mini-skirt and a red turtle-necked blouse, with a shiny red leather purse dangling on the thinnest of strings over her shoulder. Her mascara-covered eyes, her glazed eyes, her bright blue eyes...

*It's the cook.*

Ferret turned around so she wouldn't recognize him. He waited as the couple passed by and headed out the front door into sunlight.

Then he followed.

They made their way down the street to a parking lot in the center of the block. Ferret ducked behind a Rolls as the man in the sport coat glanced quickly around, opening a passenger door for Gin, and then walked around the car, a black Nova, jingling his keys. Gin didn't open the door for him. He unlocked it and climbed inside. And then they sat there and talked. Ferret watched as they both made motions with their mouths and hands, avoiding each other's eyes. He couldn't tell if they were arguing or giving one another directions. It appeared to be an argument, judging from Gin's hand motions — she kept accidentally slapping the fuzzy dice that drooped from the rear-view mirror with the back of a hand.

Ferret waited, praying that his Seven of Clubs wouldn't start the car.

Gin slipped a strap from her shoulder.

And then she quickly stepped out of the car and headed towards him.

Ferret pivoted, crab-walking on his heels to keep the Rolls between them as she made her way past his cover. He kept an eye on her through the tinted windows of the car: she blew hair out of her face with a curled lip and rolled her eyes—obviously relieved about something. And she was wearing a new purse—green, not red. They'd made a trade. Ferret considered snatching the purse to find out what was hiding inside.

And then the dude revved up his car.

He jumped, rushing towards the Nova. The man didn't even see him coming. He was at the driver's side door and swinging it open, whipping Trickster's serrated edge into the guy's face before he knew what hit him. The guy panicked and held Gin's purse in one hand—absurdly trying to hold Ferret at bay with its leather—while he tried to get the stick-shift into first gear with his other hand. The engine made strange high pitched grinding noises as he shoved the stick into the wrong slots. Ferret jumped up on the edge of the floorboards and held the roof for leverage just in case the car took off—leaning back like a skydiver at a plane's exit before the jump— and then lunged forward, driving the blade past the purse and into the guy's chest with all his weight. The engine screamed.

Ferret let go of Trickster's handle and stared deep into the man's fluttering eyes as the Nova's engine roared at an alarming volume. He noticed that the man had pounded his foot down on the accelerator, as if to run away from the death that had already overtaken him. Ferret punched at his kneecap, and the foot fell off the pedal, stamping down on the floorboards instead. As the engine came to an idle, Ferret used two hands to drag the knife through the man's bony chest from left to right, snapping through the cartilage in the middle, and then cutting a cool slice diagonally down into the ease of his abdomen.

"Lucky you," Ferret whispered, backing away from his new card.

The gushing wound formed a dripping seven of gore.

Not very original, but better than nothing.

Ferret reached into his backpack and pulled out his Polaroid camera. He had to take the shot right away, before the blood pooled together into an unreadable blot. "Smile," he said, and pressed the button.

The camera spit out the picture, as Ferret made his way around to the passenger's side. He sat down and blew on it to hurry up the development, looking out through the windshield, checking that no one was around. They weren't. He still had some time.

He waved the picture like a fan against the breath from his lips. The dice on the mirror were all fives and twos.

"Lucky you," he said as he lifted them off the rear-view mirror and placed them around the guy's neck like bizarre jewelry. He took another shot for posterity. "Lucky me." The photo spit out of the camera like a plasticene tongue. "Aren't we a pair of cards?"

He stared at the double sevens on the guy and laughed.

Ferret heard a noise. The kid who was grabbing his crotch on the dance floor was now in the parking lot, bending over to pick up the keys he'd dropped beside the Rolls. Ferret pulled the dead guy towards him and pushed him down onto the floor of the passenger side. Then he climbed behind the wheel and stepped on the gas.

As the tires hit the street, he grabbed Gin's red purse and shoved it between his thighs.

# Play Dead

♥ ♥ ♥ ♥ ♥ ♥  Q  ♥ ♥ ♥ ♥ ♥ ♥

"It's check-out time," Winston had said when Johnny stepped off the elevator. That meant that his stay in Room 505 was over. He didn't expect it to be permanent anyway. It was obvious that Nebo didn't want Johnny hanging around his new casino until game time, "advertising."

The room had been expertly cleaned by the maid in his absence. He could tell because the blankets had been removed from the mirrors and made on the bed as if he'd never slept there. Panicking, he opened his drawer: the equipment Winston had given him remained untouched. He sighed in relief and sat on the bed, opening up the Bicycle deck of cards by twisting the plastic like the wrap that covers a cigarette pack. Then he sniffed the box, inhaling the fumes of old pasteboard and cheap plastic. Good.

Since the Bikes were brand new, the Ace of Spades was right on top. Simple and ominous, the black head of the spade consumed the white of the card. Behind it, the rest of the pips followed in order, Two through King. He removed them. Spades, his suit, low to high, fresh out of the pack. One by one he laid them out on his bed, side by side.

*Spades.* A fitting suit for a man who had just buried his first body.

He stared at them, wondering how the hell he was gonna "capture life" with the Polaroid and craft thirteen cards as beautiful as the ones on his bed. It seemed impossible. The deck was already perfect.

He picked up the Ace and studied the shape of the spade closely, holding it so near to his eyes that it became blurry.

And then he set it back down. He was sure the ideas would come—just like cards themselves, it was up to the luck of the draw. He had faith. It would happen.

But not the first four. Johnny picked up the Ace, Two, Three, and Four of Spades, and shoved them back into the box. Those cards, according to Winston, were already done, care of Axe, and Johnny was already way behind the other players. So he'd have to start his own suit from the Five of Spades and keep Axe's cards in the game as if they were his own.

And for even more inspiration, Winston had given Johnny a sickening peek at Axe's contribution, fueling the nausea in Johnny's elevator stomach:

Four dead bodies. Not Shorty's rats as he'd expected, but two black women and two black men. All with close-up photographs of their groins. Genitalia butchered and stuffed in various orifices and wounds in their bodies. Winston had called them "Spayed Spades." And that, according to Winston, was why Axe had been taken out of the game. Folded like the white sheet he could have worn. Because he wasn't playing the game right—he'd captured too much life too soon. And Nebo especially hated racism, having some African blood in him himself.

Even so, the cards were to be played.

Now Johnny knew what "capturing life" meant.

Death. Murder. Creative killing.

Each death in its proper place, at a level corresponding to the hierarchy of cards.

Johnny wasn't sure he was up for it. He'd never killed anyone before, and he didn't know if he ever could. The sight of Axe's chest was bad enough. Maybe he'd end up the same way, too. He knew the game was risky, but *murder*?

The pill waited in the dresser drawer.

Johnny gathered up his suit and slid it back in the box. Next, he grabbed the fresh trash bag from the can in the corner of his room and shoved the items from the drawer into it. He put the suicide pill into the little denim coin-pocket inside the regular pocket of his jeans. Then he took what he could from the bathroom—the razor, bloodied toothbrush, and soap—and a pillow from the bed, and shoved them on top of the goods in his bag. He knew he might be needing them, if Violet was upset at him for losing her in The Bucket.

He made his way down the hall to the elevators and went down to the casino. The games were still roaring as if he'd never left. He turned to look back at the poker pit—remembering that he still had a pocketful of Violet's cash—only it didn't seem so attractive anymore. The whole scene looked boring and childish. Like Nebo had said: minimal risk. A game for wannabes, punks playing with themselves. They weren't real gamblers, only players, destined to lose. Because in such petty games the players themselves were being played.

And that's when Johnny realized that, yes, he could kill to play Nebo's game. Because he couldn't go back to what he was before. He'd already buried the bodies and seen the cards and holed up with the man behind the mirrors. He was in. In deeper than ever.

And he couldn't afford to doubt himself anymore.

He felt like a man crawling his way out of a playpen full of writhing newborns as he made his way across the casino floor, heading toward the wide open mouth of The Bucket's front entrance. The progressive slot read-out was now in the eighty-thousands. No one had won the jackpot. Johnny doubted anyone ever did.

But Violet was still sitting there, wearing her corny black leather jacket, her face drawn and blank as she pulled on the single arm of a bandit like a little girl tugging on the sleeve of her father. He wondered if she'd ever gotten up from that seat. Whether she alone had more than doubled the progressive jackpot. Whether she even knew it was daylight.

"Violet," Johnny said, placing a palm on her shoulder. "What are you still doing here?" He rubbed sleep from his eyes. "Still feeding this thing all your money?"

"Winnin'," she replied, not looking up. Her voice was coarse from too many menthols.

Johnny noticed she had a plastic cup in her lap, filled to the brim with quarters. Her jackpot tray was half-full, too. "Some things eat your money. Other things eat your soul."

"Pah," she said gruffly. "I never had no soul to take, Johnny. And slowly but surely, I'm takin' this joint for all it's worth." She reached forward and picked up a small glass beside her slot machine. Ice with a dead cherry in it. Taking a cube of ice into her mouth, she slurped on it. Johnny could hear it cracking against her dentures. "What's up? You ain't thinkin' about moseying, are ya?"

"We've been here for an entire day," he said, wondering if he sounded guilty. Violet looked like shit—zombied-out. This was his fault, for ditching her.

"Here." She handed him her bucket of quarters. "I only got so many hands. You take this and play that machine over there, while I play out the rest. Soon as I'm out, we'll leave."

Johnny took the quarters. But he didn't play them. He just pulled up a nearby stool, and watched her, waiting.

She kept hitting cherries and the occasional five-dollar payoff, while the progressive digits above her machine kept churning higher and higher.

*Sky's the limit*, Johnny reminded himself. *Until somebody wins.*

He turned in his stool, clutching his bag on his lap, and looked out through The Bucket's ever-open mouth. The sun was warbling in waves of desert heat on the horizon, like a gold coin melting in the sky. If the sky was the limit, Johnny wondered just how far he could go.

# Play Dead

*The hearts are getting old.*

As he chewed on the last of his breakfast meat, The Preacher couldn't stop thinking about how true that was. He needed to hurry up and finish. To get the entire suit done, so he could repay the Lord the money he owed him. And wash the blood from his hands.

But his cause was righteous. And he would stay the course.

He dropped his plate on his pillow, and then reached down beneath the cot to scoot out his duffel bag. Digging inside, he found what he was looking for, his plastic grocery bag, heavy and knotted tightly at one end. He tucked it inside his jacket, holding it against his chest with the pit of his arm. It felt squishy.

Then he stood and entered the soup kitchen. He looked behind the counter and saw Gin, scraping black grease from the grill with a Brillo. "Good morning, young lady."

She didn't look up. Sweat was beading on her nose. "What's so good about it?"

"Why," the Preacher said, setting the bag down on the counter but keeping it hidden from sight beneath his coat, "every morning is a good morning when you wake up with the Lord!"

"Yeah," Gin replied, blowing her hair with a curled lip. "Whatever."

The Preacher smiled. "Don't look so glum, dear. Maybe I can cheer your spirits."

Gin dropped the Brillo and faced him, wiping black stains down her apron. "Listen, why don't you go sell it somewhere else…"

The Preacher cocked his head and blinked. "Don't get me wrong. I'm just offerin' to help."

Gin looked at the slop around the kitchen. She reached inside her back pocket and pulled out a crumpled pack of Benson and Hedges. She motioned at a stack of egg cartons on a metallic tray. "If you really want to help, you can start by putting all that food back in the walk-in freezer." She tapped a cigarette out from the pack. "And then maybe help me do those dishes back there."

The Preacher nodded. "Gladly." He pulled the bag in his coat against him again and moved around the counter.

Gin popped the cigarette into her mouth and grinned. "Me, I'm taking a break."

"Much deserved, young lady. Much deserved." He grabbed a carton of eggs with a free hand. "See, I knew I could lift up your spirits. And that's what the Lord can do for you, too—he's always willing to lend a helping hand..."

The aluminum door slammed shut on its springs. Gin was outside.

The Preacher dropped his smile and moved into the freezer, gently pulling the door closed behind him. The closet-sized room was so cold he could see his breath. He made his way to the back of the freezer, where sacks the size of tall dwarfs leaned together. The bags read FRENCH FRIES, and there were about ten of them, stacked side by side.

The preacher took the warm plastic bag out from his coat and slipped it behind the french fry sacks, deep into the corner where no one was likely to find it for awhile. It steamed from the heat of his armpits. He waited for it to evaporate.

Then he quickly exited the freezer, his lungs burning from the cold.

As fast as he could, he piled the rest of the food into the crook of an arm and loaded it into the freezer, hurrying to get the job done.

Gin returned. "Hey," she said, setting a palm on her hip. "You really are helping me, aren't you?"

"You got that right, young lady. It's my mission to help those in need."

She smiled. "Well, then." She tightened her apron as she brushed past him. "It's your mission to pile these pots and pans back by the sink, too." She returned to scraping the grill.

The Preacher grabbed a tall aluminum pot and carried it back to the sink. "What's for dinner tonight? French fries?"

"Nope. Casserole."

He grabbed a pile of soup spoons and spatulas black with grime. Sadly: "God be praised."

Gin chuckled. "What's the matter, don't trust the chef?"

"No, his cooking is fine." The Preacher dropped the silverware inside the pot he'd moved. "Fine enough for the Lord's supper."

Gin stopped scrubbing to turn her eyes up toward the ceiling. "I haven't forgotten Easter, have I?"

The Preacher laughed. "Not at all, young lady. And how could you? You're a good Christian woman, are you not?"

"Well...sure." She returned to scraping, trying to drown out his voice with her iron sponge.

The Preacher was right behind her. His voice deepened. "You do love God, don'tcha dear?"

She turned, startled at his proximity, her Brillo pad was raised like an absurd weapon. She blinked as they stared at each other and then lowered it by her side, rolling her eyes. "Is that all you ever talk about? The Lord this and God that? Gimme a break. Please."

The Preacher leaned so close to her face she could feel his spittle misting her lips: "Out of the abundance of the heart, the mouth speaketh."

She blinked saliva droplets from her eyelids. "Huh?"

"Matthew twelve, thirty-four."

"Oh." Gin swallowed, faked a smile. "I thought you were trying to tell me that you had a crush on me, Preacher." She weakly managed a wink.

His mouth dropped open. His face flushed bright pink.

She twisted around. "That's all the help I need from you right now." She looked over her shoulder. "Thanks a lot for all the help, Preacher. I really appreciate it."

He stood there, mouth agape, while Gin shook her ass in his face, scraping the grill with renewed vigor, putting her whole body into it. "I said thanks," she repeated, her voice stressed.

The Preacher closed his eyes. "*Harlot*," he muttered under his breath.

"Pardon me?"

The Preacher stormed away, ignoring her. He didn't have time to show her the error of her ways just now. He'd already accomplished one mission, and he had to get back to his deck. New cards were waitingand he wanted to get back to the Lord's work immediately.

Not every heart in his suit could be kept waiting on ice, like those he'd tucked away inside the walk-in freezer.

# part Three
# DIAMONDS

# A ♦

Violet dropped her purse on the sofa like a moneybag from a bank robbery and all the quarters jingled noisily inside. She slid the black leather jacket from her shoulders and it dropped to the carpet like a heavy wet backpack. Following close behind, Johnny nearly tripped on her long coat before picking the leather up and hanging it on the rack beside other jackets she probably shouldn't be wearing—frilly overgowns and high school letter jackets. No fashion sense; every get-up like an uncertain disguise. Not that fashion mattered much to Johnny, but it gave the impression that Violet really didn't know who she was. And she was much too old for that.

Violet was already in the kitchen, making a drink. Johnny watched her from the distance of her bar, wondering if drinking was a good idea. He knew she was exhausted—probably already completely wasted from the free drinks that The Bucket had given her while she poured her life into that one slot machine. He doubted that she actually won much—all those quarters could have been bought from the cashier's cage. Johnny didn't understand what Violet saw in slots—it was a game for monkeys, conditioned to keep pulling the lever for another peanut—but she religiously played the bandit, like praying before an altar, confident something would happen if she just kept on trying.

Violet sat down on the stool opposite him, and passed him a tumbler with ice. She was pouring before he could say a word. "Did you have a good time?"

"The best," Johnny said, thinking about Gin, but not recalling much. He dug into his pocket, proud to still have most of the money she'd lent him. He tossed it on the bar. "There ya go. Didn't win much; lost a bit at blackjack."

Violet ignored it, saddling up on the stool and tossing back her whiskey. She seemed far too serious—almost depressed.

He cocked his head to one side. "You look like you could use some shut-eye."

She grinned falsely, leaning forward and forcing a wink. "Like this?" She made a face like Popeye. "Or like this?" She switched eyes.

# play Dead

Johnny shook his head and took the offered drink. He watched as she straightened herself on the stool and tried to keep her balance. He noticed movement behind her lips, like her gums were wrestling with her dentures. Her eyes were glazed as day-old donuts, staring at him.

"You've gotta be tired, Violet. You played all night, non-stop."

Her mouth clopped. "Didn't you?"

Johnny nodded. The game was constant, and he figured he always *would* be playing till the final hand.

Violet blinked, refilling their glasses. "Why don't we go over to the couch? My ass is killing me."

She stood up, rubbing her butt. They made their way over to the living room, Johnny carrying the bottle and cautiously standing by her side in case she fell. But she seemed to be fine—not quite as drunk as he'd suspected. Just dazed from the night's gambling. Her constitution amazed him.

She fell into a cushion and sighed, keeping her drink expertly balanced. Johnny sat beside her, scooching forward on the brown vinyl, trying not to get too comfortable.

They drank silently. Johnny stared at the painting of dogs cheating at Tarot.

"Ya know," Violet said, leaning back and looking him over. "You sure look a heckuva lot like my ex in that outfit. All slick and pretty."

Johnny smiled. He didn't like being called pretty, but it didn't sound bad the way Violet said it. "Tell me about him."

Violet swirled the ice in her glass, keeping her eyes on him. They were bloodshot, yellow, but gleaming. "Dutch was really a player, just like you. In his prime he could outbet the best of them. He was a rock. Had a poker face that wouldn't budge. Never. Not even in the sack." She swigged, ice smacking against her false teeth.

Johnny felt himself blushing. He wasn't sure he wanted to know about this.

"You should have seen him, Johnny. You woulda liked my Dutch. He was a lot like you. Lost his streak big time once, though. Just like you. Real down on his luck. Had to hock away everything we had just to stay afloat. And, well, with me bein' with child and all..." She started looking around the coffee table for her cigarettes. Johnny gave her one of his, and she took

134

it, not caring about the difference in brands. "I miss him," she said, trying to get the lighter to work.

Johnny frowned. "With child? I didn't know you had a..."

She put down the lighter and set the unlit cigarette in the ashtray. "And I never saw him...ever again."

He looked over at her. She wasn't crying, but sniffling, pooling tears trapped in the thick lining of her eyes. She didn't blink them out, and Johnny knew she wouldn't let them spill. She'd probably gone through this one too many times before — if she couldn't control her feelings, she sure as hell had mastered her body. She stiffened.

He didn't know what to do except try to hold her. He leaned forward and pulled her sideways against his chest, the leather uncomfortably squeaking beneath them as they just sat there. Johnny felt like he was hugging a statue. She was cold, but she somehow made him feel warm inside. The scent of lilacs and dried feminine sweat was strong in his nose, like freshly-cut fruit. Her skin was softer than he imagined.

"I'm itchy all over," she finally said, breaking the silence. She moved her head the slightest bit toward his, the skin beneath her right ear folding as her eyes peered over in his direction. "I feel like I should still be pulling levers. It's funny, ya know. Every slot has the potential to hit the jackpot at least once. I bet whoever's sitting there now just won the progressive. 'Cause I can still hear jackpot bells."

Johnny knew the feeling. The Action always lingered when you left the table — almost like a hangover, but more like the buzz of guilt after a one-night stand. And the notion clinging to the back of the brain like a tumor whispering that you should still be there, still in the game, because if you weren't, someone else would take your place. And the *luck* that was just waiting to be had.

"It's okay," he said softly and kissed her cheek.

Violet blinked — and kept her eyes closed.

Johnny held her for a long time while she fell gently to sleep. Soon her breath was frighteningly shallow, and he let her go — he thought that this was probably what death was like, a slow release of one's grip on consciousness. But she kept breathing, her chest stilling and then chugging in sudden bursts, as if her sleeping body was trying to catch up with her dreams. Satisfied that he hadn't disturbed her, he leaned forward and took the cigarette she'd left in the ashtray, lighting it and watching her sleep.

Violet must have had a tougher life than his own, Johnny thought, watching the barely-perceptible stir of her nostrils. He didn't feel sorry for Dutch at all. And he was thankful that he himself hadn't ever married, because he couldn't imagine how much worse off he'd be if he was responsible for fucking up more lives than just his own.

But he *would* be fucking up lives by playing Butcher Boy. He'd have to kill people. People who might have wives like Violet. Whole families and friends that depended on them.

He doubted he could go through with it.

And then he thought about his own fucked up life—with absolutely no one in it. Except Violet. And Gin. Maybe if he played to win, he could make his own life better with all that money. And then he could help out Violet and Gin somehow. Maybe nothing else mattered except for the people that meant something to you. Everyone else was irrelevant. Maybe he really could kill anonymous strangers for the sake of helping out himself and the people he knew. When it came down to it, the whole world was playing to win—and that meant beating you no matter what the cost—in order to survive. Life and death was the name of the game. It had always been that way: a cutthroat game of survival. That's why Johnny started gambling in the first place. Because it was all the same.

Violet's chin dropped open with a ripping snore. He looked at her gaping mouth, and saw that her dentures were lolling sideways on her tongue, strangely clamped shut between her two lumpy pink gums in a skeleton-white smile.

He plucked the false teeth out, wincing at how awfully dry they felt before setting them in the icy tumbler on the coffee table. She seemed to breathe easier. Her lungs were heaving now. Dreams had brought her away from that dead-shallow breathing that had bothered him so much.

Johnny rubbed his eyes and ran his hands through his hair. The morning sunlight was making the living room yellow and pink. He felt out of time.

None of this seemed real to him anymore. He never had thoughts like this—questioning himself. The game of his life had some pretty solid rules, and now they all had spun away, like some kid's game that he'd outgrown. Everything was gone, and anything went now. And just who did he think he was fooling, thinking that he could actually kill someone? Was he really that desperate? Or did he actually *want* to play it that way—just to play by Nebo's rules because they were the only things concrete and certain in his life anymore?

He poured whiskey into his glass, clouding the melted ice there, and took another drink. He had to get his head straight and just play it by ear. He honestly didn't know what he would do until the time came, like always. Sometimes you just had to wait until the cards were dealt before you knew how much you'd be willing to risk.

He ran his tongue through the gap in his mouth, leaning back, smoking and staring at Violet's corny painting of gambling dogs. *Spades*, he thought, considering the possibilities. *Spades*.

Inspiration hit him like the face of a cold metal shovel in the forehead.

# play Dead

"Welcome to the club," Ferret said to fresh dirt, climbing back into the black Chevy Nova and quietly shutting the door. He had to keep the windows rolled down to air out the dead guy's stench, but the blood wasn't too bad—the padding of the floormats caught most of it, and he'd buried them with the body, covering up his face and wounds with them. That way the gravel wouldn't ruin his creation.

He was exhausted, and thought about just sleeping in the car right there, effectively out of sight, obscured by the tall hills of sand and gravel behind Nebo's Shanty. But it was safer to put as much distance as he could between Nebo and himself, if he was unlucky enough to be spotted. Because he knew that Nebo could do far worse to him than the cops or prison ever could if he got caught on his property and Nebo was linked to his crimes. Winston had said that if it came down to it, the cops would be taken care of: or Ferret would have to take care of himself with a certain pill he'd been given. Ferret doubted Nebo would really pull the cops' strings just to save his neck—and he doubted he himself would have what it took to swallow Winston's pill. So he watched his back. Getting caught was one chance he wasn't willing to take.

He drove aimlessly around Vegas, trying to think things through. He still had a little less than half a suit to go, and he was running out of ideas. He knew he'd been taking more lifeforce than he should have for the lower cards, but some lives were worth a heckuva lot more than others on the social scale, too, and not just the food chain. Everything was game for the game. The order of the cards was really just a question of value. And Ferret had his own values, like 'em or not.

And the guy he'd just taken, as luck would have it (and he had faith it would), was worth quite a bit. Not only to society and Nebo, but to Ferret, too. Maybe worth too much.

The cook's red purse had some very interesting contents. Photographs— packets of them. Crude maps like blueprints of various buildings. Copies of long contracts and letters. A yellow pocket-sized notepad filled with all sorts of interesting scribbling. And every scrap of it was somehow related to Nebo Tarrochi.

He turned a corner and drove past a McDonald's. His stomach growled but it was too late to turn around. He figured he'd pull into the next one. It had been awhile since he'd driven a car, and he enjoyed the power of it. The longer he drove, the more he felt like he was in control of the world around him. He made a mental note to make sure he used the drive thru on the next fast food joint he passed. The dead guy's wallet was burning a hole in his pocket, and he wanted to spend some of his cash soon, before he gambled it all away.

Ferret figured he should probably hand everything he'd found in the purse over to Winston. But that would be like passing a Royal Flush over to the guy sitting next to you, just so you could go take a leak. Ferret knew that he held some important cards now. He just wasn't quite sure how to play them yet. But he'd find out. From the cook. She had more things on the griddle than hotcakes. She was brewing something big, and he'd figure out what she *really* had cooking if it killed him. Or her.

The dead guy's name was Silas—which didn't make much sense to Ferret, because he sighed an awful damned lot when Trickster poked into his heart. One big blood-gurgling *siiiigh-iiiigh-iiigh-gh* when all the air seeped out of his lungs from the new hole he'd opened up. Sigh-more would have been a better name.

And old Sigh-more had a press card. A news reporter for *The Sun*. Ferret remembered the cash he'd flashed at the cook in the Lucky Seven Club. He was paying for the inside scoop on Nebo—probably working up some story about him, though Ferret didn't know why he'd be so stupid as to expose a guy as rich as Nebo. He would have ended up dead either way. Ferret was just doing him a favor, making it quick. The guy should have thanked him.

*Jackpot*, Ferret thought, sighting a Burger Queen. He pulled into the drive-thru and ordered a club sandwich. The adolescent clerk didn't even notice the dirt-caked blood on his hands, or the spilled purse by his side when he passed him his food and took his money.

# Play Dead

He ate while he drove, searching for a place to park and get some shut-eye. He didn't want to go back to the shelter now that he had his own place to crash on a set of wheels, but he had to give Winston his next card. And find out more about Gin, the cook.

But first he wanted to sleep and enjoy his newfound home. And think about how he was going to deal with the new deck he'd just been handed by Lady Luck.

"The game," Winston said, frisbeeing his hat onto a nearby sofa cushion, "is getting out of control." With pack in hand, he flicked his wrist and caught a cigarette between his teeth. Flicking his Zippo as if the flame sparked from a fingertip, he lit up. All these magician-like motions were meant to show Nebo that he was still in charge, even if the players weren't.

Nebo sat cross-legged on the sofa in the foyer of his penthouse apartment, ignoring the hat that had been tossed beside him. He steepled his fingers before his face and pressed his palms together, popping all ten of his knuckles in one sharp *CLACK*. "No need to worry, my friend. It's all in the cards. Fate. It's natural for us to desire control, but we cannot let our momentary desires interfere with our ultimate goal. For Fate is more in control than we usually suspect. What seems random to us, is merely part of Fate's master plan. Let our players continue. Do not stop them."

He looked over Winston's shoulder, studying the framed set of rare "transformation" playing cards he'd bought at an auction in Paris—a set rumored to be published on the side by a printer who worked for Cotta in 1804 and was subsequently killed, his art censored for its crude means of transforming the pips into depictions of grotesque sexual positions through tricks of pen-and-ink: the spades were upturned and spread asses, diamonds were penetrated pink vulva, the clubs breasts or balls, and so on, each card its own pornographic scene. The deck was tame by modern standards, but more shocking than the current "nudies" in that it proved beyond a doubt that the same rules for romance existed centuries ago as they did today— where anything goes in pursuit of pleasure. Nebo wondered if his players would be able to work so creatively.

"I don't understand," Winston continued, looking for an ashtray that wasn't polished spotless. "Weren't they supposed to wait until they got to the face cards before they started killing people? Wasn't that the plan?"

Nebo sighed, upset by the disturbance of his thoughts. "There is no *plan* anymore, Winston. It's all up to the players. If we stop them now or censor them in any way, we'll stifle their creativity. And as you know, honest, raw creativity is essential."

Winston nodded. "Understood." He dragged on his cigarette and held the smoke. Then he blew. "I guess what bothers me is that we led The Preacher into offing Axe for doing the same thing: getting outta control, killin' folks too early in the game and so forth. And Frieze is gonna take awhile to get up the guts to…"

Nebo brought a single finger to his lips to shush him. "Fate, Winston. You have to have faith in Fate." Nebo stood up and played with the creases in his pants. "Axe was a different story. Bad karma. Bad vibes. The deck was unbalanced. We needed Frieze to make it work. And I'm confident he will restore the balance."

He walked over to another framed deck—Renaissance Court Tarot—and examined the artistry. The depictions were artful, exquisite, and wholly inno-cent. As close to *natural* as any of the decks he collected. Each figure had its own identity, in a time when everyone knew their place and the rules were clear-cut. But not any more…

"I suppose you're right, Nebo." Winston took his place on the sofa, smoking and watching him closely. "Frieze is a good player. I just hope he catches up soon. I'm eager to see if this deck is gonna work."

Nebo twisted his neck to confront Winston. "Don't start doubting it now, Winston. We both need to believe in the laws of chance, in order to wield the deck."

Winston crossed his legs and met his stare. "Oh, I believe all right. I just think that if the players don't control themselves a little bit, they're bound to screw up. And if that happens then our fate will end up being a life-long prison sentence."

Nebo smiled, determined to cool Winston down. "The police will not be a problem. And besides, as long as we have our deck by then, it won't really matter where we are. Will it?"

"No," Winston replied, picking up his hat and examining the sweat-stained rim. "I suppose not."

"Remember what I told you about Fortune. Fortune feeds on life, and likewise, life feeds on Fortune. They depend upon each other in order to exist. Like love and hate, or life and death, both are inextricably tied together. And our cards—so purely made from an ignorant and innate desire to survive—will capture the very essence of that potent energy that binds the two. We'll have the very *hunger* that Fortune has for life and vice-versa. And once we have that deck," Nebo said, surveying the cards on the walls that surrounded them as if they were mere children's drawings, "we will have the most powerful deck of prophecy cards ever created. Indeed, perhaps the very power of Fate itself."

Winston swallowed any argument. He didn't quite buy into Nebo's crazy logic, but he trusted him more than any man in the universe—enough to put up with the occasional insane rant. He knew what Nebo was capable of—how Nebo had beat Fate at its own game so often that he'd easily earned more wealth and power than he'd ever imagined possible. He sounded terribly corny when he got into these moods of his—whenever he visited his own private museum of cards—but Nebo had always been right before, and Winston had no reason to doubt that he wasn't right about the Butcher Boy cards now.

He actually didn't *believe* in all of his malarkey about controlling Fate with the cards and so on. But it was well worth it to humor Nebo. They'd been on similar expeditions together before, for much the same reasons—visits with hidden priests in Egypt to throw knucklebones; trips to deep Persia to have Tarot readings on a whim; journeys into the Brazilian rain forest for spear-dropping…all games of prophecy. And while none of them had actually *worked*, Nebo had managed to win subsequent business coups and real estate bargains with a consistency so predictable that Winston wasn't quite sure *what* had happened in those silly fortune-telling ventures. The scheme behind Butcher Boy was probably the wildest he'd ever heard of, but Winston trusted the method behind the madness—Nebo was charmed, and did his research on top of it. And Winston was rewarded for his assistance and feigned belief in more ways than one.

Nebo sat by his side, his voice stunningly warm and hopeful. "Oh, don't get me wrong, Winston. I have my questions about the deck, too. It's only natural to wonder how we can control such power." Nebo cracked his knuckles again. "But I'm sure that once they sit down with it in their hands and play the game, we'll understand its power much better."

Winston nodded. *If we ever get that far*.

Nebo lowered his head, seeking eye contact. "You don't look so certain."

"Oh, I believe," Winston replied. "I believe in you one-hundred percent. It's just the players that I'm worried about."

Nebo placed a hand on Winston's knee. "Relax. Let the cards fall where they may." He squeezed his knee. "Besides," Nebo said, removing his hand because he knew how uncomfortable it made Winston to be touched, "if there wasn't any risk involved it wouldn't be any *fun* now, would it?"

*Fun for who?* Winston asked himself, staring at his cigarette as if the flame at its tip might have the answer.

Shorty sat in the stands, watching the Little League baseball game as if he were the parent of the scrawniest kid out on the field, rooting and hooting and hollering along with the crowd. One of the parents had been barbecuing beside the bleachers, and free hot dogs were passed around. Shorty grabbed two, and swallowed each one with two bites a piece. He'd been sitting there all day—forgetting how long a baseball game could last—especially with children on the field who constantly dropped the ball. It was nearly dusk by the time the game ended, and Shorty kept his seat, watching the parents hug their children regardless of whether they won or lost, and must have heard at least three separate people say it wasn't whether you won or lost but how you played the game that really mattered.

Shorty thought both were *equally* important.

Cars were started and the field was almost entirely clouded by the dust they left in their wake as they left the gravel lot behind the bleachers. Shorty moved up to the top bleacher, to better see the field: a big white diamond of chalk which had been trampled on by filthy cleats and sliding jerseys. But it was clearly a perfect diamond, even beneath the cloud of settling dust.

Then, in the far corner of the field, he spotted what he knew he'd find. One of the players was hopping the shoulder-high fence in the backfield— tossing his aluminum baseball bat over the fence and jumping down into the parking lot of the high school that loomed behind the unused scoreboard. Shorty wasn't sure which kid it was—he had a black jersey with the number 8 on it—which was *perfect*—but he couldn't remember the kid making any significant plays in the game. Just a little nobody. A bench-sitter from the losing team, walking home from a game that his parents hadn't even bothered to come watch.

Shorty rose, picking up his paper bag. He jogged obnoxiously down the bleachers, rattling them with each step. He'd gotten a lot heavier than when he was a kid, watching his big brother play ball. It felt good to make the wood bleachers sag and shudder beneath his large steps. He was a big boy now, and he liked how it felt to be bigger than a bleacher.

The kid was almost out of sight, and Shorty had to jog to keep up with him, making sure he tagged second base on his way across the field, leaving the giant chalk diamond in the dust behind him as he made his way toward his next card, the Eight of Diamonds, near the top of the pips.

It took him a moment to hop the fence. Being older and bigger meant being clumsier and heavier, too. But he made it, nearly spilling his bag on the sharp twisting metal that ran the ridge of the fence. He thought about all those cards he'd made with things that sharp—especially that hooker, Candy, with the diamond necklace—but he knew he had to be creative if he wanted to play the game. So now he was ready for something that he *knew* would earn him a lot of chips for Butcher Boy. Eight heavy lumps of coal. The stuff diamonds were made out of, according to the man at the pawn shop. Crushed coal.

The high school was a tall brick building, not very different in appearance than the homeless shelter. Shorty remembered going to school in a similar building—they all seemed the same—and having to take Special Education classes because the teachers said he was slow. But he wasn't slow at all. He was *fast* when he needed to be—when it counted—in games like "Smear the Queer" and "Dog Pile" and "Tag the Fag," where everyone would gang up and chase him around the hallways and the playgrounds. And they never caught him. He was *fast*. Fast as *The Flash* from the comic books. And as far as dumb school stuff went, he knew he wasn't slow—he was just stupid. Or so his father had said.

He turned around a corner of the square school building, and saw the kid doing a crazy thing: tossing his baseball glove into a basketball hoop. The court was hidden in a U-shaped cul-de-sac of the building. Shorty stood there and watched him for awhile: he'd do jump shots on his cleats which made loud scraping sounds against the tarmac which echoed against the walls of the school like a dozen fingernails on a dozen blackboards. The kid made quite a few of his attempts at scoring points and whenever he did he'd cheer himself and raise his fists in victory.

Shorty walked closer toward him.

The kid heard him and turned, blushing. His hair stood out in blond spikes from beneath his oddly-cocked baseball cap. His face looked scared.

"Maybe you'd be better at basketball than Little League," Shorty said, smiling. He liked the kid. He reminded Shorty of himself—private and not quite sure what he liked to do.

The kid looked even more frightened as Shorty came up in front of him. Afraid, or just shy, Shorty couldn't tell which. Either way, the kid definitely didn't feel very comfortable. "Did you see me play?" the kid asked.

"I think so."

Number Eight smiled, easing up. "Then you know I struck out in the first inning and sat the bench the whole day. What a waste. Do you play basketball?"

Shorty lied: "Sure I do, kid."

The kid frowned. "You're not very tall." Then he smiled. "I bet I could beat you at a game of one-on-one."

"Oh yeah?" Shorty just heard the word *bet*. Loud and clear.

"Yeah. How about a game of horse?"

"Horse? I don't play the horses. Just cards. But why don't we bet on throwing stuff into the hoop?"

The kid lit up. "Free throws?"

"Sure! Free throws! Why not?"

Eager, the kid stood at the top of the key and poised himself with his mitt, judging the shot. Then he tossed the glove sky-high and it bounced flatly against the backboard and fell onto the court with a *THWAP*. A complete miss. He blushed again. "Your turn."

Shorty was opening his grocery bag. "I got a better idea." He crouched down beside him at the top of the free throw area and unloaded eight lumps of coal, each the size of a softball. "See...let's use these—they're round."

The kid looked down at Shorty. He made a face. "Rocks?"

"Why not?"

A little disappointed, the kid shrugged. "Okay, go for it, dude. I bet you can't play basketball at all."

Shorty heard the word *bet* again. He felt the energy thumping in his chest.

147

He picked up one of the larger blocks of coal and mimicked the kid, getting ready to shoot. The kid stood on one side of the post, like a player getting ready to catch a missed foul shot. Shorty made a few practice moves, warming up his arm. Then he looked at the kid. "Sure you wanna bet me on this one? It'll be a free throw, but it might cost you a lot anyway."

"I'm sure," the kid said, missing the joke, keeping his eyes on the rim. "Go for it."

Shorty snapped his arm back and threw the coal squarely into the kid's face. It struck his forehead and bounced off, leaving a solid black smear in its wake as the kid fell backwards, smacking his head on the concrete. Shorty picked up another piece of coal and moved over to where the kid fell, holding his head and crying.

He casually dropped the coal onto the kid's stomach. "Eat it."

The kid just stared at him, stunned. His eyes were thrashing in wide pools of pain.

"Eat that fucking coal, kid, and swallow it whole or I'll bash your friggin' brains in."

The kid bawled, grabbing the coal and pressing it lightly against his lips. He made swallowing motions, which looked more like kisses than anything else — going through the impossible movements out of fear. "*I...I can't...it's too...too big!*"

Shorty turned and quickly loaded the remaining seven pieces into the crook of his arm like ammunition for a snowball fight. When he turned back, the kid had the coal over his head, his arm wavering and ready to throw while his eyes dizzily tried to target Shorty.

Shorty dove, falling right on top of the kid, spilling his coal onto the basketball court. The kid tried to wrestle with him, but Shorty was *fast*, fast as he'd always been on the playground, fast as he was in draw poker, and he had Number Eight's arms pinned behind his back in no time at all. He picked up a clump of coal with a free hand and pressed it firmly into the tiny orifice of the kid's mouth mashing the teeth and gums inside. The black rock made a gritty splintering noise as he ground it into his face. He kept pressing while the kid choked on the rock, vomiting black and green crud up through the webwork of Shorty's fingers and out his nose. Soon it fit neatly into his windpipe.

"*See?*" Shorty grunted, reaching for the next piece while the kid's eyes fluttered and his legs shook. "*See?* You can do it! You ate it! You *ate* it! It wasn't too big at all!"

The kid was long gone. Shorty continued working each lump of coal inside—the job getting easier as the kid's soft muscles loosened—until all eight pieces were crammed down Number Eight's face and his throat and cheeks were unnaturally lumpy and puffed like a Christmas stocking of thin flesh.

Then Shorty picked up the kid's aluminum baseball bat and swung hard—eight times—making extraordinary diamonds.

# Play Dead

Johnny walked into the shelter and felt almost embarrassed by his cleanliness. The skins of the ones who showed up for dinner were all covered with a gray sheen the color of car exhaust from bagging the streets all day. Many stank of alcohol—Johnny knew that most of them panhandled outside casinos for booze money, having long given up the game that got them there in the first place. But Johnny was a player again, and from the hungry looks they shot him when he stepped ahead of the line in the kitchen, he knew they could tell that he was back in the Action. Their faces didn't express jealousy, but something like the pulse of hatred, throbbing red behind their eyes.

Gin motioned at him from behind a man with a long grey beard and a stained and faded turquoise football shirt that read MI MI DO INS down the sleeve. She winked at Johnny, nodded toward the back door, and kept working, eager to get through the line. Johnny knew her nod said to meet her outside afterwards, on her usual smoke break. And she looked like she could use one—dark rings encircled her eyes.

He searched the line, and then returned to the cots. Winston wasn't around, which Johnny figured. But he was looking for Shorty, anyway. He wasn't anywhere near his cot, and Johnny couldn't guess where he might be—Shorty never missed dinner; he enjoyed eating too much to skip a free meal. And Johnny didn't think he'd found a job. Shorty wasn't the type to give a damn about such things.

Habitually, Johnny tongued the gap in his teeth and walked over to his own cot. He noticed that someone else had been sleeping in it—the green Army blanket covers were matted with hard white stains. Maybe food, but probably puke or pus or jism. Sickened, he didn't bother reclaiming his space. For he suddenly realized with total certainty that his days here were finally over. Sure, he'd have to return to give Winston his cards whenever he actually got around to making them—but for now it was time to settle somewhere else. With Violet. Or, if his lucky streak continued, with Gin. Either way, being back at the shelter after so long made him never want to be there again. Which gave him yet another desperate reason to win at Butcher Boy.

A few cots away, Johnny recognized The Preacher, who was chewing on his Spam, holding it in front of his lips with cautious dirty fingers like the Eucharist. He stared Johnny back as if looking right through him, chewing on his plastic meat with the side-jaw ruminations of a cow. The ever-moving jaw reminded Johnny of the Preacher's nightly sermons, something Johnny did *not* miss at all. He avoided his eyes, wondering if he'd suckered any of the other bums into following him.

Shorty stormed into the shelter with an aluminum bang of the door. His eyes squinted when they locked on Johnny's, then turned vapid and cloudy as doll's eyes. He kept walking toward the soup line, clutching his grocery sack against his chest like a teddy bear, pretending not to have seen Johnny.

Curious, Johnny followed, taking his place in line behind Shorty. He whispered over his shoulder: "What's happening, man?"

Shorty's back muscles tightened, refusing to twist himself around. He gripped awkwardly on the paper bag. Looking over his shoulder, Johnny noticed that his arms and hands were smeared with black grime. He looked like a coal miner on a lunch break, and Johnny felt a twinge of guilt—Shorty used to take better care of himself, and Frieze wondered if his recent absence from the shelter had something to do with the change. Johnny patted his shoulder. "Where you been, Shorty?"

No answer. Johnny patiently waited. Something sizzled on the grill down the line, and Johnny's mouth watered. He'd eaten at Violet's, but just standing in line for Gin's cooking made his stomach groan. It wasn't quite hunger. Staring at Shorty's back, he wondered if his missing tooth was to blame— with an extra hole in his mouth, he had twice as many reasons to fill it.

"Hell-*lllooo*-o. Anybody home?"

No reply.

Johnny didn't have the patience for this waiting game. He cut in front of Shorty in line and forced eye contact. "Listen, if you're mad at me for not hangin' around this dump lately, or somethin', you're crazy. You'd get out of here, too, if you could, wouldn't ya?"

# Play Dead

Shorty stared right through his eyes as if watching some movie projected onto the inside wall of Johnny's skull. But his eyes reflected zombie emptiness and static—the same doll-eyed look from before.

Johnny grabbed his arm, head-cocked and smiling. "C'mon..."

Shorty slapped his palm away, lightning-quick as karate. He squinted his eyes again. Then he finally spoke with a voice that sounded wholly unfamiliar to Johnny: "You're a player now, Johnny. In the game. That means we can't be friends. It's every man for himself and I don't want nothin' to do with you anymore."

Johnny dropped his smile. He smirked. "Fine, Shorty. If you wanna play it that way, fine." He looked him up and down, trying to shame him. "But tell me one thing: who are the other players? I need to know who else I can't be friends with anymore."

Shorty whispered, conscious of the others in line. "Listen. The only other players are you and Axe and I don't know who else. Go ask Win..."

"Axe folded a long time ago, Shorty."

Shorty squinted like Clint Eastwood.

"And I think you knew that. In fact, I think you've always known more than you're lettin' on." Johnny took a step away and then turned back. "You might be able to fool everyone else around here with that Dumbo routine you pull, but not me anymore. I *know* you. Like a friend. And if you're playin' Butcher Boy, then you can't afford to be so slow." Johnny backed away. "You're a good con, though, so keep it up. I'll see ya at the game when the time comes, Killer." He turned and heard Shorty crinkle up his bag with a hug.

He felt The Preacher glaring guilt at him as he went out the door to meet Gin. She hadn't finished working the line yet, but Johnny needed a cigarette. And some fresh air. He lit up a Winston, and leaned back against the shelter's warm brick walls, heaving his lungs.

Johnny couldn't believe how Shorty had turned on him. He was a different person altogether. Maybe for the better, but considering the rules of the game they were playing, Johnny didn't think so. He wondered just what the man was capable of, not only in everyday life, but in Butcher Boy, as well. How creative were his cards? How far had he gotten in the deck? He thought about the look in his eyes when Shorty had shown him the rules for the card game: eager, feral...excited and alive. He'd probably be just as hungry in the real game.

Gin finally came outside. With a sigh she popped a cigarette between her lips. Johnny was quick with a match for her. She dragged and held it, eyes closed.

"Tough crowd, eh?"

She blew. "You should know." She leaned against the wall beside him.

It was getting dark out, but Johnny could see her just fine. Her face gleamed, but her exhaustion was etched on her face in shadows. She looked almost like a sketch in graffiti, her features chiseled into the brick wall that supported her.

And she seemed very distant to Johnny, considering how close they'd been the night before. He wanted to kiss her when she came outside. He didn't know why, but it felt wrong doing it here at the shelter, especially while she was working. So he just watched her, wondering if she felt the same way...or if he'd done something wrong that night they were together, something so stupid that it forced her to leave in the middle of the night.

"You workin' The Bucket tonight?"

"Nope," she said, her pursed lips streaming smoke. "Got two days off." She turned her head, her hair sticking to the fabric of the bricks. "Why? You wanna do somethin' later, Johnny?"

He smiled. Maybe things weren't as bad as he thought. And maybe she'd actually consider his proposition. "Oh yeah," he said, moving close to her. "I really need your help."

She blew smoke and Johnny couldn't tell if it was meant to go into his eyes. "So what else is new?" Then she pecked him on the cheek with a tight ring of lip. "What you got in mind?"

"I'll can't tell you here."

She shook her head. "You're always playing some game, aren't you, Johnny Frieze? Always a mystery." She leaned into him gently and tongued his ear. Whispered: "I think that's what I like about you."

Johnny moved to hold her.

She pulled away, digging under her apron and then handing him a set of keys. "Wait in my car out back. It's a red Ford Fiesta, you can't miss it. I'll be done cleaning things up in about an hour. Then we can talk."

*Keys*, Johnny thought, nodding seriously and pocketing them. *Trust*.

She stamped out her cigarette and went back inside to join the sounds of hissing steam and clanging pots.

Johnny lit another cigarette and made his way to the back of the shelter, feet crunching gravel with each step. Their grind sounded louder than usual to him. He wondered if that meant he was gaining weight. Far behind the dumpsters where he'd once played Butcher Boy with Shorty were a few cars, parked in careless angles against one another. He sighted the red Ford Fiesta behind a yellow El Camino and three cars over from a black Chevy Nova which he barely noticed, parked awkwardly over the curb as if eager for a quick getaway.

The Preacher thought he could taste the frozen steam of his meaty hearts on the skin of his dinner as he watched Johnny Frieze enter and leave the shelter like a bandit. It had been awhile since he'd seen the man — and he wondered what sins he had been committing in the mean time. He surely needed to be saved. Surely.

But now was not the time to think of salvation.

He stood and returned his paper plate to the overflowing green trash can in the kitchen. He saw Gin by the sink, scrubbing large pots with her back to him. The harlot was shaking the upside-down, heart-shaped flesh that stuck out from beneath the knot of her apron strings, he knew, to spite him. And to tempt the others. The Preacher knew what spells she weaved over the other desperate unsaved men at the shelter — feeding both their stomachs and their lust for flesh in the lunch lines — instilling sinful thoughts and dreams in their souls with the succubus-like body they could not have. Like the great Whore who sitteth upon many waters…Babylon, Mother of Whores…The queen of sin in the soup kitchen…

*The Queen of Hearts* in The Preacher's deck.

Soon. He was very close now, anxious to get to the face cards. As the Lord's chosen warrior in these iniquitous times, he was eager to redeem the abominable sin that surrounded him. Especially his own. The blood he had spilled in this mission had not yet been cleansed. He was still soiled, unclean. He could not wash his hands like Pilate. Sinning to battle sinners was a damnable act, but a necessary one in the age of Armageddon, in the time of the Tribulation, at the end of the world where nothing but sin and sinners remained. Including himself.

But if he won at the devil's game — and returned the money he'd win to the house of the Lord — he knew he would be redeemed. If he was unsuccessful, he would commit the ultimate sacrifice — the purification of himself by sacrifice — in the name of the Lord. *Blessed are the pure in heart: for they shall see God…*

# Play Dead

He returned to his cot and retrieved his duffel bag. It was time to move on to his next card for the Lord. The Nine of Hearts.

He had prepared himself in the usual way—reading every verse in the Bible which corresponded with the number of his card, seeking God's hidden and private messages. As he walked from his cot he counted his steps in nines, mentally reciting each memorized verse with every step before moving on to the next one: *...the tree of life also in the midst of the garden, and the tree of knowledge of good and evil...Am I my brother's keeper?...Few and evil have the days of the years of my life been...Behold also, the gallows fifty cubits high...Doth Job fear God for naught?...They are drunken, but not with wine...If thine eye offend thee, pluck it out...Make to yourselves friends of the mammon of unrighteousness; that when ye fail, they may receive you into everlasting habitations...The heart is deceitful above all things, and desperately wicked...*

And soon he was downtown. He saw nines in the sideways glances he received on the technicolored city streets, smiling nines, rounded noses, eyes with mustaches and beards beneath which formed nines in neon shadows. A hooker dressed like a cat with nine lives. A German junkie on Ninth Street uttered "nein" with upraised arms and angst when he saw The Preacher approaching. Nines were everywhere on building doorways and billboards for phone sex. Nines were in the craters on the moon. Nines in belt buckles and necklaces with silver heart pendants. In the curving of breasts and the bulging crotches of pants. On license plates and back alley graffiti. Nines of sin surrounding him, spinning, flashing nines, hooking into him with their gnarled barbs; temptations, veiled attempts to tear him away from his pursuit of the true and perfect and *predestined* Nine of Hearts.

The Preacher stepped into modest front doors of the Lariat Hotel and Casino on Ninth Street. His Nine of Hearts was inside, though he wasn't sure where. After dutifully killing Axe days ago, he had come upon his Nine of Hearts almost accidentally. But he knew that nothing the Lord sent him was accidental: he received his message during his mission to save the sinning youths who rushed into sacred matrimony for the sake of requiting their lust at the PAIR-O-DICE MARRIAGE CHAPEL. The wedding party of nine for

Mr. and Mrs. Regis Hart (according to the registry, which also listed this address), who had kicked him out of the false church for preaching the wages of sin before their wedding. They had refused to listen to him then, passing a bottle of Vodka between one another outside the heart-shaped entrance to the chapel and calling him names. But now he would show them. If they would not *hear* then, they would *see* now.

It was simply a matter of knocking on the doors of the honeymoon suites on the sixth floor.

Room 609 opened the door and the flash between meeting eyes registered familiarity: Regis Hart himself, hair wet and stinking of booze. He was in a bathrobe instead of a tux this time. He opened his mouth but The Preacher was already inside, ramming into his chest with his duffel bag to knock the wind out of the throat he was already slashing with the butcher knife he'd stolen from Gin's kitchen the day he helped wash dishes. Blood foamed and bubbled in the slit he'd made. He shut the door behind him. Peeking around the corner of the hallway inside, he wasn't certain if what he saw was real or not: he discovered not only Mrs. Hart, but the entire wedding party, gathered across and around a shiny red heart-shaped bed. Their bodies seemed pink and translucent: naked and writhing in orgy. The whole scene looked like a muscular beating heart. Green bottles of champagne were all over the floor—one arm stood straight up from the undulating pile of flesh to pour more onto them, a living fountain of sin. If this was real, then God had sent him to the right place.

"Sacrilege," he whispered and crept toward them. Everyone's eyes were closed. Slowly he made his way through the pile with his knife, not knowing who was who or where he was cutting, but he swung the blade until all of the lusty motion stilled and the only sound that remained was the steady drip of the giant leaking heart from the silk mattress onto the pink shag floor.

He looked at what he had done. Some of the bodies were clothed. They may have been sleeping. Perhaps he had envisioned their debaucherous dreams. It didn't matter. They had certainly sinned. The Lord wanted him to rid the world of their souls.

Still, it was all too messy for its own card.

# Play Dead

He removed and arranged all nine of their hearts—two parallel rows of four and one in the center—inside the deep red heart-shaped sunken tub in the bathroom. He retrieved the Polaroid from his duffel bag, and quickly took two snapshots, as he'd always done: one for Winston, one for himself.

The first photograph fell onto the white tile of the bathroom floor. The Preacher leaned over to pick it up, and the rest of his growing deck—the duplicate photographs he always kept in his left breast pocket, right over his own ever-beating heart—spilled out and sprawled across the bloodied floor.

He cursed and began to pick them up, one by one, swiping the blood from their shiny surfaces on a nearby towel. He thought of the time his nose bled, when he was hit square in the face with a tennis shoe.

And then he noticed that, taken together, the cards made a pattern all their own—spelling out a message direct from God Himself. Beside his Nine lay a sideways Seven A Six. Nine-Seven-Six—from his distance the pips arranged in the center of each card blurred into lines that seemed to spell God's warning.

*H-E-L-L.*

The Preacher dropped down and prayed for forgiveness.

Gin let him drive the Fiesta back to her apartment—an elongated studio pad above a Laundromat with slanted walls from the rooftop and windows peering out at strangely flat angles like suicidal doors to the roof. The hum and heat of the machines below could be felt through the floor. The egg yolk-colored walls were sparse with movie posters that curled at the edges, revealing bright white rectangles beneath. Nicotine stains. A worn loveseat functioned as a couch, with a theater-sized ashtray stand beside it and a coffee table in front, low enough for resting legs. All this positioned like a throne before the tiniest television set Johnny had ever seen, smack in the middle of a tightly-packed bookshelf full of dog-eared paperbacks. He liked it.

"Have a seat," she said, opening the door to a refrigerator an arm's length from the front door. "Beer?"

Johnny sat down, feeling hard wood press through the fabric beneath his butt. A familiar feeling. "Got anything stronger?"

She was already capping two. "'Fraid not. I don't get a lotta high class guests like yourself to entertain." She slipped the necks of both bottles between her fingers. "Besides, why buy spirits when they're free at the casinos?"

"Beer's fine," Johnny said, taking one from her splayed hand.

Gin dropped beside him, their hips lightly brushing. She wrapped an arm across the loveseat's back behind him and tossed her hair to one side. Curious, she stared at his profile. Johnny self-consciously sipped his beer. He could see her blinking in his peripheral vision. "So why are we here?" she finally said.

He didn't know where to begin, so he kept his mouth wrapped on the bottle's hole. Then he lit a cigarette, while she patiently waited. "Um...you know that 'job' I was tellin' you about?"

"Yeah," she nodded, smugly, "I figured it had somethin' to do with that. What about it? You outta cash already?"

159

# Play Dead

Johnny rubbed his pocket—she was right, his pockets were empty. He'd given Violet back her wad. "Well, yeah, but..."

"And you think I got money to loan ya, right?" She slid her arm out from behind him and crossed it over her chest. "You've got guts, Johnny, I gotta give you that..."

Johnny faced her, shoulders slumped. "No, I'm not here to borrow money." He shook his head, hoping she heard the honesty in his voice. "I've gotta ask you a favor."

"Oh, then it's worse." She smiled.

Johnny turned serious. "Maybe it is." He sipped on his beer and sucked on his Winston, keeping it stuck between his lips while he spoke: "I'm in a game, Gin. A big-time game, and my so-called 'job' is to..." He paused. *To what? Kill people?* "Well, my job right now is just to *get ready* to play the game. To prepare the deck."

"I don't follow." Her face said she was trying.

Johnny stood up from the couch and began to pace, avoiding her eyes when he carelessly spilled ash down his pants and onto her floor. "Listen. You know your boss at the Bucket—Nebo Tarrochi—right?"

"Uh-huh." Gin tucked a leg beneath her, paying attention. "Who doesn't?"

"Well old Nebo is setting up this really wild game with a bunch of losers like myself, people from the shelter. A poker game. A *really* wild poker game, called Butcher Boy." He pivoted. "You're a dealer. Ever heard of it?"

Gin's eyebrows were scrunched into weird angles. "Butcher Boy?" She shook her head. "Nope. Sounds like some kind of male bonding crap to me."

Johnny bent over the ashtray stand and put out his cigarette, smirking.

"What's this got to do with Tarrochi, and how'd you manage to get hooked up with him, anyway? He's one of the richest men in the country, for cryin' out loud. You gotta be carrying a lot of weight to play poker with him."

"Well, like I was saying, I gotta work for him in a way. And he isn't exactly *playing*—more like running the show. See, there are four players, and each one has to make up his own suit of cards. Thirteen a piece, before we even sit down to play. I think he wants to add them to his collection..."

"What do you mean, 'make up cards'? How the hell do you do that?"

160

*This*, Johnny thought, *is the tricky part*. He returned to his seat beside her and placed a hand on her knee. Gin's head was bent down as if straining to hear what he was about to say. Johnny didn't know what to do: how do you tell someone close to you that you've essentially been hired to kill people?

"Creatively," he replied, for lack of a better answer.

Gin's head dropped lower, chin angled at his crotch. Then she thrust it upward and rolled her eyes as if examining the ceiling for cobwebs. "Just tell me, Johnny." She eyed a corner as if spotting a nest of spiders. "The whole story."

So he did, starting with Winston and Axe, and ending on his visit with Nebo after Gin had left him alone in bed that night at The Bucket. He explained the rules of the game and described the sick cards Axe had already made as examples of exactly what "making up cards" really meant. He didn't tell her about Violet—somehow he was more embarrassed to admit he'd been sleeping at another woman's house than to admit he had buried a body with its chest gutted out. Telling her this story made him feel sick to his stomach—he was on dangerous ground here, like confessing to the cops—but it felt so good to tell the truth and be up front with Gin that he couldn't stop his voice box from streaming out his thoughts on its own accord. But the story was coming out smooth and he could tell that she wasn't horrified—wasn't sickened or ashamed of him. He could tell by the look in her eyes. It was as if she had already vaguely known. She seemed to be more concerned with the fact that he was talking honestly with her than with what he was saying.

And in the middle of the story, she held his hand.

Afterwards, she sat silent, staring at the bookcase as though watching the empty TV screen. Johnny noticed that their beers were empty, so he retrieved two more. When his back was turned she finally spoke. "A million dollars, eh?"

"Yup." He passed her a bottle and lit a cigarette. "One million bucks."

"And you haven't made any cards yet? Just buried a body, right?"

She made it sound so trivial. "Yeah, isn't that enough?"

She sighed and blew her bangs. "I don't know, Johnny. I don't know. So what are you going to do? There's no way out of this game, I'm guessing. Not with Tarrochi running the show."

Johnny looked at her, puzzled. How did she know so much about Nebo?

"I mean," she continued, "he must have selected you and the other players on the hunch that you *would* be willing to kill without giving it a second thought. And to die trying to win. He's a smart guy; doesn't take any risks unless he's pretty sure he'll be on the winning side of things. He must have seen something in you—thought you were *really* that desperate."

"I was," Johnny said, remembering. "But then I thought about you." He tugged on his beer. Suddenly, he felt comfortable talking this way. They'd shared worse secrets. It was just like playing poker: sometimes it paid to show what you were holding. "I couldn't look you in the face if I sunk that low. Hell, I was so desperate I might even have killed you." He dove into her eyes, confronting her with the possibilities. "And I'm just not willing to go that far."

Gin slid her fingers into his hair and bristled his scalp. "You're a good guy, Johnny." She kissed him lightly before leaning back and swigging from the cold bottle he'd given her. She sighed. "Geez. You gamblers. The games you play. Crazy stuff. I don't get it." Her eyes found his, questioning, shifting as if looking for the answer somewhere on his face.

"I dunno, Gin." He sipped. "I guess when it comes right down to it, gambling's really just a drive to keep winning and winning until you lose something really important. Shit, I didn't know who I was—money ain't that important to me—I just wanted to *win* and I thought money was the only way of telling a winner from a loser. But I never knew that until I lost it all. And I almost lost what I felt for you. Hell, I didn't even *know* what I felt about anything until all this crap hit me." He smoked, wondering how stupid he sounded. "All I'm sayin' is, you don't realize what you're doin till you *really* lose—till you hit rock bottom. They don't call it that for nothin'—it crushes you. And that ain't all about money, either."

She faced him, silly eyes philosophically posed. "No, Johnny. I don't think so. I've seen a lot of losers. And they all got the same looks on their faces, whether they're in the food line or sitting at the blackjack tables. And let me tell you: it's not losing that's the problem. Everybody loses. It's thinking that *just surviving* is itself a win."

Johnny raised an eyebrow, tonguing the soft tissue of his gums. He put out his cigarette, only half-smoked. "You got a point there."

Gin curled into him, all bones. "So what are you gonna do?"

"Well," Johnny said, looking down at the blond hair that tickled his chin, "that's what I meant by needing your help."

# Play Dead

In the front seat of the black Nova, Ferret scooped cold french fries from the bottom of his bag and watched. He'd allow his eyes to drift over the green neon letters of the Laundromat sign (which in the darkness read LAU RAT), and occasionally he'd glance at the manic college kids and the depressive welfare families which folded their clothes on opposite sides of the spinning washers inside. But he never took his mind off the couple upstairs, who he knew were exchanging their own sort of dirty laundry. As soon as the lighted door-shaped windows above went out, he grabbed his camera and headed toward the small hallway which he'd seen Gin and her new dude enter.

As he climbed the concrete stairwell, Ferret thought about the man she was with. Might be another reporter, another Sigh-more. But probably not. What would a reporter be doing at the shelter? If he was doing some sort of story, Ferret doubted he'd have stayed very long...but Ferret had seen this guy, Johnny something, for at least two weeks. Nobody would put themselves through bad food and worse cots with a bunch of stinking bums on purpose. She was gonna sucker him into working for her somehow. Maybe do some more snooping for her while she played cook.

There was only one door at the top of the stairs—he couldn't be sure if it was a hallway or not, because the apartment seemed to take up the entire top floor. He flattened his head against the wood and listened.

*Sloshing water. Shaking metal. A raspy SNAP-SNAP-SNAP.*

The Laundromat below. Or the sounds of sex. He couldn't tell the difference.

He tried the obese brass knob. Locked.

Instead of breaking in, he sat down on the top step—setting the camera between his legs—and waited. It might be too soon; following her—and now her new accomplice—all day had made him impatient. He had to give them time, time to get so far into one another that the surprise of his entrance would give him precious extra moments to move. Reaching over to his hip, he fingered the jagged backside of Trickster, his knife, counting off the seconds with each barb.

His original plan was to force the woman to talk and then turn her into a card—something like a club sandwich maybe—but then this new guy stepped into the picture. So he knew she was trouble, and he'd have to deal with it now, if he ever wanted to use the goods on Nebo without her making them public first.

Enough waiting. He leaned forward to stand, gripping his camera with a free hand.

And the door swung open, knob slamming into his left eye in a red and black flash and the realization that he could do nothing but fall, tumble, fall.

Ferret came to with his hands and feet strapped with strange-colored belts to the bedposts. His head hurt like hell, so he didn't bother struggling. Wincing, he tried to figure out his situation. The room was dark—shadows cast green by the Laundromat's neon letters surrounded him.

A chair creaked and then Johnny was standing over him, shaking his green grinning face.

Ferret snarled. "You're Johnny, right?"

"Fuck you," Johnny said, lighting a cigarette with a bright match. The flame turned his face deep shiny brown. The tobacco crinkled as it took. "Just...fuck you." Blinking smoke from his eyes, he twisted the match between his fingers, conjuring flame, and then sharply flicked it onto Ferret.

It landed on his cheek, right below his pulsing and puffy left eye. He sucked air and held it, stupidly watching as the orange dance of light fluttered and singed his eyelashes. Realizing what he was doing, he popeyed his lower lip and blew as hard as he could to put it out. Instead, it tumbled back into his quickly shut lid, still burning. But it was out by the time he had the guts to bat it away with a snap of his head and a hardcore blink that stung like hell.

His eyes watered madly. "*You sssssshittt!*"

Johnny's voice was calm, deep. "Shut up or I'll gag you."

"Fu..." Now Ferret struggled. No slack in the belts, which sawed into the soft tissue above his wrists and ankles, and he couldn't get any leverage from the water that sloshed in the bed beneath him. When he tired of thrashing, he realized he was pinned atop a waterbed, which seemed like a really dumb place to tie somebody up. But it was working, unfortunately. Which was even dumber. Ferret craned his neck to see if Trickster was still on his belt. Maybe he could work it to pop the bed. But nothing happened.

He looked for the girl. Nowhere. "Where's that fuckin' cook, asshole?"

Johnny melodramatically sighed and raised a bent finger with several pairs of panties dangling.

Ferret made a face.

And then Johnny dropped them over his mouth. He lunged and grabbed his chin, forcing it open and holding his head still. With an erect finger, he pressed the panties into Ferret's mouth, carefully, so that he couldn't bite. His throat made muffled choking sounds while his chest heaved and the cloth plugged up his windpipe. He continued stuffing.

Ferret's body was shuddering as he screamed and struggled for escape. Johnny peered down at him with a look of disgust and outrage. "I told you to shut up," he said, letting go of Ferret's chin and pinching his nostrils.

"Don't kill him, Johnny."

He turned and saw Gin's shadow standing in the small hallway that separated the bedroom. He shrugged, and he could see her silhouette cock a hip in defiance. Using Ferret's chest for leverage, he stood and walked over to her while Ferret's nostrils thrashed and his lungs hacked the underwear out of his throat.

It took Ferret awhile to recover from the burning agony, but eventually tore his eyes open and spotted the couple standing shoulder-to-shoulder beside the bed, staring at him with their arms crossed.

Johnny lifted his arm and lit another cigarette with the butt of the first one, before setting it down on a tray somewhere above Ferret's head on a night stand. "Why are you after us?"

Ferret just stared. He wasn't about to tell them shit, and his throat hurt too much to even tell them that.

"I mean, I know who you are," Johnny continued. "I've seen you at the shelter. And I saw your car there, too. And out front, here, just as I was putting out the lights. You must be one dumb fucking idiot to think we wouldn't even notice you running across the lot."

Ferret leaned his head away from them and spit the taste of laundry detergent from his lips. It drooled down his cheek, soothingly cool. Pain thrummed all over his face. And he was beginning to smell something in the room, too. Beer and sweat. Just like the shelter. He hated it.

"You talk," Johnny said, plucking the Winston from between his lips and holding it close to Ferret's flesh. "Or you burn."

Whispering Gin: "Johnny…"

Ferret's eyes glazed. "Yug…" his throat snapped. He swallowed. Blood? "*Yuuu currder. Dunkil me.*"

"I won't kill you." Johnny moved the burning tip closer to his face. His sweat gleamed pumpkin-skin orange. "But you sure won't leave here livin' very good."

Ferret squirmed. Broke: "*Ghokay, ogay!*"

Johnny pulled away, plugging the cig between his lips. "So talk."

His throat hurt, but he knew he had to be clear: "I…" He swallowed pain. "I found something of hers," he lied, attempting to motion his head at Gin. "In an alley. It looked important so I thought I should give it back to her."

"What?" Gin asked, stiffening.

Ferret winked. Painful, but eagerly. "Red purse."

Gin looked at Johnny, then slowly brought her head back to meet Ferret's eyes. Her lips were twisting on each other.

Johnny didn't notice. "Uh-huh," he said, walking out of the room.

Gin stared at him, head cocked to one side as if listening for Johnny's return. She leaned forward and whispered. "Where?"

He followed suit, keeping his voice low. "I told you. In an alley."

She grabbed his arm and dug her nails into it. Her voice strained and crackled with tiny high notes. "Bull*shit*. How the *hell* did you know it was mine?"

"Saw you…"

Johnny coughed, standing in the doorway. "Smi-iii-llle."

Gin backed away.

# Play Dead

The room flashed with brightwhite. Blinding. Ferret blinked—eyes very sticky and raw—and realized that Johnny had his camera in between his hands. It spat its photograph out like a black and white tongue. Johnny plucked it violently and tossed it onto Ferret's chest. "I think I know why you came up here, asshole. Not to return some dumb purse, but because you're a *player*, aren't ya?"

Ferret frowned.

"You're into Nebo's game, right? Don't lie. I know what's up." He pondered the Polaroid camera in his hands. "I'm well acquainted with this brand." He took another snapshot. Ferret winced at the blinding light. "Get the picture?"

Ferret cocked his head slowly, blinking, then got it. "You're in the game, too. A player."

"Yup." He tossed the photo next to the other one. "And I think I'm seeing spades."

The developing photographs felt much too heavy on his chest, like bricks.

"*Spades*," Johnny hissed, moving closer and showing Ferret Trickster's edge. "*Spades*."

Ferret thrashed with all his might.

He cut the belt over Ferret's left arm.

Ferret was thrashing so hard, eyes clenched in a grimace of fear and pain, that his own arm swung out and slapped him over the face and crunched his nose. He held his arm up in front of his face, too scared to look, trying to prevent Johnny from stabbing him. But when nothing happened he opened his good eye and froze.

Johnny had an eyebrow raised, picking at a fingernail with the tip of Ferret's knife.

Ferret's muscles dropped and he reached up with his free hand to rub the sore bone in his nose. "What the hell is going on here?"

Johnny shrugged. "I can't be killing no fellow player. What fun would that be?"

Ferret looked at Gin. She looked just as confused as he did. "Say what?"

"I can't kill you. Rules say hands off the other players. You know that, don'tcha?"

"Umm…" Ferret's head angled slyly. "Yeah. That's right."

"And that means you shouldn't be fuckin' with *us*, either. Now, I realize that you probably didn't know I was in the game before you came up here with this here camera and hunting knife, but now that you know, you know better. Don't you?"

Ferret began loosening the belt on his other wrist. "Uh-huh," he said, not paying much attention and still not quite believing how easily he was being set free. His face and hands numbly throbbed while he considered his options. "I guess so."

"Because," Johnny continued, not bothering to help him while he sat up and quickly worked the buckles from his ankles, "all this was just to show you that I *will* kill you next time I find you snooping around me or Gin here. You know how it works: if you break the rules, you fold. Just like Axe did." Johnny tucked the blade end of Ferret's knife into his armpit to light a cigarette. "I should know. I buried him."

"Right," Ferret said, sitting up, and looking dumbfounded. "You're the dude that took his place in the game. I get it now." He turned defiantly, sitting up straight and flexing his muscles. The neon green fell into his new wounds and reflected shiny black. "But that don't mean I ain't gonna beat you in the game itself, Johnny. Maybe you shoulda killed me when you had the chance to save your skin." He smiled and nodded like a vulture over fresh kill.

Johnny streamed smoke through his nostrils. "And maybe you should fucking shut your trap before I do kill ya." He fingered Gin's hand. "Got another beer, honey?"

She made a face at him, and he couldn't tell if it was at calling her honey or in response to what he had just done. She just nodded vaguely, as if answering a spirit, and left the room. Johnny faced Ferret. He looked pathetic—stunned and bloodied. "Beer?"

Ferret turned only his eyes to face him. "I do not drink alcohol." He swallowed and ground his teeth, eyes locked on Johnny's. "Ever."

Johnny pouted his lips. "Fine. Just thought I'd be sociable."

Ferret's eyes narrowed. "Why? You one of those jerks who think all red men are lushes?"

"Nope," Johnny said as Gin returned with a green bottle. "Just thought it'd help you with the pain." He swallowed beer. Then he passed Ferret his camera. "You take that and just get out of here, all right? And don't let me see you again."

Ferret snatched the camera from his fingers as if Johnny would pull it back away. He stood, shaking blood back into his wrists and feet. "What about my Trickster?"

"Excuse me?"

"My knife, what about my knife?" He held out an open palm. "It's mine."

Johnny toyed with it on his lap. "I dunno if I trust you yet. And I want your name first. In case Winston gives me shit."

The skin beneath Ferret's chin was shaking. Johnny thought he could see the bruise of his eye pulsing like a heart in his eyesocket. Signs of anger, need. He'd seen it in plenty of poker games.

"They call me Ferret."

Johnny looked up and down his skinny frame and chuckled. "Figures."

He thrust his palm out—veins purple-black webs on the muscular strands of his forearm. "The knife."

"I want your word, too, that you won't be botherin' me no more."

Ferret's eyes drifted. "You have my word."

"Good." Johnny stood and walked to the window. "You can get your knife on your way out," he said, opening the pane and tossing it into the square of night. Ferret's wounded eyes creased open and winced when the metal dinked the sidewalk below like hollow glass.

His voice was amazingly calm: "You *bastard*." He pivoted like a soldier and stormed out of the bedroom.

Gin opened her mouth as he breezed by the loveseat, ignoring her. "*Purse*," she whispered sharply, but Ferret was already out the door and running down the stairs.

Johnny came out and sat beside her, beer in one hand and photographs in the other. He passed them to Gin. "He forgot these."

She didn't bother looking at them, keeping her eyes on his. "You're just gonna let him go. Just like that."

He chugged from the beer bottle. They could hear the Nova revving loudly outside. "We had no choice, Gin. But we sure as hell shook him up. He won't be coming around here no more, that's for sure. Heck, some *good* has come out of this. I know two of the other players now, Shorty and Ferret. And maybe he'll hesitate when he puts other people in the same position he was in, making cards. If his creativity drops, that'll lower his stake. But either way, we won't have to worry about him anymore."

Gin twisted awkwardly. "How can you be so sure? He was gonna *kill* us, Johnny. Kill us! Good thing you spotted him, or we wouldn't be sitting here right now." She leaned away from him, turning up a palm between them. "I can't believe you just fucking let him walk away."

"Players are true to two things, Gin. The rules of the game and their word. Don't ask me to explain it, but those two things are all a player's got if he wants to keep his rep. And besides, Ferret has just as much to lose by killin' us as we would if we tried to kill him just now. Nebo won't allow it. And we're sittin' at Nebo's table. House rules: if the players became cards, then there'd be no one left to play."

She rubbed her face with both hands. "I'm trying to understand. But this is happening so damned fast."

He held her thigh. It was hot. "I know it is. But that wasn't nothin'. This game is real scary, Gin, and I'm kinda sorry I got you involved. It's going to be like this until its over. Maybe not people creepin' up on us like that Ferret fucker, but we gotta watch our backs. I'm playing with desperate men. And that includes Nebo." He squeezed her leg. "Thanks for helping me. I owe you the world, and when I win this game I'm gonna give it to you."

Gin finally looked down at the photographs in her hand, her mind drifting away from Johnny's words. Ferret was framed in fear, eyes wide in the first shot like a still from a horror movie. The second photo was a close-up so full of shadows and blurred that she couldn't make out much of Ferret's face, except for his nose and eyes…the eyes like fists clenched shut, a thin line of pupil peering through the red crack like the guts of an oyster. And Gin recalled feeling much the same way when Johnny was moving toward him with the knife, his voice hissing deeply like someone else's: *Spades…Spades….*

"You really were about to kill him, weren't you?"

Lifting his hand, he stared at his beer and then picked at the label. "Yes," he said. "I was."

She glanced at him. Looked back at the photos.

Johnny peeled the label clean off. "It was really strange, Gin. I actually *saw* possible cards when I was comin' at him with that damned knife. I saw Spades. Spades were in his eyes. In the shape of his head on that pencil neck of his. Even in the shadows his head was like one giant Spade, a leaf waiting to be plucked." He looked at the label in his palm and began folding it. "And that knife: one sharp Spade, right in the palm of my hand."

"Stop it, Johnny. You're scaring me."

Johnny dropped the label. He had curved the edges into an arrow, tore the bottom, and shaped the gummy paper into a perfect Spade. Without realizing it. "You know," Johnny said, patting Gin on the leg. "I think I'm beginning to scare me, too."

Gin lit a cigarette, staring at the photograph. "So I guess I'm in this with you now, eh? I mean, shit, now Nebo's gonna know if Ferret tells your pal Winston about what happened here tonight."

Johnny shrugged. "Maybe I'll beat him to it. Give him a different story."

She raised the photograph closer to her face. Johnny looked over at her and cocked his head. "What is it?"

"Well," she said, eyebrows furrowing, "I think I'm seeing Spades in this picture, too."

Johnny blew air through his nose, a stifled laugh. "No you're not. I was just a little crazy…"

"I'm serious," Gin continued, her eyebrows raising with her lips. "I see Spades, all right. Five of them." She passed him the photo, tracing the shadows around Ferret's nose.

Johnny sighed in confirmation. "Amazing," he said, shaking his head from side to side as if trying to erase the image of Ferret's bruises from his eyes.

# Play Dead

Winston sat on his bunk, wishing the whole thing was over with. He was getting tired of the place with its constant undercurrent of filth: a lingering taste in the back of his throat and a thin film he could feel on his skin. His clothes were beginning to smell funny and he thought he was catching some virus from the constant hacking and coughing of the regular bums who lived there, sleeping day and night, waking only to piss or eat. He felt no pity.

The Preacher had given him his latest card without even bothering to explain the story behind all those disembodied hearts. Winston accepted it with a nod, holding back his desire for control, giving fate its due. But if anyone was getting out of hand, it was The Preacher. "I hope you cleaned up real good," was all Winston could say to him before tucking the card inside his pocket and looking the other way. It didn't matter: Nebo owned the Lariat Hotel, and they'd already covered his tracks for him. Winston knew how lucky they were that The Preacher had killed all those people at the Lariat instead of someplace else where he was likely to get caught. But then again, Winston was beginning to wonder how much luck had to do with anything anymore. It couldn't be a coincidence. But it could be *Fate*.

Johnny entered through the front door, eyes locking on Winston's with a bang the second the aluminum door slammed behind him. He appeared *changed* somehow: his clothes were different; he was clean and shaven; his walk was sure-footed and upright. But his eyes had been altered. Deep and darker than before. Thick lines in the skin over them.

Winston smiled. "You did it."

Johnny just stared at him, reaching into his back pocket and withdrawing a photograph. He passed it over, face down, like a bad hand.

Winston examined the photo while Johnny sat on the opposite bunk, burying his hands in his dark blond hair and staring at the floor.

"This is pretty blurry kid. You musta been in a rush, eh?" He eyeballed the picture. A human face in shadows—Johnny, he realized, was already into taking human lives. Just like the others. Fate was still at work. "Sloppy, but

understandable for your first card. Still, I don't…oh, here it is. I see it."
Winston spotted the number 5. The flat black eyebrow capped a curving
thick line of shadow which traced around the nose beneath and inscribed a
wobbly black 5. In the puffed, blackened. and purpled eye beside it, a com-
bination of shadows and bruise crookedly cast the shape of a spade. "Not
bad, Johnny. Not bad at all." Winston twisted it sideways. "You really
rearranged this guy's face. Really good work. I'm surprised you got the light
to do all this. First I've seen that happen."

"Me, too," Johnny mumbled.

Winston tucked it into his pocket behind the cold plastic of The
Preacher's photo and his cigarette pack. He withdrew it, passing a smoke to
Johnny and lighting his own. "I'm sure you'll get a decent stack of chips
from Nebo for this one."

Johnny shook his head. "Listen, I don't care about the game right now.
You gotta have a talk with that bastard named Ferret."

"Excuse me?"

"Ferret. That Indian guy. One of the players."

"How do you know…"

"We had a little talk the other day. Seems he wanted to make a card out
of me. And the girl I was with, too."

"Let me guess," Winston said, leaning back. "You're still messin' around
with that cook. What's her name, again—Gin?"

"Yes, Gin. We're seeing each other off and on."

Winston leaned forward again, eyes squinting. "So what happened,
Johnny? *She* doesn't know about the game, now, does she?"

Johnny smoked Winston's cigarette. "Nope." He leaned forward. "I managed to convince her that Ferret came to collect a gambling debt from me.
She bought the story. Doesn't have a clue. But I don't want that little fucker
coming around me any more, okay? He's a jerk and I don't trust him."
Johnny pointed the hot end of the cigarette at him for punctuation: "I don't
want to have to even see him till game time. Tell him to stay away."

Winston found it hard to believe that Ferret had inadvertently picked
another player for his next card in the deck. But he reminded himself of Fate.

# Play Dead

"I'll tell him, Johnny. But this changes things. Now you two know each other. That might screw up the game. I'll have to talk with Nebo."

"Ferret knows the deal, all right. Hell, I wouldn't be surprised if he knew I was a player all along. Trying to win the game by cheating." Johnny smoked. "You watch him."

"Will do." Winston crossed his arms. "But you've got worse things to worry about. You're still way behind in the deck. You've got some catching up to do. Keep going in the direction you started. I like what I see."

Johnny sighed, and stood up. "Right." He nodded and began to walk back toward the front door.

"And Johnny," Winston called, stopping him. "Don't you let that little girlie find out about our game. There's been enough screw-ups, already. If you really like her, keep her out of it. Got it?"

Johnny nodded and then quickly walked out the door without saying a word.

Winston heard something crackle behind him, and turned to see Ferret approaching, twisting his neck from side to side to get bone noises out from his spine. He looked like he'd been in a boxing match—his eye was black and bruised. "What the hell happened to you, Ferret?"

Ferret sat beside him, casting sideways glances around the shelter. "My last card put up a little bit of a fight. But I got the little bugger." He reached out and put a card into Winston's breast pocket and patted it. "It was worth it. You'll see."

Winston scowled. "I'll be the judge of that," he said, reaching up to his pocket.

Ferret raised a hand to stop him. "Not right now, Winston. I've got news. You're new player, Johnny what's-his-face, is shackin' up with that girl who works in the kitchen. Know her?"

Winston dropped his hand. "Yeah? So?"

"So? So she knows, man, she *knows*." Again, Ferret cracked his neck.

Winston waved the idea away. "She doesn't know shit. And the only way she might have found out is because you tried to take another player out of the game, you fuck-up."

176

Ferret's eyes danced. "Wha...wait a minute."

"No, you wait. I heard about your little mix-up with Johnny Frieze. You stay away from the other players, got it? Or you're gonna fold. I'm not gonna tell you again."

"But Winston, she knows. I was there..."

"Johnny covered your ass. Had the sense to tell her that you were there to collect a gambling debt. That's all." He reached into his pocket and grabbed his pack of cigarettes with Ferret's latest picture. He popped a cigarette magician-style into his mouth but didn't look at the photograph. "No thanks to you."

"A gambling debt?" Ferret rubbed his black eye. Winced. "Hey, wait." He stood up. "I guess I'll have to prove it to you. Stay right here."

Winston shrugged and smoked his cigarette, taking the free moment to examine Ferret's latest card. The upside-down face of a dead child with gray eyes rolled back in their sockets stared up at him, and Winston had to hold back his stomach. The kid was wearing black mouse ears, like something from Disneyland. A long metal shaft—the black handle of Ferret's survival knife—stuck out of the center of the top of his skull. His head rested in a puddle of blood on a sidewalk, droplets trailing over to the number 10 sloppily finger-painted on the cement in the upper corner of the photograph.

"Here." Ferret had returned, and was passing Winston a manila envelope.

"Hold on, hold on." Winston looked up at him, refusing to take the package. "What the hell is this supposed to be?" he asked, showing him the photo.

"Isn't it obvious? My next card, The Ten of Clubs."

Winston just stared at him.

Ferret looked down at the picture. "Oh, shit, you've got it upside-down." He plucked it out of Winston's fingers and turned it around for him. "See, this kid is ten years old. And a Mouseketeer. He looks just like a club, doesn't he, with those dumb big ears on his little head?"

Winston studied it and then put it back in his pocket, shaking his head. "Running out of ideas, Ferret?"

"What?" He cocked his head and it crackled.

"Don't try to sham me. That card sucks. Poor kid. Victim of a lame-brained idiot. You better start trying a little harder to be creative if you want any chips for the game."

"But…"

"Ferret," Winston said, staring him down. "This is not good."

Ferret swallowed, and Winston could see his neck muscles tighten. He raised his hands. "Fine. Forget the card. The face cards will be better, you'll see…"

Winston kept his eyes on his. "They better be."

"But here, you'll like what's in here a lot better." He tossed the manila envelope on the blanket beside Winston's thigh.

"What's this, the kid's birth certificate? His membership card in the Mickey Mouse Club?"

Ferret nervously laughed. "No, it's proof that that cook lady knows more than she's saying. I found it in her apartment."

Winston rolled his eyes and opened the envelope. His mouth fell open when he saw what it contained. He could sense Ferret waiting patiently, his goofy smile widening while he shuffled quickly through the papers. Winston could feel his face flushing red. These were things that nobody—not even Winston—was supposed to know.

Finally, he looked up at Ferret and sealed the envelope. "Okay," he said, closing his eyes again slowly and swallowing his anger at Fate. "Kill her."

Gin was being very open, Johnny thought while idly watching her dress. She played her hands open, stud poker-style, and he liked it—this was how partners, he guessed, were supposed to act. She had shared her feelings about the game with him and had already begun helping him make the cards. But it wasn't just her game plan that got to Johnny; she was honest about her feelings for him, too, and had offered him everything she had as if it were his own: her apartment, her car, her food…even her body. While he sat on the bed, she dressed up in her Bucket of Bucks uniform as if her nudity were routine, as if they'd been living together for years, and she even pretended not to notice him blushing. But he was. Not from embarrassment, really. Just because he wasn't sure what his end of the bargain was supposed to be, or whether he was holding it up. Sure, he had to play the game, but what else did he have to offer her besides the money afterward, if he won? She had said she loved him. Maybe that's what she wanted. Regardless, he had to trust her words. Not something he was used to doing.

Dressed, she tossed him her keys, and he drove her to The Bucket.

Sighting the tall building at the end of the Strip, Gin lit a last-minute cigarette, getting what nicotine she could into her system before work. "So Winston bought the card, eh?" she said, breaking the silence.

"Yup, just like I told you." Johnny stopped at a red light. "Ferret was so scared that he *looked* dead. Good thing the photo was so blurry and close-up, though. Winston mighta recognized him."

She spoke smoke: "Hope he doesn't notice the bruise on his face and make the connection."

"Me, too." Johnny turned into the lot. "But so far so good."

Gin stared at the building like he was taking her into the gates of a prison. "I hope so. 'Cause if Nebo catches on to me, I'm dead."

Johnny looked over at her, spotting the four-leaf clover over her breast. "Nah, you've got good luck. Besides, I already told you what I said to him: Ferret came to collect a gambling debt. If they confront you, tell 'em that."

He parked by the front entrance. Gin continued smoking, staring at him. "I can't be seen around here. You better go."

She cocked her head, sizing him up. A lip raised in a smile. "You hate this, don't you?"

"Hate what?"

The sexy grin widened. "Cheating at cards."

Johnny faked a laugh. "Right." He leaned over to kiss her, but she nuzzled his neck instead. Johnny petted her hair and talked into her ear: "It ain't cheating if you don't get caught. Now you get out of here. I'll pick you up at two tonight. And then we'll get busy on the next one."

"I think I'm looking forward to that." She rolled her eyes as she leaned back and snuck the final drag from her cigarette like a teenager in a school bathroom before leaping out of the car and slamming the door. She ran up the steps and into the mouth of the casino, not bothering to wave or look back. Her green uniform joined the other glitzy colors, a rainbow absorbing all light.

Johnny drove to Violet's. Knocking on her door felt like coming home to family.

"C'mon in, Johnny," she called from behind the door as if she'd been waiting for him. "It's open."

He entered. Violet was sitting at her bar, grinding fruit into her blender, and Johnny could smell the pungent odor of her truth serum drink from where he stood. Her eyes were bright when she smiled at him, but Johnny thought she looked artificial with her dentures back in place. When she had passed out in his arms the night before it had been as if he'd seen her back stage. Now she was in full costume. Acting.

"C'mon over here and try some serum. I've added a new ingredient, and I wanna hear what you've been up to."

Johnny obeyed. He had the clothes she'd given him the other day tucked under an arm and set them on the couch. The clothes Gin had bought him— "gifts" she'd said that morning—felt good on his skin, but still he gave Violet her due. "Thanks for the cool outfit, Violet. Dutch was a lucky man, and I appreciate it."

She frowned and waved at him, and then turned off the blender. "Eh?"

He pointed at the sofa. "Thanks for the clothes the other day."

"Oh," she nodded, all business. "I see you're back in the swing. Good for you. Glad I could be of service." She poured two tumblers and raised one in toast. "Here's to change."

They drank to it.

"So," she smacked her lips, eyeing him. "Gotcher self a new woman, I see."

Johnny instantly blushed. "How…"

"Just look at that get-up you're in. Looks like someone's been shoppin' and I sure as hell know it wasn't *you*. 'Sides." She paused to swig. "You got lipstick on your collar, lover boy."

Johnny awkwardly rubbed his neck.

"Knew it would happen. Read it in the cards." She winked. "Can't say I didn't try none, though."

Johnny felt like a kid, so he dug a cigarette out and quickly lit it. His ears felt hot while she stared at him, grinning. "You mean to tell me," he finally said, puffing, "that those Tarot cards of yours predicted that I'd get lucky?"

"Nope," she replied, joining him in a smoke. "Them cards didn't say nothin' you didn't tell 'em first. Your *fate* did."

"Right."

"Wanna bet?"

"You forgetting who you're talking to? Damn straight, I'll betcha. Deal 'em out. I want to see this, and I'm gonna *remember* this time."

Violet was already capping off his tumbler with more serum. She shook her head. "Only you would wanna bet against your own fate."

"I'm *serious*," Johnny said. "Let's bet. What's the stake? I don't have any money right now, but if that's what you want…"

"Far as the Tarot's concerned, Johnny-boy, your life is at stake. Not your money. But if you really need to bet something, how's about betting me something stupid like…I dunno…"

"Favors," Johnny finished for her. "We'll bet favors."

Violet was retrieving her rubber-banded Tarot deck from beneath a small stack of old *TV Guides* on the bar. "Favors it is," she said, unwrapping the cards.

Johnny watched as she shuffled the deck—tall as a triple-blackjack deck—expertly steepling and shoving the cards together in her small hands like a dealer at a table. The cards seemed stiff as cardboard; they didn't make much sound as they slapped together, as if they were falling into their proper places without argument. Then she held it in her palm before Johnny. "Go ahead, you remember what to do."

"Actually," Johnny said, remembering only his hangover from that night. "I don't. Am I supposed to ask you some question about my love life or something?"

She shook her head. "Nah, that question-and-answer stuff is for babies. You just think about your life, and the cards might provide you with more information. I don't need to know what it is." She nodded at the deck in her palm. "Just tap the top, three times."

He did so, chuckling. "This is like a bad magic trick, Violet."

She raised an eyebrow over a darkly diluted eye. "It's your life we're talking about here." She shuffled again. "I'm not manipulating the cards in any way. I'm just shuffling once to let the cards find their proper order, now that they've felt you."

She set the pack down and looked up at him. "Are you sure you want to know?"

Johnny lit a smoke. "I'm not sure about much of anything anymore, Violet. And I'm not quite sure you know what *you're* doing either. So what do we got to lose?"

"Favors, Johnny. Remember?"

"Right." He blinked smoke from an eye. "Deal."

She turned over four cards, then two more face down, in the shape of a toppled cross. Johnny didn't recognize the cards much, but he did spot the card he knew she'd pull on him: Death. He looked down at the corny drawing of the skeletal reaper and held back a snicker. "Figures," he said, thinking of low budget horror flicks. "I bet the deck is stacked with them."

"What're you bettin' now?"

"Nothin'." He stamped out his cigarette and swallowed more of Violet's truth serum. Banana booze and tobacco tar didn't mix too good. "So when am I gonna die?"

Violet laughed. "That death card there doesn't mean you're gonna die. None of these face-up cards do. Most of these here cards are just about your current predicament. So unless I'm sittin' here with a zombie, you should be good to go. These cards aren't perfect—they just tell a story, so to speak, about your life. So let me see if I can read it to you."

"Shoot."

"Okay," she leaned over the bar, examining the cards. "This first one here on your far left is Death, but like I said, it don't mean you're gonna die. Because it's on the left, it's about your recent past, and means you've lost something important to you. Like all your money, right?"

"Oh. Uh-huh." He nodded. "True."

"Of course it's true. Okay. The one next to it represents you." She pointed at it, and Johnny noticed a knight holding a sword as big as his body, dressed up in gaudy armor and a loincloth.

"I'm Conan the Barbarian?"

"Nope," Violet replied, ignoring the joke. "You're the King of Swords. Normally this would mean that you're fair, creative, powerful, and even wise. Ha! But because it's upside-down, it means that you've got a mean streak in ya, and you're not to be trusted. The King of Swords is a bastard, always plotting and tricking folks with his hidden agenda. Sound about right, Johnny?"

He smiled, flashing the gap between his teeth. "If you say so."

"Well," she said, "it could mean that you're just confused right now, following the wrong track, and that you're trying to reverse it with some sort of scheme. It depends on your outlook—optimistic or pessimistic—either way, this card's saying something about your character."

Johnny's eyes roamed to the card beside it: a man pulling one stick out of a pile and holding it like an arrow. "What about the next?"

"Your current goal. The Seven of Wands. Hmm…it indicates valor, success in competition. In a nutshell, winning. But you have to be true to your heart if it's gonna work."

"Lucky seven, eh?"

"Yup." She smiled. "An admirable goal. You don't exactly have big dreams, Johnny, but good enough for the likes of you, you crafty some-bitch." She paused to take a drink. "The next card, though, is supposed to tell us what's currently blocking you from reaching that goal. Let's see...the King of Pentacles."

Johnny craned his neck to look. Another Conan, decked out in jewelry this time, holding a long golden rod and a giant encircled star—the kind he'd seen on gas station signs and satanic rock albums—only more artful, the size of a bowling ball in Conan's palm. "Hey," he said, comparing it to the card that had represented himself. "This dude's upside-down, too."

"Right. Whoever he is, this guy is standing in your way. A real bastard, this king. He cheats, he's corrupt, and gives in too easily to his vices. Supposed to be stupid, too; makes a lot of mistakes. Wastes his talent, most often on gambling. Go figure."

"Sounds more like myself than the other card did."

"Could be you are your own obstacle. Hey, nothing's written in stone here. I'm just tellin' you what I see. It's up to you to see how it applies to your own life, though."

He motioned at the face-down cards. "Hmm. So what have I got in the hole here? Jacks or better, I hope."

"Very funny. These two cards have to do with the future. The one on the bottom is the way you'll overcome your current obstacle, and the one on top predicts the outcome. Let's check 'em out." She flipped the one on the bottom first.

Johnny eagerly looked down at the card—a smiling man with a funky hat and motley outfit, holding two balls with pentacles on them as if about to juggle. "A Joker? Are Joker's wild?"

"Well, not exactly." She traced her fingers around the two balls the figure was holding, a line that crazy-eighted infinity. "This is the Two of Pentacles, and symbolizes balance. You'll have to juggle many things at the same time to reach your goal, and you'll find success and harmony if you can pull it off. But it takes determination, not to mention coordination. It's a tough card."

"So what will happen if I do juggle things like this? What's the—what did you call it? The outcome?"

She flipped the final card. It was upside-down, like the other face cards. Only this one had a statuesque muscular nude on it, with a long white beard. He was blowing a brass horn twice the size of his head in the direction of the mountain tops behind him. Clouds like ghosts filled the sky. "What is it?"

Violet coughed. "This is the Last Judgment. A pretty vague card. Open-ended. Reversed like it is, it means that delay and confusion make matters worse; you should bring your business—whatever it may be—to a close as soon as possible, to avoid more problems than you already have."

He looked up at her. "You're saying I'm fucked."

She avoided his eyes. "I'm not sayin' nothin' of the sort. I'm saying that your future is yet to be written. Unknown. You've got too much shit going on at once which you'll need to juggle into order. It's all up to you, though, to tell if you win or lose in the long run. Maybe neither will happen, which can be good sometimes." She reached for the blender and poured the rest of her pulpy concoction into her glass and took a sip, giving him time to consider the cards on the table.

Johnny fingered his chin. "Well, I guess I win the bet."

Violet nearly choked on her drink. "Say *what*? This whole spread meant something to you—you know it's tellin' the truth."

"Maybe, but it doesn't say anything about my love life, now, does it?"

Violet cocked her head. "You tell me."

"No-no. You don't get off that easy."

"Neither do you, Johnny. It's your life, not mine. But maybe I'll do you a favor anyway. Besides, the cards don't tell us much directly. Fate isn't as eager to tell us about what it has in store as you'd think."

"What do you mean? Just how do these stupid things work?" He raised a hand. "Not that I believe in any of this bullshit; just curious."

She was lighting a menthol cigarette, motioning at the cards. "Each card is like a cup. It holds the past, present, and future. But that future is empty until you tap the deck, which is when these cups are filled with your own fate."

185

"So that would make you the bartender," Johnny said, passing her his empty glass.

She didn't get it. "Not really. I'm more like the person who drinks from the cups and tells you what the stuff inside tastes like."

Johnny reached for the uncapped bottle of vodka beside the blender, and poured himself a shot. "Do I taste good? Or do I got no taste?"

"I dunno, Johnny. Damned if that wasn't the strangest spread I ever read. So open. Nothing's certain in your life, so anything's possible, good and bad. But I'd be careful if I were you—something's gonna happen real soon."

"I bet it is." He teased the Last Judgment with his palm. "So where'd you get these cards, anyway? This stuff is from the Dark Ages. Who makes 'em anymore?"

"This here is a genu-wine deck. Not some kid's game. They're hand-printed, hand-made. You can tell by the initials on each card." She began collecting them to put the deck away. "I've heard strange stories about the people who make these decks, though." She winked and rubber-banded the deck. "Like, in order to give the cards their power, the artist has to channel the spirits of Fate and what not..."

"Uh-oh. Here comes the mystical bologna."

"Bologna or not, I'm just tellin' you what I know. The power in these cards has to come from somewhere. The artist just lets the spirits work through him. Kinda like in that movie, *Ghostbusters*: the artist captures their energy in the cards. I've heard that a lot of 'em go psycho after the experience. Anyway, when you tapped the deck, they sucked a part of you inside, too, to keep 'em alive. It's kinda like feeding the tigers at the zoo."

Johnny drew the connection: *the artist captures their energy in cards.* Was Johnny supposed to be that artist? Was Nebo making some bizarre sort of Tarot deck?

"Listen, Violet. About that favor..."

♦ ♦ ♦ ♦ ♦ ♦   Q   ♦ ♦ ♦ ♦ ♦ ♦

Gin stepped out of the mouth of the casino, scanning the streets for Johnny and her red Fiesta. They were nowhere around, which she expected. It had been a slow night at the tables, and Danny, her pit boss, let her off a half hour early. But she had hoped Johnny might be waiting, and for some reason, was surprised that he wasn't. Almost upset.

Some people walked by, laughing. No Johnny. She lit a cigarette and leaned against a large pillar, shielding herself in the shadows it cast. Gin didn't want to be here at all, and the night had dragged on infinitely; she felt as though Danny was always spying over her back, and the observation cameras constantly seemed pointed at her beneath their domed housings. Paranoid or not, the players all played like stooges; like losers sent to keep an eye on her. Even on break, she was never unaccompanied. Except now.

"I've got your purse," Ferret whispered with the flash of his bruised face as he passed her on the sidewalk and kept walking.

It took her a second to understand. Then she jogged to catch up with him, cigarette bouncing heavily between her lips. "Hey! Wait up!"

He didn't face her until she was by his side. He stopped in his tracks, all grins. "Yes?"

Gin whispered, though she had no reason to: "I want that purse back."

"It'll cost ya." He cracked his neck and fingered the tip of Trickster below his belt. She didn't see it.

"I figured that. I'll pay, if it's reasonable. But don't think I don't have the original copies of everything that was in there. And first I want to know how you *really* got it. There's no way you found it in some alley."

He returned to walking and Gin kept up with him.

"Have you heard back from Sigh-more?" Ferret asked coyly.

"Who?" She tossed her cigarette.

"That reporter."

"No, I haven't. He's been missing…" She cursed. "You did it, didn't you? You robbed him; maybe even killed him."

"None of that matters," Ferret said, turning at the corner of the Casino. "Let's talk about you." He led her to the parking lot, where hundreds of cars gleamed, empty and hollow in shadows like artificial gems. "I want to know what you intended on doing with all that juicy stuff in that purse."

Gin looked around, wondering if Johnny had come yet, whether he might be parked somewhere in the lot. Nervous, she fished another cigarette out of the swamp of her pocketbook. "Um, that's none of your business."

Ferret looked up the night sky, idly searching stars. "But it is."

Gin stopped, loudly scraping a heel against the tarmac. "Fine. Forget it. Keep the purse. I don't need those copies anyway. You can do whatever you want with that stuff." Ferret paused, but did not turn around. "But I know you're in that game with Nebo, and can't get out of it. So there's nothing you can do. All that information can't help you one bit—you're screwed." She pivoted to head back to the casino and wait for Johnny.

"I can tell Nebo all about it," Ferret called over his shoulder. "You won't only get fired. You'll be killed. And Johnny can't do shit to stop him, because just like me, he's in the game, too."

She stopped. They stood there, back to back across the lot, ten paces or so away like a pistol duel.

Then she returned to where he stood. "Okay. What do you want?"

He lifted a finger to his lips to shush her and led her to the black Nova. Gin immediately recognized the reporter's car as he opened the door for her. "We'll talk in here, where it's private."

She paused. She knew she shouldn't be doing this. Johnny was on his way to pick her up; not only might he not find her out front, but Ferret could easily try to drive away. Still, she had no choice. This was the only opportunity she'd have to set things straight with Ferret. She slid a long leg inside, and sat against the familiar leather. Ferret slammed the door, and Gin double-checked to make sure it was unlocked if she needed a quick getaway.

While Ferret made his way quickly around the black hood of the Nova, Gin scanned the car for the purse, hoping she could grab the evidence and run. She saw nothing but crumpled and greasy fast-food sacks. Pooling stains of shadow which could have been Silas' blood. White and pink fuzzy dice, turning seven. The dots on the dice were cut-outs from what appeared to be cards—club shapes, arranged in fours and threes on each side.

Ferret climbed inside, jingling keys in his hand.

"You start this car," Gin quickly said, "and I'm outta here."

Ferret pulled the door shut behind him and slid the keys into the ignition. He kept his hand there, and turned his head to face her. His neck cracked. "Do you really have any choice?"

Urgently: "Johnny's coming to pick me up any minute now. And if I'm not here, he knows who to blame. Johnny meant it when he said he'd kill you. I'm more important to him than that stupid game."

"I doubt you're worth more than a million dollars," Ferret said, clucking his tongue. "But I wasn't planning on going anywhere anyway. Now," he dropped his hand from the ignition, and reached down with the other to grip Trickster's handle where she couldn't see it. "Talk."

"Let me see the papers first."

Ferret smiled. His eyes trailed down to her uniform, lingering over her chest. "You know, you look pretty good in that outfit," he said. He motioned at the logo above her left breast. "Nice buckets."

The muscles in Gin's jaw clenched on their own accord.

He raised a stiff index finger. "I especially like *that*," he said, jabbing her in the four-leaf clover over her nipple. Pain sang up the left side of her ribcage.

*"That's it!"* She angrily yanked on the doorknob, and clambered for escape. The dome light above flickered yellow as Ferret quickly wrapped an arm around her shoulders and brought Trickster's edge to her throat, pulling her backwards against his chest. She struggled, and then felt the blade tweak her skin. A slight hot and wet trickle ran down her collar. Not too much blood, but just enough to scare her. "Okay, okay, okay," she whispered in fear of her voice giving the knife something more to cut. She gave up control of her muscles, and he pulled her back.

Hot breath in her ear canal: "Shut the door."

She obeyed, knife at neck.

"Don't try that again," Ferret whispered. Gin did not reply. He let his

189

hand drift down her blouse, awkwardly cupping her left breast and lifting its weight so he could see the four leaf clover from over her shoulder. "Yes," Ferret's voice calmly said as he squeezed tightly, "my Queen of Clubs. My wonderful Queen of Clubs…"

Gin swallowed slowly, trying to pull her neck back as far away from the blade as possible. She refused to look down at what he was doing. It hurt, but she could take it. His razor stubble scratched on her cheek. "Clubs?" she asked, trying to stall him.

"*Green* clubs. So beautiful. And unexpected." He caressed them with his thumb, gently pressing the thick fabric patch against the stiffening nub of her nipple beneath. "A good luck charm if there ever was one."

Gin recognized the tone of his voice—like Johnny's manic *Spades…Spades…Spades.*

She got an idea. "Those aren't clubs, honey. Clubs have *three* leaves. And what your playing with has four." Her voice sounded terribly fake; a cheap attempt at strength.

"I know, your highness," Ferret replied, lifting the knife and trailing its tip down her chest. "One lucky club too many." He angled the tip against the emblem. "And that means one will just have to go."

She gently closed the lids over her eyes. Her voice was hardly there: "Please, no…"

And then the scouring pad of Ferret's beard scraped sharply against her cheek and ear, the knife arcing quickly in a yellow flash before her eyes as his arms flung back and she sprang forward, twisting to see another man's hands around his shoulders, forcing him out of the car.

Gin grabbed her neck, brought her hand back. Bloody. But not drenched. She looked up and Ferret's head suddenly smashed against the glass of the windshield outside with a loud crack, startling her. His eyes stared blankly at her, empty, as his nostrils streamed blood down the glass.

Dizzy, she leaned over to the open door. "Johnny, oh my God, you just…"

The Preacher leaned his head inside the car. "Are you okay, Ma'am?"

It took her a second to recognize him. "You…"

"He's been lusting after you. Following you all day, like the lamb to the slaughter. I kept an eye on him, though. The Lord told me to." The Preacher's eyes widened when he saw the blood on her neck. "Are you sure you're okay?"

"Yes," Gin said, collecting her pocketbook and casting glances into the back seat for the evidence Ferret had stolen. "I'm fine." She tried the glove compartment. No luck. He hadn't brought it with him—probably never intended to hand it over at all.

"Well you best be going," The Preacher said, dragging Ferret by the shoulders into the driver's seat. "He won't be very friendly when he wakes up."

"Right." Gin got out of the car, and slammed the door. "Thanks Preacher," she said as she came around the other side of the Nova, and leaned over to kiss his sweaty forehead. "I owe you one."

The Preacher visibly writhed.

Gin rushed back to the front of the Bucket, to try and find Johnny.

Meanwhile, the Preacher set Ferret behind the wheel, lifting his head back so he wouldn't fall on the horn. Then he punched him squarely in the jaw, which audibly cracked. "The harlot is *mine*, you cheatin' sinner. You won't steal her from me." He hit him again, right on top of the bruised eye like a target Johnny had painted on him. *"Mine."*

Ferret's head flopped to one side as if he'd killed him. The Preacher panicked and gently rested a palm against the center of his chest. He could feel a pulse. His heartbeat. His *heart*. Calling for his fingers to clench down in-between the thin ribs there. Hot blood thrashing against the wall of skin and bone beneath his palm...

The Preacher forced himself to let go. He knew he couldn't take Ferret out of the game. He shut the door, and casually walked in Gin's general direction, wondering where she ran off to. Just outside the front entrance of the casino, he saw her legs flash as she bent inside the Fiesta with Johnny. They hugged.

"The Queen gathers another heart," he uttered as they drove away. Pressing the photographs in his breast pocket closer to his own heart, he began to pray in time with its beat. It felt much the same as Ferret's. Drowning. Thrashing to be free.

191

# Play Dead

♦ ♦ ♦ ♦ ♦ ♦
♦ ♦ ♦ K ♦ ♦ ♦

"Geez," Gin said as Johnny dabbed the cut on her neck with a paper towel. She leaned back against the kitchen sink and groaned. "You sound like you're mad at *me*, instead of Ferret."

"Well, why the hell did you follow him to his car, anyway?" Blood oozed beneath the pressure of his fingers. "Wait—hold still." Frowning, he smeared the wound clean, but blood kept coming up. "He really cut you good. You're lucky he didn't catch an artery here or something. Hell, you're lucky period."

"Must be my four leaf clover," Gin grimaced.

"Here, hold this on there." He pressed her hand against a fresh square of thick paper towels. "I think it's clean now, though who knows what kinda shit he had on his knife. I doubt Ferret keeps it very clean." He started digging through drawers. "Got any tape or something?"

"Let's just leave it open," she said. "The air will help it heal."

He opened a silverware drawer. Looked at her wincing. Slammed it. "Fine, Gin. You take care of yourself. I can't always look after you, you know? There's only so much fucking bullshit I can juggle at once."

She faced him, elbow cocked as she held her neck. She blinked a few times. "So that's it. You feel responsible for me."

He blinked back. "Well I did get you into all this."

"Just stop right there. I knew what I was getting into when I agreed to help you play this game, and I know what I'm doing now. You don't have to act like you're my father or something. We're partners in this, but we both are pulling our own weight, too. Otherwise, what's the sense, right?"

Johnny filled his lungs with air. Held it. Blew. "I guess so." He grabbed a pack of menthols from the stovetop and lit one. "You just scared the shit out of me, that's all." He stared at her over a screen of smoke. "Please don't do that again."

She nodded with her whole body, not wanting to bend her neck.

Johnny sighed and rubbed his eyes. "It's getting late. We should hit the sack."

"I can't possibly sleep after what just happened." Gin walked into the living room, dropping on the loveseat. "How about a beer?"

Johnny grabbed two. Sat beside her.

"Listen, Ferret is still gonna come after me when he recovers from The Preacher's beating. I don't know why, but he's out to get me."

"We'll get him first," Johnny said, bending a bottle cap between thumb and index finger. He dropped the crimped metal in the ashtray. "Winston had his chance to deal with him. Now it's my turn."

Gin lifted her hand and the makeshift gauze stuck to her neck, a brown button of coagulated blood holding it in place. She put the free hand on Johnny's leg. "Don't. You might get — what — disqualified?"

"Well Ferret should be after pulling this crap. But I don't think that'll stop him. He's too unpredictable. Might try to take us out before Nebo catches up with him."

"Listen, Johnny, before you go any further." She looked for her cigarettes. Spotting them on the oven, she stood to retrieve them. "We gotta talk." She tapped a smoke, lit, and twisted. "About Ferret."

His eyebrows crinkled. "What about him?"

She turned away, plucking off the paper towel, and fingering the wound. "I don't know where to begin. It's just…he's got something on me."

"Oh yeah?" Johnny smoked and nodded. "I know what he's got." He watched her turn to face him, splayed fingers on her neck as if feeling for a pulse. "Your purse, right?"

Her eyes widened, dilated.

"Bet you thought I forgot what he said when he was here. What was in it, Gin?" He sipped on his beer, waiting for an answer.

"I…" She looked down at the floor, then back up. "Why didn't you say anything?"

Johnny rubbed his forehead with a palm. "I knew you'd tell me sooner or later. Thought I'd taken care of whatever the problem was when I talked to Winston, though." He arched his eyebrows as if stretching the exhaustion out of his scalp. "I know you're not a cop or something, or else you woulda stopped all this by now. But something's going down, and we might as well

193

get it out of the way now." He made impatient signs with his fingers. "So come on, come clean."

"Where do I start?" She returned to the seat beside him and stared at the tiny blank gray TV screen in front of her while she spoke, as if catching him up on some imaginary mini-series on the tube across from them: "I needed money. Big time. I don't have much talent, but when I was in school I was good at research. Not just diggin' in the library, but finding people, getting the truth out them, stuff like that. I wanted to be a journalist, and I was good at it, but, shit, everyone wants to be on the news, right?"

Johnny shrugged. "Not me."

She ignored him: "Anyway, I could find anything. *Anything*. Except a job. Crazy, right?" She lit another cigarette, barely stopping her story. "So I sorta went freelance. Not for the news, but for companies and stuff. You know, people willing to really *pay* for stuff. Kinda like a private eye, only without the office and everything. The trick is to be unknown; only an idiot would have a listing in the phone book, telling the world that they're a snoop. It isn't a steady job, but I prefer it that way. Get to set my own hours, and can pull out of a job if it gets too scary. Anyway, the money is easy, really—you just find an angle, look for people who could really use the info if they only knew about it, dig up the dirt, and then hand it to them on a silver platter without their asking for it. They pay more that way, actually. Like a bonus for opening their eyes…"

"Wait," Johnny interrupted. "You want me to believe that you're a private detective who *makes up* your own cases? Give me a break."

She turned from the TV. "I know it's sounds hokey, but it's true. Fact is, clients prefer it that way. I'm anonymous. And like I tell 'em, if you need to investigate something you already suspect to be true in the first place, then why hire a private eye? That's when you need a lawyer, not a gumshoe."

"Listen to you!" Johnny was chuckling. "You're cute, you know that?"

She frowned. "Don't call me cute, Johnny."

He held up his hands in defense. "Okay, I believe you. So what's that got to do with Ferret? You investigating him, or what?"

"Not Ferret," Gin said flatly. "Nebo."

"*Nebo?*" He spilled ash on his lap. "You're crazy! Do you know what he'd do to you if he found out?"

"I know better than you do, probably."

Johnny's nostrils flared as he stared at her, his eyes shifting in confusion.

"Nebo is the most powerful man in this state. And he's been buying off the city for real estate. That's why I finagled a job at The Bucket and the shelter; he owns both."

"Nebo owns the homeless shelter?"

"Yeah. Part of his deal with the government." She took a deep drag. "I won't go into the details, but there are a ton of people willing to pay for the stuff I've got on him. Real estate companies would kill to know this stuff. But the stuff I actually found is so big that I wanted to give the news a try first. I already tried selling it to one reporter, but Ferret got to him first."

"*What?*"

"That's what I'm trying to tell you. He got a hold of the info I gave to a dude from the *The Sun*. I don't know how, or what he's gonna do with it, but if he tells Winston…"

"You'll be killed." Johnny said. "I'm surprised you're even here to tell me this right now. Winston's gotta know. That's why Ferret came after you—he had permission. Good thing The Preacher has a crush on you, or you'd be a goner."

She fingered her neck and guffawed. "The Preacher. He really gives me the creeps. Always wanting to help me. But I can't say I'm not thankful for being saved."

Johnny stood, not having enough energy to laugh. "So what's your plan now? You're not gonna expose Butcher Boy, are you?"

She gave him the most serious face he'd seen. "You know better than that, Johnny. I'm in it with you, to the end. I didn't even *know* about Butcher Boy until I got to know you. And frankly, you're right. I knew I was in over my head, and I was going to close shop as soon as I heard back from *The Sun*. But Silas never contacted me."

"And so you kept up your cover in the soup kitchen and at the blackjack table. I get it." He closed his eyes. "Damn, this is too much. I'm too tired for this crap."

She pulled him against her, holding his back tightly. "I know it's heavy, Johnny. I didn't tell you because I was finished with investigating Nebo. And I thought that with what I know about how he operates, I could help you win the game."

He buried his head in her neck, lips gracing her fresh wound. "You still can, Gin." He kissed the gash. His tongue felt like a spade in his mouth. "And I can help you get your neck out of the wringer."

She tightened her embrace. He could feel the shudder of a chuckle in her lungs. "You know, I've always wanted a partner."

Johnny inhaled her hair. It smelled like the carpeted hallway of The Bucket. Greedy green. He ran the spade of his tongue against the lobe of her ear, and gently whispered. "Well, I don't know how to break this to you, partner." He moved the hair free of her ear to get in closer. Gin hummed, her chest vibrating warmly against him. He kissed her earlobe. "But I'm going to have to kill you now."

Gin lightly laughed with her lungs.

Johnny saw Spades.

# Part Four
# SPADES

# A ♠

Eyeing the shelter for the other players, Johnny pressed his only remaining front tooth, and he could feel it bending in its soft socket. His gums made a slight shredding sound; the fiber that held the tooth in place was dying. He knew he'd be losing it soon. That morning's sink session had resulted in the bloodiest toothbrush yet, and his puffy abscessed gums had been leaking salty yellowish liquid all day. Tonguing it, playing with the tooth in its socket, was his unconscious way of enjoying the tooth while it lasted, but he knew he was only quickening its eventual loss.

"Well," Winston said, interrupting him with a puff of smoke. "Don't you have something for me?"

"I think you'll be surprised by this one," Johnny said, passing Winston the Six of Spades.

Unmistakably Gin, limbs starfished over a grass lawn. Her head twisted sideways to show off the wound on her neck, gurgling blood. Pips from shoulder to hips, six sharp garden shovels stuck out of her chest, three beside three, handles forming solid parallel lines. The angle of the shot revealed a rectangle of brown dirt cut into the grass above her head, a splintered wooden pole sticking out of the earth: a freshly-dug grave.

"Nice," Winston said, fanning his lap with the photograph. "I see you finally came to your senses with this chicky."

Johnny ignored Winston's grin. "It wasn't easy," he said sadly. "But she was on to me. She knew Ferret wasn't visiting to collect a gambling debt. And she knew all about Butcher Boy—I don't know how she found out, but she knew."

Winston raised an eyebrow. "We've been watching her. Seems she's been sticking her nose where it don't belong into Nebo's affairs." He slid the photograph into his breast pocket and withdrew a pack of cigarettes. He tapped a few out of the cut end of the pack like round white skyscrapers and offered one to Johnny.

"Nah," he said, tonguing his loose tooth, "I'm thinking about quitting."

# Play Dead

Winston shook his head and lit one up for himself. "Right." His face clouded with fresh smoke, and Winston blinked behind it. "You're not a quitter, Johnny."

"Maybe, maybe not." He pressed hard on his tooth and the shredding of his gums sounded like a spade cutting dirt inside his skull. "Fuck it. Give me one."

Winston smiled and nodded, already having one free from the pack and sliding it between his fingers like a magician. "You know," he said, watching Johnny closely as he set fire to the end of his smoke, "you're still five or six cards behind the others. You gotta catch up as fast as you can, so the game can go on as scheduled. Think you can do that for me?"

Johnny thought about Gin. "After what I just did, Winston, I can do anything. Because I really got nothin' left to lose anymore." He smoked. "You'll get your cards. Give me a few days, and I'll bring you two or three next time. The ideas are coming real easy now that I've started. Almost like the cards themselves are telling me what to do."

Winston patted him on the back. "I knew you'd work out, Johnny. You're a real player." He lifted his hand off his shoulder and toyed with his cigarette. "Just make sure you cover your tracks. We can only do so much to keep the cops away. And the more you rush, the easier it is to slip up."

"Just like any poker game," Johnny said, standing.

Winston nodded. "Listen, Johnny, I wanted to tell ya: you're doing real good. If you ever need more supplies—or if you need a woman to take that cook's place—you just let me know, and I'll see what I can do. That's my job, after all. To take care of you players." He tipped his hat. "Now get to it, Johnny. The game is sooner than you think."

"Sure thing," Johnny said, almost tagging the word "boss" onto the end of his sentence. He chuckled to himself while tonguing his gums and made his way out the front door. He walked around the concrete prison-like walls of the shelter and spotted Ferret's Nova beside the Fiesta he had parked in Gin's old spot earlier. And then he saw Ferret, sitting with his legs crossed on the hood, waiting. He looked exhausted, as if his wounds were draining him of all his strength: his face was badly bruised, his cheeks and forehead stained with large puddles of purple and yellow. The damage Johnny had given his eye was healing, but The Preacher had done far more to his face than Johnny had. His grinning mouth was split down the middle, like a sideways pair of extra lips, puckering red glass at Johnny: "Where's your woman?" Ferret asked.

"Gin's not coming to work today," Johnny said, reaching into his pocket. He tossed the extra photograph he'd taken onto the black hood beside Ferret's lap. Ferret's face folded in weird flaps as he glanced down at the picture of Gin's butchered body.

Johnny crossed his arms and waited.

Ferret finally looked up, peering deeply into Johnny's squinting eyes. "Nice work," he finally said. "Couldn't have done it better myself."

Johnny just nodded. "She was more trouble than she was worth. And really distracting, if you know what I mean."

"Oh yeah," Ferret said, twisting his wounded lips into a double-smile. "Oh yeah."

"Listen," Johnny said, popping a cigarette into his mouth and offering one to Ferret. Ferret waved the pack away as if scared of them, and Johnny recalled his fear of fire and the lit end he'd scared him with on Gin's waterbed. Johnny shrugged and lit his own, letting the flame linger before his face awhile to watch Ferret squirm. "I want to apologize for banging you up like I did. We're players, and we should know better, right? So let's call a truce." Johnny puffed, sizing up Ferret's looks. "Are we square, man?"

Ferret rolled his eyes downward, staring at Gin's card. "Shit," he said, not raising his eyes. "Only if I can keep this picture, I guess."

Johnny blew smoke from his nose. "Sure thing. It's a dupe. Just for you."

Ferret lazily flopped a palm out, and they shook. Gambler's honor. "Until the game then."

Squeezing his hand tightly, Johnny repeated: "Until the game."

# Play Dead

♠ ♠

Shorty looked at himself in the full-length mirror, curiously eyeing the features of his own face. He raised a hand to stroke his beard and traced a finger up his temples with the other, as if reshaping a clay bust of himself. But the person that faced him behind the glass wouldn't budge.

He had changed. Somehow, his face had changed when he wasn't paying attention. It had gotten older on its own accord—he looked more like his father than himself: dark rings around sunken eyes, jutting cheekbones angling his jaw like a fish, and fat, drooping ears. Shorty tugged on one of the lobes, trying to put it back the way it used to be.

Another face appeared beside his own in the mirror. "Can I help you, sir?"

Shorty kept his eyes glued to his own reflection. "I guess not," he said pressing the unmoving bones of his temples. His skin felt like a rubber mat draped over someone else's skull: his father's, teeth perpetually grinning.

The man slipped between Shorty and the mirror, blocking his vision. "If you're not going to buy anything, Sir, I'm going to have to ask you to leave." He prodded his cheek with a tongue and raised an eyebrow.

Shorty looked him up and down. The man wore a brown suit with a red tie. A gold watch and several effeminate rings. No name tag, though most of the other salesmen were wearing one. "What's your name?" Shorty asked.

"Stanley." The man cocked a hip, his suit pants swishing as he did so. "And you might be...?"

Shorty lowered his head, waiting for the salesman to finish his sentence.

The man twisted his palms likewise, waiting for Shorty.

"I'm looking for Jack," Shorty plainly said, breaking the man's stare to survey the rest of the department store. There were mirrors all around the building, right below the ceiling. Mirrors on every post. Mirrors on the walls and three-way mirrors in every corner. Mirrors everywhere. Just like the casinos.

"I think you have the wrong place," Stanley replied. "No one named Jack works here."

Shorty's face crinkled. "What? C'mon, this has gotta be the place."

The salesman shook his head. "I'm sorry. No Jacks here." He examined Shorty's attire with a scowl. "You might try the other end of the mall."

Shorty started walking, not bothering to turn around. He was too busy trying to capture himself in as many of the mirrors that surrounded him as possible. But his eyes could only find one at a time, and he couldn't shake the feeling that his father was out there in the mirrors that he *couldn't* see, multiplying, a whole crowd of fathers swarming together beneath the surface of the shiny ocean of mirrors. Gathering their strength to chase him from close behind like a school of piranha.

He stepped out of Piker's and emptied his lungs, twisting around to make sure that his father wouldn't follow him out. Satisfied that his reflections were still trapped in the department store, he walked the long concourse of the mall—the lettered sign of the other department store loomed at the opposite end from where he stood like a series of shaped suns on the horizon: BETTER BUYS.

And then he noticed the mirrors on the ceiling. Mirrors dripping lights, reflecting the necks of all the people walking in front of him. He craned his own neck upward, spotting himself standing there in the middle of the mall with his grocery bag. Losing his balance, he pulled his eyes away and spun around: more mirrors, everywhere, surrounding him. Mirrors lined the walls of the McDonald's on his left. Mirrors in the Optic Vision on his right. Mirrors reflecting mirrors.

He ran, no longer frightened by his father but by *himself*, reflected in every pane of glass. He felt trapped in a prison without walls, a house of infinite possibilities, of infinite Shorties living secret lives...

He almost ran right past the jewelry store that read DIAMONDS in large, mirrored lettering.

Shorty forced himself to stop and took a seat on the hardwood bench in the middle of the hall. He sat there, closing his eyes, clutching his bag, trying to convince himself that he was still Shorty, not his father, not someone else, just Shorty, the player, the gambler, the winner of Butcher Boy...

He opened his eyes. DIAMONDS.

Standing, Shorty slowly cut through the passers-by and entered the jewelry store. There were no shoppers inside, just two men in fancy suits standing behind a long row of glass cases (mirrored inside) like a barrier to stop him. Their faces instantly lit up with a practiced smile and then retracted as Shorty entered. The two men shot each other a glance, as if arguing over which one would get stuck serving their new customer. That glance said it all; Shorty knew he didn't belong in a place like this. But he kept his eyes stuck on theirs, avoiding the mirrors that surrounded him like bright spotlights.

The man on his left cocked his head and faked a smile. "And how can I help you this afternoon?"

Shorty looked down at his chest. No name tag. The other salesman—pretending to rearrange the rings in their cases—was nameless, too. "Um, is Jack here?"

"Jack?" The man looked over at the other. "You know Jack?"

Shorty smiled. "Is he here?"

"No," the guy said, checking a Rolex. "Jack doesn't come in for another hour. Was he working on something for you, or…?"

"Not yet," Shorty said with a broadened smile. "But I need him for a diamond."

"Perhaps I can help you," the salesman said. "I'm…"

Shorty dared to break away from his eyes and chance a look at the mirrors. Diamonds surrounded him, reflected in their glass-and-mirror cases. Rings and chains and bracelets, all draped over a deep plush felt as green as a blackjack table. Shorty crouched down to better see the diamond rings, their large clear and glinting rocks showering his eyes with kaleidoscopic color. And behind it all, in the background of his vision like a blurry painting, his own face had returned to the mirror.

A hand slipped in to block him. "…this here is our finest, and I'm sure your…um…*significant other*…would just *love* it." The hand craned and plucked a gem from the felt and snaked its way back out of the case.

Shorty frowned, loudly crunching his bag against his chest as he stood. The man behind the counter continued talking as he fingered the ring, but Shorty couldn't hear him any longer. He was thinking of his mother and father, dead, buried hand-in-hand back in Reno in Tinhorn Gardens Cemetery, still waiting for Shorty to hit it big and buy them a decent tombstone. Still waiting for Shorty to win at Butcher Boy.

He looked up at the salesman, tears blurring the bright lights in the shop into puddles of red and green. "Daddy never bought Mom a *real* diamond," he said, cocking his head. "I promise, I *promise*, Mommy. I'll buy that as soon as I win."

The salesman frowned while the other sauntered over for back-up.

Shorty twisted his shoulders and charged out of the store, entering the crowded aisles of the mall. He was crying and didn't even realize it until the tears made a splattering sound on his grocery bag. He didn't care about the mirrors anymore—they no longer scared him, because he now realized that no matter how many reflections surrounded him, no matter how many ghosts of his father tried to haunt him, no matter how many *significant others* encircled him, he was utterly alone and always had been ever since he came to Vegas.

Shorty returned to the wooden bench and sat down, waiting for Jack—his Jack of DIAMONDS—to show up for work. Reaching inside his pocket, he pulled out his practice deck with the Jack already right on top. Using its bent corner, he picked his teeth, flexing the card up so that he could see its red and yellow face while he did so.

In the face card he saw what might have been himself at an earlier age. And he realized that not all mirrors were made of glass.

Jack was closing up the jewelry store: pulling out trays of diamonds and sliding them into a large file cabinet-like safe. Shorty—playing poker solitaire on the darkened bench of the mall—patiently waited, occasionally glancing up through the chain-link security mesh that Jack had pulled down over the store entrance. His Jack was a hard worker—had made quite a few sales— and was himself as finely dressed in his pin-striped suit as royalty. He wore a Rolex and several rings; decked out in his expensive shoes and dutch-curled blonde hair, he was not only a salesman, but also a model for his wares. From his distance, though, Shorty found his eyes to be the most striking: grotesquely large and heavily-lidded with blue rings. He looked just like the picture on the card.

And he was trapped behind the chain-link door. Out of reach. Forbidden.

# Play Dead

Shorty scooped up his cards and dropped them in his grocery bag, keeping his eyes on Jack inside the store. He half-jogged over to the entrance — which reminded him of the cargo nets he could never climb in Junior High — and gripped the chain, rattling it to get his attention.

"We're closed," Jack said, not looking up from behind the counter.

"I need you to make me a trade," Shorty said eagerly.

Jack looked up, not making eye contact, but studying Shorty's body. "Go away or I'll call mall security."

"Wait, wait, just look at what I have..." Shorty bent over and dug inside his bag.

Jack approached the chained entrance, and fiddled with a drawstring.

Shorty stood up, his mother's necklace in his palm: "See, this has gotta be worth a lot of..."

Jack grinned. Then he noisily dropped down the secondary door — aluminum slats like metallic garage panels clattering between them — shutting Shorty out.

Shorty ran. He knew exactly where to go. Having seen Jack magically appear in the shop for his shift hours before, he realized that there was a back entrance, and had scouted it out while Jack was trying to con two lovers into buying overpriced wedding rings. Behind all the shops in the mall was a labyrinthine passageway: walls of gray cinderblock and white spackle, unfinished and sterile as a prison hallway. Shorty opened the unmarked brown door and entered the maze. He writhed his way through the passageways, finding the back door to the diamond store and back-tracking around the corner, so he could catch his Jack by surprise. Just like in cards, when you'd keep your Ace in the hole, and bet like it was still buried in the deck.

He heard voices and snuck a peek around the gray brick corner.

Jack was locking the door to the shop, a security guard in a black uniform standing beside him. He had a gun in a brown leather holster and was holding a large tan sack, like the moneybags Shorty had seen only in cartoons.

Shorty ducked back to his original position, cursing under his breath. He'd have to follow his Jack of Diamonds home. He turned, and made his way back through the labyrinthine tunnels, hearing more voices behind him.

Doors along the passageway were opening—people in suits stepping into his way and locking up—and it took Shorty a moment to realize that most of the shops were closing down now—the whole *mall* was closing—and maybe, just maybe that department store, Piker's, was closing, too, *opening up its back door to let his father out into the hallways…*

"Hey…" someone behind him called, and Shorty ran, not looking back, pedaling his feet just like he did when his father would chase him out of the bedroom. He turned a corner and spotted a restroom sign. Breathing heavily, he barged inside.

Dark and empty. One yellowing porcelain sink-and-mirror beside a pissed-on toilet seat. The toilet was making a running noise, as if it had just been flushed. An aluminum mop bucket leaked gray water into a puddle which trickled into the drain beneath it.

Shorty leaned against the door, listening to the voices pass by, wondering if his father was still out there.

Soon they faded, and Shorty placed his hand on the knob.

The door swung open, nearly pulling him with it, and Shorty snapped his hand backwards, spilling against the mop bucket in the corner. His grocery sack landed in the puddle with a wet *thwack*.

"Oops, I'm…*You!*" The face in the doorway squinted sickly.

Shorty dove and grabbed the man by the collar, pulling him inside: it was Stanley, the salesman from the department store. Only this time he was all alone—without Shorty's father in the mirrors for backup. Stanley grunted in his grip, but Shorty already had his hair in his fist and was bringing his skull down against the seat of the toilet. The white disk cracked off its hinges, a large oval spilling tiny beads of urine and blood onto the concrete floor. Shorty thought of cracked clams.

Stanley fell on his side, a tiny purple dot growing rapidly in the center of the large pink welt on his temple.

Shorty moved slowly. He picked his grocery sack out of its puddle, and the bottom fell out, scattering goods all over the floor. He picked the camera up first, checking to make sure it was still dry. Anger pulsed in his eyes, dimming the room with each strobing heartbeat. He turned around and locked the door.

# Play Dead

Stanley moaned.

Shorty looked at himself in the mirror. Tiny bullets of sweat were in the folds of skin above and below his tired eyes. His beard looked full and alive, each hair standing on end.

He looked like himself again.

Setting the camera on the back of the still-running toilet, he grabbed the mirror by its sides. It was heavy, but slipped easily out of place. Carefully, he held it horizontally over the sink, looking down his nose to see his own reflection—the stubble under his chin, his flaring nostrils, his dark and widening eyes—as he brought the back of the mirror against the rim of the sink. It cracked neatly in half, making a sound like folded cardboard. Stepping over to Stanley, he fingered its exposed edge. It was sharp enough to do the trick. What had his mother always said to his dad when they needed to do something they didn't want to for money? "Jack, honey, you know how it is: *Necessity is the mother of avengin'*." Or something like that. Shorty thought of her smiling voice whispering that phrase in his ear as he straddled Stanley's body and brought the mirror neatly down into his stomach.

It went into him easier than he thought it would, like a butterknife cutting a sandwich.

The salesman's eyes burbled open and discovered only his own horrified reflection staring back at him. His sight trailing down to abstractly gaze at the red and yellow goo squishing up from his gut at the bottom of the mirror.

"Here, Jack," Shorty said as he grabbed the mop and put its handle into the man's out-thrust, clenching palm. "This will have to do." The man's hand obeyed on its own accord—a large diamond ring coming into view as its fingers twisted around the wooden pole. His shoulders eased down, and he gently rested his head on the floor. The bruise on his forehead was spreading purple fingers towards his eyes. Shorty knew he'd have to act fast. He picked up his camera, and adjusted the mirror with a free hand to make sure it would make an equally bisected reflection in the card, just like the face card.

"Gotcha, Dad," he said as he pressed the red button on the camera. The light from the Polaroid's flashbulb slapped and caught on the skin of his eyes like the blazing facet of a diamond. "I gotcha."

Johnny opened up Violet's Tarot deck while she poured thick drinks from her blender. The top card was of a man hanging upside-down by his ankles from a rope, a hangman's noose over his foot. He turned it over—right side up, the dude looked like a dancer, leg cocked beneath him as if he had nothing in the world to worry about.

"So," Johnny said watching Violet light up a cigarette. "When did you paint these here cards?"

Violet kept smoking, turning her eyes on him. They stared at each other for a moment, reading one another's poker faces. Finally, Violet broke: "How'd ya know I did 'em, Sherlock?"

Johnny nodded down at the deck in his hands. "The initials in the corner. Too small to read, but the same handwriting as the signature on that painting in the living room of the dogs. Betcha thought I didn't see that those dogs were playing with Tarot cards, either."

Violet chuckled in the back of her throat—a guttural sound that rattled her dentures. "Not bad, Johnny-boy. Not bad at all. You're pretty good at readin' folks. You know when to call a spade a spade. That's the gambler in ya."

It felt good to hear Violet say that. He smiled, reaching for his cigarettes.

"And when you win that game of yours," she continued, "you better buy me some new garden tools."

Johnny laughed so loud his teeth whistled.

Gin stepped into the dining room wearing the frilly robe that Johnny himself had worn on his first night at Violet's. She dug under her ears with a pink towel, right above the large bandage taped over her neck. "What's so funny out here? Is he flirting with you again, Violet?"

"Yup," she said smiling over at Johnny. "Your boy here's just one big flirt. You better watch him, or I'm liable to take him from ya."

Johnny was blushing behind his cigarette, winking at Violet. "I'm yours."

Gin sat down beside Johnny at the bar, and the three of them looked in opposite directions, grinning. Gin nervously scratched her stomach beneath the robe.

Violet swallowed her drink. "Are you sure you're all right, honey?"

"Much better now. Thanks for letting me use the shower—all that red stuff Johnny poured on me was giving me the creeps. That and those rusty little shovels bent under my shirt. So itchy!"

"It had to look real. You know that," Johnny said, smoking. "And getting you out of the picture is worth a little food coloring on your stomach, ain't it?"

Gin nodded.

"Well you didn't have to dig the hell out of my backyard," Violet said. "My neighbors must be talking up a storm."

Johnny leaned over his arms on the bar. "Shit, I didn't think of that…"

"Here, sweetie." Violet poured Gin a glass and slid it over to her. "Don't worry none, Johnny. I'll just tell 'em I took in some boarders, a student couple taking art classes at the college. They'll believe it."

"They better," Johnny replied. His new loose tooth felt sideways in his mouth, scraping the inside of his lip when he talked. He tongued it, and it shifted in its socket with a clicking noise only he could hear. He toyed with it like a trigger in his jawbone. "What about Winston? I know he's your bookie. But does he know where you live? We're not gonna get any surprise visits from him, are we?"

Gin's eyes widened. "That bastard's your bookie?"

She nodded impatiently at Gin, her eyes glued to Johnny's. "He don't know nothin' but to meet me at the Shanty every Monday morning, and how to count my money. He won't know crap."

Johnny nodded. Everything seemed to be in order for their hustle. "Well I gotta catch up on my suit. Winston says the others are near their face cards already."

Gin sighed.

"I don't quite get all this," Violet said, leaning forward. "I mean, I get the general gist: you guys gotta fake a buncha pictures and all that, playin' dead and foolin' Nebo into thinking they're for real. But how are you gonna find folks willin' to pose for you like Gin did, with all that shit stickin' out of her chest like a gardener gone berserk? I just don't see it happening."

Both of them faced her at the same time.

Her face blanched—pale purple to powder white. "Oh no. No ya don't. Not me. I ain't gonna be your dummy."

Johnny cocked his head. Violet tore her eyes away. "No. No-siree. Uhn-uh. Not happening."

Gin looked at Johnny, shrugging with a pout. "If she won't do it, she won't do it."

Johnny signaled her to hold on with his palm. "Violet? Remember our wager? You owe me a favor." He leaned toward her, trying to regain eye contact. "You're not welchin' on our little bet, are you?"

She rolled an eye up at him. "You know damned well I'm not. Lettin' your girlie and you stay with me is favor enough. But I ain't gonna be one of your spade cards, Johnny. I just don't got it in me."

"And why not?"

"'Cuz Winston'll see it right away. He'll know it's me."

"We can fix that," Johnny said. "Hell, we can make it look like you don't even *have* a face, if you want us to."

She shook *no* with her head, frowning seriously, looking something like one of the dogs in her painting. "Nope, he'd know. He'd sense it. I've known the bastard for years." She was staring at the floor as if ashamed.

Gin had a hand on Johnny's thigh. "Don't push her…"

"Violet, look at me."

Hesitantly, she obeyed.

"That's not it at all, is it?" Johnny searched her face. She looked pale, the color receding from her natural splotches. "You're thinking about something else. Something's scarin' you."

Gin's grip tightened on his leg, fingernails pressing into bone.

She stared at the floor. "Damn you, Johnny." She refused to look up, her head hung low. "You're too damned good at spotting people for your own good." She wiggled her lips. "Gamblers. Why do I put up with 'em?"

Johnny stared her down, reminded by her voice of her ex-husband, Dutch. "Spill it, Violet. What gives?"

211

Her head snapped up and she flashed him an impetuous face. "You think you're so smart, you tell me."

"This ain't no quiz show, Violet. I've got no idea. But there's something going on here, isn't there? What's going down?"

She blinked. "I'm close enough to death as it is. And you want me to practice."

"Uh," Gin released Johnny's leg and stood, scratching her stomach again. "I'm gonna dry my hair."

They ignored her, staring each other down.

Violet lit up another cigarette. Johnny could smell the mint in the air. "This might sound corny to you, Johnny. But to tell ya the truth, I don't want to lose myself in the card."

"Say what?"

"Like the Tarot. You remember. When you tap the deck, it feeds off part of you."

Johnny leaned back. "Give me a break, Violet. You'd just be posin' for a picture, that's all."

"Not if the card is meant to be played. And it's more than that, too. You wanna know what scares me, Johnny? What really scares me shitless?"

"What?"

"You do." She stood up, tapping an ash in the nearby tray. "Nothin' personal. But like I told you, when an artist makes a card, they channel the Fates. And that's playin' with fire, 'cuz you never know who's really in charge of the creatin'." She took a deep drag. "I know, because I've done it." She nodded at the Tarot deck Johnny had been playing with earlier. "You don't think I'm *that* good of an artist, do you? Hell, no. I didn't make them cards all by myself."

"You mean to tell me you honestly believe in all that mumbo-jumbo? C'mon!" Johnny reconsidered her logic while he took a hit from his smoke. "Even if it's true, what I'm doin' for Nebo is just a sick game. It ain't nothin' like the Tarot."

"Ain't it?"

They had another staring match. Johnny thought about the other cards he'd done, how he'd literally seen the very Spades he was creating: in Ferret's eyes, in Gin's chest, everywhere around him. It was all in the details, when he paid close attention: potential spades, waiting to be made. Violet raised a good question and Johnny knew it. Who was really in charge of doing the creating? Johnny didn't believe that he was actually possessed by the Fates or channeling dead spirits or anything so corny...but was he *in charge*? Not altogether.

Gin returned in a jersey T-shirt and blue jeans. She was scratching her chest and stomach. "You really did a number on my body with those shovels, Johnny. Really rough. Good thing I'm dead already, 'cause I don't think I wanna go through that again. I got little scratches all over the goddamned place." She parted a gap in her robe and showed them a puckering line of scar beside her navel. "Don't look too good either."

Johnny didn't need to look at Violet. He could feel the heat of her glare.

Violet, monotone: "There's some lotion in the medicine chest, dear."

"Just what I need." She winked at Johnny and returned to the bathroom.

Johnny needed another cigarette. "*Bullshit*," he said, though he didn't sound like he meant it at all. He pressed his tooth for the pain, trying to remember cutting Gin up, but unable to conjure the memory. His gaze turned to the Tarot deck, with its hanging man doing an upside-down jig. His grin was a smiling frown—a cocky paradox like the Joker in a deck of cards: wild, everything and nothing at once. "This is all just bullshit."

# Play Dead

Violet's ad in the college paper — "models wanted for experimental photographer" — turned up spades. Too many of them. She received at least twenty-five phone calls, and only barely managed to whittle the volunteers down to four or five willing to play dead for Johnny's photographs. And that number *didn't* include herself, because — as she insistently reminded Johnny — "I ain't no dog, and I'll never roll over and play dead for nobody."

Gin and Johnny had collaborated for two afternoons to plan the cards. They drank gallons of coffee and went through at least two cartons of cigarettes, inventing on paper the best designs they could come up with, in hopes that Johnny would get the highest stake possible on game day. Johnny appreciated the help — he was a player, not a preparer. He didn't think he was very creative when it came to "planning." If he had been, he probably never would have chosen a life of gambling — or the loss that came with it.

Gin, on the other hand, was quite creative, and Johnny figured her talent came from her job as a freelance investigator. She was obsessive, intense regarding the details, entirely wrapped up in trying to imagine each card beforehand. The process was simple: Johnny would lay the proper spade from his practice deck down on Violet's bar, and Gin would stare at it, rattling off the first thing that came to her mind. Johnny took notes on her free associations, and occasionally pursued an idea more deeply, asking her follow-up questions. Violet — when she wasn't yakking on the phone with a prospective model — would toss an idea or two into the pot, as well. Johnny would write these down, but didn't put much stake in them, since they all related to the tarot in one way or another. And he didn't even want to *think* about Nebo's twisted plans for the deck.

When the day came to first meet their models — "Spay-day" Violet called it, giving Johnny enough cash to pay the models before heading out to The Shanty — Johnny spent the morning looking back over their notes. By this time, a lot of scribbles and doodles in the shape of spades covered the page, a great deal of his handwriting was illegible, and most of the ideas looked pretty pathetic in writing. He wasn't quite sure they were ready. But as Gin reminded him, everything would work out and more ideas would come once they started posing people for the cards. "Just like research," she'd said, "where just doing it is half the inspiration." Still, Johnny wanted to get the game plan straight in his head. He looked over his practice deck and tried to remember what the notes were supposed to mean. The underlined parts of the random notes read something like this:

SEVEN—a crying skull—an M or W—7 aspen leaves or Xmas trees—lucky seven

EIGHT—eating, ate—5 up, 3 down—octopus arrows—crazy eights

NINE—letter H—suspenders—"suffering" (tarot)—comma—not much here

TEN—decimal—deck-a (cards?)—percent—tennispades....

"We're fucked," Johnny said, looking up from the list at Gin.

"Whatta ya mean?" Gin sat beside Johnny on the brown vinyl sofa, scratching her stomach with a vague look on her face—a wide open double arch of eyebrows.

"I mean we're *screwed*. None of this makes any sense to me anymore. Look here." He pointed down at the list with a dirty fingertip, "'A crying skull.' Just what the hell is that supposed to mean?"

Gin withdrew the Seven of Spades from Johnny's Bicycle deck. "See," she said, tracing the pattern of the pips on the card with a long, red-painted nail, "The two spades on top look like the eyes of a skull, and the four running down from 'em—two on each side—look like teardrops. Don't they? And here, the one in the middle: it looks like a bony nose."

"I don't see it at all."

Gin picked a pen up from the coffee table and scribbled a line around the upper pips, inscribing a circle roughly corresponding to the shape of a human head. "See now?"

Johnny looked at the card. He saw the crying skull, but thought it looked childishly crude: a crayon drawing by a psychotic five-year-old. He scratched the whiskers of an upturned chin with the card, and looked down his nose at Gin. "Uh-huh. Don't you think you're stretching it just a little bit?"

She crossed her legs. "Well…isn't that what being creative is all about? Taking what's already there and stretching it around until you got something new?"

"There's a difference between bein' creative and just bein' plain old hard up."

The door knocked. Gin grinned. She bounced out of Violet's sofa and opened the door. A kid decked out in punk rock gear with jet black bangs spiked over his eyes and an earring in the shape of a skull stood in front of her, trying to peek over her shoulder. Johnny thought he looked like an underage kid trying to look old enough to sneak into a bar. "I'm here for the modeling job," he said, his voice in the form of a curious question.

Gin's face lit up. She took him by the pale hand and led him inside the living room, her smile wide and toothy. "Johnny, I'd like you to meet Lucky Seven."

The boy reached forward. "Nice to meet you, sir."

Johnny cocked an eyebrow as they shook. "You ready to die, kid?"

Lucky Seven brushed the hair from his eyes and flashed an artificial smile. Black stains dribbled down his cheeks—tattooed tears, Johnny quickly realized. "As ready as always," the kid said, puffing his cheeks apathetically.

Johnny looked down at Gin's circle on the card: *a crying skull*. He looked back up at the punk, not quite believing his luck. The kid blinked. His eyelids were blackened with mascara and eye-liner in death-mask perfection. Not quite enough tears leaked in ink from his blood-shot eyes, but Johnny could fix that.

"Gin," Johnny said, standing up, "why don't you go get some of Violet's make-up for our Seven of Spades here?"

She was already in the bathroom, digging through drawers.

Johnny curled up at the foot of the sofa, reviewing the Polaroids on Violet's purple satin quilt. Gin looked down at him from the leather couch above.

"Listen to that," she whispered. "Violet's snoring."

216

Johnny hummed in agreement, wondering if she forgot to remove her dentures. He slipped the Spades out of his bicycle deck and spanked them down one by one beside their appropriate photographs as if playing Solitaire. "You think Winston's gonna buy these?"

"Of course he will," Gin replied. She didn't look at the cards. She didn't have to. The shots had gone perfectly. Much better than they'd planned. Every model had shown up at the doorstep with something subtle about them that supplemented their original ideas—like the punk kid with the tattooed teardrops, or the woman whose eyes looked *naturally* insane when they buckled her up in a sheet-turned-straitjacket for the Crazy Eight. "Those cards are perfect."

"But don't you think it's just a bit too coincidental that these models fit the cards perfectly? I mean—shit—we couldn't come up with half of the ideas they did, just by being themselves."

"Truth is stranger than fiction, eh?"

"No, it's not that. It's just...I dunno...*weird*."

He could hear her scratching, pondering. "It's not coincidence. You're just lucky, Johnny. Charmed. That's all."

He rolled over to look up at her, and caught a flash of smooth shins, gliding together as she rubbed her feet above him. "But I don't *feel* lucky at all. It's more like these cards want to make themselves. Like Violet was tellin' me: I'm not in charge. *They* are."

Gin smirked. "Give me a break. You're not buying into that fortune-teller horse shit now, too, are you?"

Johnny tilted his head to stare up at the ceiling. A blank white slate. "I don't know."

He heard her rustling around above him, the leather sofa making strange crumpling and squeaking noises. He turned to look up at her again, but Gin was on her way down to him, rolling down from the sofa and sliding onto Johnny's chest. She was warm, soft. Naked.

"Wha…"

Gin's mouth stifled the question from his lips, catching his curled tongue with her own. She slickened the dry washboard of the roof of his mouth with

217

its tip, then licked the gap between his front teeth. Johnny did the same to the soft underside of her tongue, lapping the smooth flaps of skin there while she discovered and applied pressure to his new loose tooth, shifting its roots. The tooth signed Morse Code messages he couldn't understand up his jaw-line and into his brain. He licked her tongue, urging her to continue.

Gin began working his underwear down his thighs with one hand while gently brushing the hair around his ears with the other, carefully keeping her breasts pressed tightly against his ribs, their tips like hard plastic buttons. Using a toe, she slid the elastic band of his shorts around his ankles and over his feet.

Johnny rolled her sideways, onto her back, softly stretching her arms up over her head, gentling holding them splayed by gripping the bones of her wrists. Her hands clenched and unclenched, pawing air. She writhed beneath him, gliding the smooth flat canopy of flesh that stretched over her pelvis against his pulsing groin, teasing him with the rim of her navel as she gyrated. Johnny released her wrists to dig his fingers into a thatch of blond hair, bringing her tiny earlobe to his lips like a mouth to a kiss. He probed and Gin squirmed.

Arms free, she reached for something from her toppled purse by the foot of the sofa, and then slid both hands down her stomach, teasing Johnny's penis with the sharp tips of her fingernails. He prodded her ear as deep as he could with his tongue, letting her know he liked it. He didn't even feel the condom being slid onto him, only felt the grip of her palms, tightening. She guided him inside her, gracefully, never stopping the established rhythm of her always grinding hips. She was tight and wet around him—holding him in her grip like a greased blood pressure sleeve—their pulses thumping together hard and then releasing.

He pulled out of her to stop himself from letting go too quickly and crouched between her legs, running his flickering tongue down from her shoulders to her breasts, lapping at her nipple as she lifted her hips and twisted away. Gin's tit slipped free of his mouth and he kneeled up behind her, his hands sliding down to her hips, gently squeezing down on the tight, smooth sides of her ass—and her fingers were already there, sliding him inside, cupping his hard testicles and squeezing gently, urging him to buck against her. She craned her neck and Johnny opened his eyes...

To see the cards and photographs, clinging to the sweat on her back, glinting flashes of light in the darkness.

To see spades.

She rocked awhile and then moaned, pounding angrily against him. Johnny held on, staring at the cards that glistened on her back like black-and-white tattoos. Gin's hair whipped one off her shoulderblade as she thrashed her head from side to side, bucking.

Johnny released a hand to pick one of the cards from her back. The card made a shredding sound, like the removal of a bandage. Gin groaned. He brought the spade to his mouth and licked the sweat from its face. He tasted Gin—salty, menthol, plastic.

Johnny let himself fall forward while Gin continued to fuck, the muscles of her cheeks tight and flexing against his abdomen as he felt the cold plastic of the cards and photographs against his chest. He reached around Gin— a card in each hand—and pressed their cool surface against the pink tips of her nipples.

Gin moaned, arching her back.

He brought the cards back to his mouth one at a time, licking them, and then sticking them like stamps to the supple underbelly of her dangling, sloshing breasts. The edges tickled her nipples, cutting against the spongy, purple flesh like wide fingernails.

He reached underneath to caress the tight muscles of her flexing stomach.

Gin grunted—a guttural groan he could feel inside her. Violently, she pulled on him.

Johnny prodded the source of her pain—the thin scars on her stomach and chest—the wounds he'd made with Violet's garden spades. He traced the sharp edges of his fingernails across their length. The scabs peeled, flecking down from his palms.

Gin was still mumbling with each thrust. Her eyes were tight slits of mascara, teary in the corners. She looked pained. And yet intensely beautiful.

Johnny reached for the Polaroid camera on the coffee table.

# Play Dead

Gin quickened her pace, rhythmically punching her butt back into his hips like a giant sweaty boxing glove, nearly pushing him back on his ankles. She snapped her head from side to side, and Johnny could feel those motions echoed inside of her. She was still mumbling, uttering something angry and hateful with each rising thrust of breath.

Her wet ass spread before him like the two heavy leaves of a spade.

He shot his picture just as he exploded in pleasure.

But Gin wasn't finished yet. She had slid one of the cards down from her tits, and was pressing it against her clitoris, its plastic shell crumpling and popping from the pressure of her fingers, its plastic edge scraping the condom on the underside of Johnny's softening member. And she was still uttering what sounded like curses as she groaned and beat her rear end against him. He leaned forward, trying to hear her words. His ears rang and drummed with blood, but he couldn't make out what she was saying.

He only knew that Violet was no longer snoring.

And that the photograph that spat out from the mouth of the camera had landed on Gin's undulating back. Developing as she whimpered then roared in orgasm, black-and-white to color.

"No slip-ups, right?"

"Right," Johnny answered, not quite sure.

Winston frowned, fanning the five photographs in his grip like a poker hand that Johnny had just dealt. Showing him only the black-and-white backs of the Polaroids, Winston scanned their edges, shuffled them, and arranged them in the order of a straight flush; Spades, Jack high.

Johnny nervously set fire to the end of a cigarette. He wished he had a drink to kill the flavor of urine that was collecting on his tongue from the shelter's odors. Another to kill the pain in his jaw from the tooth he'd lost in the sink earlier that morning. And another to quench the uneasiness tickling up the back of his skull as Winston closely examined his faked cards.

Winston shook his head, sadly. His hat made a wispy shifting sound on his head.

Johnny double-puffed his cigarette, leaning forward with a noisy creak of the cot they sat on. "What's the matter." It was a statement, not a question.

Winston tsk-ed, tipping his hat to reveal eyebrows raised over closed eyes. He was swallowing again, and Johnny recognized these tell-tale signs of his anger.

"*What?*"

"I'm afraid," Winston said, opening his eyes to probe Johnny's, "that this is the best damned set of cards I've seen yet. The other players are gonna *kill you* when they see how many chips you're gonna get for these."

Johnny's chest burst out nervous bubbles of laughter.

Winston grinned. "I especially like your Jack of Spades, here." Winston fanned the hand again, pointing down at the gory puddle of red on the right side of the model's face where an eyeball should have been. "A *One-Eyed* Jack. I'm surprised no one else thought of doing that yet."

Johnny raised an eyebrow. "Me, too." It had seemed like such an obvious way to do the card. Johnny recalled how the model—a round-shouldered, biker type—had one lazy eye that seemed to follow behind the other eye's trail like a retarded second cousin as it scanned the haphazard junk on the walls of Violet's living room.

Winston slapped Johnny's back. "I knew you'd work out, my man. You're pretty much all caught up with other players now."

"Glad to hear it." Johnny wondered just how far the others were.

Winston toyed with his belt buckle—a well-polished silver slab with a racehorse on it. "So the game's a go, then, for Sunday."

His eyes shot open. "Sunday? *This* Sunday?"

Winston stood. "Yup. Six days. Judging by how quickly you did your latest, I'm sure you can come up with the rest of your suit by then."

Johnny's mind was racing. He needed to find two more models in less than six days. A Queen and a King. And they had to be better than the rest.

"C'mon," Winston said, patting Johnny's tense shoulder. "Let's grab some grub."

Johnny obeyed, though he sickened at the thought of digesting the shelter's food again. Violet was spoiling him, and he liked it that way. But he supposed it was best to show his face around, to let the other players know Winston was on his side…and that he was still in the game.

The line was short, and Johnny and Winston stood their places silently, waiting.

Shorty passed by—struggling to balance his paper plate—and didn't even notice Johnny. He figured Shorty was avoiding him on purpose—he'd said before that they could no longer be friends since Johnny was a player now—and that suited Johnny just fine. But he couldn't ignore the ring that Shorty was wearing, a large, shining gem in contrast to the waste matter on his paper plate: a diamond ring.

Johnny nudged Winston, nodding at the jewelry.

Winston shrugged—cautious to discuss anything about the game while others stood nearby. He whispered: "He says it's for his parents in Reno. Stole it off his last card."

Johnny frowned. How could Shorty walk around in a *homeless shelter* with an expensive diamond ring on his hand for everyone to see? And why hadn't he gambled it away by now?

The line moved forward, and Johnny half-expected to see Gin there, winking at him. In her place, The Preacher stood behind the counter, spooning runny clumps of bright red meatloaf onto their paper plates. After topping them off with a gray gravy and a cheap excuse for a biscuit, he'd routinely make the sign of the cross over the food, mumbling a prayer.

"Praise the Lord," The Preacher said, lifting the sagging plates up to hand to them.

He recognized Johnny immediately, and turned to glare at Winston. His mouth was twisted in a bespittled sneer. A droplet of saliva landed in his plate.

Winston to Johnny: "Preacher here took over after your girl, um, quit. Nice of him to volunteer, eh?"

The Preacher supplemented his speech as if it were a distraction, "Anything for the Lord." He kept his eyes glued to Winston's, trying to communicate something secret.

Winston mimicked him, reaching for his plate. "Praise the Lord."

The Preacher blinked. Then he sprung. Spilling both of their plates down onto the counter, The Preacher leaned forward and gripped the outside edge of the countertop with both of his hands. "*It's you*," he grunted, staring in disbelief at Johnny, pulling back on the counter as if to break it in half.

Johnny retracted his jaw. "Sure is. Last I checked, anyway."

"You! I know what you did. Ferret showed me your card." His chin began gibbering, bubbles of spit popping in the corners of his purpling lips: "*You stole my heart, you bastard!*"

Now Johnny knew who the third player for Sunday's game was, and why he was following Gin that night he saved her from Ferret—not because he had a crush on her, as Gin believed, but because she was supposed to be The Preacher's card, not Ferret's. He was saving her only to kill her himself.

Johnny snatched his nearly empty plate and backed away, not bothering to answer The Preacher's glare with anything but a coy lift of his lips. *Good thing I beat you to it*, he thought.

Winston was instantly in the player's face, like a Marine drill sergeant, the brim of his hat tapping against The Preacher's forehead. Johnny watched as he grumbled at him to *shut the fuck up* if he wanted to stay in the game.

# Play Dead

Winston slowly peeled himself away from The Preacher's accusatory stare, the look on his face daring The Preacher to say another word. Together, Winston and Johnny walked back toward the room of cots.

"*Damn you*," The Preacher uttered, slapping a new scoop of red meatloaf into a plate for the next man in line. "*Damn you to Hell*," he repeated, blessing the next person's plate with another imaginary cross.

Johnny pretended not to hear his curses, and looked down at his food. "Wonder how meatloaf cooked with fire and brimstone tastes?"

Winston rolled his eyes at him. He'd left his own plate on the counter, and was tapping a cigarette out of a pack magician-style and popping it into his mouth.

As they walked along the cots amidst the sound of smacking lips and drooling "yums," Johnny spotted Ferret, mouth agape atop a balled-up green blanket. Dark bruises were still evident on his face, and his large nose quivered with a snore. Johnny considered adding a new bruise to his collection, since he'd shown another player—The Preacher—his card. But Johnny knew it was his own fault for making the duplicate and giving it to him in the first place—and he knew it was better to make them all think Gin was dead, then to have them stalking her for their cards. Besides, it sometimes paid to show your hand before the next deal.

The coincidence bothered him, though—two players (three, if he included himself), all going after the same woman to make a card for Nebo's deck. Again, he felt as though maybe the cards were creating themselves. Perhaps Fate—if it existed—didn't approve of cheating?

"That's weird," Johnny said to Winston. "Look at Ferret. He's sleeping through lunch."

Winston smoked. "The fucker's been sick lately. Always bitchin' about migraines and what not like a little girl. And I've had enough of his shit. He better get his act together or he's foldin'." He puffed in punctuation.

Johnny recalled that Ferret had his own car—that outdated black Nova—and he wondered what he was even doing at the shelter in the first place. Probably came to turn in a card, Johnny figured. He wondered what it could be. He wondered what *everyone's* cards would look like on game day. What had they done? What were they capable of inventing? Winston had said that Johnny's latest batch was far better than anything they'd turned in. If Winston wasn't lying—which he could have been—Johnny wondered just how creative the other players were, and just how crafty they'd be when it came down to playing the game itself.

And he wondered if they—like himself—were even remotely in charge of what they were doing anymore.

They sat down at Winston's cot. Johnny picked what appeared to be a stringy vein out of his meatloaf and took a bite. It was difficult to chew. The holes between his teeth throbbed as the meat plugged into the gaps with each bite.

Johnny looked at the thick bulge of photographs behind the fabric of Winston's breast pocket and wondered what awaited him Sunday.

# Play Dead

The Preacher scrubbed blackened crisps from the bottom of his meatloaf pan with a green pad of steel wool. He thought about what he had witnessed today, thanks to God's favor. A lesson had been learned—one that remained to be taught: *Thou shalt not steal.*

The new player, Johnny, had stolen from him. Stolen the Queen right from his deck. Stolen the blessed food right from his hands. Stolen his hope.

He was a thief, a robber of not only the Lord's servant, but the Lord himself. He'd taken the name of the Baptist, the name of Jesus' disciple, the name of one of the Gospels: John. And he'd taken the body of Christ into his mouth as if it were merely a soup cracker.

The Preacher twisted the hot water knob on the large aluminum sink that reflected his image and scalded the soapy grime from the bottom of the pan. Every last morsel of the food he'd blessed had been eaten, taken into the mouths and stomachs of the needy sinners. He'd received compliments on the meal—and he knew that he had saved some souls on this day, giving them communion, the body of Christ, the blessed *heart* of Jesus, body and blood of the Savior, manifest in the many hearts he'd sacrificed and collected and ground into the meatloaf. These poor souls were God's children, though they did not know it. And today, a victorious warrior for God, he'd saved all of their rotten souls, whether they wanted it or not.

Including the pilfering sinner named Johnny.

He hoped the communion the thief had taken in sacrilege was burning a hole in his stomach. Like holy water on a demon. A silver cross on the undead.

But for the others, he hoped he had repaid his debt to the Lord.

The change in his plans was discomforting, but he knew—like Job and Abraham—that he had to sacrifice his own desires for his servitude. The hearts were originally meant for his Queen. He'd planned on stuffing her with them—filling her empty shell of a soul with the one thing that her lust ignored—the hearts of those she damned—the beating engine of God in everyone's chest which she herself did not possess. But in reflection, The

Preacher recalled that now, as always, the Lord worked in mysterious ways. And he was always with him. This mass communion of the Lord's sacred hearts for the homeless was much better than his previous plan. Instead of damning one woman—Queen of Whores, whose vanquishment had been stolen from him by an undeserving sinner—he'd saved the souls of the innocent. Souls who were victims of the world's vice, not knowing better to save themselves.

Still, The Preacher cursed himself for letting Gin go that night when Ferret, too, had tried to steal her from him. He knew he should have jumped ahead in the deck and made her card right then, right in the car, right when he had the chance. But he didn't have his hearts with him that night. And Johnny had beaten him to it—stealing her right out from under him. He set the meatloaf pot in the drain, and asked the Lord not only for forgiveness for his doubting, but also whether he should punish this thief of the Lord who had disobeyed his commandment: Thou shalt not steal.

*Thou shalt not kill* echoed back in his mind in reply.

"Except for you, my Lord," he added aloud.

*And* THOU *shalt not steal, Preacher.*

And he suddenly realized that the Lord had taught him a lesson he hadn't seen coming...that it was *himself* who had stolen from the Lord—the money he'd gambled away from his church before he had ever come here to this new mission. If the new player, Johnny, had stolen from him at all, it was to teach him the evil of his own ways, to remind him that he himself had a debt to pay the Lord. Johnny was a message-bearer, a mouthpiece for the Lord.

Now he knew how the Lord had felt when he'd robbed him. Paying him back with the souls he had just blessed with the Holy Communion was not enough to undo what he had once done. He had to complete his mission—to repay God with the money he'd win from the poker game—in order to make up for his sin.

Or give God what remained if he lost: to sacrifice himself. Because if he couldn't repay what he owed the Lord, he'd rather not live any longer.

Win or lose, though, he knew that this time the game would be played on his own. Although the Lord was in his soul, he could not count on the Lord to play the game for him, like he had before, and lost it all. This time it would be his own decisions that would make or break him. He was calling the shots. It was a heavy burden—but one he was willing to take.

Only two cards left...

Something clicked. The Preacher opened his eyes to see Shorty snapping his fingers in front of his face like a hypnotist. "Hey, Preach. Great meal. I've never had meatloaf like that before. What'd you put in it?"

"Bless you, my son," Preacher replied, reaching a hand out to caress Shorty's cheek.

Shorty stumbled backwards, The Preacher's fingernail scratching his face. "Ouch!" He rubbed his face with a ringed finger. "Hey, none of that. Just wanted to say thanks."

"You have the Lord to thank. Not me." The Preacher smiled at him.

Shorty said, "Whatever," and walked away.

The Preacher watched him leave, happy for his saved soul, genuinely pleased with sharing the body and blood of the Lord with the cleansed sinner. He knew that he'd tricked them all—like cheating at cards—by sneaking His hearts into their food. But there was no other way. Miracles—like causing the blind to see or resurrecting the dead—were *forced* upon their receivers. Like an unexplainable accident that only God understood.

And as Shorty left the kitchen, his eyes couldn't help but focus on the thin red line he'd accidentally drawn on Shorty's cheek with his fingernail. The scratch was an omen—the blood that rose to the skin, a reminder. A new lesson had been learned.

And once again it had to do with Johnny Frieze.

Elsewhere in the shelter, vomit splattered wetly on the floor.

Johnny needed a break from walking. Violet's house seemed much farther away from the shelter than it had the day he'd ran its distance after burying Axe's body. Today the sun was a bright white disk behind a protein gray sky—a rare cool day for Vegas—its feeble light dulling the edges of everything he looked at. But it made him tired.

Reaching a busy corner of the Strip, he sat on a purple and white bench beside the crosswalk outside The Circus Casino. Traffic lights dangled and clicked audibly overhead. A newspaper machine stood beside him, brimming with cheap flyers for phone sex and escort services. It was red, with the word FREE etched over its handle. Tourists and losers passed by, eyes glued to the unnecessary flashing lights on the Strip, ignoring both Johnny and the red box he sat beside. Thinking of his night with Gin, he slipped the crumpled glossy photograph from his back pocket and looked down at its chemical colors. The round white surface of the sun glared out at him, censoring his vision of anything but the perfectly tapering V of Gin's spiny back. He curled the photograph's edges and stared at the pornographic image, admiring its accidental genius: in the shadows, it resembled a fleshy Ace of Spades.

*How easy*, his mind urged. *How easy it would be to exchange this for Axe's Ace of Spades in the deck.*

He still wasn't used to the idea of having to play Axe's old cards for his suit. They not only disgusted him: what bothered him more was that they weren't his creations at all. It was like painting a portrait, only to have someone else's signature in its corner. But then again, time was running out. He'd have to come up with even more cards to fill out his suit if he wanted to replace Axe's cards. More models. In less than a week. He still had the King and Queen to go.

Besides. He wanted to keep this photograph. His Ace in the hole, so to speak. It inspired him. And just like his gold tooth had once helped him keep his confidence, so, too, would this card. Because no matter what happened—

win or lose—in the long run, he'd always have something to fall back on. A rich visual memory of Gin's desire.

A small crowd of pale-legged tourists and men in polyester business suits approached him, clustered together from the opposite side where a street sign mutated from a solid red DON'T WALK into a flashing green WALK. Johnny pocketed the photo, thinking how crazy it was that Vegas brought so many different types of people together, yanking them free of their normal surroundings to pitch them around in this playland, this Show—transforming somewhat normal folks into oddities that played off one another in contrasting fashions, mannerisms, and dialects—like a brimming carload of strange clowns at the circus.

*WALK. WALK. WALK.*

Johnny wasn't ready to leave yet, no matter what the street sign told him to do.

He fished his practice deck from a pocket, rifled inside the torn cardboard box, and tapped out his remaining burden: the Queen and King of Spades.

They hadn't quite planned for these cards yet, figuring that they'd have plenty of time to produce them. And since these were face cards—*people*—Johnny had assumed they'd be the simplest photos to pose and capture. But now, sitting there in the middle of the Show like a film extra, he was drawing blanks.

*Let it ride. The card will make itself. Just like the others…*

He focused his eyes on the Queen in his palm, one large Spade floating over her shoulder like a thought balloon—like the memory Johnny couldn't wash from his eyes of sex. The Queen's sharp angles, thick eyelids, and tiny pinch of a nose reminded him of Gin so much that he couldn't see her as anyone else. Unlike the other face cards—which carried weapons and pikes and swords— Queen Gin held a single, purple-leaved, wilting flower—a violet—close against her breast as if it had sprouted there naturally—simultaneously living and dying as its stem twisted and drooped skyward. Johnny squinted, imagined the Queen in pain—and her face mimicked this exquisitely—as she yanked the flower free from her own nipple. The colors of the card relaxed in the gray sunlight of Vegas, and she began to look like a beautiful gardener looking for a place to plant her sad flower, a place that captured the most sunlight, holding the roots of the blossom gently but awkwardly in her grasp as it struggled up toward the Spade symbol, a black, melting sun above.

He recalled how hard she'd loved him that night on Violet's floor. How she muttered inaudible words like angry curses. What was she saying?

Johnny blinked. A thought—a memory—clicked behind his eyes: *Was I the one who was grunting curses?*

It could have been him. He recalled digging his nails into Gin's scars, as if to tear her stomach out. And he thought he knew why—because making the cards all day had frustrated him so much that he'd found himself actually *wanting* to kill the models at times, an idle thought between clicks of the shutter as he saw Spades in potentially lethal wounds and bruises across their artificially posed bodies. He hated the lack of control—hated the way the cards were *making themselves* as if he weren't even a part of the process.

Another crowd passed him by, more drunken clowns on their way to The Circus.

He switched cards, eager to get his mind off the insane paths it was following. He wasn't sure exactly what they'd do for their Queen, but he figured Gin might be game to play dead again, possibly disguised with one of Violet's wigs, one of her motley outfits, and a ton of her terrible make up.

The King of Spades was a perfect mate for the Queen—their faces nearly a mirror for one another. Except the King was holding a long sword, entranced by its edge, the blue lines of his beard effectively removed from his face as if he'd just finished shaving but forgot the hair beneath his chin. But his eyes were suicidally cold, black. Like the Suicide King—the King of Hearts with an axe buried in his own head—which was responsible for his losing his gold tooth and getting him into this game in the first place. Johnny began to see himself in the card—disguised with mustache and beard dangling from his chin. In his imagination he felt like a cheap fake trying to fool his own reflection in the sword he held before his nose. He was the King of not only Spades but Swords, the Tarot card Violet had said represented him—a tricky, plotting bastard—confused, upside-down, following the wrong tracks—easily led astray, as always, again...

# Play Dead

Johnny angrily shoved the cards back into their box. The cards weren't only creating themselves. They were changing *him*.

Another group passed by, someone at its center singing "Viva Las Vegas" in a deep, hammy voice. The gray sky seemed to dissipate, a golden puddle of light spreading out around them like a supernatural spotlight. The corny singer stepped free from the passers-by, lifting a gold-buckled snakeskin boot to the empty spot on the bench beside Johnny. The man in jet-black hair leaned over the white creases of his polyestered knee and tightened the buckle.

An Elvis impersonator.

Elvis faced Johnny behind thick rose-colored glasses, snarling. "Vi-vaaaa....*vi-vaaaa!*"

"Las Vegas," Johnny flatly finished, smelling the residue of gin and tonic in the air between them.

Raising a thick black eyebrow, Elvis looked down at Johnny's deck of cards and then sat beside him, his abdomen sagging as he snapped dollar-signed cufflinks.

"Looking for work?" Johnny asked the King.

"Always," Elvis said, his face pathetically serious. "Not much work for the dead these days."

Johnny took a moment to grin and peruse the blue-gray sky, his eyes flickering madly as if hopelessly searching for limits.

Elvis was a nice guy. He trusted Johnny's promise that the money was at his studio—Violet's apartment—and was kind enough to not bother singing when they made their way off the strip and into the suburban backroads and gravel alleyways together. It was like another world out here, another city surrounding the Show, as if the condominiums and ranch-styled houses were a backstage entrance to the desert that surrounded Vegas. And Elvis seemed a bit too anxious to drop his act and costume, loosening his collar and draping his wide-lapelled jacket over an unsleeved arm as they walked together, Johnny spewing the same old lies he'd told the other models about being an art student doing a "card series." He'd read these lines so often from his mental script that he easily fell into the part. And that made him more than a little bit nervous. So nervous he almost believed the bullshit, feeling more like an impostor than the Elvis wannabe himself.

They turned down an alley that divided a new condominium complex, tall walls of bright yellow stucco towering on either side, protecting the tiny yards they sheltered. They could barely hear the whisper of sprinklers behind them. Occasionally, the stucco bent diagonally inward for a parked car and a green, padlocked door. Elvis and Johnny crunched the gravel with their shoes, their voices echoing off the walls like someone else's.

A new voice suddenly joined in the rebounding conversation: "You gonna do this one for real?"

They both jolted and twisted. The Preacher stood three paces behind them, wiping the sweat from his forehead with a dirty sock and dropping his duffel bag onto the gravel.

Johnny didn't like being followed. Or surprised. He felt himself blushing—in *anger*. "What the fuck do you want, Preacher?"

The Preacher bridged the gap between them. "I got you fingered, Johnny. The Lord showed me the light."

"Who's this supposed to be?" Elvis asked with a sweaty sneer arching over a starched white collar.

Johnny shrugged, stepping closer to The Preacher, hoping he wasn't stupid enough to answer.

The Preacher had the sense to whisper. "Nice trick with the neck, but I'd seen that cut the Ferret gave your girlfriend that night. And I know you didn't finish the job, 'cause experience tells me there weren't nearly enough blood drippin' from them little toy shovels you used."

Johnny ground his teeth. They seemed to collapse into the gaps between them, tearing free of their gums.

Elvis leaned against a wall with an out-thrust palm, cocking his hip while he lit a Marlboro. He pretended not to be listening and made his way into one of the carports. Johnny heard a zipper. Running water. Elvis said "Ahhh..."

Johnny moved forward. "What do you think you're doin', Preacher?"

He held up a hand to stop him. "Now I know you don't know me from Adam—praise the Lord—but I'm an old-fashioned player." The Preacher licked his grinning lips. "I believe in justice. It's the Lord's way. Sure, he forgave Judas as he sat at the table for the Last Supper. But if a man cheats at the *card table*, Lord knows he should be shot, last meal or not."

Johnny squinted, feeling like something from a B-grade Western. "But you're not accusin' me of cheating." He smiled, almost laughing at the corniness of it all. "Are you?"

The Preacher squinted back, pulling his butcher's knife around from his back. "You don't play by the rules, son, you don't play at all."

Johnny blanched at the sight of the knife, which glinted in the sun so brightly it nearly blinded him. He shielded his eyes, holding a hand out for protection. "And the rules say you can't mess with the other players..."

The Preacher grinned. He turned the knife in his palm, holding the handle outward. "I ain't gonna do nothin' of the sort. I just want you to prove to me that you're playin' fairly."

Johnny peered down at the wooden handle, reminded of the King of Spades' sword. "I don't follow."

"Show me you're really *playing* the game—not some cheating sinner— and I'll abide by the rules." He motioned with the knife, nodding in the direction where Elvis was pissing. "Prove it to me, and I'll take your word that my Queen of Hearts—the harlot you stole right out from under me—is in God's hands now, and not your own lusty paws of sin."

Johnny defiantly looked down at the knife. "I don't have to prove anything to you."

Something metallically clicked behind him. They both looked away to see Elvis, motioning a stiff arm with his gaudy white polyester jacket balled around his hand. He rolled his cigarette from one side of his mouth to the other. "Elvis likes his guns, boys." He came up beside Johnny, motioning at The Preacher's blade. "Now you just go ahead and drop it."

The Preacher frowned, but didn't move.

Johnny started laughing. "Praise the Lord!"

Elvis pivoted, taking aim at Johnny. "Not so fast, my man. Soon as we ditch this weirdo, you're gonna take me to that studio of yours and give me all that money you promised."

Johnny froze and ground his teeth again.

The Preacher's eyes folded in, black pupils rolling around beneath the lids like wet rubber as he slowly lowered the blade. "Studio?"

Elvis spit the butt from his lips, training the gun back and forth between the two players. "*Move.*"

Johnny obeyed when the gun was off him, gripping the handle of the butcher's knife and arcing it up into Elvis' forearm and continuing up into the soft underside of his jaw. He released the handle—its brown end sticking from the bottom of Elvis' head like the long stem of a spade—and dove into his chest, knocking him to the ground.

The Preacher was backing away from the scene, crossing himself over and over, thanking the Lord for his salvation.

Johnny sat up and saw Elvis' right eye roll back in its socket. The other kept its pupil on Johnny, the iris purpling with fresh blood, steady as the first plum that hits in a slot machine. He thought he could see the very tip of the knife glinting behind the lens, holding the orb in place.

Something gurgled. Johnny looked down past his bubbling throat to see his bleeding arm spill out from under the folds of his white jacket, which was spreading with a deep red spade. Elvis' hand was empty, twitching fingers cocked in mockery of a gun. A stiff thumbs up.

Johnny gripped Elvis by the shoulders and shook him madly. Spittle flew out of his mouth as he screamed into his face: "You *fuck*! You *stupid* fuck! Look what you made me do, you fuckin'...*fuck*!" Tears started to run from his eyes as he shook him, staring down into his crazy-cocked and coloring eyeballs, the blood puddling in the soft valley beneath his Adam's apple.

A hand fell on his shoulder. Johnny looked up to see The Preacher, sweating forehead canted up to the bright blue sky in prayer. His free hand offered Johnny his Polaroid camera. "Forgive me Lord for ever doubting this Christian soldier you've sent us…"

# Play Dead

"Thank God," Violet said when she opened the door and saw Johnny standing there, dazed. "You're back. We've been wondering what took you so long."

Johnny stumbled inside. He felt homeless again, like his first night at the shelter. Empty and worthless. Undeserving of the few friends he had. Reduced by a momentary act of panic into a cold-blooded killer.

Two college kids were sitting on the sofa, nervously smoking cigarettes. Johnny sat beside them, patting his pockets for his own cigarette pack. Recalling that he'd smoked the entire pack on his way to Violet's place, he stole a Pall Mall from the kids' pack on the coffee table. They tried to keep their cool, but were blatantly put-off by Johnny's clothes and smell. "Lemme guess," Johnny said, not bothering to look at them. "Our King and Queen of Spades."

"Right," Violet said, staring down at him and frowning, trying to figure out what his problem was. "They called this morning, hoping they weren't too late." Violet feigned a smile at the kids. "They were awfully lucky."

"Who isn't?" Johnny asked, inhaling smoke with each breath. "Got a drink?"

Violet moved toward the bar. "How about you two? Wanna try some of my trusty truth serum?"

The girl in cut-off jeans and a tank top declined. The boy in athletic shorts that read WILSON and a flannel red-and-blue shirt buttoned all the way up to the collar, convict-style, perked up. "I'll try anything." Violet was already chopping bananas into the liquid at the bottom of her blender. "Why do you call it truth serum?"

"'Cause the truth is," Johnny said glibly, "life sucks. Take one sip, and you'll agree the next morning."

"Cool," the kid said.

The blender groaned and hacked. It reminded Johnny of Elvis' gurgling throat. He turned and made eye contact with the boy: "Too bad you're not gonna have the chance to find out." He flexed the muscles in his face, pressing what was left of his teeth together. More had loosened, and even his jaw felt like it would soon collapse and fall right off its hinges.

The kid cracked his knuckles. "Whatta you mean?"

"I already did my King. Thanks for comin', but we don't need you."

The boy's face flushed, and he looked back over at Violet—who hadn't heard a thing, thanks to the churning blender. He licked his lips, staring at the spinning liquid as if it contained forbidden fruit.

"Get out," Johnny said, his voice as polite as he could force it.

The girl beside him began packing her cigarettes into her purse, but Johnny gripped her arm. "You can stay. I might still need you."

The boy slammed the door behind him.

"What's goin' on?" Violet asked, returning to the living room.

"Nothin'. I already did my King." He released the girl's arm, and she responded by lighting another cigarette, though her first still burned in the GREAT SMOKY MOUNTAINS ashtray on the coffee table. Johnny heard an exaggerated roar of a car engine outside. The squeal of tires.

Violet was handing out tall glasses of her concoction—giving the girl one even though she hadn't asked for it. "What do you mean, you already did your King?"

"Just what I said," Johnny said, snuffing out the Pall Mall. "Where the hell is Gin?"

"Sleepin'," Violet said, sipping. "Truth is, she's not feeling too well. Guess I'm in charge of things today." She lit a cigarette and stood over them. "What'd you guys do last night, anyway? Raid my liquor cabinet?"

The girl looked over at Johnny as though she were part of the conversation.

Johnny recalled how he hadn't heard Violet snoring that night he and Gin lovingly wrestled on the floor. He just grinned at her: *you know* exactly *what we were doing*.

His twisted lips looked more like a grimace of pain to Violet than a smile. "How are *you* feeling? You don't look so good."

Johnny chugged the tall glass of pulpy liquor to the bottom and smacked his lips. "Getting better. Got another?"

She rolled her eyes at the girl. "He knows damned well where it is."

Johnny sighed, stood. He made his way over to the bar, pointing with his eyes over to the girl on the couch, and Violet got the message. She sat beside her. "So tell me, Shirley. What do you do?"

Johnny phased their voices out as he poured himself a glass and chugged the remainder straight from the blender. The buzz wasn't killing the guilt—the lingering absurdity of what had happened—yet. He made his way into Violet's bedroom to check on Gin.

The room glowed a sickly gray-yellow from the slats of sunlight that beamed in through Violet's vertical blinds. Everything smelled like lilacs—he could even taste them—as though clusters of the pungent flower were stuck in his molars. A mound beneath purple satin sheets, Gin was a straight rectangular box on the bed, her arms stiffly pressed against her sides, her legs tightly clamped together. Her mouth was wide open, but she didn't appear to be breathing. Johnny sat beside her shoulder, the bed sinking with his weight. She didn't stir. He noticed deep black rings around her eyes—even sleeping, she looked exhausted. Or worse: dead.

He gently shook her shoulder. Gin surfaced from sleep in slow-motion blinks, her eyes empty cups dipping into the color of the bedroom's light but coming up empty, not registering any difference between the dark behind her lids and the world outside.

"Gin," he said. His guilt was intensifying along with the ringing in his ears. He felt responsible for her weakness—as if everything he'd recently touched was deconstructing. "I'm sorry, Gin," was all he could say, stealing a Benson and Hedges from her pack on the bedside table.

She answered with a deep groan. The same sound he'd heard when they'd made painful love.

"What is it?" Johnny asked, setting his glass down and leaning an ear to her mouth.

Lips parting: "Crr...cruhh"

Johnny moved so close he could feel her lips on his ears. Cold fruit. "Hmmm?"

Her breath spun and spiraled into his ear: *"Carrr-rd."*

Johnny sat up, scowling. "Card?"

She flopped an elbow up and weakly pulled the purple sheet down from her neck.

The first thing he saw was the scratches he'd given her, spread open like cancerous slits down both sides of her chest. Some of the scabs were wet. Rust and green.

"Holy *shit*," he said as they blurred into choppy geometric shapes: Spades. Six of them. As if the garden tools he'd scratched her with had branded her chest with pips of infection.

Dizzy panic. He tossed the sheet back over her, his fingers brushing cold flesh. "We gotta get you to a hospital, Gin."

She seemed to come to life then. "Nee-no-no-no," she murmured with a thick dry tongue. "No-nee-no-nee…"

"You're sick, Gin. Really sick." He reached down to grab her. "C'mon, let's go…"

She gripped his arm. Her hand was cold, stiff. Urgent and high-pitched, she whispered what could have been a muffled scream: "Noo-oo. Nee-no. *Nee*-no."

*Nebo*.

Johnny recalled what she'd found out about the game runner's real estate holdings. He figured Nebo probably owned the hospital, too: that would explain Gin's resistance. "Well out of town, then. Someplace. A private doctor, maybe?"

She released his arm, the muscles in her face relaxing, catching rays of light. "I bee-kay. Vile-ta-care…"

"She's right, you know," Violet was saying, suddenly behind him, "I'll take care of her. She'll be fine. But you've got business to finish."

Johnny closed his eyes. Nodded. He clenched his face painfully tight. But he couldn't get her wounds out of his sight. "I'm sorry…"

Violet squeezed a hand on his shoulder. "C'mon, Johnny. Your Queen awaits. Let's let Gin sit this hand out, and get some rest."

He lowered his head. Gin was drifting off again. "Give me a second."

Violet gave his collarbone another soft squeeze, and then shut the door behind her.

# Play Dead

"*Loser*," he uttered under his breath, pounding his thigh with a fist.

He dug his hands in his hair, clawing at the fissures of his scalp with his fingernails, trying to squeeze something real back into his skull with the pain. All he could think of was how he was losing again. He'd lost his money long ago. That was nothing. Then he'd lost his guts: forced into cheating at cards. And he couldn't even do that right, losing the one thing that kept him above the other players, the one thing that kept him sane—knowing that he didn't have to resort to murder.

And now he felt like he was losing the one thing that kept him in the game: Gin.

*And what had she told him?* He tore his hands free of his hair, taking a clump of strawberry blond with them. *It ain't losing. It's thinking that just surviving is itself a win.*

Johnny slipped a fist inside his mouth. Clamped a loose tooth between finger and thumb. Gently tugged an incisor free. He could barely feel it. His mouth flooded with warm salty blood.

He placed the tooth in the valley between her breasts, over her heart.

It looked like a tiny white spade.

He swallowed the hot liquid in his mouth. "I'm gonna win this game for you, Gin." He swallowed again. "You better get better." Gulped. "You better *survive*, Gin, 'cause I'm gonna fucking *win* this game if it kills me."

Nebo loosened his tie while Winston tore the plastic free from a new deck of table cards with the BUCKET OF BUCKS shamrock logo on back.

"Cheap, but effective," Nebo said, his deep voice shaking Winston. "Soon we'll have the real thing. And we will no longer simply be playing poker."

Winston shuffled, nearly spilling the slippery deck from his fingers. "I'm not so sure we should be doing this quite yet," he said, searching the almond color of Nebo's eyes.

"*Sometimes*," Nebo replied, sipping a brown liquid from a snifter, "Sometimes you have to take your chances. But the game is on Sunday, and I don't want to chance having him screw it all up. We can have no delays. The time is now—I can feel it."

Winston stopped shuffling, trying to contain the slick cards into something he could handle. "I could be wrong, you know. I don't know for sure if he's dying. He might just be sick."

Nebo's eyes rolled down to the deck in Winston's hands. "Deal."

Winston sighed and slapped the deck down on the table. Nebo used two long fingers to cut, barely touching the cards as if by virtue of their cheap plastic and mass production they were something diseased. Winston recovered the deck and tossed the cards, five each.

Neither one of them picked up their hands.

Winston leaned forward. "I'm sure I could sneak Ferret into the hospital. Get him checked out. See if he'll be able to make it. Maybe he just needs some medicine, I dunno…"

"Now, now. You said Ferret might as well already be dead. He hasn't gotten out of his cot all week. What did you call him? 'Down for the count?' That won't do." Nebo took a large gulp from his snifter. "I want my players alert and alive come game day. And if he's been out cold all week—nearly in a coma from that beating someone gave him—*with a card still left to create*—then I don't want him in the game." He picked up his hand, studied it.

Winston did likewise, but only went through the motions, momentarily ignoring the cards he'd been dealt. He retrieved a cigarette from his pack and lit it, cautiously, taking his time. This was a serious game. He didn't want to make any mistakes.

"You're sure Ferret didn't get in a fist fight with one of the other players? Maybe over a card game or something?"

"They wouldn't dare," Winston said, distractedly. "The players know better. I've warned 'em about doing that, at least a dozen times." Winston smoked. "If you ask me, I think one of his cards put up a fight he wasn't expecting."

"By the way," Nebo said, snarling at the smoke cloud which drifted his way. "How is the deck coming along? Has Frieze finally caught up?"

"Johnny's doing fine. Better than we expected, even." Winston paired up the Nines in his hand. Considered his discards. "His cards are much better than the others'. Shorty's running a close second. He keeps to himself, though. Who knows what's going on inside his head? His cards are quite bizarre. Never knew he had it in him."

"And The Preacher?" Nebo plucked two cards from his hand and tossed them face down between them. "Still with us, heart and soul?"

"Oh yeah," Winston replied, his stomach churning with the memory of his Nine of Hearts. "And cooking at the shelter, to boot." He counted the number of cards Nebo had chucked—two—which meant he was probably holding a three-of-a-kind, at best. Winston held on to his Nines, keeping an Ace kicker for luck and discarding the junk that remained.

By the time he was finished, Nebo was pouring himself another brandy. Cigarette in mouth, Winston palmed the deck and dealt out the draw cards—two to each of them.

"Now remember," Nebo said, leaning back in his chair as if he already knew which cards he'd drawn, "the trick with Ferret will be to capture the lifeforce of the creator himself. We need to keep the potency in the cards. If this is going to work, you'll need to make a card out of the card-maker. In Ferret's case, the King of Clubs."

Winston counted his cards: he'd drawn a Nine and an Ace. Full house. He grinned. "You act like I'm the one that's gonna do it. This game ain't over yet."

Nebo flipped his hand without looking down: three Deuces. Not even curious, he then turned the draw cards: Two of Spades and Seven of Clubs. Four Deuces. Four-of-a-kind. He smiled.

"Damn," Winston said, slapping his cards on the table. "You win."

"Of course I do," Nebo said, cocking his chin as he sipped on his brandy. "I always win."

Winston grumbled, sweeping the cards on the table together like a kid retrieving his marbles.

"Oh, don't look so glum, Winston. You'll make a fine player. And this will make for a much more interesting game come Sunday." Nebo couldn't stop smiling. "I'm sure you'll be much craftier than Ferret ever could."

Winston torched another cigarette with the butt of his first one. "Okay," he said, puffing. "You won the game. So I gotta take his place, not you. I gotta make a card outta him. Fine." More puffing. "But I still don't like the idea. What happened to all that crap you said about letting Fate do its own thing?"

Nebo blinked smoke from his eyes. "Who says it isn't, my friend? Didn't Fate just decide which one of us would take his place? Won't Fate dictate what happens this Sunday?"

"I dunno," Winston said uneasily. He poured himself a glass of Nebo's brandy. He noticed that his hands were shaking. "This feels a lot like cheating to me. And I don't know if I'm up for it."

Nebo lowered his head. "I'm afraid you have no choice." He cracked his knuckles. "And as far as cheating goes, this is one game where deception is not a factor of play. Cheating just *can't happen*. No one can cheat Fate. Not even me."

Winston quickly swallowed his drink, wondering. Wondering how Fate had managed to cheat *him* out of running things and into actually playing the Clubs in Butcher Boy. Wondering whether it would cheat him once again come Sunday. Wondering whether Nebo would spare his life if he happened to lose.

# Play Dead

The game was on. Johnny was ready.

He entered Nebo's BUCKET OF BUCKS Sunday morning without fear. He knew this could be his death day—if he lost. But he was certain he'd win. He *had to*. It was in the cards.

He'd prepared for the game both mentally and physically—playing practice hands of Butcher Boy with Violet while Gin stayed in the bedroom, recovering. When he turned in his Queen and King that week, Winston repeated his confidence in Johnny's likelihood of getting the highest stake of chips for his creativity. Especially for Johnny's King—the photo of the dead Elvis impersonator he'd taken with The Preacher's camera—which Winston called his "crowning achievement," best of the batch.

Johnny walked past the blackjack tables, and spotted the table Gin had beat him at the last time he was inside The Bucket. The curving tabletop was covered with deep green plastic, not unlike a body bag. Most of the tables on this side of the pit were similarly shrouded with plastic and dimmed lights— table games were dead on Sunday mornings—and Johnny couldn't help feeling lonely as he passed Gin's table by. He stopped in his tracks and dug into his breast pocket for a cigarette. Benson and Hedges. Gin's brand. Menthols. He didn't like it much, but its flavor kept Gin in his mouth and in the back of his mind. Because he was playing the game for her now, not just himself. He lit the long filtered cigarette and deeply inhaled its cold musty mint, holding it in his lungs like a drug as he dug into his back pocket and examined his private photograph, the fleshy Ace of Spades.

He heard slot machine jackpot bells ripple away from him, like a wave of luck washing across the casino floor.

He felt the security cameras humming electric above.

Pocketing the photograph, he made his way to the prison-barred registration counter, as Winston had instructed. The clerk asked him for his name. "Johnny Spades," he said—the password Winston had given him—and the woman behind the counter punched it into her computer. Her eyes wrenched

244

open when his entry came up on the screen, and she quickly slid him an envelope she'd retrieved from a drawer. Johnny took it, feeling a key and folded paper inside as he stared at the clerk's uniform—the shamrock and rainbow on her breast reminding him of Gin.

"You've got a casino credit of a thousand dollars," the clerk said, smiling. "You can bring this to the cashier's cage to claim it." She handed him a slip of paper with gold-embossed printing.

Johnny thanked her and made his way to the bar. He ordered a gin-and-tonic, and tore open the envelope. The key spilled out: Room 2110. The letter read: "Go to your room immediately, and prepare. Game begins at seven in the penthouse. You may enjoy the casino beforehand with your credit. You may also order any food you like, free of charge. Live it up while you can." Underlined, beside Winston's signature: "DO NOT LEAVE THE CASINO."

Johnny slammed his drink and obeyed, heading towards the elevators.

*The sky's the limit.* The phrase came back to him as he pressed the button and the elevator sailed upward. *The sky's the limit.* Only it sounded more like *disguise* the limit in his mind when the elevator came to a halt on the twenty-first floor.

He made his way down the deathly silent hallway, walking on what felt like a green carpet of money straight off a counterfeiter's press.

On the bed in Room 2110, a suit waited for him: black pin-stripes, backed up with a charcoal gray shirt, a bold white tie with gold stitching, thick black socks, well-polished leather shoes, new underwear still in its plastic bag, and a white silk handkerchief.

Johnny got the hint. Nebo didn't want the players running around his casino in their homeless get-ups. Maybe he wanted to spoil them a little before the game—make them comfortable, give them a taste of the rich life, make them itchy for tonight's Action. Maybe. But Johnny figured something else was going on. It bothered him that Nebo knew what size shoes he wore. The suit was snazzy, sure, but it looked like a funeral suit, too, all wrapped in dry cleaner's plastic on the bed's cushy quilt.

Johnny stripped naked. He smoked another one of Gin's menthol cigarettes, laying on the bed with his photograph of their sex. It didn't give him an erection—it never had. He didn't care that Nebo might be watching behind the mirror. He closed his eyes and pressed the cold photograph against his chest, prodding the gaps between his teeth with his tongue, digging it into the hollow sockets of healing gum. The pain felt good. A reminder.

He decided not to go downstairs to the tables—wanting to keep his mind straight, focused on the game instead. He mentally went over his game plan—considering ways of breaking the other players, thinking about their strengths and weaknesses. Getting hungry, he slipped on a robe from the bathroom, and phoned for room service. Knowing he'd be tempted all day by Nebo's credit, he had the operator put the whole bankroll Nebo had spotted him on the stupidest thing he could think of—a Keno card—like a thousand dollar Lotto ticket which he knew would never hit. When the food came, the room attendant handed him the card, winning numbers marked in black crayon and his amazing wager marked in red. He'd picked one through thirteen. None of them were winners. Johnny smiled. "Viva Las Vegas," he said as he shut the door on the baffled man in the Bucket of Bucks uniform. High rollers usually gave tips. Not Johnny. Not anymore.

He ate as much of the pepper steak as his mouth could stand, the television keeping him company with sports results. Afterwards, he picked the gristle from his teeth with the corner of the Suicide king, occasionally cutting his gums with its sharp edge, yellow-red pus streaking stains beside the King's sword. He thought of Elvis. Himself.

He fell asleep studying the Bible he'd discovered in his bedside table. A wake up call he hadn't ordered rang in his ears around 5:30. When he answered the phone, his mouth was inflamed and puffy, as if he'd chewed on a fistful of razors in his dreams. He took a long shower, letting the hot bullets of hard water wash the sores in his mouth. He decided not to shave. After he brushed his teeth, screaming, he chewed three complimentary aspirins, massaging the powder into his gums with an index finger.

The suit was heaven. Almost enough to make him forget about his throbbing mouth.

He smoked. Nearly seven o'clock. He hoped the number was lucky for him.

Johnny slipped his Polaroid of Gin's backside into his suit jacket pocket like an expensive leather wallet. He pocketed his practice deck, along with two packs of Gin's cigarettes. Digging the contents from his jeans on the floor, he retrieved the things he'd brought with him that morning, just in case. Just in case *he lost*. He tried not to think about the Suicide King — sword stuck beneath his crown as if trying to prod it free from his skull — as he balled up his old clothes and tossed them into the wastebasket.

He checked himself one last time in the mirror. He smiled to check his teeth. The gums were white and purple.

"You're on," he watched his lips say, as he accepted an unspoken challenge and headed for the door.

He knew Nebo was watching.

The elevator went all the way up to Nebo's penthouse on its own accord. The card key Winston had once used was unnecessary.

A blond waitress in black net stockings and a tight green bikini greeted him, handing him a fizzing glass. She smiled and led him through the foyer, past cards behind shiny glass frames that reflected the two of them. Johnny watched the shift and shimmy of the waitresses' ass — smooth creases of flesh slipping in and out of the fold of her green panties — as she turned a corner and opened a large door.

The game room.

The room was surprisingly sparse. A hexagonal mahogany table covered with green felt stood at the center of the room, surrounded with plush leather chairs. Directly above the table's center, a black dome hung from the ceiling — a camera, Johnny figured, though he didn't see the need for them. The floor was bright white — hard linoleum tiles without patterns. No one was sitting down. Johnny instantly spotted Shorty, whose eyes were glued to the waitress' heavy breasts. His suit looked silly on his large shoulders, sleeves rising high on his forearms when he nervously sipped his drink. He looked like an overgrown kid who still needed his mother to dress him. His tie was crooked, knotted strangely at his neck. The Preacher — similarly dressed, but much more in control of his attire — was kneeling in a corner, facing the blank white walls, whispering prayers. His hands were gripping a

247

black leather Bible. Ferret wasn't present. *Probably overslept*, he thought, remembering how sickly he looked, snoring on his cot in the shelter when he turned in his last card.

The waitress quietly stood by a makeshift bar beside the room's door, waiting.

Johnny slipped a cigarette between his lips. Lit it. Walked over to Shorty. "You ready, pal?"

Shorty kept his eyes on the blond. "I ain't your pal."

"Rats," Johnny said, grinning slyly. "I thought we could partner up and beat these losers at their own game. Maybe make a deal—whoever wins helps the other out. Then we can split the winnings. Somethin' like that."

Shorty blinked. "No can do."

Johnny pulled the cigarette from his lips with a V of his fingers. "You know what, Shorty? I *bet* you can."

His eyes broke from the woman, rolling over to Johnny's own. He squinted. "Say what?"

Johnny winked. "I'll bet you that diamond ring on your finger that you can."

Confusion swarmed Shorty's face, his eyebrows twisting into question marks. "Can wha...?"

The doors swung open, Winston and Nebo entering side by side. Nebo had a long black box in his left hand, carried like a book.

Johnny heard The Preacher's voice echo from the far corner of the room: "Amen," as he shuffled to his feet.

"Welcome," Nebo said, his face all smiles—his eyes glistening and dilated, as if drugged with anticipation. "Please, be seated."

Johnny took the chair with its back to the door. The Preacher sat on his right—Shorty on his left. That suited him just fine.

Winston sat directly opposite of Johnny. Nebo sat on his right, next to Shorty.

"What gives?" Johnny asked, looking around the room. "Where's Ferret?"

Nebo ignored him, gingerly setting the long black box on the green felt of the card table. The waitress had begun setting drinks down in front of them. Johnny couldn't take his eyes off the box—leatherbound—sharp corners. To Johnny it looked like a coffin. He knew it contained the cards each of them made. So many lives. So much death.

Winston coughed. "Ferret had to fold. I'm taking his spot."

All three players simultaneously looked over at him. Winston avoided their eyes, tapping a cigarette butt against the edge of the table to pack the leaves down to their filter. "Anyone got a problem with that?"

Johnny looked over at Shorty. Then at The Preacher. Both stared down at the table. He could tell their thoughts paralleled his own. Not only were they quickly reminded of just how life-and-death this game was, but now it had taken an unpredictable turn. The game wouldn't play like they'd expected with Ferret out of the picture. Johnny's mind raced through his experiences with Winston—possible ways to break his concentration, if need be. But he didn't really know how to make him crack.

"Wait just a minute," Johnny finally said, grasping at straws. "Mr. Tarrochi, this ain't right."

Nebo lifted an eyebrow, but he didn't look up from his box.

"We *earned* these seats," Johnny said, casting glances at the other players for support. "We made that deck. Each and every card. Winston here didn't do jack shit, except collect them."

The room was quiet. Winston just stared at Johnny, his face painted with anger.

"We're wasting time," Nebo said, cutting the tension with his voice. "Winston earned his seat, gentlemen, as you'll soon find out. He has every right to sit here, and he's to be treated as an equal to each of you. If he loses," Nebo said, unlatching his box, "he dies."

Winston closed his eyes and swallowed.

"It's customary," Nebo said, caressing the black leather creases of the box in front of him like a Christmas gift he couldn't open yet, "to review the rules in a game such as this, before play begins. Butcher Boy is a simple game. I shall deal. One round only. This is how it works: the deck is dealt face-up to each player in turn until a pair is attained, upon which the card is given to the player who made the pair. When that happens, betting will take place, just as it does in regular poker. The deal resumes, left to right, stopping whenever another card comes up that can pair or match any hand showing. When a matching card comes up, it is given to the player who holds its mate. Again, that player will begin a series of bets, and then the deal will resume accordingly. The game ends when one player receives a four-of-a-kind. That player will win the purse I've promised."

Nebo looked each player in the eye, one at a time. "Each of you deserves to win. I know how much you've suffered and struggled in preparation for this game. How much creativity and dedication you've put into these cards we are about to play with." Again, he stroked the leather box. Then he scanned their faces, proudly grimacing at each of them. "And for both your loyalty and hard work, I've decided to reward you by altering the rules in your favor. The player with the *lowest* hand showing at the end of the game will also be spared his life. Only the remaining two will die."

Johnny stroked the stubble on his chin. Nebo's voice was almost monotonous, dead as he stated both the rules of the game and their possible deaths in the same tone of voice. Johnny's chances of winning—*and* dying—were now fifty-fifty.

"Any questions?"

"Yeah," Johnny asked after an unbearable silence. "Why favor the loser?"

"Losing's just as hard as winning. And besides," he grinned, "I hate mediocrity. Any other questions?"

The players faced off, glancing at one another as if hoping someone would find a loophole out of the "dying" part.

Nebo cracked his knuckles. "Okay, then. Let us begin by staking each player with the appropriate amount of chips. I've decided that each of you should get an equal amount."

Johnny: "*What?*"

Everyone looked up, save The Preacher, to whom money was irrelevant. Even Winston looked surprised, one eyebrow raised in curiosity.

Nebo held up a hand to silence him. "I admit, all of your individual creations were unique—some better than others—but since each of you are equally responsible for creating the most remarkable deck ever produced, you should each be equally rewarded. I'm sure none of you will mind that I've upped the total purse to two million dollars, will you?"

Shorty grumbled. The Preacher remained silent, his eyes focused on the ceiling above, impatiently waiting for the game to begin. Johnny frowned, staring at Winston, who was patiently examining the patterns burning on the end of his own cigarette.

"After all," Nebo continued. "Only those who win will be able to spend it. The betting has no influence on the outcome, actually. These chips are merely tokens to show you that the pot is indeed for real." The blond waitress distributed four racks of black casino chips with rainbowed rings at their center to each player. "You each now have five hundred thousand dollars in plastic. But do try to concentrate on the game and not the stake. As gamblers, I'm sure you already know that money is really nothing more than a way of keeping score."

*Until you're down to zero*, Johnny thought, tonguing the holes between his teeth.

"Let us play," The Preacher said, as if he'd just joined the congregation.

# Play Dead

Johnny was entranced with the cards.

Nebo tossed the bodies around the table, slowly, relishing each image as it landed before the appropriate player, its color lending depth to the frame which contained it, like a psychedelic grave cutting down into the green felt of the table. Each card was bordered in black; red numbers and suit symbols in opposing corners defined each card's value. In some cases these symbols were unnecessary—the first two doctored photographs dealt were clearly a Jack of Diamonds and a Six of Clubs—but others were impossible to distinguish without deep study.

Like the first card Johnny received: a puddle of red lumps, arranged in the shape of the letter H. Only after reading the computer-generated pips in its corners—9♥—did Johnny recognize the organs for what they were: nine disembodied human hearts, dangling veins and arteries like parts violently torn free from a car engine.

Another card landed beside his Nine—he tried to keep his eyes glued to the number—K♣—but he couldn't help recognizing Ferret's battered face, eyes rolled skyward as he was engulfed in red flames and black smoke. Three car tires encircled him—one around the neck, and two around each arm—his charred, blackened flesh entirely filling in the gaps—melting rubber and man into the shape of a dark club as he burned...

Johnny gagged, pressing down on his gums with a thumb to override the nausea with pain, looking away from his cards, eyes involuntarily training on the other player's hands: bodies with limbs arranged in impossible angles; close-ups of pale white faces with their throats slit; various wounds shaped in the form of numbers and suits...all murder, cold and sterilized by the plastic coating and framed black border of the cards. And he saw his own Spades, fitting perfectly in the mix as if he'd really killed his models, as if he had committed the same atrocities as those he was sitting with. Which he had—but only once. Accidentally.

"Ah," Nebo said, flipping a card over to Winston. "A pair of Jacks."

Winston grinned under his hat, peering out at Johnny, pleased with the reaction his one and only contribution to the deck—Ferret—had caused. As if shaking Johnny up were more important than the pair of boys he'd just been dealt—more important than the two Jacks and the Ten of Diamonds which brought him one step closer than anyone else to winning.

"I'm surprised you got your hands dirty, Mr. Clean." Johnny faced him off, happy to take his eyes from the table. He tried to put on his best poker face, but Winston stared him down with a pearly smile till it felt like a cheap transparent mask on his features.

Winston fingered his black poker chips. Tossed a small stack into the center of the table. "Ten thou," he said, turning to The Preacher.

The Preacher matched him. He was holding a Seven and a Six, eagerly awaiting for his third card. "I'm with you," he said, nodding at Winston. "And so is the Lord."

It took Johnny a few moments to realize that it was his turn to see the bet. All eyes were on him, impatient. He tried to keep his hand in his mind, refusing to look at the cards. He knew he was holding nothing. But in Butcher Boy, if you folded, you died. So he saw the bet, even though it was all so arbitrary. Who would fold? What did betting matter? They might as well be spinning the chamber of a revolver in a game of Russian Roulette. Nonetheless, the sound of his chips clicking together made it feel right and he wasn't about to complain..

Shorty was already following suit, tossing a stack of black disks in with the others. His eyes were alert, quick. Johnny noticed he was holding an Ace of Hearts and the Three of Spades—one of Axe's old cards.

"Interesting," Nebo said. "Quite interesting. This is much more exciting than I anticipated."

Johnny stared at him. Nebo's face had lost its stern features—his cheeks glowed with red, his eyes were furtive and dancing. Like a child who first discovers video. Hypnotized by the game.

Nebo eagerly continued the deal, sliding The Preacher his due card, then Johnny and Shorty. No matches came up. Nebo paused to narrate the potential hands that were showing while the players considered one another's cards.

"Jacks. Possible straight. Nothing. Nothing." He started the cycle again with Winston.

But Johnny got his card—catching another King. Spades. "Pair of Kings beats Jacks," Nebo said, stopping the deal and announcing the obvious. "Bet."

Shorty laughed at Johnny's card while he nervously rubbed his suit pants beneath the table. "Elvis? The King? You offed The *King?*"

"Who says rock and roll will never die?" Winston asked, grinning. He slid the handkerchief out of his breast pocket and wiped sweat from his forehead.

Johnny didn't have to look at the photo. It was tattooed in his memory. "Another ten," he said, ignoring their banter, tossing the chips in the pot and happy to be ahead in the game. But he knew that a pair of Kings didn't mean jack shit at this point. It was too early to tell. He longed for a regular game of draw—where a player didn't depend on the cards for his game, but played with the players themselves. Again, Johnny hated not being in control. The cards that were making their way around the table had made themselves. He could accept that. Even the King he'd killed. But not having anything to do with the *play*...not being able to keep his cards to himself, not being able to bluff or play out of the hole...that bugged the shit out of him.

But it was only just beginning. He could feel the Action. *Fuck the cards,* Johnny thought, getting itchy. *I'm gonna play this my way.*

The players called him.

The deal continued, Nebo dealing and reading the obvious, trying to stir up the excitement. "Eight of Hearts...Jacks get nothing. Six of Hearts...pair up, Preacher."

He tossed in ten thousand. All three of them saw the bet.

"Two of Clubs...Kings' got a partner. Two pair bets, Johnny."

He only bet ten. The players matched. Nebo peeled another card. To Shorty: "Ace of Spades with a possible flush! Pair of Aces bets."

Shorty eagerly sat up, his breasts absurdly jiggling. "I'm gonna kick all your asses," he said, tossing ten more chips in the growing pot.

"Not bad, Short stuff," Johnny said, jealous of his hand. "Possible flush of four Spades, with two Aces showin'. Can't get better than that." He grabbed his glass—so wet with condensation it almost slipped out from his grip. He smiled at the other players, raising his glass in a toast. "And it *won't*." By the time it was his turn to meet Shorty's bet, he set down his drink and tapped a long menthol cigarette against the edge of the table, mocking Winston's earlier move. He waited.

"You gonna bet?" The Preacher asked. He nervously lifted and dropped some chips in his palm. "We ain't got all day, sinner."

Johnny lit up. Then he blew smoke in The Preacher's direction, purposely stalling to rattle his nerves. "Look who's talking! The *wagers* of sin are death, Preacher. The *wagers* of sin are death."

The Preacher snarled. "Don't you dare take the word of God in vain, blasphemer."

"Count your blessings, Preacher. 'Cause you ain't gonna have none left when I get through with you." Johnny French-inhaled as he tossed in his ten chips, plunking one at a time from his palm with a flip of his thumb. He looked over Winston's cards. Shorty's. The Preacher's. "And I'll raise all you losers another dime." He tossed in ten thousand more, turning his face to challenge Shorty personally as he repeated the tiddlywinks maneuver with his chips. He knew how much it riled Shorty when the Action started churning. He'd drop the slow and retarded routine and be right on top of things, eager to get in the game. But maybe there was only so much Action Shorty could handle. A threshold. After all, Johnny figured, Shorty might be able to channel that energy into his game, but that didn't mean that he could *control* it…

Shorty met his raise with a slap of his chips on the table. "You're going down, friend."

Johnny, pouting, babying up his voice: "I thought we weren't friends no more, Short stuff."

Shorty's head cocked slowly backwards on its own accord as he tried to read Johnny's intention on his face. Angrily, he broke contact and faced Winston. "It's ten more to you."

"The boy can count!" Winston said, joining Johnny in the tease.

Johnny leaned closer to Shorty. "I bet you still like me. I *bet* you like me lots."

Shorty's face was turning red.

# Play Dead

"Well *I* don't like ya, boy," The Preacher said, matching the bet and calling.

Nebo was gauging the amount of cards left in the deck. "Now's when things really get interesting," he said, already tossing the next card in the air.

Winston caught a Jack of Clubs, right off the fly. That gave him a three-of-a-kind. Silence filled the room. It was getting close. Almost half the deck had been dealt, nearly half the money was now in the pot, and Winston was now one card away from winning. Preacher had the lowest hand—a possible straight if the cards were lucky enough to hit right. Johnny and Shorty were caught in the middle: their lives depended on one Jack, still buried in the deck. Now any deal could be their last one. And each card was likely to match something that was already out on the table.

Johnny ground his teeth, violently plugging the gaps with the tip of his tongue. He missed the taste of gold. He lit up another menthol to quench it. "What are the odds, bookie?"

Winston had been smiling at Nebo when he heard him. Slowly, he faced Johnny, tossing in a handful of chips without looking. "Fifteen thousand," he said, "to your one measly life, loser."

The Preacher saw his bet.

"Don't get testy," Johnny said, still in a staring contest with Winston. He'd never seen Winston so intense: he wasn't a player like the others, and was obviously working hard at acting like one. "I just think you forgot to factor beginner's luck into your equation."

Shorty snickered, rubbing his hands on his pants again.

"Are you in, funny boy?" Winston asked, his face flushing.

Johnny and Shorty called.

Nebo turned the Six of Spades, flipping it over beside The Preacher's other Six. "Praise the Lord," he said, nabbing a three of a kind, not realizing that he'd moved out of the "low hand win" position. "This," The Preacher said, lifting the card by the corner to show everyone, "is my lucky card." He turned it Johnny's way, snidely grinning.

It was Gin, playing dead, shovels sticking from her chest like daggers.

Johnny's leg began to shake. He snuffed out his cigarette and pulled another one from his pocket. "Get that out of my face, Preacher."

"Sinner," The Preacher was saying, pushing the card closer to Johnny's face like a talisman. "I forgive you. But the Lord never will."

Johnny batted the card away with a fist against The Preacher's wrist. The Preacher laughed and set it down beside his other sixes. Then he bet. "Twenty."

Johnny took his time, smoking his cigarette with eyes closed. Shorty was anxious to bet, playing with his chips. Johnny opened his eyes and faced The Preacher, grinning. "Do you really think that bothers me, Preacher? That card ain't nothin'. Wait'll you see *my* lucky card. " He reached into his pocket and pulled out his extra Ace of Spades—the meaty one of Gin's brilliantly shiny buttocks. He set it down beside The Preacher's Sixes—a mock four-of-a-kind. "It's a wild one, ain't it, Preach?"

The Preacher turned deep red, clutching the Bible beside his chips. He recognized the heart-shaped figure as curved hips, the texture at its center as carnal penetration, turned upside-down below him. He slapped the Bible down on top of the cards, covering up the sin. His lower lip twitched, spit spilling over its rim: "Lusting sinner, you will remove that pornography from this table, or so help me God, I'll cut your throat."

Nebo saw the butcher's knife The Preacher was drawing. "You'll do no such thing," he calmly said, standing up. "If you win, I'll give you the pleasure, but right now we've got a game to play."

The Preacher kept his eyes on Johnny, red like coals.

"You heard him," Johnny said. "Play."

"Put the knife on the table," Nebo said, moving to the bar to fix himself a drink. The waitress was gone. "In fact, since this is a gentleman's game, if *anyone* here is holding a weapon, I want it. Now. Or the game's off." He poured a brandy with his back to them, waiting.

By the time he turned around, two knives and a small pistol were on the table like extra chips beside the pot.

"Very good." He sipped his brandy and walked up behind Johnny. "Sir, be a gentleman, would you, and remove that extra card from the table?"

Johnny obeyed, lifting the Bible and politely handing it to The Preacher whose face had flushed redder than any of the cards on the table. He picked up his Polaroid, gave it a glance, and pocketed it. "Where were we? Let's see. It was my bet, right?"

Nebo collected the weaponry and carried it over to the bar, placing it inside a cabinet and turning a key.

"Your bet," Shorty said. "Hurry up."

Johnny saw that Shorty, too, was shaken up by the sight of sex—his nervous habit of rubbing his pants sounded something like masturbation beneath the card table.

Nebo returned to his seat, the skin around his cheeks tightening as he clenched his teeth in anger. "Let us continue. The Preacher has three Sixes. It's Johnny's turn to either see the bet...or fold." He emphasized the last word like a threat.

"I'll see his triple Sixes," Johnny said, leaning an elbow over by The Preacher as he tossed in his chips, whispering from the corner of his mouth: "Figures you drew the *devil's* number, reverend."

The Preacher's eyes shot open, and he looked disbelievingly down at his cards. The numbers 666 curled and writhed on the table. "This can't be! No, Lord, no!"

Nebo rapped his knuckles on the table. "Please."

"But..." The Preacher anxiously faced all the players—even Johnny—as if begging for it not to be true. Johnny lifted a lip. The Preacher dropped his head in his hands, covering the tears that began to spill from his eyes. "Dear Lord..." his voice raised in pitch but lowered in volume, spewing an urgent prayer.

Shorty and Winston quickly called the bet, eager to get on with things.

Nebo was quick to flip the next card. He grinned up at Johnny. "King of Diamonds."

"Yes!" Johnny quickly tossed in thirty chips, avoiding the picture on the card—a body in mirror image, a line of red and yellow guts bisecting the frame. Shorty's work.

"I'm the King of Kings," Johnny said.

The Preacher didn't catch the intended double meaning, his hands clawing at his temples. Johnny thought he heard him saying "Such as I have give I thee" over and over under his breath.

Shorty matched the bet, scratching his legs. "You might be winnin', Johnny, but so am I. Look, I got the lowest hand here."

Johnny winked. "Told ya we could do it, partner. I win the bet."

Shorty scratched more quickly, shaking his head at the table like a Quaker on LSD.

Winston tossed his own chips in. "Game's not over till it's over." He faced The Preacher—who reached forward and turned his three Sixes over one at a time, still muttering bible verses with a whisper. "I'm really gettin' sick of your crap," Winston said, swallowing spit. "You in or not, Preacher?"

Hands shaking so hard they rattled the chips like bones, he saw the bet.

Johnny surveyed the table, lighting up one of Gin's cigarettes for luck. Everyone was on edge, except himself. The cards no longer bothered him— they *all* seemed like cheap fakes, forgeries, and toys now. Even the players seemed faked, clichéd stereotypes, actors in bad costumes. The Kings on the table proved it to him: the deck was his. He'd win. He knew if he shook everyone up, luck would go in his favor. Just like in regular poker, back before he ever got involved in all this: players fooled themselves if they thought they could control the fate of the deck. It was the players who got played. Johnny knew that whoever mastered the players would master the draw, seducing Lady Luck his way—she was only attracted to those who could keep their cool. Those who made her look good. Those who made others jealous, envious, covetous.

Nebo's face colored a deep olive. He turned the card from the top of the deck.

Johnny instantly recognized the flash of red between Nebo's manipulating fingers.

*The Suicide King.*

Johnny fell back against his chair, as if Lady Luck had jumped on his lap to rape him. The other players just stared, not quite believing what was happening. He thought he could hear their eyelids wetly blinking in astonishment in the room's sudden silence.

Nebo grinned knowingly, nodding, passing the winning card over to Johnny like an award.

# Play Dead

Winston suddenly swung a hand out, grasping Nebo tightly by the elbow. "Hold on…"

Johnny looked up. Winston's head was bowed, eyes squinting tightly as he leaned forward, looking down at the table, closely examining Johnny's lips…

Johnny sighed, smoking. "You lost. Face it, Winston."

Winston motioned with his chin, his eyes black bullets beneath the lids. "What brand you smokin' there, Johnny?"

Johnny blew smoke in Winston's direction. He didn't blink. "Gin's. Got a problem with that?"

Nebo pulled his arm out of Winston's grip. He sighed. "Don't shame me, Winston. I know you're not as experienced as these fellows, but you know better than to be a sore loser."

"But he's cheating," Winston said, his face wrinkling. "Why would he be smoking his girlfriend's cigarettes if she was long dead? I *know* Johnny Frieze. Read him like a book. And the truth is, he's a sponge. Smokes whatever you give him. And I'm thinkin', Nebo, that maybe she gave him that very pack…"

Shorty was twisting the ring on his finger. "Mommy…"

"And I'm thinkin' he mighta faked her card, after all. Listen, Nebo. It makes sense. He's never been nothin' but a no-good con artist anyway, and …"

The Preacher laid hands on Winston: "Have faith. He's a thief, a fornicator, and a killer. A vicious, ruthless sinner. I, too, thought he was a cheater. But I saw him carve up Elvis like a turkey. My own eyes are stained with his murderous sin. God alone knows what sins far worse he's committed. Survival on this living hell called Earth is his damnation. We have a greater calling. You, my friend, are going to join me in hell…" The Preacher had slid his fingers up to Winston's throat.

Shorty cried.

A gunshot ricocheted off the linoleum floor, splinters snapping from the leg of Johnny's chair as the bullet whizzed past his shoes. But Johnny didn't break, cigarette casually held between his fingers as he continued to smoke, eyes turning carelessly up to Nebo.

The players froze.

Nebo lifted the gun out from under the table, and turned it on Winston. "I asked you kindly. Now sit back, relax, and shut the *fuck* up."

Winston hesitantly obeyed, eyes focused on the gun's sight.

Nebo whipped the pistol around. "That goes for everyone."

Johnny sucked smoke into his lungs. Held it. Blew. He looked down at the huge pile of black chips and then back up at the dealer. "I haven't won jack shit, have I Nebo?"

Nebo was all smiles. "That's what I like about you, Johnny. You're a good guesser." Nebo nodded, glancing around the table. "And you happen to be right. You lose. You *all* lose." Nebo was cautiously digging inside his jacket pocket with a free hand. "I'm the one with the highest four-of-a-kind." He withdrew four cards and tossed them on the table. "Four wild cards. Read 'em and weep."

Each card read JOKER down its side in crisp red lettering. A black border framed a photograph of each player sitting at the table. Johnny saw himself in the top card, bird's eye view of his neck craned up—veins standing out as if begging to be slit—as he leaned back from a poker table. His old gold tooth glimmered in his mouth like buried treasure.

"Figures," Johnny said, stamping out his cigarette. "You're the cheater. The welcher."

"Oh no," Nebo said, sipping from his brandy, gun steady in his other hand. "I may be a lot of things, but I'm no cheater. You can't cheat Fate, Johnny. Winston might be right—maybe you did fix your cards. Maybe you did try to fuck me. But I'm willing to wager that it didn't work."

Johnny didn't spill. He lit another cigarette, ignoring the pistol in his face.

Winston: "You gotta be kidding, Nebo. This ain't right. You cheated *me*..."

With a twist of the wrist, Nebo pointed and snapped back the trigger. Winston's hat sprayed backwards, a chunk of scalp and brain caught inside its suede hull as his body fell out of his chair, knees slamming the table with a sharp THUMP which spilled everyone's chips. When the jarring echo of the gunfire faded from their ears, everyone could hear the slow trickle of blood on the linoleum.

The Preacher dropped down on his knees to give last rites. Johnny watched as he made the sign of the cross with two fingers over Winston's

261

still breathing chest. Something red and yellow was in-between his fingers—held in reverence like the Eucharist. It took Johnny two seconds to realize what he was holding: the pill each one of them had been given, the suicide pill, in case they found themselves in trouble.

Nebo saw it, too.

The Preacher prayed silently, holding the pill between his thumbs and slowly bringing it to his lips. Nebo held his gun on him, watching, waiting.

He let him swallow and wallow in his own prayers while he cowered beside Winston, his lips softly chanting: "Such as I have give I thee, such as I have give I thee, such as I have give I thee…" His voice drowned down to a manic whisper.

Johnny's teeth were clenched so tight that they all felt ready to collapse in his mouth. He stared at the ashtray where what remained of Winston's cigarette still burned, the gold letters of its logo browning to a crisp as the smoke danced around the filter.

Shorty gripped down on the edge of the table, blinking madly. "I don't get it, Nebo," he said. "I don't get it. Me and Johnny here, we won, fair and square. You gonna let us go now, or what?"

"Let me guess," Johnny said, his voice so calm it sounded like someone else's in his mouth.

Nebo, his voice oddly warm: "I'd like that Johnny."

"This wasn't about the game at all, was it? The deck's for something else. Like the Tarot. Except with *real bodies*." It sounded obvious when he said it, but Shorty's reaction was total surprise, his jaw dropping so far that a string of drool spilled over his lower lip.

"And?"

"And somehow these cards," Johnny said, fingering the Kings on the felt in front of him, "are gonna predict the future or some corny gypsy bullshit like that." He thought of Gin's research on him. "Probably need 'em for the other games you play: real estate and government crap."

Nebo cocked his head sideways. "Corny? Why, not at all. If anything's corny, Johnny, it's playing poker—a child's game compared to what I can do with these cards. I won't simply predict the future like a fortune teller—I can *create it* by dealing them out. I can control chance, Fate. Real estate is nothing. This deck means I can control anyone and anything in existence."

Johnny lit another cigarette. Inhaled the memory of Gin, hoping it would last forever.

Nebo turned passionate, punctuating his sentences with the end of the gun. "You gamblers are all alike—playing cards as if it were a career, as if the cards weren't playing you all along. I make my living off of you idiots. But did you ever wonder, who holds those cards? Did it even occur to you that—even when you've got a Royal Flush right there in your palm—that maybe you're not *really* holding them?"

Johnny nodded. "But you do."

Nebo shook his head impatiently. "I do now, thanks to you." He looked down at the table. "These cards hold life, Johnny. Life. And fortune."

Johnny looked over at Shorty. Then looked back, confused.

Nebo pointed down at The Preacher with his gun. "Look down there. See how his legs are shaking? See how he's in the throes of death, even as we speak?"

"How can't I?"

Nebo motioned with the gun, dramatically cocking it as he trained the barrel on The Preacher's forehead, the muscles around his eyes crumpling down as he aimed. "Tell me, who's holding his cards right now?"

Johnny, smoking: "I don't follow."

"Living is like being dealt a hand of cards. You play 'em your whole life. But when it comes down to it, the game can end at any time. But not because of *chance*. Because of *Fate*, which is really the same thing—only with a name, with a purpose." He leaned over and pressed the gun against The Preacher's forehead, burrowing back folds of skin. "I could shoot The Preacher right now or I could let him take his own life, but either way his game is over when *Fate says it is*. Fate pulls the trigger. Fate put the pill in his mouth. Fate played his cards out tonight, not him."

Johnny finally understood completely. And he saw his way out. "And these cards give you the power of Fate. Because by taking pictures of death, they captured the moment when Fate shows its cards."

"Exactly. You're a good player Johnny. Got a good eye. I'm gonna hate having to kill you. But…"

Johnny held his four Kings up with both hands. "But if I were to, say, rip these cards right now, you wouldn't have shit left to play with."

Nebo snapped up, stiff-arming the gun across the table. "Don't you even think about it, Frieze…"

"You might shoot me. Or you might lose your deck. Either way, it's all in the cards, right?"

Nebo, cocking. "Put it down *now*."

"Shorty," Johnny said, tearing his eyes free from the barrel of the gun for only a second of eye contact. "Do what I'm doing. Get ready to rip." He moved the cards in front of the gun and kept them there, like a shield, daring Nebo to shoot his own deck.

"Don't listen to him," Nebo said, finger trembling on the trigger.

Johnny, quickly: "Shorty you copy me *now*, or we're both gonna die."

Shorty shook his head, looking at both men, not sure who to believe.

"I bet you a million bucks you don't have the balls to rip up those cards."

Shorty reached for his Aces.

Nebo turned the gun on him and fired. But Johnny was already moving, hands under the table and lifting, bringing the table up like a wall in front of him, tumbling it over onto Nebo as he tried to stand. Shorty fell backwards in his chair, the bullet nicking his shoulder.

Nebo fired again, a hole punching through the bottom of the table and whizzing past Johnny's ear. He jumped down on the bottom of the table, knocking the wind out of Nebo. The gun slid across the floor, spinning through a puddle of Winston's blood and trailing a red letter S in its wake. Johnny dove, grasped its hot wet handle, and twisted.

Nebo was trying to stand, the table toppling the grotesque photographs all around him like a collapsing house of cards in an earthquake as he lumbered up from his knees.

Johnny pointed the gun up at the black security dome—sighting the video cameras that electronically wheezed above him—aiming right at his own reflection on its plastic housing—and fired.

Violet was waiting at her bar, already pouring two glasses of her truth serum when he opened the door. The apartment was dead silent.

He lit a Benson and Hedges before he sat down. He looked into her eyes. "She's dead, isn't she?"

Violet nodded. She was wearing one of Gin's pajama tops like a blouse, tucked into a black leather skirt that showed the whites and purple webs on her legs. She didn't bother asking about the game—she knew he'd win. She knew all along.

Johnny took the drink and finished it with one swallow. He could instantly feel the alcoholic fruit soaking up the acids in his stomach and working its magic on him. He set the glass back down on a tan-stained cardboard coaster in the shape of a daisy. "I knew it right after I saw Winston's card. Remember how I told you about that dude they call the Ferret? How he snuck up on us at Gin's apartment and I punched his face in?"

Violet pursed her lips. "I remember. Same guy who tried to kidnap her, right?"

"Right. Well, Winston turned him into a card—made him the King of Clubs. I didn't get it right away, but Nebo said something later on that got me to thinkin'. He knew I'd fixed my suit, and it didn't matter to him. He knew that I knew all about his real estate business, too, and that didn't bug him either. Not at all. And he said that I couldn't cheat Fate. That it wouldn't work."

Violet swallowed, moving her lips as if she were sucking the cigarette she held inches away from them. But she wasn't smoking. She stared down at the bar.

"And he was right. It didn't work. *Fate won*. I made a card out of Ferret's bruised face, and he died. I made a card out of Gin—faked the whole damned thing—and *she* died!" Johnny smoked his cigarette, staring at Violet as if accusing her of their deaths. "And I can't help thinking about the other seven pictures I took—all those college kids, not more than twenty years old.

I wouldn't doubt if they're dropping dead over their notebooks right now."

A tear spilled down from the purple rim of Violet's left eye, trailing mascara.

"And you *knew* they would die, Violet. That's why you wouldn't pose for me. Because you knew, didn't you."

Her voice was deep. "Johnny…don't…not like this…"

"And the only way I figure you knew that'd happen is because of those Tarot cards you made. Sure, you tried to warn me. You told me all about their power, and what the real deal was when it came down to makin' them. But you didn't tell me everything you knew. You didn't tell me the entire truth."

"I couldn't have stopped you either way," she said, her voice soft and delicate and sorry. "You'd already started the cycle. I couldn't change Fate."

Johnny angrily grabbed the Tarot deck from the corner of the bar, where it rested beneath the *TV Guide*. He snapped off its pink rubber band with a yank of his thumb. It fell beside a bottle of rum like a dead worm.

Violet sounded frightened. She was still crying. "Please, Johnny…*Please*. It's all over now."

Johnny picked the Death card from the bottom of her Tarot deck. He ran his fingers over its surface, feeling its texture as if reading Braille. "Is it?" he asked. "Is it ever really over, Violet?" With the nail of his index finger, Johnny began scraping the paint from the card, scratching the face right off Death. It flecked easily beneath the plane of his finger.

There—beneath the cheap paint—an old black-and-white photograph, yellowed with age—a young man with his hair greased back 50's-style, horn-rimmed glasses over his nose—a wide-lapelled suit jacket with diamond patterns on it over a bony frame—a black hole between the lapels where his heart once had been.

Violet shook her head *no*, denying the reality before her.

"It's your husband, Dutch, isn't it?"

She shook her head more quickly. The blood was purpling in the splotches on her face as if Johnny had struck her.

"Tell me, Violet. I wanna hear you say it." He tossed the card down in front of her and lit another cigarette off the butt of the first one.

She picked up the photograph and pressed it against her tearing eyes, covering up her shame. "You're right, Johnny. It's him. You don't really think Nebo invented Butcher Boy, do you? He wasn't the first. And neither was I." She dropped the photo face down on the bar and reached for her cigarette pack. She blinked rapidly, as if trying desperately to regain her old attitude. "Fate's a funny thing, Johnny. Really funny. You know better than anyone else how it can make or break you. But it isn't just that." She paused to light up. "It *needs* people, just like people need it."

Johnny nodded, completely understanding.

"I won. Long ago, I won. Just like you did today. I had no choice in the matter. And I'm guessing you didn't either. It just *happened*, right?"

"Sorta."

She stared at him. "Don't hate me Johnny. I did what I could to protect you."

"*You coulda saved Gin.*"

The tears were welling up again. "I couldn't. Really. The cards make themselves. That's just the way it is."

"But we could have stopped them, dammit…"

Violet picked up the Tarot deck in a thin fist of bone, shaking it madly. "*These* were all that could have saved her, Johnny. And they didn't. They simply decided not to, just like they did with my Dutch." The deck bent like cheap paper in her fist. "*These* kept the cops away from you. *These* kept your lucky streak up. *These* even helped you win today. But they didn't want to help Gin. Sometimes…" she spilled the deck on the bar, looking down at her dead Dutch, scratched out of Death. "Sometimes I think Fate gets jealous."

Johnny reached for the tall bottle of rum beside the blender. He capped it, and chugged straight from its neck. Then he passed it to Violet, wiping his lips on his bicep.

She took it, sizing him up and trying to change the subject. "So you gonna show me the new deck, or what?"

Johnny opened his suit jacket and slid the black leather case free from its satin pocket.

Her eyes widened. "Nice touch," she said, lifting the bottle in toast.

"Congrats." She drank in large gulps.

Johnny caressed the black leather of Nebo's case. "Ya know, I think you're right, Violet. Fate does get jealous. It's only got so much to give."

She nodded, both eyes blinking in affirmation, tipped bottle perched awkwardly on purple lips.

Johnny pulled Nebo's gun out from the small of his back and aimed.

Michael A. Arnzen

Gin was right: surviving alone was not a win.

Johnny rewound the videotape he'd discovered in the rafters above Nebo's gambling room and studied the game again, taking notes on how the cards played out. Every draw from the deck—every card, every hand—had a hidden purpose, a higher meaning, a message that Johnny alone could deduce. Each was an instruction for wielding the power of the deck. Each was a clue.

And each time he watched the story pan out on Violet's wide-screen TV, the ending remained the same: Johnny, pistol pointed directly at himself—at the viewer behind the camera—followed by a blast of gunfire that rattled the speakers—and ending in a flash of black. It always ended in black. Spade black.

He'd won. What happened afterwards didn't really matter. He couldn't remember much—just that he'd awakened dazed and alone in Violet's apartment, a cashier's check from the Bucket in his wallet and the deck in its long black box on his chest like a book he'd fallen asleep reading.

But whenever that videotape went black he played out the possibilities. What could have happened. What should have happened. What might have happened. What could have gone better—what could have gone wrong. Inventing stories to fill in the gaps in his memory like dreams play out the possibilities of night:

*The gun barrel confronts him. The inevitable blast roars inside of his ears and light blares between his eyes as if his head was the chamber of the pistol all along. The screen flickers: red to black, red to black...*

Johnny points the gun down at Nebo's forehead. The Suicide King is stuck to his cheek like a bad tattoo. Johnny sees himself in the card and fires. The card still sticks when his face explodes. Shorty tries to run. Johnny shoots him in the back, and he sprawls across the floor.

He collects the chips. The cards. Puts them in the box. Retrieves the videotape from inside the shattered plastic dome on the ceiling. Spends some time drinking gin, smoking menthols, photographing the dead bodies with a

269

# Play Dead

Polaroid camera. Goes down to the cashier's cage and cashes in. The cashier says "Congratulations, Mr. Spades." He climbs into Gin's Fiesta. Drives to Violet's. Finds out the truth. Shoots her just 'cause it feels like the right thing to do. Things come full circle. Finishes off the rum. Takes her photo. Tries to make enough Spade cards out of the pictures of all those bodies in his pocket to switch with the ones Axe had planted in the deck. Later, he passes out on her couch, entranced with the way the dogs cheat at Tarot…

*The gun barrel confronts him. The inevitable blast roars inside of his ears and light blares between his eyes as if his head was the chamber of the pistol all along. The screen flickers: red to black, red to black…*

Johnny points the gun down at Nebo's forehead. Makes him beg. Nebo feigns prayer, but instead reaches for the cards that are scattered about around him, muttering incantations. Johnny feels his arm moving up towards his own temple on its own accord. Placing the hot tip of the gun beside his eye socket. Smells gunsmoke. Trigger finger closing. Nebo's calling the shots, wielding the deck.

Shorty dives and saves him just in time. The bullet misses his head by only so much. He loses a few more teeth when his chin hits the floor beneath Shorty's weight. Meanwhile, Nebo is at the bar, unlocking the cabinet where earlier he'd stashed everybody's weapons. Johnny fires only because he has to. Afterwards, he makes good on his bet with Shorty—the bet that said they'd partner up and beat Nebo at his own game—and they split the pot between them. They part ways. Johnny gets the videotape and cashes in downstairs.

But when he's talking to Violet about the real deal, he spots motion reflected in the rum bottle she's drinking from. He turns and aims. Shorty's in his sights, a sharp diamond cutter jutting from the hand arced over his head. Johnny shoots—figuring a million bucks wasn't enough for Shorty. Maybe he wanted the deck, too.

Johnny and Violet get drunk afterwards. They play with the cards. Maybe play with some bodies, too. Later, Johnny passes out on her couch, dizzily watching the dogs cheat at Tarot. In the morning Violet is nowhere to be found…

270

*The gun barrel confronts him. The inevitable blast roars inside of his ears and light blares between his eyes as if his head was the chamber of the pistol all along. The screen flickers: red to black, red to black...*

Johnny points the gun down at Nebo's forehead. But it's too late: a burst of whitelight like an insanely huge flashbulb blinds his eyes. Vision returns and he's trapped inside a room of glass. He can't shoot his way out. This is because his gun has been transformed into a long sword. He's wearing a colorful motley outfit, like royalty. Something heavy on his head: a crown of plastic, jeweled with black poker chips and studded with his own spade-like teeth.

Whenever he looks down he sees only his own reflection, cut off at the stomach.

A dark shape perpetually hangs over his shoulder, digging into his peripheral vision for eternity, like a cancerous lump in the eye. He lifts up the sword. Entranced with the reflection of his changed face in its flat metal surface, he sees what constantly haunts him—the moon, a black spade.

With open eyes, he stares into the sword and dreams.

*The sky's the limit.*

However it really ends, it always ends the same: Violet's deck is mysteriously gone. Her dentures are in his mouth. The moon is out and everything's black.

However it really ends depends on how Johnny plays the cards he's dealing out on the table before him, knowing full well that—as Fate would have it—no matter how dead his cards might be, their lifeforce remains eternally trapped in their dark frames.

But surviving is not enough.

*The gun barrel confronts him. The inevitable blast roars inside of his ears and light blares between his eyes as if his head was the chamber of the pistol all along. The screen flickers: red to black, red to black...*

He deals.

# About the Author

MICHAEL ARNZEN has been publishing ground-breaking horror fiction and dark poetry since 1989. His first novel, Grave Markings (Dell/Abyss, 1994) received both the Bram Stoker and International Horror Guild awards, and was recently reprinted in a fine leather-bound tenth anniversary edition (Delirium, 2004). His latest books are a flash fiction collection, 100 Jolts: Shockingly Short Stories (Raw Dog Screaming, 2004) and a poetry book, Freakcidents (Shocklines, 2005). Arnzen holds a PhD in English from the University of Oregon and is presently an Associate Professor at Seton Hill University, where he teaches horror and suspense fiction in the country's only graduate program in Writing Popular Fiction.